Dornford Yates is the pseudonym of ⬚⬚⬚⬚⬚⬚⬚⬚⬚⬚⬚⬚⬚⬚ into a middle-class Victorian fam⬚⬚⬚⬚⬚⬚⬚⬚⬚⬚⬚⬚⬚ together enough money to send hir⬚⬚⬚⬚⬚⬚⬚⬚⬚⬚⬚ solicitor, he qualified for the Bar but gave up legal work in favour of his great passion for writing. As a consequence of education and experience, Yates' books feature the genteel life, a nostalgic glimpse at Edwardian decadence and a number of swindling solicitors. In his heyday and as a testament to the fine writing in his novels, Dornford Yates' work was placed in the bestseller list. Indeed, 'Berry' is one of the great comic creations of twentieth-century fiction, and 'Chandos' titles were successfully adapted for television.

Finding the English climate utterly unbearable, Yates chose to live in the French Pyrénées for eighteen years before moving on to Rhodesia where he died in 1960.

ADÈLE AND CO.
AND BERRY CAME TOO
B-BERRY AND I LOOK BACK
BERRY AND CO.
THE BERRY SCENE
BLIND CORNER
BLOOD ROYAL
THE BROTHER OF DAPHNE
COST PRICE
THE COURTS OF IDLENESS
AN EYE FOR A TOOTH
FIRE BELOW
GALE WARNING
THE HOUSE THAT BERRY BUILT
JONAH AND CO.
NE'ER DO WELL
PERISHABLE GOODS
RED IN THE MORNING
SHE FELL AMONG THIEVES
SHE PAINTED HER FACE

DORNFORD YATES

AS BERRY AND I WERE SAYING

HOUSE OF
STRATUS

This edition published in 2001 by House of Stratus, an imprint of Stratus Holdings plc, 24c Old Burlington Street, London, W1X 1RL, UK.

www.houseofstratus.com

Typeset, printed and bound by House of Stratus.

A catalogue record for this book is available from the British Library.

ISBN 0-7551-0036-0

'Golden lads and girls all must,
As chimney-sweepers, come to dust.'

To all those golden lads and girls and chimney-sweepers, to whose personalities so many of my characters owe their creation.

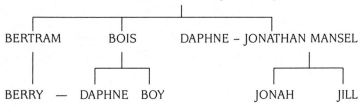

BERTRAM PLEYDELL
(of White Ladies, in the County of Hampshire)

BERTRAM   BOIS   DAPHNE – JONATHAN MANSEL

BERRY — DAPHNE BOY   JONAH   JILL

NOTE

In writing this memoir, I have endeavoured to do two things. The first is, except as an author, to suppress my personality: the second is to report nothing which will not interest either my customers or the world at large. Occasionally, I have given persons or places names which are not theirs: this, against my will, but not my judgment. Sometimes, too, I am not quite sure of my dates. For these failings, I must beg to be excused. Of 'Berry's monographs', portions are matters of opinion, and portions are matters of fact. The latter are strictly true. If ever I state a fact for which I cannot vouch, I say as much. Whether this memoir proves the proverb that 'Truth is stranger than Fiction', I do not know. But I have nothing exaggerated, 'nothing extenuated, Nor set down aught in malice'. Witnesses swear to tell 'the truth, the whole truth and nothing but the truth'. I could not take such an oath, for, even at this distance of time, I have, in some cases, no right to tell 'the whole truth'. But I can honestly say that I have told 'nothing but the truth'.

DORNFORD YATES

"Don't talk to me," said Berry, "about reminiscences. A year or two back I compiled an arresting record of great events. Naturally unconversant with the trivial and sordid details of publication, I charged you with the duty of presenting my memoir to a hungry world. Need I say that you failed me? With the result that an immense public has been denied a great privilege and enduring entertainment of a rare and refreshing kind."

"Dress it up as you please," said I. "But what are the facts? No firm would have dared to publish the memoir you wrote. Jonah and I devoured it, with tears running down our cheeks. But you can't print stuff like that."

"Stuff?" said Berry.

"Stuff. For one thing alone, at least six writs for libel would have been issued at once. Then, again, it was far too short. Thirty-one thousand words won't make a book. And it's no good arguing. I know what I'm talking about."

"Then why return to my vomit? Why bring the matter up?"

"Because I have something in mind. I, too, have memories – some of them entertaining, most of them dull. Now if we combined yours and mine, we might make a book. We should have to expurgate yours: unless you consent to that, I'm not going to play. But if that is done and the two are added together, one of these days a volume might be produced."

Berry leaned back, fixed his eyes upon the ceiling and fingered his chin.

"None but the great," he said, "should write their reminiscences. For a lesser man to do so, it is a gross impertinence. Who cares where he was born or went to school?

1

Or what his nurses smelt like, or why he fell off his pony in 1894? That is the paltry level to which the stuffed shirt descends: he will give to the world such rubbish, because *he* values it. These things are a presumption we *must* avoid. But there are memoirs of another sort. Provided he suppresses his own personality, any man, be he Privy Councillor or bricklayer's labourer, has a clear right to set down things he remembers and impressions he has received. And that is what we shall do. You were behind the scenes in more than one *cause célèbre*. I was familiar with Paris in 1902. You were a guest, more than once, of the famous Madame de B—. The girl-friend who taught me backgammon was born in the lengthy reign of King George the Third. Such things are side-lights on history and may be set down without shame. But we must be very careful."

"I entirely agree," said I. "And I think we might have a stab."

"Oh, darling, what at?" cried Jill, coming into the room.

"I know," said Daphne, behind her. "A book."

Berry addressed me, frowning.

"Ignore the ungodly," he said. "You were saying we might have a stab."

"But we must be critical. And we can't be critical, until we've finished the thing. Then we read it over and knock it about. And, if what survives passes muster, I'll see it through. But I'm damned if I'll pad. If, when it's done, it's too short, it'll have to be scrapped."

"We shall have to make notes," said Berry. "Whenever we think of a thing, we must put it down. Write down Calais, someone. That was where George Brummel stayed. I was sick in the street at Calais when I was four."

"Disgusting brute," said Daphne.

"No blasphemy, please," said Berry. "Already the jewelled wheel of my memory is beginning to turn. I remember one night at Covent Garden – "

"Wash out," said I. "You can't introduce K G."

"Why not?" said Berry. "It was a great institution. In the Covent Garden Balls the flame of Vauxhall and Cremorne flickered for the last time. And could anything have been more English? Caruso, Melba – however world-famous the singer, once a fortnight he or she had to give place, because young men and maidens desired to dance in the theatre in which they were booked to sing. And Dan Godfrey held the stage and the whole of the stalls were floored."

"If you put it like that," said I... "But no remembering one night."

"I suppose you're right," said Berry, wistfully. "But I can't help feeling that one or two episodes might be with decency set out. Shall I ever forget when Ruby wore your top-hat?"

"Oh, Boy," said Jill.

"May I suggest," said I, "that you confine your memory to your own dunghills? In any event, what Ruby wore is hardly a side-light on history."

"I know, I know. But I decline to subscribe to a slab of unleavened bread. Such things are indigestible."

"Yes, but your idea of leaven..."

"Nonsense," said Berry, "nonsense. Listen to this.

"Among the more subtle disasters occasioned by the first Great War was the loss by Paris of her personality. From being a city breathing *joie de vivre*, she became a bore. This will be denied – not by Frenchmen, who know the truth, but by those visitors who were not acquainted with Paris before the outbreak of war. The very name is a lure: and, since they know no better, they are well satisfied. But the real Paris has been dead for nearly forty years.

"Entering the city in the old days, you were immediately affected by her care-free atmosphere. This was compelling – and incomparable. She never could have worn the comfortable majesty of London: but, though she wasn't really, she always seemed to be *en fête*. Festival was in the air. Her gaiety was infectious. Everyone gave the glad eye, as a matter of course.

3

And very nice, too. If it did nothing else, it did the heart good. And her people were so understanding. About two o'clock of one morning I left Montmartre."

"Do be careful," said Daphne.

"I left," said Berry, "in what is called solitary state." He looked round defiantly. "Now it had been expedient that during the revelry I should – no matter why – assume a false nose. This was an admirable appendage, for it was not only striking, but comfortable – so comfortable that after a while I forgot that I had it on. And so I returned from the unique inconsequence of Montmartre to the quiet solemnity of the Place Vendôme, still wearing this emblem of genial festivity. When I paid the driver of my cab, he raised his hat. When I entered my hotel, the night-porter bowed. But neither, by word or look, gave me the slightest indication that he found my appearance in any way abnormal: and it was not until I was confronted with the reflection of my countenance in the privacy of my room that I realized that the dignity with which I had invested my orders had been considerably embarrassed. Well, there you are. The French were entirely natural – impatient of any restriction, but always ready to share what joy there was. Every day was an adventure. A trivial *contretemps* was a matter of infinite jest. Paris was gay. Of course she had her faults. And the strict have called her hard names. But the *joie de vivre* of Paris was a cordial such as I never tasted anywhere else. It was not for sale: it ran in the streets, as the wine used to run on high days years ago. And it made glad the heart of man."

My brother-in-law looked round.

"You must admit that that is unexceptionable."

"Most restrained," said I.

"Well, now it's your turn. What about the Old Bailey? Of course it'll let the side down, but if, as you suggest, the sheep's to lie down with the goat – "

"Why," said Jill, "because he was at the Bar – "

"He didn't have to haunt the Criminal Courts."

"He didn't" – indignantly. "Besides – "

"My darling," said I, "don't try and take the brute on. As he knows, by the purest chance I have seen more of the Old Bailey than have most Common Lawyers. I was present at and sometimes concerned in cases, to be admitted to which some people would have paid very high. And, honestly, looking back, I don't think they would have been wrong, for much of what I witnessed is today remarkable. A lot of novels are written which deal with crime; and descriptions are sometimes given of the Court and its procedure. And when I read them, I wonder whether the Court has changed. But I don't think it has.

"About the proceedings at the Old Bailey, there is very seldom anything dramatic. As a rule, they are almost painfully matter-of-fact. Sometimes the atmosphere is sordid: but it's always intensely real. You get right down to the bone. And that is why, though I was very glad when my time in Treasury Chambers came to an end, I cannot regret what I saw, for it was the real thing."

"Go on," said my sister. "I'm getting all worked up."

"Begin at the beginning," said Berry, "and don't leave anything out."

"Well, don't blame me," said I, "if you don't like it.

"Old Bailey is the name of a street which runs from Newgate Street to Ludgate Hill. The Central Criminal Court has always stood in this street. Before it was known as the Central Criminal Court, it was called Old Bailey Sessions Court; and that is, I suppose, how it came by its name. For many years the court-house formed part of the building known as Newgate or Newgate Prison, the most famous jail in the world. Claude Duval, Henry Esmond, Defoe, Jack Sheppard, Lord George Gordon, Fagin and many other famous or infamous people all lay within its walls.

"Now in 1902 Newgate was pulled down, and the Old Bailey with it: and on the site of Newgate the present Old Bailey was built. But in 1901, Coles Willing, who preceded Forsyth as our solicitor, took me to see the old court."

"You were very young," said my sister.

"Fifteen," said I. "But he knew I was bound for the Bar and he wanted me to see the old court before it went. And I'm awfully glad I did.

"He took me in by a door which Counsel used and I sat with him at a table in front of Counsel at which solicitors sat.

"At the moment there was nothing doing, so I looked well about me, while Willing began to talk to a Treasury Counsel he knew. It was a winter's afternoon, and the court was lighted by gas. It was very close and seemed to be very full. But the jury-box was empty, as was the dock, and only an Alderman, robed, lolled on the Bench. (No Judge may sit alone at the Old Bailey; that is to say, another Commissioner must always be in the building: an Alderman, as being a Justice of the Peace, will do.) On the Bench was a long divan and a row of davenports. On the carpet on the floor of the Bench were lying sweet herbs, and a posy of flowers lay on the Judge's desk. (To this day you may see the same things; they are a survival of the time when Newgate was full of jail-fever, and it was hoped that, with herbs and flowers about him, the Judge would be spared.) What hangings there were were dingy and all the woodwork was soiled. In the body of the court there seemed to be no room to spare, and the aisles were crowded. Looking up at the mouth of the public gallery, I saw only a sea of faces: it was Hogarthian: the occupants must, I think, have been crouching on the top of one another.

"Suddenly there were two loud raps, and one of the ushers cried, 'Be uncovered in Court.'

"Everyone stood up, and the Judge walked on to the Bench."

"Hawkins?" said Berry.

"No," said I, "I wish I could say it was: but Mr Justice Hawkins had already retired. I put him in *Lower Than Vermin*. He was a damned good Judge, such as they don't breed today. But he was hard on Counsel. Tireless himself, he'd sit till two in the morning, with never a window open, because he hated draughts. And he was mad about racing – Mr Justice Hawkins never was known to miss an important race. But in this particular case, Mr Justice Phillimore was on the Bench."

"Give me strength," said Berry.

"Yes, he was a corker," said I. "I'll give you that. He was a Puritan. His Puritanism oozed – and got under everyone's skin. The things prisoners said to him would have made a gangster blush: and they very, very seldom abused a Judge. Ridley shared that distinction. But, then, he used to buy it, as Phillimore did. But Phillimore was a good Judge, while Ridley was a bad one. But I'm getting away from my tale."

"Never mind that," said Berry. "More of Ridley."

"Well, one reminiscence," said I. "Danckwerts, QC, was appearing in the Court of Appeal – not the Judge of today, but his father. And Danckwerts' estimate of Ridley was very low. 'My lords,' says Danckwerts, 'this is an appeal from my Lord Chief Justice, sitting as a Divisional Court.' (A Divisional Court consists of two Judges, sitting together.) Old Lord Justice Vaughan-Williams took him up. 'But, Mr Danckwerts, that were impossible, that my Lord Chief Justice should sit as a Divisional Court.' Danckwerts looked round at his junior, sitting behind. Then he turned to the Bench. 'I beg your lordships' pardon. M' learned junior reminds me that Mr Justice Ridley was also present.' "

"O-oh," cried Jill, with a hand to her pretty mouth.

"I can't swear to that, for I didn't hear it myself. But I knew Danckwerts and I knew Ridley – not to speak to, of course – and I have no doubt at all that it's perfectly true. And now let's go back.

"Phillimore took his seat. Then some door was opened and a jury began to return. They'd been considering their verdict. When they had entered their box, the prisoner appeared in the dock. He was a small, compact man, and looked rather like a coachman, which in fact he was. The court was more crowded than ever, for people had been coming in. Then the jurymen answered to their names. When that was over, the Clerk of Arraigns rose. He was sitting directly below the Judge. He addressed the foreman of the jury.

" 'Gentlemen of the jury,' he said, 'are you agreed upon your verdict?'

"The foreman rose and replied.

" 'We are.'

" 'Do you find the prisoner guilty or not guilty?'

" 'Guilty.'

"A rustle ran round the court.

" 'And that is the verdict of you all?'

" 'Yes.'

"Coles was whispering to counsel.

" 'What's the charge?'

" 'Murder.'

" 'Oh, my God,' breathed Coles, and got half out of his seat.

" 'No, no, man. It's too late now.'

"Coles sank back and laid a hand on my arm.

"The Clerk of Arraigns 'called on' the prisoner.

" 'You have been found guilty of murder. Have you anything to say why the Court should not give you judgment of death?'

"The prisoner replied.

" 'No, sir.'

"Then an usher or the Judge's Crier made a proclamation, calling upon all to keep silence 'upon pain of imprisonment'. As he did so, the doors of the court were locked. I think I shall always hear the clash of the wards.

"I looked at the Judge.

"Standing behind him, his clerk had laid the black cap on his wig. I can't remember whether it was a square or a circle of silk, but it hung down all round his face and hid his wig, and I must confess that it lent his countenance a truly terrible aspect. By his side was standing his chaplain, gowned in black. He addressed the prisoner by name and then passed sentence of death in the world-famous words. And when he had done, the chaplain said 'Amen'.

"For a moment the silence persisted: then everyone seemed to stir. A warder touched the prisoner on the shoulder. At once he turned away from the bar, to disappear down the stairs.

"When I looked at the Bench again, the black cap and the chaplain were gone and the Judge was leaning down to talk to the Clerk of Arraigns.

"And so I can truthfully say that I saw and heard a poor man sentenced to death, while he was standing at the bar at which Jack Sheppard once stood. But I am more than glad to be able to add that he was later reprieved."

"Two warders?" said Berry.

"Always two. Sometimes more. For a woman, wardresses."

"Does the death sentence worry the prisoner?"

"I've only once seen that – and I've seen and heard it passed a good many times."

"Does it worry the Judge?"

"I only know of one case. And then the prisoner made a Masonic sign. The Judge was a Mason, too: and it shook him up. He'd no right to do it, of course."

"Coles Willing was worried?"

"Yes. He never meant me to hear such a thing as that."

"But it didn't worry you?"

"I'm afraid it didn't," said I. "It never has. It's a very solemn moment. I can't exactly describe it; but you have the impression that Time is standing still."

"I couldn't bear it," said Jill. "The poor, poor man."

"I'm sure you couldn't, my sweet. But don't forget that he's bought it. He showed his victim no mercy – don't forget that."

"Well, that's history," said Daphne.

"A side-light on history," I said. "The dock went to Madame Tussaud's. And now it's Berry's turn."

"Don't rush me," said Berry. "My gorge hasn't fallen yet. And where did the davenports go to? The National Sporting Club? Of course, all this crime stuff is going to debase the book."

"Don't be absurd," said Daphne. "The value of it is that it's perfectly true."

"Do you suggest," said her husband, "that that virtue will not distinguish such contributions as I am permitted to make?"

"Er, no," said Daphne.

"I should hope not," said Berry. "It is not my practice to deceive. If a fellow asks me for a fish – well, he mayn't get Rainbow Trout, but he won't get a serpent. I remember one night at Cannes. I'd just won three francs at *Boule*. Goo-goo was showing Boy – "

"I don't remember Goo-goo," I said.

"Oh, you must remember Goo-goo. The best legs in – Or was it *Chocolat*?"

"Go on," said Jill, squeezing my arm. "She was showing Boy…"

"Well, Aquamarine and Boy were – "

"It was agreed," said I, "that we should suppress our personalities. You've given Paris a show. What about incomparable London Town?"

"Ah," said Berry. "That was a city, that was. What did Blucher say, as he rode through the roaring streets after Waterloo? 'What a city to sack!' So completely German – he was our guest – and so completely true. She was a fine old jade… Weather could not tarnish her magnificence. Grave or gay, there was always a majesty about her that nothing could take away. I think I saw her at her best one morning in June…

"Within the week King George the Fifth of England was to be crowned. So his subjects repaired to London, and London was very full. All for whom room could be found were staying within her gates. Since the weather was set fair, it follows that the streets were congested all day long: and when I say congested,

I mean it – never before or since have I seen such a weight of traffic in London's lanes. And the traffic was gay, for every taxi was open and there wasn't a bus on the streets with a covered top. Silk hats and flowered dresses and parasols, nosegays and button-holes – and the great sun lighting it all from a cloudless sky. It was, indeed, a brilliant spectacle: but it was more than that, for its brilliance was rarefied." Berry turned and looked at me. "Is 'rarefied' right?"

"I can't imagine," said I, "a more appropriate word."

"Good. Now the thing was this. The peers had been summoned, as usual, to attend the Coronation in state: and all who still had their state coaches were asked to bring them to Town and drive to the Abbey in those fine equipages. As many as could complied. The state coaches were greased and furbished and sent to London by rail: liveries were procured: handsome horses were found. But the horses of 1911 were not accustomed to drawing an old state coach and many had hardly seen the London streets; and so it was felt that such equipages must be 'run in', if I may put it that way, before the day of the Coronation itself – with the very happy result that, on every day of that week, one had the unforgettable privilege of seeing them adding to the traffic which congested the West End streets. The wigged coachman, square on his hammercloth, clad in his gorgeous, eighteenth-century dress – scarlet or blue or yellow, all laced with gold; two powdered footmen on the tail-board – the Duke of Wellington had three – similarly attired, and the great coach, its coats-of-arms glowing in the sunshine, flashing and swaying behind its handsome pair. Museum pieces in action, period stuff, 'mucking in' with the buses and taxis and private cars... It was a sight for sore eyes, and that's the truth.

"One morning I had an appointment in Rutland Gate. I had to see old John —, much earlier than I liked. But he was run off his feet and could give me no other time. I left his house at ten and, crossing Kensington Road, I boarded a bus. I got a good seat on the top and settled down. My next appointment was at Hill's at half-past eleven o'clock. Yes, I was going to have my hair cut. Ordinarily such a journey to Old Bond Street would have taken a quarter of an hour: on that lovely June morning it took nearly an hour and a half: but not one moment was dull. Hyde Park Corner presented an astonishing sight, an ocean of traffic as far as the eye could see, full of slow-moving currents sliding all ways and giving place to cross currents from time to time. How the police controlled it, I've no idea. It was most remarkable. We proceeded along Piccadilly, the blocks becoming longer in duration the further we went. But that didn't matter to me, for Piccadilly was glorious, the Green Park was looking its best, there wasn't a cloud in the sky and all the world was in a holiday humour. At last we reached Old Bond Street and I got down. I walked along to Hill's, and there was Brown all ready to do his stuff."

"Brown," said I, "was one of the old school."

"So he was," said Berry. "Brown was an institution. He commanded my great respect. A first-rate master-barber and a most charming man."

"He ought to have written his reminiscences."

"So he ought," said Berry. " 'Member how old Lord — used to slip him a penny at Christmas and say 'Here's half a crown'? Which reminds me, that very morning a nice-looking fellow comes up, while Brown's drying my hair. 'May I speak to Brown?' says he. 'Of course,' I said. So he asks if Brown can take him that afternoon. Brown says no, he's sorry, he's booked right up. 'But,' he says, 'I can take you in five minutes' time, sir. My next appointment isn't till half past twelve.' 'No, no,' said the man, 'not now.' I saw him glance down. 'I must go home first. Are you sure you can't fit me in this afternoon?' Brown shook his head. 'I'm very sorry, sir.' Well, he made some other appointment and went his way. As Brown picked up his brushes, 'D'you know, sir,' he said, 'why he wouldn't be done after you?' 'I assume,' said I, 'I assume he's got an engagement.' Brown smiled. 'No, sir,' he said. 'But he won't sit down in those trousers. He's certain pairs of trousers in which he will not sit down. Spoils their set, he says.' He was perfectly right, of course: but few would have cared to be so particular.

"Well, Brown finished me off, and I put on my collar and tie and he slid me into my coat. Then I thanked him and said goodbye and left the shop. I decided to walk to the Club. So I strolled back to Piccadilly. I got to the corner of Old Bond Street and stood there a moment, wondering how to cross. 'Waiting for you, sir,' said a voice. It was a bus conductor, laughing all over his face. By God, it was the bus I had left half an hour before. And it hadn't broken down: it was only waiting to move."

"What ever," said Jill, "what ever did people do? People, I mean, who simply had to get there."

"They walked or they went underground. Of course, no end of appointments simply went west. But nobody seemed to mind. Those were the tolerant days. I never had a passport till 1919. Before the first war, you could walk into Victoria Station, take a ticket for Constantinople and alight there three days later without any fuss. For a five-pound note you could spend a whole week at Lucerne. The journey both ways was included and so were all sorts of excursions about the Lake. And fed like a fighting cock. And the stuff that was sold in the shops was very good. On the outbreak of war I purchased a pair of braces – simple webbing and leather – for eighteen pence. And I gave up wearing those braces in 1938. That's twenty-four years' service for eighteen pence. Is anyone going to deny that those were the days?"

"No one," said everyone.

Berry regarded his wife.

"One evening we dined with old Stakely. He used to give his dinners at The Berkeley, because he lived in chambers in

Jermyn Street. He stopped me the following week, as I was leaving the Club. 'How much champagne,' he said, 'did we drink on Thursday last?' It was a dinner for eight. After a slight calculation, 'I'd put it at six,' I said. 'That's what I make it,' he said. He began to laugh. 'They render my bill on Mondays. On Monday last they never rendered a bill. I stopped at The Berkeley on Tuesday, to ask them why. They sent for the Manager. "That's quite right, sir," he says. "You had cause for complaint." "I know," said I. "The woodcock was overdone." (It had been – very slightly, and Stakely had made a fuss.) "What of that?" says I. "It was overdone, sir, and you had cause for complaint. In that case we make no charge." "But the champagne," I said. The Manager bowed. "Sir," he said, "the dinner was not as it should be. Next time you honour us there will be no fault." Now that's what I call service. And it paid them hand over fist, for all of us swore by The Berkeley from that time on.'

"No one will believe that," said Daphne.

"What does that matter?" said Berry. "We know it's true."

"Berry's right," said I. "Whether people believe us or not is their affair. And if they don't, I can't blame them, for times have changed. A novel cost four and sixpence before the first war: whether I wrote it or Kipling, the price was the same. A bottle of excellent whiskey cost four and sixpence, too."

"One night," said Berry, "I had come up for some dinner. I think it was at The Goldsmiths' – I can't be sure. Anyway, I met David —: he was an ARA. When the show was over, he asked me and one or two others back for a drink. He lived in St John's Wood, as many artists did. It was not a very big house, but it was most attractive. And he had some beautiful things.

"After he'd shown us round –

" 'Who's your landlord?' said someone. 'Or is this house your own?'

" 'Well, I haven't bought it,' says David, 'and who my landlord is, I haven't the faintest idea. I've lived here for twenty-two years and I've never been asked for rent.'

"As soon as we could speak –

" 'And rates?' says somebody.

"David shook his head.

"'Never a penny,' he said. 'I think I'm off the map.'

"And that was a damned nice house – in — Road."

"Incredible," said Daphne.

"But true," said Berry. "People used to live and let live before the first war. I remember it well." He looked at me. "Carry on, partner," he said.

"Not after that," said I. "I propose to retire."

"That's right," said my sister, rising. "It's nearly half past twelve."

"Have a heart," said Berry. "The golden fountain is just beginning to play." Again, he regarded me. " 'Member that night in Venice when you and the Duchess got lost?"

"Neither do you," said I. "Besides, it's my turn."

"Yes?" said my wife.

"Rowed past her palace," said Berry. "And never found out their mistake for nearly an hour and a half. That's Venice – that was."

"Oh, Boy," said Jill.

"That," said I, "is romance. And romance is a tale whose scene and incidents are remote from everyday life."

Daphne had reached the door.

"Do remember," she said, "that Pony's coming tomorrow at ten o'clock."

"My God, so he is," said Berry. "Blast his neck." He got to his feet. "Spain's the country, you know. No business is done in Spain before mid-day. I mean, that gives you a chance."

*

"I knew there was something," said Jill. "Wigs. Last night you said that the black cap covered the Judge's wig. I always thought that Judges never wore anything but those very big wigs."

"Oh, no, my sweet," said Berry. "Judges are almost invariably clothed. I suppose it's a question of dignity."

"Boy, you know what I mean."

"So does he," said I. "Never mind. It is a mistake to think that Judges always wear what is called 'the full-bottomed wig'. Artists often make it – who illustrate tales, I mean. And I've seen it made on the screen. There are, in fact, three wigs which are worn by the Bench and the Bar. One is the full-bottomed wig, which is the one you mean. A Judge never wears that in court. He used to wear it in court, when he was charging the Grand Jury: but now the Grand Jury has been done away with. He wears it in Church and on ceremonial occasions. A Queen's Counsel wears the same wig, but never in court, except on the one occasion when he is making his bow on his appointment. He, too, wears it only on ceremonial occasions. The second wig is the ordinary barrister's wig, such as I used to wear, with curls upon either side and two little tails behind. The 'stuff gownsman' has no other wig: and Queen's Counsel wear the same wig when they are in court. The third is the Judge's wig. This is exactly the same shape as the barrister's wig, and it has two tails behind, but it has no curls."

"Usedn't you to say that a wig always gave you a headache?"

"So it did," said I, "if I had to wear it all day. That was because my hair was very thick. It wasn't the fault of the wig. Hold a wig to the light and it looks like a rather thick web: so the air comes through all right. But if a wig fits as it should, it compresses your hair: so that, if your hair is thick, no air can get to the scalp. If I'd been in court all day and was dining out, I always tried to get to Hill's to have a shampoo, for my hair was just like tow, for want of air. That's why so many counsel go bald: it's worse than a field-service cap."

"What about women barristers?"

"Oblige me," said Berry, "by not referring to that cult. Women on a jury were bad enough, but a woman barrister..."

"I'm afraid I agree," said I. "By the grace of God, I was confronted with neither, for in my time they weren't allowed. I desire to do no injustice; but I had six years of the law, and nothing will ever convince me that a woman should serve on a jury or go to the Bar. I decline to state my reasons: but, of what experience I had, I know I'm right."

"Some may," said Berry, "have truly legal brains: some may be accomplished advocates: but they are women – not men: as such – "

"That'll do," said Daphne. "I couldn't agree with you more. But that will do."

"Well, I've seen them at it," said I. "Not women barristers, but women defending themselves, examining, cross-examining and addressing the Court. And they were very able."

"You mean the 'suffragettes'?"

"That's right. The militant suffragists. The ones I'm thinking of were the Pankhursts. Although repeatedly told, they refused to obey the rules of evidence: and when they addressed the Court, which they did for hours, ten tenths of what they said had nothing to do with the charge: and at the end of this spate of irrelevance they had worked themselves up until they burst into tears. It was a most lamentable exhibition. The authority of the Court flouted, hours of time wasted, latitude invariably abused. That sort of thing sends you mad. And lawyers shouldn't get mad. But they're all human. My God, how we hated those women."

"They took advantage of their sex?"

"My sweet, you said it. There are some jobs in which the sexes must not be mixed. And the Law is one of them."

"I confess," said Berry, "that I was but a Justice of the Peace: but I held that insignificant position for nearly thirty years. I don't think you could say that I was pronouncedly susceptible, and few, I think, would deny that I was a male. But, if there had

17

appeared before me two female advocates – one a damned good-looker, with an engaging address and what I believe is called 'it' in a marked degree, and the other a blear-eyed hag, with a full-bottomed face and an offensive air – to adjust the scales of Justice would have been very hard. *Ex uno disce omnes.* Judges, at present, are males; and unless they've tea in their veins, they're bound to be affected in just the same way. If either of you two beauties put on wigs and gowns and walked into the Court of Appeal, they'd have to hold the Lords Justices down on the Bench."

"Thank you, darling," said Daphne. She turned to me. "Boy, please tell us more of the suffragettes."

"So he shall," said Berry. "But let me subscribe a preface to what he is going to say.

"In the years immediately preceding the first great war, the period of militant suffragist disturbance was gradually displaced by a period of militant suffragist outrage. All over the country, attempts, frequently wholly successful, were made to destroy by fire buildings of note. Several lovely old churches were burned to the ground. But churches were easy money, for the house of God cares for itself by night. A bomb was placed and exploded in Westminster Abbey, damaging the Coronation Chair. The greens of well-known golf-courses were ravaged beyond repair. One summer evening half the windows of Old Bond Street were smashed to smithereens, to the great provocation of their owners and of all who passed that way. His Majesty's mails were burned, to the loss and inconvenience of His subjects, high and low. The running of The Derby was interfered with and at Tattenham Corner the King's horse was brought down. As a result of this vulgar and intolerable behaviour, the tide of the public temper was running high, and, had a plebiscite been taken in 1913, there can be no shadow of doubt that the voting against Women's Suffrage would have been at least fifty to one. Then, in the twinkling of an eye, came the first great war. And throughout that war the women of

England pulled far more than their weight. With the result that, when the war was over and the electors were asked whether women should have the vote, most people felt they deserved it – and said as much. But the British memory is notoriously short. And so, in the fullness of time, it came about that the women who inspired and directed conduct so monstrous as to kill their cause, are now most honourably mentioned as creditors to whom all women owe their right to vote."

"That's perfectly true," said I. "But for the war, the movement would have been smashed. The British Public would have smashed it, for they would have taken the law into their own hands. Take that famous Derby alone. The King's horse was lying fifth and couldn't, I think, have won. But if Craganour, the favourite, had fallen, the anger of England would have known no bounds. I almost wish he had, for he only won to be disqualified."

"In favour of Aboyeur," said Berry. "Give me strength."

"One is forced to assume," said I, "that the Stewards were temporarily insane."

"An unfortunate moment for such a blinding attack."

"I agree, but there you are. And it's all over now."

"Don't run out," said Daphne. "You were going to speak of the suffragettes."

"As you will," said I.

"In the autumn of 1908 I became a solicitor's pupil: my tutor was the Senior Partner of the Solicitors to the Commissioner of Police. At the end of one year I left, to be called to the Bar. H G Muskett had never had a pupil before and, being a stern man, rather naturally regarded me with grave suspicion. This, I contrived to allay, and we soon became good friends and I went with him everywhere. One of his many duties was to appear for the Crown at Bow Street, when militant suffragists were required to answer charges of obstruction and assault in the vicinity of the Palace of Westminster.

"We had already appeared on several occasions, when Mrs Pankhurst announced that on a certain evening in June she proposed to lead a great number of her adherents from Trafalgar Square to the Houses of Parliament. She was at once informed by the Commissioner of Police that she and her followers would not be permitted to approach the Palace of Westminster. This notice, she ignored. On the evening before the day she had fixed for the demonstration, the Commissioner rang up Muskett and suggested that, since many arrests would almost certainly be made, it would be as well for him to see for himself the kind of conduct for which it would be his duty to prosecute the offenders at Bow Street on the following morning. Muskett agreed, and it was then arranged that he should join the Commissioner at Cannon Row Police Station at, I think, eight o'clock. Muskett then asked if he could bring me, and the Commissioner said yes."

"This conversation," said Berry, "was on a private line?"

"Yes," said I. "As well as the ordinary telephone, we had a private line to Scotland Yard. The operators were, of course, police."

"Speed or secrecy?"

"Both. There were certain conversations one didn't wish overheard."

Daphne put in her oar.

"For years after you entered that office, darling, you were terribly quiet."

"That's right," said Jill.

"The first day I came," said I, "Muskett said, 'You will see and hear many things in this office which you must never repeat.' He stopped there and looked at me. Then, 'I never speak twice,' he said. 'You needn't be afraid, sir,' I said. 'I shall never talk.' And then, after that, for a year I was in Treasury Chambers. I think, perhaps, those two years rather tied up my tongue."

"I'll give you this," said Berry – "you kept your word."

"Thank you," said I. "I know you'd've done the same."

"And now," said Jill, "go on with the suffragettes."

"Well, we dined early, walked across the park and then across Whitehall to Cannon Row. It was a perfect evening: more people were about than usual, because, I suppose, they wanted to see the show: and there were a lot of police. The militant suffragist rally was in Trafalgar Square, and the latest news at Cannon Row was that the women were about to march. Almost at once the Commissioner arrived. I was introduced, and we then proceeded, all three, under police escort to an island in the middle of Whitehall, quite close to Parliament Square. As we gained the island, a police cordon was being drawn about fifteen paces further on across Whitehall. There were mounted police waiting in Parliament Square, but they didn't want to use them if they could help it, because, on former occasions, the horses had been stabbed with hat-pins, and things like that."

"The filthy beasts," cried Jill.

"I entirely agree. That was vile."

"Well, there were police reserves all over the place, and Superintendent Wells was on horseback moving from spot to spot. Inspector Jarvis, a very nice man whose age was about forty-five, was in charge of the cordon and was standing just in front. There still was plenty of light, and after a little we saw the procession approaching along Whitehall. Onlookers were approaching with it, on the pavements on either side. The procession was led by Mrs Pankhurst. I think her daughters were behind her, but I can't be sure. They passed us and had almost reached the cordon, when Jarvis stepped forward. 'Good evening, Mrs Pankhurst,' he said, for they knew one another well. 'I'm afraid you know that we can't let you and these ladies go any further.' Whilst he was speaking the women behind Mrs Pankhurst were moving half-right and half-left, so that, by the time the conversation was over, there was a thick line of women confronting the cordon of police. 'I demand,' said Mrs Pankhurst, 'to be allowed to pass.' 'I'm sorry, Mrs Pankhurst,' says Jarvis. 'But you were advised that you and your supporters

21

would not be permitted to approach the Houses of Parliament, and we are here tonight to prevent any such attempt.' 'You refuse to let me go by?' 'I'm afraid that's so,' says Jarvis. 'Very well,' says Mrs Pankhurst – and swung to the jaw. I saw her do it. She hit him a swinging blow as hard as she could. I heard her hand meet his face, and his cap fell off. One of his men picked it up, and he put it back on his head. Then he took hold of her arm. 'I'm sorry,' he said, 'but I shall have to take you to Cannon Row.' She went quietly. But, as she was arrested, her followers went for the police. Screaming 'Votes for Women', they flung themselves at the cordon, fighting like so many beasts. It was a shocking scene, and, had I not seen it, I never would have believed that educated women could so degrade themselves. Indeed, I decline to believe that any woman, however low and vile, has ever so behaved, unless she was drunk. And these women were not drunk. Arrests were made right and left, and a constant stream of women was flowing to Cannon Row. Some fought and struggled, demanding to be 'let alone': others went quietly enough. Police reinforcements continually filled the gaps in the cordon, and were assailed in their turn. After about half an hour we left the scene. In that time I only saw one woman roughly used. She had been arrested and was resisting savagely. The constable who was taking her to Cannon Row, took her by the shoulders and shook her. He was immediately reproved: but he had my sympathy. The woman had laid his face open from temple to chin."

"My God, what with?" said my sister.

"Her nails, my sweet."

Daphne covered her face.

"Well, there we are. As you have seen, I never forgot that night. The next morning at Bow Street, nearly one hundred women were due to appear. On charges of assault and obstruction. Of such were the Militant Suffragists.

"One or two flashes from Bow Street, where they invariably appeared.

"The interruption to the ordinary work of the Court – or perhaps I should call it 'the addition' – was serious. More than once the Magistrate sat until ten o'clock at night, to try and dispose of the charges with which he was overwhelmed. And we, of course, had to be there. It wasn't so bad for me, but Muskett was on his feet for nearly the whole of the time.

"On one occasion the women subpoenaed the Chancellor of the Exchequer and the Home Secretary. I don't know why they were allowed to get away with it, for neither of the Ministers was in a position to give any evidence of any kind regarding the offences with which the women were charged. But they only wanted them to serve as cock-shies. We were rather worried as to how the Home Secretary, Herbert Gladstone, would show up, for he had the reputation of being a weak and foolish man. Naturally enough, we were in no way uneasy about Lloyd George, who was the Chancellor of the Exchequer. Never were expectations so falsified. Gladstone did terribly well. He was firm and dignified, and more than one of his answers was very much to the point and made everyone laugh. But the figure Lloyd George cut was almost contemptible. His demeanour was craven, and he tried to be funny and failed – and laughed at everything he said. Nobody else did. I can't explain this, and never met anyone who could.

"On another occasion, the militant suffragist leaders were defended by —, QC, an Irishman. His eloquence was undoubted. Lack of material never embarrassed him. This was as well, for there were, of course, no answers to the charges of obstruction and assault. He was, I suppose, accustomed to making bricks without straw. So he made a most admirable speech – but his peroration included a comparison which I would give much to forget. No English paper printed it, so that only those who heard it can repeat what he said. It was, to be frank, sheer blasphemy of the most atrocious sort. Had I not heard it, I never would have believed that any Christian would have spoken a sentence so shocking in open court. It was by no means a question of taste: it was a question of instinct. The effect of his words was most painful. Incredulous horror was reflected by every face. The Magistrate, Curtis Bennett, went white to the lips: Muskett turned red as fire: I thought the Magistrate's Clerk was going to faint: Wells, who was sitting beside me, went purple: and everyone present seemed to have stopped breathing, as though they were expecting the hand of God to strike. Their demeanour shook —. He faltered in his speech, and his voice, so to speak, tailed off. Then he recovered, added a word or two, asking for his clients' discharge, and resumed his seat. Had the matter been brought to the notice of the Bar Council, I sometimes think that he would have been disbarred. But the blasphemy was so shocking that nobody, I suppose, was minded to repeat it. I know I wouldn't have repeated it for any money.

"Superintendent Cresswell Wells of 'A' Division of the Metropolitan Police was a first-rate officer, a well-known and popular figure and a very nice man. To me, he was always kindness itself. On one of the days on which we were dealing with the militant suffragists at Bow Street, when the Magistrate adjourned for luncheon, Muskett and I hastened to the old Gaiety Restaurant, which did you very well. We had hardly taken our seats, when I noticed that I had forgotten to replace my wrist-watch, which I had laid on the pile of towels before me, before I washed my hands."

"Even," said Berry, "even a blue-based baboon – "

"I know," said I. "It was the act of a fool. I never did it again."

"Go on, Boy," said Jill.

"Well, I went straight back to the lavatory, to find the watch gone: and the liveried attendant swore that he had not seen it. I'd no time to pursue the matter, but, as you may remember, it was a very nice watch. We got back to Bow Street a few minutes before two o'clock and I took my usual place between Muskett and Wells. Naturally enough, I told Wells about my loss. He listened to me. Then he beckoned to Jarvis, another friend of mine. He spoke with him for a moment and added 'Go yourself'. Twenty minutes later he laid my wristwatch beside me with a quiet smile."

"What had happened?" said Daphne.

"I never asked. When the Court rose, of course I thanked them both. But as neither offered any explanation, I left it there."

"Oh, I couldn't have borne it," said Jill.

"My sweet," said Berry, "your husband's not always a fool. Two of the biggest shots in 'A' Division had, between them, effected the return of some stolen property. Had Boy inquired how they had done it, his stock would have fallen very low."

"Look here," I said, "I'm afraid we're breaking our rule."

"No, we're not," said Berry. "Let's have some more about stolen property. Why is it so seldom recovered?"

"You mean, in robberies of consequence?"

"Yes."

"Because in all such robberies the disposal of the swag is arranged before the robbery is done. The fence is all ready to receive it and pass it on. (At least, this is how it was in 1909.) A big receiver will have his own appraiser, waiting to value the stuff. Then someone else picks it up… Twenty-four hours later it's lying in Amsterdam. Or, if there's a hitch, it may go into a Safe Deposit. It is the fence that matters. If there were no receivers, there wouldn't be any thefts. No big ones, I mean. Now here's a simple, illuminating case. On a wet autumn evening, three men were standing in a row, regarding a jeweller's window in the Waterloo Road. The man in the middle was a fence, and the other two were thieves. They'd brought the fence along, to have a look at the stuff which they proposed to steal – and to say what he'd pay them for it. Apparently, they were satisfied; for that night the job was done, and an hour or so later the stuff was handed over in the bar-parlour of a pub in Notting Dale."

"Did they go down?"

"No action was taken – I think, by our advice. The information was full, but the evidence was too thin."

"What does that mean?" said my wife.

"Evidence is information which can be given in Court. Most information can't be, because it's hearsay or the informer can't be called. But it's almost invariably true. If all information were evidence, not one defendant in fifty thousand would get off. I'm speaking of forty years ago, but, so far as indictable offences were concerned, unless the police were dead certain, they never made an arrest."

"Which means that no innocent man was ever sent down?"

"Yes."

"What about poor Adolph Beck?"

"That was a case of pardonably mistaken identity. Beck was the very image of the man who committed the crime. There was...one other case. But, by the grace of God, no damage was done."

"Proceed," said Berry.

I hesitated. Then – "I shall have to leave out a little."

"Even now?"

"Even now. However, I'll do my best, for it is an astonishing tale. I wasn't in the case, but I knew rather more about it than most people did.

"A man of means dwelt at his country place. This was known as The Grange. He kept no men-servants, though the house was solitary. He was broad and strong and courageous. One night he was sitting at dinner with his wife and his sister-in-law. The dining-room windows gave to a terrace: the windows were shut, but the curtains were not drawn, although it was dark. A shot was fired from the terrace, and the bullet went by his head. Wisely enough, he didn't go for the windows, but, instead, rushed from the room, through the hall and down a passage. This led to the terrace from which the shot had been fired. He was out to get the man, unarmed though he was. But the man was out to get him. He must have known the house, for he was in the passage before his victim was. And he had a knife in his hand. They grappled in the passage, and staggered and swayed, still grappled, into the hall. There the women were gathered, helpless and horrified – the wife, the sister-in-law and one of the maids. And there, before their eyes, the husband was stabbed to death. His murderer turned and ran the way he had come.

"The house had no telephone, and I don't think the police had cars. So it was quite a long time before they arrived. Of course they did all they could, but all wheels turned more slowly in 1909. It was two nights later that a constable was walking his beat in a neighbouring town. He was passing a yard which was shut by iron-barred gates. As usual, he threw the beam of his lantern round the yard. And he saw a man. He asked him what he was doing. The man's answers didn't satisfy him, so he had him out of the yard and marched him off. The station-sergeant wasn't any better satisfied than his subordinate, so the man was charged and detained. 'Loitering on enclosed premises with intent to commit a felony.' Early the following morning, this particular police-station received the description of the man who had murdered the master of The Grange. And when they looked again at the man they had put in a cell – well, he tallied with the description in every way.

"It was the deadest case I ever knew. He was put up for identification and all three women instantly picked him out. It appeared that he was a cousin of the dead man, that he was a ne'er-do-well, that he knew The Grange and, by the dead man's orders, had recently been turned from its doors. He bore such traces of the struggle as you would expect to find: his coat was torn, his arms were bruised and his hands were cut. The account he gave of his movements could hardly be checked. When asked about the cuts on his hands, he said he had broken the window of a baker's shop in order to steal a loaf. He couldn't give the name of the village, and, though inquiries were made, no baker's shop was found to confirm his report. When asked about his movements upon the fatal night, he said he was in the bar of a certain public house. This was too far from The Grange for him to have committed the crime. When seen, the landlord denied this. On second thoughts, however, the landlord said he was there. In other words, his evidence was unsatisfactory. And this particular landlord was very well known to the police, as a most unscrupulous man. The revolver and knife, of course, had disappeared.

"Well, the man was committed for trial and was later tried. He went into the witness-box and denied that he was the man. His only witness was the landlord, who came unwillingly to Court and went to pieces in the box. The Judge summed up against him, and the jury retired. Everyone thought they'd be out for a quarter of an hour. They weren't. They were out for four hours. And then they came back and found the fellow 'Not guilty'. So he was released.

"Everyone was astounded. As I have said, it was the deadest case. But juries will be juries, and that was that.

"When the tumult had died, something – I don't know what – came to the knowledge of the police. Two months later another man was arrested and, to everyone's amazement, charged with the crime. There was quite a lot against him. He was proved to have been in the vicinity of The Grange on the night of the crime. In his possession was a revolver: a bullet fired from this was found to bear exactly the markings which were borne by the bullet which was taken from the dining-room's wall. Finally, when he was stood side by side with the man who had been acquitted, it was immediately seen that no man could tell them apart. They were facsimiles.

"Now I don't want to sound old-fashioned, but it has always been my honest belief that God Himself intervened and directed that jury to spare that first man's life. There is no other explanation. It was the deadest case."

"That *is* history," said Daphne.

"I don't go as far as that: but, at least, it's true."

"What did you leave out?" said Jill.

"Nothing of consequence, darling, as your inquiry shows."

"Who was the Judge?" said Berry.

"I can't remember. God knows it wasn't his fault. But it must have shaken him up."

"Let's have some more about receivers."

"It's your turn now."

"One more – featuring 'the fence'."

"Give me some port," said I. "My throat's getting sore."

Berry replenished my glass with tawny port.

"If," he said, "you knew how to produce your voice…"

"I know," said I, "I know. Strangely enough, it never got sore at the Bar."

"You never had a big enough brief."

"There's something in that," said I.

"Rot," said Jill. "Boy's got the most powerful voice I've ever heard."

"That is irrelevant, but true. The fog-horn type. When he was calling Nobby, the Vicar's nose used to bleed. And now for the receiver: he always interested me."

"Not half as much," said I, "as he interested the police. But the receiver was always extremely hard to hit.

"When I left Muskett's office, after one year with him, I was called to the Bar. The following day I entered Treasury Chambers – as a pupil, of course. And there I spent one year.

"One day a case came in – The King against Goldschmidt: and when I opened the brief I found it was 'Cammy' Goldschmidt, a most notorious fence. We'd been laying for him for years, for he was behind four-fifths of the really big things. But he wasn't charged with receiving: he was charged with harbouring, a little known offence. Harbouring is comforting a man whom you know to have committed a felony. For harbouring, you can get two years' hard labour: but for receiving you can be sent to penal servitude for fourteen years.

"Well, the thing was this. The police were unable to get Cammy on a charge of receiving, because he was too damned shrewd: but they were always ready, in case he should put a foot wrong. And now that was what he had done.

"Cammy Goldschmidt lived in style. He'd a very nice house in Hampstead, he kept his carriage and horses and he dressed in Savile Row. One rainy night an old lag came to his door, with a cart and horse. His arrival was reported to Cammy – by the butler or parlour-maid. And, though he was very much vexed, Cammy thought it best to go to the door himself. Now Cammy's instinct was to send the fellow away: but the lag knew rather too much, and, if he had turned nasty, it might not have been so good. So Cammy allowed him to stay and to sleep in a stable with his horse. But the horse and cart had been stolen, as Cammy very well knew. God knows how these things get round, but somebody talked – with the happy result that the biggest receiver in London was sent for trial on a charge of harbouring a thief.

"From our point of view, it was a rotten case. In the first place, one's sympathy is always with the hunted, and one finds it hard to blame a man who has given shelter to such unfortunates. In the second place, the case against Cammy was almost painfully thin, and the witnesses for the Crown were by no means above reproach. Still, it was so very important that such a receiver as Cammy should be out of action – if only for two or three months, that the Director of Public Prosecutions determined to have a stab.

"Cammy was confident. He instructed Charles Gill, QC, a very eminent counsel and a master of the art of defence. Indeed, I must frankly confess that, if I had been offering odds, I'd have given twenty to one against the Crown. What was so galling was that City of London juries are very shrewd. And had the jury, in whose charge Cammy would be, had the faintest idea of the truth, they would have sent him down without leaving the box. But they wouldn't know the truth, and we couldn't put them wise.

"Now, about this case, there was one curious thing. Among our witnesses – we only had two or three – was a man to whom Cammy had once given great offence. That was probably why he was bearing witness against him. Now this witness knew perfectly well who Cammy was: and he knew, as did all of us, that it was almost grotesque that so important a receiver of stolen goods should be arraigned only upon such a trifling charge. But that, of course, was neither here nor there. Cammy was charged with harbouring: and any reference to his activities as a receiver could not be allowed.

"Before the Judge took his seat, Gill approached Travers Humphreys, who was appearing for the Crown. 'You probably know,' he said, 'that one of your witnesses dislikes my client very much.' 'Yes,' says Humphreys, 'I do.' 'Well, you'll be careful, won't you, to keep his nose to his proof?' 'I promise you that.'

"The case was tried by Bosanquet. He was the Common Serjeant – a first-rate lawyer and a delightful man. He was aged and pale as death, and there were times when he sat so still and so silent that a man might be pardoned for thinking that he was dead. I once heard this unusual appearance commented upon – by a lady who had hoped for six months, to whom of his wisdom he had given five years. 'You – old corpse,' she said. And Bosanquet led the laughter against himself.

"Well, he came on to the Bench and Cammy entered the dock. He was something over-dressed. The cut of his morning dress left nothing to be desired, but the slip to his waistcoat, his button-hole and his patent-leather boots looked out of place. He was given a chair, and sat on it, lolling and smiling and watching Gill.

"The Crown presented its case, and it was painfully clear that the jury was unimpressed. I never remember a jury that looked so bored.

"The last witness we called was Cammy's enemy. Humphreys was as good as his word and took the greatest care to 'keep his nose to his proof'."

"What does that mean?" said Jill.

"A witness' proof is a statement of what he is going to say. It is by no means a statement of all he knows. But it is a statement of all that he is allowed to say in any particular case.

"Now the evidence he gave was not of great importance: it certainly rounded our case, but it did Cammy's next to no harm. It was very short, and very soon Humphreys sat down. And then Gill made a mistake…

"I know that's a big thing to say, for Gill was a brilliant man, whose little finger was thicker than my loins. But I can't help that. Perhaps it was Homer nodding. Be that as it may, he made a bad mistake. He failed to leave well alone. In other words, he rose to cross-examine a witness who had done his case no harm, who he knew was dangerous."

"But that's elementary," said Berry.

"I know. I hate to say it of Gill, for nobody could have been kinder than he was to me. He asked me to enter his Chambers, which I always felt was a very high compliment. He was almost the finest cross-examiner of his day. But that was nothing. I have sat beside him and seen him extended. And Gill extended made a man hold his breath. By the sheer force of his tremendous personality, I have seen him bend to his will five most hostile Justices of the Peace. Not a jury, mark you. Five cultured English gentlemen, accustomed to dispensing justice. And against their better judgment, he made those men grant bail. It was a great achievement, and only a very great man could have brought it about.

"And now we'll go back to Cammy.

"Gill rose to cross-examine. And these were his only words. 'In fact, you know very little about it?' The witness laughed. Then he pointed at Cammy. 'I only know he's the biggest receiver in London – an' so does everyone else.'

" 'Stand down,' says Bosanquet, sternly.

"The witness left the box.

"But the damage was done. At the witness' words, the jury sat up as one man. It was just as though they had had an electric shock. And Cammy turned a very unpleasant green.

"When he summed up the case, the Judge did his best. He told the jury plainly that the witness had no right to say what he did and that they must put his words right out of their minds. But he might as well have told the sun to stand still. At any rate, good as he was, he wasn't up to Joshua's standard.

"The jury retired, and Gill sat comforting himself with the reflection that he would have little difficulty in getting the conviction quashed by the Court of Criminal Appeal.

"And then the jury returned – and blew his hopes sky-high. They found Cammy guilty, of course. But they added a rider. 'We should like to say,' said the foreman, 'that the irrelevant remark made by the witness – has in no way influenced the decision to which we have come.' Well, no one – not even Gill – could have won an appeal after that. If you remember, I said that City of London juries were very shrewd."

"My God, what a show," said Berry. "What did Bosanquet give him?"

"As far as I can remember – eighteen months."

*

"I always find it," said Berry, "matter for regret that I have never been accorded the privilege of observing an apparition. All sorts and conditions of people, whose qualifications and merits in no way compare with mine, have been so accommodated. But though, on more than one occasion, I have passed lack-lustre hours in the most sinister surroundings – because, of course, I had accepted some liar's advice – never has any apparition stalked or stumbled or floated into my view. Once I undoubtedly heard the note of a bell, but, though my host assured me that that was a phantom sound, I found myself unable to ignore the indisputable fact that there were within earshot quite thirty old-fashioned swing-bells, any one of which, had it been set in motion, could have produced the note. I am, therefore, forced to the conclusion that, while ghosts interest me, I do not interest ghosts: my addresses have been rejected: it is now, indeed, some years since I made up my mind no longer to seek the acquaintance of personalities so ungracious and so blind. But I must confess to disappointment. I've heard so many reports of spectres that have been seen and sometimes heard, of lights that have been extinguished by no known agency, of doors that were shut – and have opened, of stairs that have creaked beneath some unseen weight... Still, my disappointment is tempered by this – that only on one occasion have I been rendered such a report by a man who saw a spectre with his own eyes. His statement diminished all hearsay, once for all. For reasons which will appear, I have no hesitation in passing it on.

"I was staying at a château in France before the first war, and among the guests was a Major Andrew —, of a famous Scottish Regiment, to which the sons of his house had always gone. He was a very quiet man and kept a lot to himself: but we always got on very well, and I think he knew me better than anyone else. One thing about him stood out – he was intensely practical. His lack of imagination hit me between the eyes. This emerged from our conversation over and over again. While such a trait in a soldier used to be a good fault, I had a definite feeling that such a man would never go very far. I may have been wrong there, for he was most intelligent.

"Now it was the custom at the château for the women to retire in good time and the men to bid them good night and repair to a smoking-room. This was a spacious apartment, very well found. And there we would sit and talk for an hour or more. The company included more than one eminent man, whose light conversation was most agreeable: but one night a foolish, rich man decided to take the floor. Accordingly, he retailed a ghost story which I had been told as a child: when he had done, some other fool had to beat this well-worn tale, and for the next half hour all the old stock ghost stories were trotted out. Before they were done, the eminent men had withdrawn, and the audience gradually shrivelled, until Major — and I were almost the only two left. He had said nothing at all, and I remember thinking of the contempt with which so practical a man must have regarded such reports. Discouraged by our demeanour, the last of the fabulists made some excuse to retire, and Major — and I were left to ourselves.

"For a little we did not speak, but savoured the blessed silence which supervened. It was rather like turning off the wireless. I was just about to break this – by a singularly destructive criticism of our late tormentors, when he addressed me.

" 'I once saw an apparition.'

"I hope I didn't show it, but I never was so much astonished in all my life. It was as if an archangel had said, 'I once had an affair with a chorus-girl.' Then I realized I was on to something extremely rare – a first-hand report by a man who was quite incapable not only of lying, but of embellishing the truth.

" 'Please tell me,' I said.

" 'I'm afraid it's a rather long story.'

" 'So much the better,' said I.

" 'Well, I live in Lincolnshire. The house is too big for us, so we've shut up two-thirds of the building and live in one of the wings. Once a month, I take the carpenter with me and go round the whole of the bit we keep shut up – in case the rain's come in or something like that. One day we were on the first floor, when I opened the door of a room, and there was an old fellow, wading across the floor. He was wearing black breeches and stockings and a good-looking plum-coloured coat. He had a wig on his head and an ebony cane in his hand. His face was whimsical.

" 'Well, my first impulse was to run downstairs, to see if his legs were sticking out of the ceiling below.' (Is that or is that not the statement of a practical man?) 'Then I decided to wait and see where he went. He crossed the floor, still wading, and disappeared into a cupboard.

" 'If I'd had any sense, I should have run into the next room, but I never thought of that until too late. Instead, I called the carpenter, who was a room or two behind, and told him to take up a floor-board. Sure enough, there was another floor, about twelve inches below. So I think there can be no doubt that the apparition was treading the original floor. Then we examined the cupboard. This was very shallow, and once had been a doorway which led to the adjoining room.

" 'A few days after this my wife and I went out to tea. We went to a country house about the same size as ours, in which, as a matter of fact, my people had resided a good many years ago. But the strange thing was this – that our house was really the home of the people that lived in it now. In a word, about a hundred years ago, the two families had exchanged houses. The present owner was a contemporary of my father and he lived there with his daughter who was about my age. And though they lived very quietly, we had been asked to tea, because he wanted to meet his old friend's son.

" 'When we got there, the daughter received us and said that, to his distress, her father was not well enough to leave his bed: but he hoped very much that I would go up and see him, after I'd had some tea. So, of course, I did. Directly I saw him, I was sure that he'd never get up. He was very plainly failing... I stayed with him for a little, and we said the usual things. He was very insistent that I should see the pictures before we went: and he made me promise to ask his daughter to take us round the gallery.

" 'And so she did. And she told us about the portraits, as she went. We'd got down to George the Third, when damn it, there was the very old fellow I'd seen a week before. Coat, breeches, wig and cane, and the same whimsical face – I'd have known him anywhere. Fortunately, I held my tongue. "This," says the daughter, "is William (or Samuel or some such name). And he's always supposed to appear before one of us dies."

" 'Well, of course, he had appeared – in the house which was his own home, when he was alive. Naturally, I said nothing. Ten days later, I think, her father died.

" 'Wasn't that a queer business?'

"That's the only ghost story I ever tell, and for me its virtue lies in the fact that it was related to me by the most unimaginative man I have ever met and a man who would see no sense in telling a lie. For all that, it's hearsay. I cannot say that I've seen a spectre myself."

"At any rate," said my wife, "it's very well worth putting in."

"It's hardly a side-light on history."

"That doesn't matter," said I. "The discerning should find it of interest. In any event your own personality has been entirely subjected, if not suppressed. Which is more than I seem to do."

"No one," said Jill, "can talk about something they've seen without saying 'I'. And if they try to do it, it's awfully dull."

"There's a lot in that," said Berry. "When I was of tender years, I saw a fat Royalty get stuck in a carriage's door. I mean, people had to shove from behind – I saw it done. No, I shan't say who it was, for she was a very good sort; and she took it awfully well and laughed like anything. The point is I saw it happen: and if I say as much, the incident seems more vivid than it would seem in *oratio oblique*? Is that right, partner?"

"Perfectly right. *Oratio recta* is the more vivid of the two."

"Translation, please," said my sister.

"Straight speech, as opposed to bent: a speaker's actual words as opposed to a report of what he said."

"Take *Treasure Island*," said Berry. "That work of art would lose quite half its charm if *Jim* didn't tell it himself."

Jill looked at me.

"Is that why you always do it?"

"In my romances? Yes. At least, I suppose it is. I started like that in *Blind Corner,* and never looked back."

"Stevenson knew," said Berry. " For such tales, it is the right way. But, of course, it limits the narrator, because he can only report what he saw or heard. Don't you find that embarrassing sometimes?"

"I can't say I do," said I. "But I know what you mean. I suppose I've got into the knack. Of course, one character sometimes reports to the narrator what he has done."

"That's perfectly natural. But Stevenson did get stuck."

I laughed.

"I know. In *Treasure Island* the doctor takes over the tale. But Stevenson does it so beautifully that it does no damage at all."

"You don't always do it, Boy. Use the first person, I mean."

"Oh, no. Not in most short stories – I don't know why. And not in some of the others. *This Publican*, for instance. I couldn't have done it there."

"I hated *This Publican*," said Jill.

"The best thing I ever did."

"*Rowena* was so awful."

"True to life, my darling."

"Have you ever known a woman like that?"

"No. But she combined the worst characteristics of three women that I did know."

"Which is your worst book?" said Berry.

"That answer I keep to myself."

My sister addressed her husband.

"You are a brute," she said.

"No, he's not," said I. "Some books must be weaker than others, as every writer knows."

"An author can judge his own work?"

"If he can't, he's not a craftsman. If a silversmith makes a poor tankard, he knows it's a bad one far better than anyone else. But he must be a silversmith."

"Meaning…?"

"Many people who cannot write, write books today. For all I know, they think they're terribly good. In fact, they're beneath contempt."

"That's a true saying," said Berry. "What I don't understand is why the publisher takes such filthy tripe. He's the retailer, and the retailer must know. Bauble and Levity wouldn't accept a dud tankard."

"I know," said I, "but some retailers would."

"Listen," said Daphne. "You said just now that you could judge your own work. Don't you care what reviewers say?"

"I care very much. Whether it's good or bad, I value an honest review. So long as they're honest, I value the bad ones most. I can't pretend I enjoy them, but – well, to more than one unknown reviewer, I owe a great debt; for he has picked out some fault to which I was blind, and I've taken very good care not to – What d'you do with a fault? 'Commit' it?"

" 'Serve'," said Berry.

" 'Commit' must serve. Not to commit it again. *Punch* made me wince once; but, even while I was smarting, I was immensely obliged."

" 'Honest'?" said Jill.

"Sorry," I said. "But I'm bound to put that in. But malice can be instantly recognized and should be ignored. I don't think you got much in the old days, but now the reviewer by profession seems to be rather rare. Nowadays all sorts review books – very often, I fear, authors. And that, for obvious reasons, is utterly wrong."

"Dog eating dog?" said Berry.

"It can amount to that. And now let me please say this – reviewers as a whole have been far kinder to me than I have deserved. Of the debt I owe them, I am extremely conscious. They have, of course, helped my sales; but, what is of much more importance, they have encouraged me. Only a very few have been malicious. When they are, I summon the memory of things which real reviewers have said. St John Ervine and, for all

I said about authors, Compton Mackenzie himself, though he can't have known it was I. And *Punch* and *The Spectator*. Those are reviews that matter, when all is said and done."

"Oh, I know," said Daphne, "you mentioned *This Publican* just now. That was founded on a theory I know you hold – that a man who looks like another will be found to have the same nature."

"That, I have always maintained; and on very many occasions I've proved it true. I was taught it by a fellow of Jesus, who all his life had studied his fellow men. He was one of the founders of the OUDS, and Arthur Bourchier once told me that he was the finest amateur actor that he had ever known. To say he was of the old school is nothing at all. He might have stepped straight out of Dickens: face, manner, clothes – everything about him was forty years out of date. He was a survival of a forgotten time. Anyway, he taught me that theory, and I've always proved it true. Over and over again. You know a man called A. Ten years later, perhaps, you meet a man called B. And B resembles A very closely indeed. If you can watch B, you'll find he has the same nature, the same characteristics, the same outlook. If A was a gambler, B will gamble, too. If A was very particular about his clothes, B will be very particular about his. If A had a violent temper, B will have one, too. And so on. If B reminds you of A, and is not exactly like him, his ways will resemble A's in a lesser degree. I mean, if you didn't trust A, you'd be wiser not to trust B. Thanks to John Morris – that was the old don's name – ever since I was at Oxford I've studied my fellow men: but the six years I had of the law gave me a splendid chance of observation. Witnesses, jurymen, Judges, counsel – there was always someone to study, and so I was never dull. I mean, you can do in court what you cannot do in a restaurant or a club."

"Just as well," said Berry, "you never had any briefs."

"I had to do something while waiting for my case to be reached."

"The big shot's cases had to wait upon him."

"You are a beast," said Jill.

"He's within his rights," said I. "My practice was very slight. But, unless you were pushed or had a big chance and grasped it, the Bar was always a very steep ladder to climb. I once saw a man seize his chance."

That's rare," said Berry. "Who was it?"

"It involves a story," said I.

Berry got to his feet and filled my glass.

As he replenished his own –

"Is that very touching gesture understood?"

"Yes," said I, "and here's your very good health."

"Here's yours," said Berry. "And now we must have some more."

"You'll both have gout," said Daphne.

"What the hell?" said her husband. " Carry on."

"I was staying with the —s, near Ipswich, when I was sixteen. I was one of four boys in the house, and the weather was simply vile. After three days, Lady — was beside herself and I fancy she told Sir George that if he didn't get us out, she'd go herself. And then he had a brain-wave. The Assizes at Ipswich were on, and he drove us in and put us in the Magistrates' box. I think we all enjoyed it – I know I did. For the case was the Peasenhall murder, a *cause célèbre* of its day. A village girl had been murdered – Rose Harsent, by name, and the village blacksmith stood accused of the crime. A young man, called Ernest Wild, was counsel for the defence. Child as I was, I could see how well he did it. Henry Fielding Dickens led for the Crown. And the Judge was old 'Long Lawrance', as he was always called. Wild made his name in that case, and he never looked back. Years after, I was his junior: and I told him that I had been there. 'Rot,' says he. 'You weren't born.' 'I was:

I remember you well.' 'What was the blacksmith like?' 'He was a great, big fellow, with a clipped black beard. And he never stopped stroking his beard the whole day long.' 'Good enough,' says Wild. 'You were there. But you shouldn't have been. D'you know that fellow always remembers my birthday?' 'So he damned well ought to,' said I. Wild laughed. 'Perhaps you're right,' he said. 'But where are the nine?' Not long after that, Wild became Recorder of London: and his old opponent, Henry Dickens, was made Common Serjeant. So the young took precedence of the old."

"Was Wild a good Judge?"

"Not outstanding. He didn't live very long."

"And 'Long Lawrance'?"

"He was very sound and very popular. Towards the end, he began to grow very deaf: but he learned the lip language and hardly missed a thing. He was a great character. Being deaf, he was unable to hear his own voice, and he used to say things which he meant for his Marshal's ear, which were clearly heard by everyone else in court. He was not the best of lawyers, as he well knew. One day at Lewes, Marshall Hall was before him and was pressing a point of law. Now Marshall was a great advocate, but he was a worse lawyer than 'Long Lawrance' was: so we were all enjoying ourselves. Upon this particular point, the Judge was against Marshall Hall and told him so. But Marshall Hall persisted. At last 'Long Lawrance' got cross. 'Mr Marshall Hall,' he said, 'don't waste the time of the Court. I have told you that *I am against you.*' And then he added in what, I suppose, he intended to be an undertone, 'I may be a — fool, but I'm against you.' There was, naturally, a roar of laughter, and Marshall Hall collapsed."

"That's of value," said Berry. "A touch of nature, you know. Hadn't Marshall Hall the unfortunate reputation of getting across the Judge?"

"Yes, he had. More than once I was his junior, and he was always very kind to me. But I'm sure he'll forgive me for saying that that reputation was not altogether undeserved. But he was a very fine advocate and he had a big success. He was tall and broad and a very handsome man: and he had the most splendid presence of anyone at the Bar."

"Who was the best of them all?"

"Rufus Isaacs. Danckwerts was the finest lawyer of Bench or Bar. But Rufus Isaacs was the most brilliant advocate. He towered above his fellows. He had a great charm of manner – an irresistible charm. Juries could not withstand it. Then, again, he had an incredible memory. I never remember his referring to a note.

"The first time I ever saw him, I was still at school. Coles Willing took me to see a Trial at Bar. That is a very rare thing. It is the hearing of a criminal case in the Royal Courts of Justice, which are of course Civil Courts."

"Why and when?" said Berry.

"When there is reason to think that, by such a transfer, justice will be better served. In this particular case, The King against Whitaker Wright – "

"This *is* history," said Berry. "Whitaker Wright."

"Well, he was up for fraud. He'd been very active in the City, and his advisers felt that it would be impossible to empanel a jury at the Old Bailey which was not prejudiced. But in the Law Courts they could have 'a special jury' to try the case. And the Crown agreed.

"For more than one reason, it was, as you clearly remember, a memorable case. In the first place, Whitaker Wright was a very big noise and he lived for several years in a very big way and, when he fell, he fell with a very big crash. In the second place, throughout the case, the Judge displayed a very definite bias against the accused. I always found this strange, for Bigham was a very good Judge – he later became Lord Mersey and President of the Probate, Divorce and Admiralty Division. In the third place, Rufus Isaacs, as Attorney General, led for the Crown. Fourthly, within ten minutes of having been found guilty and sentenced to penal servitude, Whitaker Wright died by his own hand. Poison. Fifthly, after his death they found upon him a fully loaded revolver, with which he might very well have shot Bigham dead.

"I'll deal with those points in a minute. And now let's go back. Coles Willing took me into a court which was crammed. Isaacs was on his feet, summing up for the Crown. He impressed me immediately. He had a charming manner and a delightful voice. I could see him well and, though he was dealing with figures and date after date, he never once glanced at a note. (They used to say of him that, such was his power of concentration, he could ask a question in cross-examination with the answer he had in view six questions ahead. He was certainly very much feared, and many a case was settled, when the other side learned that Isaacs had been retained.) I don't know how long we'd been there, when I saw the Judge raise his eyes to look at the clock. Isaacs saw him, too, and immediately stopped. 'Your lordship is thinking of adjourning?' 'I think so, Mr Attorney. I think you'll be some time yet.' 'I'm afraid I shall, my lord.' 'Very well. Until two o'clock.' Then the Judge left the Bench, and Whitaker Wright stood up.

"I hadn't seen him till then, for he was in the well of the court. And he turned to look at the clock, so I saw him well. His face was the colour of cigar-ash, and the sneer lines, as they are called, looked as if they had been drawn by a finger dipped in blue chalk. Any one must have been sorry for such a man. About twenty-four hours later, the jury found him guilty and the Judge sent him down.

"Now, had he been at the Old Bailey, he would have been in the charge of warders, and warders know their stuff. But they don't have warders at the Law Courts: so the tipstaves looked after him, and looking after prisoners was not in their line. Consequently, each morning, when he surrendered to his bail, he was never searched. Warders might not have found the poison, but they would have found the revolver. Consequently, again, when, after his sentence, he desired to visit the lavatory, a tipstaff took him there – *and waited outside.* So Whitaker Wright took his poison without any fuss. Now the Judge may have been in no danger. Whitaker Wright may have thought of shooting himself. The fact remains that, because there was no dock, he sat where suitors sit – in the well of the court. There was no tipstaff with him, and the Judge was twelve feet away. And he must have deeply resented the bias which Bigham showed. However, he didn't do it, though a good many people thought it was in his mind."

"Otherwise, Bigham was a good Judge?"

"A first-rate Judge. Strangely enough, on one other famous occasion, he put a foot wrong. That was at the Old Bailey...

"A shocking case of child-cruelty came to be tried. What was more shocking still was that the woman indicted was gently born and bore an honourable name. The hearings in the police court had been very naturally splashed, and feeling all over England was running very high. I may be wrong, but I think the case was transferred to the Old Bailey, because it was felt that in her own County the prisoner could not have had a fair trial.

"Well, she went down: but, instead of sending her to jail, Bigham imposed a fine of fifty pounds. On the face of it, such a sentence was absurd, for it was a very bad case. What may have been in his mind was that the publicity the case had received had finished the accused, that her honourable name was now mud and that she could never again show her face in any company that knew who she was. Be that as it may, the indignation of the public knew no bounds, and the old *cliché* of there being one law for the rich and another for the poor was on every poor person's lips. For that reason alone, such a sentence was mischievous. She was tried, I think, in December, and the Drury Lane Pantomime opened on Boxing Day. In this there was a good song which a clever girl sang very well. 'I don't want to be a lady.' The last lines of every verse landed a different punch, and the last of all ran:

'And if justice can be downed
'At the price of fifty pound,
'Well, I wouldn't be that lady if I could.' "

"That was pretty hot," said Berry.

"I heard it," said I. "And the roars of applause with which it was received had to be heard to be believed. But, except for those two lapses, Bigham made an excellent Judge."

"Did they often transfer cases?"

"No. I remember a case that was postponed – for a very unusual reason."

"Proceed."

"Well, I was in the case, so I know what I know. Even now I can't say much, for it was one of those cases which are heard *in camera*. But I can tell you this – that it was the most astounding case that ever was heard. And that was Charles Gill's opinion: and he was a pretty good judge. Tolstoy never conceived a drama so savage and so sensational. The accused was a millionaire – an American millionaire. He had a fine place in England – and was arrested at his own lodge-gates. Bodkin, a splendid lawyer, appeared for the Crown. Gill and Wild, both QCs, and the head of my chambers, as their junior, were instructed for the defence. The case entailed many hearings before the Justices; and, since the head of my chambers had a great deal of work, I used to take his place. Gill lived in St James's Street, and every day he picked me up at the Club and took me down in his car. It was a long drive, and that was how I came to know him so well."

"It's strange, looking back. Gill and Wild and I used always to lunch at *The Crown*, a fine old house, where we have all lunched together time and again."

"*The Crown?*" said Jill.

"Don't knit your brows, my sweet. I've changed its name. I must do that sometimes, if I am to tell these tales.

"After lunch, Gill and I used to walk up and down the sleepy old High Street, while Wild, I rather think, dozed. Gill wouldn't let him touch the case – he did everything himself. Gill used to tell me the line which he was going to take that afternoon: and I used to make suggestions, which he heard with attention and invariably turned down. One day, during our walk, he asked a favour of me.

" 'You know,' he said, 'that they're sitting again tomorrow?'

" 'Yes.'

" 'And that tomorrow will be a very critical day?'

"I nodded.

"So it would be. The defendant was going into the box.

" 'Well,' said Gill. 'I want you to do something for me – something to help. The man is in a highly excited state. He is violently resentful. Instead of coming back to London with me, I want you to travel with him and to calm him down.'

"I stood still and closed my eyes.

" 'Almost everything else,' I said. 'I'd do a great deal for you. But I do not want to sit by the side of that man.'

" 'I ask this of you,' said Gill. 'I want you to ride with him and to let him let go to you. If he lets go to you, he won't let go in the box. For he is now in that state in which he must let off steam. Encourage him to do it – to you. If he goes it in court tomorrow – well, there's an end of the case. He won't do it to me or to Wild. But he will to you.'

" 'All right,' I said. 'For your sake. But I simply loathe the idea.'

" 'I know you do,' said Gill. He put his arm through mine. 'And I'm greatly obliged. But it's really of great importance. Just let him talk. And – and – well, deal with him as you think fit. I'll ask him to give you a lift. I'll say you want to get back, but that I'm going to stop on the way.'

"I doubt if the defendant enjoyed the drive any more than I did. But I'll say he let himself go… Gill was perfectly right. The man had to let off steam. Next day he did very well in the witness-box.

"At the end of each hearing, Bodkin and I used to stay to hear the depositions which had been taken that day read through to the respective witnesses. These, I used to check with my note, and Bodkin with his recollection. Sometimes there was a dispute about the actual words which the witness had used: but Bodkin was always very charming and, with the generosity of the Crown, nearly always gave way.

"Of his great experience, Gill had realized from the beginning that, once the case reached a jury, the defendant was doomed. That was vision. He saw, and his sight was good. Nine counsel out of ten would have decided that the accused was bound to be committed for trial and would have reserved their defence. But Gill was the tenth. So the battle royal was fought in the Petty Sessional Court. It was really fought between Gill and the Justices, for Bodkin never pressed his cases, and in this particular case the evidence spoke for itself.

"From first to last, Gill did the whole case magnificently. He was on his mettle, and, so far as I saw, he never put a foot wrong. He examined and cross-examined to perfection. I've told you already how he *made* the Bench grant bail. On the last day, he made a supreme effort to persuade them to dismiss the case. If ever I saw a case which should have gone for trial, it was this one. But Gill very nearly did it. After his truly brilliant performance, the Justices retired to consider what they should do. And then at last they came back and announced that they had come to the conclusion that it was a case for a jury to decide. I can't say we were disappointed. You may cry for the moon, but you can't be disappointed if you don't get it. Gill had made an impossible demand. His triumph lay in the fact that his demand had been considered for very nearly an hour.

"I'm afraid I've strayed from the point I was trying to make." My sister smiled.

"Always do that for me. I wouldn't have missed a word."

"You're very sweet. Well, the prisoner was sent for trial. But when the solicitors asked which Judge would try the case, to the

48

general consternation, it proved to be Phillimore. Now Phillimore was, as I've said, a Puritan. He carried to excess an outlook which was inhumanly strict. If he was trying a man for stealing a duck and the fact emerged that the prisoner had a glad eye, that prisoner was doomed. Phillimore couldn't help it; that was the way he was made. And when we learned that he was to be the Judge that would try the case – well, we knew that if he did, the man might as well plead guilty as fight so hopeless a fight.

"So Charles Gill got going. The Attorney General was approached and he at once agreed that the case was not one which Phillimore should try. And so it stood over until the next Assize.

"The fellow went down all right, as he richly deserved. But we were, at least, spared Phillimore's reactions which would have sent us mad. And Phillimore was spared, too: for he was a genuine, though most objectionable, Puritan, and I really believe that the evidence would have shortened his life."

"Did it shorten yours?"

"No. But then I am not a Puritan and I am pretty tough. But it certainly shook me. But it was the dramatic situation that hit you between the eyes. There was the play before you, complete in every detail, a stronger, more terrible play than dramatists, ancient or modern, have ever dared to create. And it wasn't a play at all. It was the real thing."

"I believe you," said Berry, "but may we have the name?"

"I'd rather not give it. But this was in 1914, and the prisoner was sentenced at Lewes at the Summer Assize. Perhaps I've said too much, but I'd like to add one thing. The magistrates granted bail. As some time must elapse before he was tried, the accused asked the Crown's permission to visit America. Now the offence with which he was charged was not an extraditable offence: so, had he declined to return, he could not have been brought back. So the Crown, rather naturally, hesitated to comply with his request. But he promised that he would return to stand his trial.

So they let him go. And he kept his word and came back – for seven years."

*

"I feel," said Berry, "that the number of persons yet alive who were acquainted with the German in his habit as he lived before the first war must be comparatively small. And very few accurate pictures of the German of that day have ever been presented. The only one I ever came across appeared in *The Caravaners*, which was written by the lady who wrote *Elizabeth and her German Garden*. In that she presented a picture of a German officer and his unfortunate wife which was so lifelike that nearly all who read it supposed it to be a lampoon. Why? Because they couldn't believe it. They simply could not believe that any educated man could he so selfish, so complacent, so foolish, so arrogant, so offensive and so *gauche*. We are, of course, a tolerant lot, and we shrink from believing that other people are brutes. That is, in a way, a good fault: but it may prove extremely expensive. In Germany's case, it did. For the average German is not only cursed with the failings which the lady in question exposed, but he is very gross and inherently cruel. There are, of course, exceptions – at least, there were. But they only proved the rule.

"And now, having said my piece, which will do about as much good as a belch in a barrage – "

"You filthy brute," said Daphne. "Why must you be so disgusting?"

"The reflection," said her husband, "that, though my estimate is true, it will not be believed, induces, as always, congestion of the emotional ducts. I do not have to tell you that this must be dealt with at once; and the violent metaphor always affords me relief. However, as having frequently visited Germany before the first war, I am in a position to recount one or two items of behaviour which I witnessed myself in a country

50

some of whose ancient cities undoubtedly fill the eye. And Boy shall contribute others…

"On one occasion, I was escorting Aunt Adela, who had been distinguishing Wiesbaden, back to her English home. About half-past one we left our compartment and sought the restaurant-car. There we were allotted two seats at a table for four. Opposite us were two Germans – in excellent cue, for the German is fond of his food, and the luncheon served in those days was always extremely good. One of the Germans had a beard.

"No doubt, the train was late, for the driver just then decided to make up time. The pace was greatly increased, and the coach began to sway and to take the points in its stride.

"Soup was served – in soup plates. Afraid to risk it, Aunt Adela and I refused. But it takes more than the whim of an engine-driver to come between a German and his food. Our two vis-à-vis got down to it – literally. Anxious to lose not a drop, they approached their noses to their plates, in order to reduce the distance which their spoons would have to cover between their plates and their mouths. This was, no doubt, common sense, but the spectacle was hardly in the nature of an *aperitif*. However, they found it great fun, and they jested as they gobbled – and sometimes missed their mouths. And then the car gave the very hell of a lurch…

"The bearded German stopped some of his soup with his face, but most with his beard. The other got his on his chest. But nothing could diminish their good humour. They simply roared with laughter, regarding each other with tears hopping down their cheeks. Then one smeared his chest with his napkin: the other dabbed at his face and then wrung out his beard into his plate. *Then he picked up his spoon again…*

"Yes, I took Aunt Adela back to our carriage there. When we reached Cologne, I bought some sandwiches."

"I can only suppose," said Daphne, "you want to make us sick."

"In a way, I do," said Berry. "At least, not you, because I know you believe. If sickness is the price of belief let unbelievers be sick. After all, dogs will be dogs: if human beings are to imitate their less attractive pursuits...

"One flash from Wiesbaden. Aunt Adela purchased a paper and, strolling into the *Tiergarten*, or Park, sat down upon a bench to read. Very soon a policeman approached her. 'What are you doing?' he said. 'I'm reading a paper,' she said. 'Then be more careful,' he said, 'and move to that seat over there.' Aunt Adela stared. 'Why?' 'Use your eyes,' said the policeman. 'Regard the back of your seat.' Aunt Adela did as she was bid. On the back of her seat was a label *To be sat upon only*. 'On that seat over there,' said the policeman, 'you may sit and read.' Aunt Adela moved, to find that this was quite true.

"I was one day in Munich, a very pleasant city, with handsome streets and buildings and really beautiful fountains, always at work. The weather was very hot. I had spent a fruitful hour at one of the galleries, for the pictures at Munich need no commendation from me. And now I was strolling idly towards my hotel. My attention was attracted by a crowd which was gathered about the basin of one of the fountains to which I have just referred. So I turned aside and walked up, to see what was going on.

"In the great marble basin was a mongrel dog. I imagine that it had been thirsty and, in its endeavours to drink, had fallen in. At any rate, there it was. It was, of course, out of its depth, for the basin was deep: and, because the rim was polished, it couldn't get out. Every time he tried, the poor fellow's paws slipped off. And in desperation he'd swim to another place. How long he'd been there, I don't know; but his strength was failing fast and it isn't too much to say that he was a drowning dog. And the crowd was watching his struggles... And waiting for the last one of all. So was a German policeman... The latter improved the occasion with all his might. Each time the dog got his paws on the basin's rim, the policeman cried, 'Move along, there, move along': and the crowd fairly roared with laughter at this display of wit. But the dog's eyes were starting, for death was very close…

"I pushed my way to the basin, got the dog by the neck and hauled him out. The crowd retired a little – I think they thought he might shake himself, and they didn't want to get wet. But he hadn't the strength to do that. He just stood still, trembling, and let me pat his head. I was suddenly aware of the silence, and looked up to meet the stares. Then, 'English', said more than one, and spat on the ground. You see, I had spoiled sport."

"The filthy swine," cried Jill: "the filthy swine."

Berry shrugged his shoulders.

"I have exaggerated nothing. The crowd was an ordinary crowd – of business men and odd women and errand boys. It must have been sixty strong. And all I have said is God's truth."

My sister lifted her voice.

"Have you nearly done with the Germans? I can't stand very much more."

"Side-lights on history," said her husband, "don't always smell very sweet. What I have just related shows the inherent cruelty which made it not only possible, but natural for German men and women to administer Belsen and other institutions with such efficiency. Provided they are not the subjects, suffering, human or animal, leaves them cold. But that is not the stuff of which fellow creatures are made.

"On another occasion, in 1913, I happened to be in Berlin. Berlin is a vulgar city – at least, what is left of it was – with nothing to recommend it, so far as I saw. I was only there for two days, but a German who was introduced to me begged to be allowed to show me the latest luxury flats. All, he said, had been taken, but none were occupied: this was because there remained some work to be done. But the city was proud of them, because they were the last word. The special idea, of course, was to impress the Englishman. As I had time to spare, I thought I might as well go.

"They stood in a quarter of fashion, and, though I've forgotten the rent, it must have been very high. The entrance was imposing, and the hall within, very fine. A marble pavement and pillars. And the flat I was shown was convenient in every way. No expense spared. It was, no doubt, the last word. Six rooms, I think, and a bathroom, very well done. The servants' bedroom was small, but would just accept two. The kitchen was well contrived. It was on the small side, but well found. Built-in dresser, range, a capacious sink, lavatory – "

"What did you say?" said Daphne.

"Lavatory," said Berry, wide-eyed. "The servants' lavatory."

"D'you mean to say it opened out of the kitchen?"

"No, my darling. It didn't open out. There weren't any walls or door. It was just there. Between the sink and the – "

"*There?*" shrieked Daphne.

"There. Complete. Porcelain pan, hardwood seat, and the cistern with chain above. I can't remember whether there was a paper – "

"But not *in* the kitchen?"

"*In* the kitchen," said Berry. "I saw it – with these two orbs. It was part of the built-in equipment...in the latest luxury flats to be built in Berlin...in the year of Our Lord 1913. And some Boche had designed that kitchen. And others had seen and approved it – and taken the flat. And if, after that, you are going to tell me that the German is a fellow creature, all I can say is that I do not agree. I mean, even the animals – "

"Now I do feel sick," said Daphne. "Positively sick."

I poured a glass of brandy and put it into her hand. She sipped it thankfully.

"And that, again," said Berry, "is God's own truth. And will anyone deny that that is a side-light on history? Manners and modes of the German...on the eve of the first great war."

"Let Boy take over," said Daphne. "After the last half hour, the Newgate Calendar will be a great relief."

"I know," said Jill. "The Temple. Boy took me there once. Fountain Court was lovely, and so was Crown Office Row."

"We mustn't write a guidebook, my sweet."

"I know. But it was so lovely."

There was a little silence. The others knew that the laying waste of The Temple had hit me extremely hard.

"There's just one thing," I said. "You'll have to tell me whether it's worth setting down."

"I'll lay it isn't," said Berry. "Besides, I've just remembered the Germans at Marienbad. Boy was there in – "

As the storm of protest subsided, I took up my tale.

"When I left Treasury Chambers, I became a Common Lawyer and went to Brick Court. Number One had just been rebuilt, for that section of the building had been condemned. And there my chambers were, on the second floor. (Oliver Goldsmith had lived and worked in Brick Court, and so had Thackeray.) The head of my chambers, Harker, had the principal room: but mine was very pleasant and looked due South.

"Now Harker and I used to arrive at Brick Court at about the same time – between, say, half-past nine and a quarter to ten. And the first thing I always did was to go to his room. I was his devil, you see, and we used to discuss the work. If I had arrived before him, I sat in front of the fire and read *The Times* till he came.

"I'd been there about two years, when I entered Brick Court one morning, as I had done – well, hundreds of times before. I walked upstairs, opened our own front door and entered the nice, square hall. At once I noticed that the clerks had moved the hat-stand – you know: a mahogany thing, with hooks for hats and coats and a rack for umbrellas or sticks. I supposed they had some good reason, so I took off my coat and hat and hung them up.

"Top-hat, of course," said Berry.

"Of course. This was before the first war. When I was a Judge's Marshal, I always wore morning dress – in the county towns, I mean. And nobody found it strange, when I walked about the streets."

"You'd be mobbed now," said Daphne.

"Yes, I suppose I should. Well, I hung up my hat and coat and walked into Harker's room, as I always did. Harker hadn't arrived, but there was a stranger there...sitting at Harker's table...staring at me...

"Well, I stared back. I mean, the man wasn't waiting – he was at work on some brief...and sitting at Harker's table...in Harker's room...

"Well, we stared at each other in silence.

"Then something made me throw a glance round. The room was different. The red leather chair was gone, and instead of the one engraving, two cartoons by Spy were above the mantelpiece.

"A frightful thought came to my mind.

" 'My God,' I said. And then, 'Tell me, is this the third floor?'

"He nodded.

" 'That's right. The third floor,' he said.

"I never remember feeling such a fool. I had walked past our front door on the second floor, and climbed to the third, there to invade the privacy of the chambers exactly above. Except for the furniture, they were exactly like ours. And much of the furniture was the same.

"Consumed with mortification, I did the best I could. I apologized abjectly, explained that I belonged to the chambers below and that for some strange reason, for which I could not account, I must have walked up three flights, instead of two.

"From being pardonably sticky, the fellow became quite civil and said it didn't matter at all. Perhaps it didn't to him: but it did to me. I bowed myself out of his room, slunk through the hall, picked up my hat and coat and stole downstairs, like a thief.

"Harker hadn't arrived, so I sat down in front of his fire and wondered what he would say, when he heard what I'd done. I was still too hot and bothered to look at *The Times*.

"About seven minutes later Harker arrived.

"I think I shall always see him, standing in the doorway of his room, with his hat on the back of his head and his overcoat over his arm, staring at me, with his hand clapped fast to his mouth.

" 'Whatever's the matter?' I said, and got to my feet.

" 'Boy,' he said, 'I've done the most awful thing. The most damned awful thing that I've ever done.'

" 'Tell me,' said I. But I didn't have to be told. I knew. His words and his demeanour were too familiar.

" 'Well,' he said, 'I entered the hall, as usual, and the first thing I noticed was that the clerks – '

" ' – had moved the hat-stand,' said I. 'You needn't go on. Ten minutes ago I did the very same thing. Walked into the chambers upstairs and into your room.'

" 'Oh, I can't believe it,' said Harker. 'And a fellow sitting at my table?'

" 'That's right,' said I. 'He didn't seem too pleased, but he thawed a bit when I crawled – as I had to do.'

" 'That's more than he did with me. His manner was just black ice. And how could I protest? I never felt such a fool in all my life.'

" 'You can hardly blame him,' said I. 'Once, yes. That is just possible. But twice in the same ten minutes...' I shook my head. 'Of course he's now convinced that we were having him on.'

"Well, there we are. That is exactly what happened. And to this day, I cannot imagine why. I went out and scanned the staircase, to see if there was something which might have misled us both. But there was nothing at all."

"That," said my sister, "is most remarkable."

"Yes," said Berry, "it is. And I think that it should go in. It's evidence of something supernatural. On that particular morning some influence was at work in Number One Brick Court. An evil spirit or something was playing his knavish tricks."

"And the man was a stranger?" said Jill.

"Yes," said I. "That he had the chambers above means nothing at all. You can live above or below a man in The Temple for five years or more – and never know him by sight. Gill's chambers were below ours. Though we used the same stairs, I never saw him there once."

"Did you ever know a coincidence in a case?"

"I did – on one occasion. No damage was done. But there were two coincidences – each of them very strange. The whole of the tale is strange, and only about one-fifth has ever been told. Perhaps, if I changed some names…"

"We'll leave that to you."

"Madame la Comtesse de B— was the most remarkable woman I ever met. Her virtues were outstanding, and she had glaring faults. Her personality was the most powerful I ever knew. I never met her until she was fifty-five, but in her youth she must have been dazzling, indeed. For her own sex, she had a profound contempt: her conversation was brilliant; her sense of humour was rare. She was immensely rich.

"One summer's day, when she was in Austria, a cable arrived from London. This was how it ran. *Have been robbed please cable me twenty pounds George Dixon.*

"Now she knew George Dixon well. He was an English prelate of the Roman Catholic Church. I came to know him, too. And I feel bound to say, although I am not a Roman Catholic, that *Monseigneur* Dixon would have greatly distinguished the English Catholic Church."

"You put him in *Anthony Lyveden* and *Valerie French*."

"Yes, I did," said I. "He was *Cardinal Forest*. In fact Dixon never lived to get the red hat. He would have had it, if Pius the Tenth hadn't died: for the latter was very fond of Dixon: he used to call him 'Dixon *meus*'. But all of that's by the way.

"Madame de B— knew Dixon very well; and she knew that he was in England, on leave from Rome. But she did not believe that the cable had come from him, for he had friends in England to whom he could have applied. Yet she dared not ignore it, in case he was the sender and needed her help. The office of origin was on the Surrey side: the address was that of a house in a London Street; but she did not know London well, so these things didn't help. And so she cabled the money. At the same time she wrote to Dixon's address in Rome, to which she knew that he would shortly return.

"In a few days' time she had another cable. This came from Rome. *No such cable was ever sent by me George Dixon*. This confirmed her suspicions that she had been fooled. And Madame de B— was the wrong sort of woman to fool.

"Now she instantly made up her mind that the fraudulent cable had been sent by a play-boy she knew very well. (Their relation was strictly moral; but her acquaintance was wide.) He was, she knew, in England at the time at which the cable was sent, and they had lately quarrelled – he and she. No doubt this was his idea of twisting her tail. She decided that he must be taught that such ideas did not pay. So she wrote to her London detective – a first-rate man.

"The detective soon reported that the address on the cable was what is known as an 'accommodation address': it was, in fact, that of a small tobacconist's shop in a street which ran a stone's throw from Waterloo. The woman and her daughter, who kept it, remembered 'Mr George Dixon' and they described the play-boy without any prompting at all. That was enough for Madame de B— , and she instructed her detective to seek a warrant at once. He respectfully replied that such information would not be enough for the Court and that identification must take place.

"Now the play-boy was French – a younger son of a very great family. He hadn't a bean, but he was one of those blokes who never sink lower than the Ritz."

"That," said my wife, "is out of one of your books. *She Fell Among Thieves*, I think."

"You're right," said I, "and I apologize. But it exactly describes him."

"It exactly describes," said Berry, "a lot of wallahs I've met. How the hell they do it, I've no idea. But you've got to hand it to them, and the fact remains."

"Well, the play-boy was French, and he was back in France. In fact, he was at the Ritz. So the mother and daughter, who kept the tobacconist's shop, were taken over to Paris at vast expense. There they were put in a taxi, to sit outside the Ritz and take a look at the people who went in and out. After about three hours the play-boy appeared. At once, both women rose up and cried out, 'That's him.'

"Well, that was good enough. The women returned to London, an information was sworn and a warrant for the playboy's arrest was issued forthwith. But the offence was not an extraditable offence. Still, the play-boy was often in England, and every boat-train was met for week after week.

"I'm afraid I'll have to go back. Before the information was sworn, a statement was taken from Dixon. No, he had not sent the cable. He'd never been robbed. Where was he at such and such a time on such and such a day – the time and day on which the false cable was sent. Well, where do you think he was? *He was walking about the mean streets that neighbour Waterloo.* That morning he'd come from Hampshire to Waterloo. He was on his way to Southampton, *en route* for Rome. And he had an hour and a half to wait for his train. So he left his luggage with a porter and went for a walk. As like as not, he passed the office of origin at the very moment at which the cable was being dispatched. *Dispatched in his name.* Perhaps you can beat that. I can't. It was, of course, the purest coincidence: but, brought out in cross-examination, it would have sounded strange."

"I'll say it would," said Berry. "They couldn't have put him in the box."

"I told them as much," said I. "And he came to me about it and asked what I thought. 'The defence may not get it,' I said, 'but if they do, I must tell you frankly they'll fairly lam it in.' 'I didn't do it,' he said. 'You don't have to tell me that, sir. But you must see that of all coincidences it is the most unfortunate that any evil spirit could have devised.' 'Perhaps,' he said, 'perhaps it won't come to that.' 'I don't think it will,' said I. And I was perfectly right.

"The weeks went by, but the play-boy stayed fast in France. 'He's afraid to return to England,' said Madame de B— . So we all thought.

"Late that summer, S F Edge, the famous racing motorist, was spending a fortnight at Ostend. One day he received a cable. *Have been robbed please cable me twenty pounds.* And the cable was signed with the name of a close friend of his. But S F Edge wasn't deceived, for the friend in question had joined him in Ostend the day before. Edge cabled to Scotland Yard – and a man was sent at once to the accommodation address…

"The culprit was a clerk in the cable office. As soon as he was arrested, he threw in his hand. He confessed to sending both cables and to having obtained twenty pounds by sending the first. He was committed for trial and presently appeared at the Old Bailey, where he pleaded guilty. Madame de B—'s solicitors sent me a watching brief. And so I saw the man. If you'd put him beside the play-boy, you could hardly have told them apart.

"So that was that. But Madame de B— wouldn't have it. She always maintained that the play-boy had sent the first cable to twist her tail."

"That was childish," said Daphne.

"Of course it was," said I. "But I said she had glaring faults."

"Dixon wasn't called?"

"No. The Crown only proceeded on the S F Edge case, and, before he was sentenced, the prisoner asked that Madame de B—'s case should be taken into account."

"So nothing about the first case ever came out?"

"Nothing. I don't think her name was mentioned. It was very much better so."

"Poor Dixon must have been thankful."

"I'm sure he was. For such a man, it was a most unpleasant position, and had the play-boy been charged – and had he come to London before Edge's cable was sent, he certainly would have been charged – well, Dixon's position would have been dreadful, indeed. For he had met the play-boy at Madame de B—'s."

"And the play-boy might have gone down?"

"He might indeed," said I. "In any event, it would have been a hell of a case."

"God bless my soul," said Berry. "How little we really know about such things. Have you got any more?"

"I remember half a coincidence. Perhaps a fair description would be 'a curious chance'. But it did concern a well-known murder case."

Berry rose and poured me a glass of port.

"I quitted Treasury Chambers in 1910: from there, as I have told you, I went to Brick Court. In Treasury Chambers I'd been Travers Humphreys' pupil. And the last thing I did with him was the Crippen case. I'll deal with that later on, but not tonight. Some three months after I'd left him, an old lady died and was buried in Camden Town. At least, that was where she died. For two or three years she had been a paying guest – with some people whose name was Balsam. She was a very paying guest, for she left Balsam all she had and he had insured her life for quite a big sum. I imagine it was the Insurance Company that asked the first questions of all and didn't like the replies. Be that as it may, two or three months later the old lady's body was exhumed. Less than a week after that the Balsams, husband

and wife, were under arrest. The charge was wilful murder. And when the Crown opened its case, it disclosed that considerable traces of arsenic had been found in the old lady's body and alleged that this terrible poison had been administered by her hosts. Now the Balsams employed a solicitor whom they knew. He lived not far from them and he was a personal friend. And he briefed Gervais Rentoul, a son of the Judge. (He wasn't a High Court Judge, but he sat at the Old Bailey and the City of London Court. He was one of the best after-dinner speakers I ever heard. He used to write his letters on the Bench. And, if ever I was before him, he always showed me a kindness which I in no way deserved. In spite of his correspondence, he always did very well. Some people were funny like that. Knowing that I wrote in my spare time, the Senior Chancery Registrar once asked me to recommend him some books. 'I get so bored in court, sitting under the Judge.') I knew Rentoul quite well. We'd been at Oxford together and he was called to the Bar a year before I. And this was his first big brief. Travers Humphreys appeared for the Crown. And the case began to take shape.

"One day, before making for The Temple, I drove to the Stores. Then I walked to St James's Park and took the train. When I entered one of the coaches, there was Travers Humphreys all by himself. I went and sat down by his side, and we passed the time of day. Presently – " 'The King against Balsam,' I said. 'Crippen repeats himself.'

" 'I wish he would,' said Humphreys. 'It's not so good.'

" 'Why, what's the trouble?' said I.

"Humphreys lowered his voice.

" 'We can't prove possession of the poison.'

" 'Oh dear,' said I.

" 'Exactly. He did it all right. You can take my word for that. But proof is another matter. If we can't prove possession, Balsam is going to get off. And he oughtn't to get off, for this is a wicked case.'

"He had my sympathy. The Balsams had been charged and at the second hearing he'd had to open the case. And now he had got to prove it. And, as things stood, he couldn't prove it. He could allege that Balsam had administered the arsenic: but when Balsam swore that he had never had any arsenic to administer, his statement could not be countered. I mean arsenic's not like flour. You can't buy it by the pound."

"In Crippen's case, you had it."

"Oh, yes. Crippen was a quack doctor. He made up drugs. And in some of the drugs he made up, he used hyoscine. And hyoscine was the poison with which he poisoned his wife.

"Well, we walked to The Temple together, and he went to Paper Buildings and I to Brick Court. I hadn't been there half an hour when my clerk came into the room. Would I speak to Mr Rentoul? I told him to put him through. Rentoul wanted to know if I'd a few minutes to spare. I said I had. 'May I come round and see you?' 'Of course.' 'You're quite alone?' 'Yes.'

"Five minutes later Gervais Rentoul arrived.

"He sat very close to me and spoke very low.

'I want your advice,' he said. 'You've been in Treasury Chambers and know the ropes. Well, I'm defending the Balsams, as you know. Now, entirely between you and me, the prosecution is stuck. They can't prove possession of the poison. And unless they can prove that, they won't get home.'

" 'I see,' I said. 'Go on.'

" 'Boy,' he said, 'this is strictly between you and me.'

" 'Of course,' said I. 'You know I never talk.'

" 'Well, the thing is this. There were fly-papers in the house for some time before her death.'

" 'The devil there were.'

" 'There were. Now should they get hold of that fact, they will suggest that the victim was poisoned by the water in which the fly-papers were soaked.'

" 'They certainly will,' said I. 'Everyone knows that – '

64

" 'Not so fast,' says Rentoul. 'Does everyone know? I know it's a popular belief that you can poison a person by giving him that water to drink. But has that ever been proved?'

" 'I believe it has,' said I. 'But that was some time ago.'

" 'The solicitor doesn't believe it, and I'm not sure.'

" 'Well, if they get it, the Crown will have its analysts and so can you.'

" 'The solicitor says we should be ready, in case they do.'

" 'What ever d'you mean?'

" 'Well, he wants to get some fly-papers and see for himself.' "I said, 'Good God.'

" 'Well, I advised against it and said I'd see what you said.'

" 'I trust you didn't mention my name.'

" 'Oh, no. But I said that you knew the ropes and that your advice would be sound.'

" 'Well, tell him this,' said I. 'Tell him to expunge the word "fly-paper" not only from his vocabulary, but from his brain – until you have won your case and the Balsams are free.'

" 'I thought you'd say that,' says Rentoul.

" 'Gervais,' I said, 'be your age. Whether anyone can die of drinking fly-paper water, I do not know: but I know I wouldn't drink it for fifty thousand pounds. And, if you purchase a fly-paper, you must sign the poison-book. That rather looks as if they were dangerous. More. Poison-books can be produced in court. And if anyone connected with Balsam were to sign a poison-book at this moment, when every paper in England is splashing this case – well, two and two do make four, and any number of people can do that simple sum.'

"Rentoul thanked me and left.

"But I've always found it strange that, within the same hour, the Crown should have told me of the door which they could not unlock, and the Defence should have come to me and shown me the key." With that, I got to my feet. "We must go to bed."

"Don't be absurd," said Daphne. "You can't leave it there. What happened?"

"That's the end of my tale," said I. "Everyone knows the rest."

"Well, I don't," said Jill. " Go on."

I sat down again.

"My advice was ignored. A few days later, casually enough no doubt, the solicitor asked one of his daughters if she was going out. She said she was. 'Then get some fly-papers,' he said. 'There seem to be a great many flies about.' That afternoon his daughter went forth to shop. On the way home she fell in with the elder Miss Balsam. The two were old friends. They were heading for home, when the solicitor's daughter stopped dead. 'Oh, there now,' she said. 'I've forgotten something. Father told me to get some fly-papers.' 'Oh,' says Miss Balsam. 'I know where you can get them. I got some for Daddy not very long ago.' So the two turned back together."

I saw Daphne cover her mouth.

"Yes," said I. "It really is rather dramatic. Miss Balsam took her friend to a chemist's shop. Her friend asked for some fly-papers. The chemist said no, he had none. 'Well, you had,' says Miss Balsam, 'because I got some here.' 'When was that?' says the chemist, staring. 'About six months ago.' 'Not here,' says the chemist. 'You've made a mistake in the shop.' 'I did,' says Miss Balsam. *And I signed the poison-book.*' So the chemist takes it down. 'What name?' he said. 'Er, Balsam.' The chemist stiffened. 'That's right,' he said. 'Balsam. And now I remember you.' He opened the book and looked back. 'On the fourth of June?' he said. 'Is that your signature?' 'Yes.' He shut the book. 'Well, I haven't got any now.' As the girls left the shop, he picked up the telephone...

"The following afternoon the Treasury sent Travers Humphreys the proof which he so much desired."

"How awful," said Jill.

"Just Fate," said I. "Fate saw that justice was done. Mrs Balsam was found 'Not Guilty'. But I saw Balsam sent down. I shouldn't have gone, but there was a man in my chambers who wanted to see the case. And they wouldn't let him in. But I was known. And so I took him there. By then it was almost over. The jury was out. But he wanted to see Balsam. Then the jury came back and Balsam re-entered the dock. And then he realized that Balsam was about to be sentenced. 'Take me out,' he whispered. 'Don't be a fool,' I whispered. 'It's too late now.' So Rentoul never made his name. But he did quite well. He was made a Police Magistrate. Marylebone, if I remember. But that was several years later, after the war."

*

"Last night," said Berry, "you made an observation which was not commonplace."

"I'm glad of that," said I.

"I don't suppose you realized it," said Berry, "but you did. And what you said reminded me of an occasion which I am happy to record. You said that Judge Rentoul used to write letters on the Bench, but you submitted that that pursuit did not affect his administration of justice."

"I could never see that it did. His summings-up were sound and he never missed any point."

"That was because his control of his brain was such that he was able to do two things at once. In the course of the first great war I was taking part in a military exercise in Egypt. And one of my duties necessitated the 'occupation' of some station upon some railway line. It was only a gesture, of course: the working of the railway went on. I walked into the telegraph office. There was the station-master dealing with a message in Morse. He was an Egyptian. Now I could read and send Morse in those far-off days; and so I stood by his side. And then I saw what he was doing. A receiver was strapped to his ear: with his right hand he was writing a message down: with his left he was sending it on to somebody else: his left was about ten letters behind his right.

I suppose you might call that killing two birds with one stone: but if you can beat it, I can't. And I saw it done."

"Incredible," said Daphne.

"But true. The art of concentration brought to a perfect pitch. We obey our brains: his brain obeyed him. After all, the biggest shots at the Bar were pretty good in that line."

"That's perfectly true," said I. "Their powers of concentration bewildered the average man. The answer is, of course, that they were supermen. Take F E Smith, for instance, afterwards Birkenhead. I've seen him come into the robing-room after an all-night sitting at the House. Cigar in his face and looking as fresh as paint. As like as not, he'd be leading in three big cases that day. He'd sum up for the plaintiff in one. The instant he'd finished a really remarkable speech, he'd leave for another court: there he'd cross-examine a defendant – and that, quite brilliantly. Whilst he was still on his feet, his clerk would be pulling his gown, for another Court was ready to hear him argue a difficult point of law. He might or might not have done by half-past four, when the Court would rise. Smith would leave at once for his chambers, there to hold consultations on three or more different cases soon to be tried. And about half-past six he would return to the House.

"I may be wrong, but I don't think that sort of life could be led by the average man. I mean, all Smith touched, he distinguished. The point of law which he argued could not have been argued so well by anyone else. (Perhaps I should except Danckwerts, for he was the greatest lawyer of them all.) I confess that nothing he did compares with the station-master's feat, but I think you may fairly say that Smith made his brain obey him. And he was but one of several, almost as good."

"Supermen all," said Berry. "About that, there can be no doubt. Their power of concentration resembled a spotlight which they could focus first upon one case and then upon another, to the complete exclusion of everything else. And now let me add a rider, which may make some people think. How was Smith able to do as much as he did? To sit up all night in the House and pull such a hell of a weight on the following day? Because he was perfectly served – waited on hand and foot. A chauffeur to drive him: a valet to help him undress and prepare his bath: other servants to produce his breakfast... Because he was spared every atom of physical effort. If he'd had to stoke his own furnace, before he could have a bath; clean his own shoes; help his wife to get breakfast and help her again to wash up before he went off; drive himself to the Temple – well, a very great man would never have left the ruck. Of such is the price of the death of domestic service. No man, they say, is a hero to his own valet. That may or may not be true. But no man becomes a hero who hasn't got one. Conceive the one and only Arthur cleaning his own boots on the eve of Vittoria."

"Or Waterloo," said Daphne.

"Ah, he was a Field-Marshal then. And I think a Field Marshal has a share in a batman today. And now it's Boy's turn. My gorge must be allowed to subside."

"You said last night," said my sister, "that you put Monseigneur Dixon into two of your books?"

"So I did."

"The portrait was unmistakable?"

"I can't say that. You see, I didn't know him so very well. But I had him full in my mind."

"And you did it again," said Berry, "with that very prince of masters, Norman Kenneth Stephen of Harrow School."

"As well you know – in the Prologue of *The Berry Scene*."

"And that *was* recognized?"

"Yes."

"Anyone else?"

"I don't think so. *Bell* in the Chandos books was inspired by the second 'first servant' I had in the first great war. He was – perfection. But every one of my characters is a composite picture of persons I've seen or known."

"Even *Aunt Harriet*?" said Jill.

69

"In *Ann*? Yes."

"*Ann*," said Berry, "is the very best short story you ever wrote. Most are tripe, so that isn't saying much. But *Ann* – "

"They aren't," shrieked Jill. "Boy's never written tripe."

"Well, mediocre, then."

"And that's untrue," said Daphne. She looked at me. "How long was your name put first?"

"On the covers of magazines? For exactly twenty years. To tell you the truth, I'm rather proud of that."

"Where was it put after that?"

"Not even inside," I said. "You see, I stopped writing short stories before I lost my place."

"Very wise," said Berry. " Did you always insist upon being given precedence?"

"I never once raised the point. The editors did as they pleased."

"Are short stories easier to write than novels?"

"I wouldn't say that they were. The two are entirely different. When I'm writing a novel, after a very few pages the book takes charge."

"That is a saying," said Daphne, "I never can understand."

"Well, I become an amanuensis. I don't know what's coming next. That's why, when American editors used to ask me for a synopsis, I never could give them one: for I'd no idea of the line which the book would take. So I used to make one up: but I always said, 'But it mayn't turn out like this' – and, of course, it never did."

"Look here," said Berry. "I am a reasonably credulous man. But I'm not a damned fool. D'you mean to sit there and tell me that, when you wrote *She Fell Among Thieves* you didn't bring *Jenny* in to be *Chandos*' second wife?"

"Certainly," said I. "I never suspected her existence, till *Chandos* saw her in the distance by the side of the pool. And, when she walked into their arms, I thought she was going to marry *Mansel*. It never occurred to me that she liked *Chandos* best."

"Well, either you're mental," said Berry, "or else you're the biggest liar I ever met."

"Let's say I'm mental," said I. "D'you remember *Blind Corner*?

"No woman in it," said Berry. "The best thing you ever did. Not that that's saying much."

"Be quiet," said Jill.

"At the end of the penultimate chapter, the faithful party is stuck. Stuck good and proper. Am I right?"

"Yes," said Berry, "I suppose you might call it 'stuck'. They're only entombed alive. Ten yards or so of their tunnel have fallen in, and they have no shovels or picks: the other way out is barred – by four bars which they cannot move: beyond the bars is a passage which leads to the bottom of a well, in which the water is rising very fast: and the well is ninety feet deep. And you call it 'being stuck'."

"Well, I wrote the last words of that chapter late one night. When I read them through the next morning, I almost lost my nerve. I remember saying aloud, 'My God, I've done it now.' For I could not see how any men *could* emerge from such a predicament. Then I calmed down. 'Well,' I said to myself, 'the book has brought me so far: the only thing I can do is to go straight on.' And so I did. And the book brought them out all right, without any fuss. And *The Times* said 'The escape from the great well is story-telling of a high order.' "

"So it was," said Berry. "I give the book best. And when you write a dud, that's the book's fault, too?"

"I suppose so," said I. "I only do as I'm told."

"But not in short stories?" said Daphne.

"Not to the same extent. I can usually see the outline. Though I don't think I did in *Ann*. I certainly never foresaw her husband's death."

"How long did *Ann* take you to write?"

DORNFORD YATES

"Exactly six weeks. I always remember that."

"That's very slow," said Berry.

"I've always been very slow. *Red in the Morning* went quickly
– I don't know why."

"A rotten title," said Berry.

"Beast," said Jill.

"Not one of my best, my darling."

"So was *This Publican*."

"To be honest," said I, "*This Publican* was one of the very
best titles I ever chose. But it was too subtle. Lots of people
thought that it was a religious book."

"I do hope," said Berry, "they sent it to their maiden aunts.
They'd have enjoyed *Rowena*, wouldn't they?"

"*Lower Than Vermin*," said Jill, "was one of your best."

I shook my head.

"Thousands didn't get it," I said. I glanced at my wrist. "Just
look at the time we've wasted. It's Berry's turn."

"But this must go in," said Daphne.

"Not into the book?"

"Of course it must," said Jill.

"I think it should," said Berry. "Among those of little taste,
you have acquired a certain low reputation for delivering the
goods. You've never written a classic, like *Forever Amber*: and
you've never rammed home sex, as every novelist should. That
very convenient epithet, so often preceding 'fool', does not
appear in any of your books. You've never belonged to The
Savage Club: you never came out of Fleet Street: you know no
other author and you know no critics at all. You've never
lectured in America. You never fought for the Communists in
the Spanish Civil War, and you have never patronized the Café
Royal. You have always lived your own life and have always sat
down to meals at the accepted time. You dislike publicity, and
you've never used your pen-name except on the covers of your
books. In short, you have broken every rule that Fleet Street lays
down. You are a black marketeer. Yet, as I say, to the less

exacting, you issue a furtive appeal. They derive an unlawful pleasure from reading your rotten books. And I think it only right that they should be shown the horrid nature of the ground upon which they venture to tread."

"I've been speaking off the record," said I.

"Bung it in," said Berry. "Mother knows best. And what's the Newgate Calendar done?"

"One moment," said Daphne. "Titles. What shall you call this book?"

"CONVERSATION PIECE," said Berry.

"Glorious," said Jill.

"So it is," said I. "And it's exactly right. Unhappily, it has been used – as the name of a play."

"What does that matter?" screamed Berry. "Is every inspiration I have to be cast into the draught?"

"If it's second-hand – yes."

"But I never knew it had been used. I created the blasted thing."

"Sorry," said I. "But it's been created before. And now try again."

Berry expired. Then –

" 'Try again.' This isn't a spelling-bee. Flashes of genius are not to be controlled. What about REGURGITATION?"

"Whatever's that mean?" said Jill.

"A gushing-back," said Berry. "You see the idea? Our memories have gushed back."

"I don't like the sound of it," said Daphne.

"Neither," said I, "do I. It's sometimes used of drains, which have been stopped up."

"I know," said Berry. "CUD."

"CUD?" screamed Daphne. "You can't call any book CUD."

"But that's what it is," said Berry. "This book is the cud which Boy and I are chewing. When a cow crops grass, it doesn't masticate; it shoves it straight into its stomach. Then it lies down, and the stomach regurgitates the grass into its mouth for it to chew. That grass is then called cud. The analogy is exact."

"You really are bestial," said Daphne.

"All right," said Berry. "You choose one."

"What about PRIVATE VIEW?"

"That's quite good," said I.

"It's one of your chapter-headings."

"I know. But it suits the book."

"I think it's rotten," said Berry. "PRIVATE VIEW. What of?"

"Well, it hasn't been used," said I, " – so far as I know."

"That doesn't surprise me," said Berry. "And I don't want to be the first. You might as well call it PUBLIC PRINT."

"Well, I think it's good," said Jill. "It is a private view of the things you both saw and heard."

"I doubt if we'll beat it," said I. "Of course, it isn't as good as CONVERSATION PIECE."

"Not in the same suburb," said Berry. "What if that has been used as the name of a play?"

"That knocks it out," said I.

Berry expired again. Then –

"What about THE BLAST IN THE BELLOWS?"

"People wouldn't get it," I said, laughing.

"I don't see what it means," said Jill.

"There you are," I said. "He has, my sweet, THE WIND IN THE WILLOWS in mind."

"PERSONAL PROPERTY," said Daphne.

"That's a very good title," said I, "but it wouldn't fit. You see, we're trying to suppress our personalities. As Berry and I were saying, before we began – "

"There you are," roared Berry. "There you are. AS BERRY AND I WERE SAYING. And can you beat that?"

"Well done," said I. "And that's how a title should come."

"Quite perfect," said Daphne.

Berry looked round.

"Let me put," he said, "an oratorical question. That means, let me say, a question which requires no answer. What would you do without me? Everything of value in this rotten book is being furnished by that dazzling and inestimable faculty – my mother-wit. And now I provide the title. While you were all scouring your brain-pans – "

"Boy said it first," said Jill.

"Give me air," cried Berry, excitedly. "Open the window, someone. 'Boy said it first.' Of course he did. But out of his vomit, I plucked this…"

For the next forty-five seconds Daphne and Jill dealt with him faithfully.

"It's disgusting," my sister concluded. "Some filthy allusion is constantly on your tongue."

"It's all emotion," said Berry. "That child-wife, sitting there, saw fit to plunge a plough-share into my bowels. They're the seat of the emotions, you know. The Sainted Paul – "

"That's quite enough," said his wife.

"All right, all right," said Berry. "Invade the liberty of the subject. Throttle free speech. And what's the Old Bailey done?"

"Not tonight," said I. "I can give you a memory of Bow Street."

"Proceed."

"It occurred before I was 'called', while I was a solicitor's pupil in Bedford Row. One Monday morning I reached the office, as usual, just before half-past nine. And I met the senior partner just going out. This was most unusual, for, in the ordinary way, he never reached the office before a quarter to ten.

"He smiled at my surprise.

" 'Trouble at Bow Street,' he said. And then, 'I shan't want you.'

"I never know what it was that made me say, 'Mayn't I come?' Never before had I questioned what Muskett said. I just felt I'd better go.

"Muskett looked faintly surprised, for his word was law. Then he said, 'Oh, well, you can if you like.'

"So I turned and fell in beside him. We walked to Holborn, there to pick up a cab.

" 'I have no papers,' said Muskett. 'I only know it's a case of assaulting the police. A pretty bad one, I gather. In Leicester Square. The Commissioner's very angry. They rang me up at my house.'

"His words set me thinking. I had been out of London that Saturday night. It wasn't 'Boat-race Night'. All the same, I had seen disorder in Leicester Square…"

" 'Boat-race Night,' " said Berry. "Those were the days. I've been chucked out of *The Empire* on 'Boat-race Night.' And, as they threw you out, they chalked your back: so that, when you returned, they could see if you were one of the blokes of whom they were tired."

"Do you treasure that memory?" said his wife.

"Yes," said Berry, "I do. I used to recall it when I was up on the Bench – and temper justice with mercy, because I knew. I was never blind, you know: never more than just nicely. But what an evening it was. Now they climb up Eros – do their best to destroy an exquisite work of art. If that had been done in my day, the squirt that did it would damned near have lost his life. Shall we continue now?"

"*You* interrupted," said Daphne.

"Nonsense," said her husband. "I accepted an invitation to enrich a statement of fact. I did so lavishly – to be rent, as the swine were rent. No, that's wrong. As the mugs were rent by the swine, when they cast their pearls before them. You know, I can't help feeling – "

"Go on, Boy."

"Well, we got to Bow Street about a quarter to ten. The bench was empty: the Magistrate would not sit before ten o'clock. As we took our seats, an Inspector appeared and said that 'the statements were on the way'. Muskett shrugged his shoulders. 'Show me the charge-sheet,' he said.

"He looked at the charge-sheet. Then he gave it to me.

"One Stephen Close, clerk, was charged with being drunk and disorderly and with assaulting the police. On Saturday night, of course.

" 'My God,' I said, 'I know him. The fellow's a friend of mine. We were at Oxford together. And he isn't a clerk at all. He's doing well at the Bar.'

"Muskett said nothing. Just then the statements arrived. As he read them, he passed them to me. It was, as he had said, 'a pretty bad case'. Stephen had been chucked out of *The Empire*. Well, that was all right – er, quite nice people were. But he had resented this treatment, and, since he was fighting drunk, the chuckers-out had been reinforced by the police. Stephen had laid out three policemen – one was still sick – and it had taken five more to get him down. He had to be strapped to a stretcher, before they could get him away. An immense crowd had gathered to watch this disgraceful scene and traffic had been interrupted...

"As I handed the statements back, 'Your friend's luck,' said Muskett, 'is out today. Marsham is sitting. And you know what Marsham is.'

"Well, something had to be done. When Stephen and I were at Oxford, I knew him very well. Though a year senior to me, he'd always been very friendly, and I liked and admired his style. We'd done odd things together. We'd chanced the proctors and visited Abingdon Fair. One night, coming back from the theatre, he was attacked by five toughs. It was he that did the damage, for he was immensely strong and he knew how to hit: but I set my back against his and gave as good as I got. He laid three out, and the other two took to their heels. And now he was at the Bar and was doing well. I hadn't seen him lately, for The Temple was off my beat. But Stephen did all things well.

The man had drive. And he was abstemious. But, if he did drink too much, the man was dangerous. The liquor went to his fists.

"As fast as I could, I poured this out to Muskett. And all the time I was talking, Muskett fingered his chin. When I had done, 'Well, I won't press it,' he said. 'But I can't alter the facts. You'd better see the Inspectors in charge of the case.'

"I was off in a flash.

"Those men were terribly good. The moment I said that he was a friend of mine, they looked at one another and said, 'Oh, well.' I said, 'He's one of the best. He's at the Bar and he's doing terribly well. If the Magistrate sends him to jail, he'll be disbarred. So if you could tone it down...'

" 'That's all right, sir,' said one. 'And he did come round to the station on Sunday afternoon. And said he was sorry. I'll bring that out.'

" 'You're very good,' I said. 'I tell you he's one of the best, but when the drink is in him, he just goes mad.'

" 'And there you're right, sir. He half killed one of my men. But, if he's a friend of yours...'

"Then an usher called for silence. As I slid back to Muskett's side, the Magistrate took his seat.

"Marsham was really a splendid magistrate. He was a great gentleman. In his youth he had gained his Blue – for cricket, I think. He was a member of a well-known County family, always distinguished for the example it set. He was a good lawyer and he knew his world. He had no need of money, and his job was not congenial to such a man: but he thought it his duty to do it, and so he did. He did it terribly well. But he was a stickler for good behaviour. For the poor, he would make allowance. For a man who should have known better, none at all. *Noblesse oblige.* Muskett was perfectly right, when he said Stephen's luck was out.

"At once the case was called and Stephen entered the dock. I dared not look at him, but I had seen him see me as he was brought into Court. Muskett rose and said he appeared for the police. And Stephen pleaded guilty.

"Then Muskett presented the case...

"Now Muskett was a just man, and he always presented his cases extremely well. The militant suffragists, for instance, sent him half out of his mind, but he always presented their cases without emotion. He was stern, but scrupulously fair. In Stephen's case, he knew his client was angry – I mean, the Commissioner of Police. For that reason he had been sent for. In the ordinary case of assault, the police-inspectors managed the matter themselves: apart from what Muskett might say, his mere appearance declared the gravity of the case. Yet, upon this occasion, he far more than kept his word. 'I won't press it.' His short address to the Magistrate could hardly have been bettered by some counsel briefed for the defence. Yet Muskett had never been at Oxford and had never had any of those things we call advantages. So his gesture was handsome, indeed. And he made it for my sake. And the two inspectors played up. They slurred the assaults and they mentioned that Stephen had come to the station on Sunday, to say how sorry he was."

"That's too easy," said Berry. "Besides, they all do that. Don't tell me that weighed with Marsham."

"I quite agree. But it showed they were trying to help. Stephen, of course, said nothing. Then the case was closed, and Marsham sat back in his chair. And then he let go. I'll say he dressed Stephen down. With a tongue like a pickled rod, he lashed him right and left. Right up to the last, I thought he'd send him to jail. But he didn't. Twenty-five pounds and costs – and Stephen was clear.

"Well, that was all right: but, as Arthur would have said, it was a damned nice thing – the nearest run thing you ever saw in your life. And if, on that Monday morning, I had been one minute later in reaching Bedford Row; if some strange intuition, for which I cannot account, had not bid me ask Muskett to let me come, Stephen would have gone down for a month or six weeks. And had he been sent to prison, he must have been disbarred."

"I hope and believe," said Berry, "that he sought you out forthwith and stood you the finest dinner that Scotts could serve. Three dozen oysters apiece, a succulent *tournedos*, Stilton to follow, and all washed down with champagne."

"Steady," said I. "I deserved no credit at all. If I hadn't done what I could, I should have been a sweep of the vilest sort. To Muskett, the credit: because I pleaded for Stephen, he risked his employer's wrath. And to the police: they had every right to be cross: because I asked them to do so, they toned their evidence down."

"The fact remains," said Berry, "that if you hadn't gone all out – done your best with Muskett and done your best with the police, Master Stephen Close would have been sent to jail. Is that so, or not?"

"Oh, yes," said I. "You can't get away from that. With Marsham on the bench, he wouldn't have had a hope."

"Hard labour?"

"Without a doubt. I think he'd have got six weeks."

"And been disbarred?"

"Automatically."

"His career finished, as soon as it had begun?"

"Yes."

"And you were the *deus ex machina*?"

"I happened to be cast for that role."

"Doesn't one dine and wine a friend in need?"

I shrugged my shoulders.

"It didn't work out like that."

"How did it work out? As students of human nature, let's hear the truth."

"Ten days later," I said, "I attended a conference. This was in Paper Buildings. On my way back to the office, I ran straight into Stephen by Inner Temple Hall. We naturally stopped, for I hadn't seen him since. 'Hullo, Stephen,' I said. He looked me up and down. 'I suppose you expect me,' he said, 'to thank you for saving my life.' I confess that my smile faded: but though I was off my balance, I managed to keep my head. 'You're wrong,' I said. 'I expect nothing of you. But I can tell you this – that, if I hadn't been there, you wouldn't be here in The Temple talking to me. You would be stitching mail-bags in Wormwood Scrubs.' Then I stepped to one side and left him."

Jill's hand stole into mine.

"For years I couldn't fathom behaviour so gross. And then one day I got it. 'Neither a borrower, nor a lender be; For loan oft loses both itself and friend.' Shakespeare is always right. As you know, there are many men who, if you lend them money, will hate you for the rest of your life. Why? Because they know that they are beholden to you. And there you have it. As a result of my interference, Stephen was beholden to me. And that, he could not forgive."

"Words fail me," said my sister.

"I'm glad of that. I'd rather you didn't comment. Besides, it's ancient history. All this happened quite forty years ago."

" 'Forty years on,' " said Berry. " 'Loved the ally with the heart of a brother.' Never mind. I trust what Marsham said appeared in the press."

"I can't remember," I said. "The police toned it so much that the case wasn't splashed. But about that, I do nothing. How it is today, I don't know: but in those days to approach a reporter was to cut your throat."

"What d'you mean?" said Jill.

"The reporter's sense of duty was very high. He was trusted by his paper to report what he thought his paper should know. And any attempt to induce him to leave something out was an attempt to make him betray his trust. Incidentally, it showed him at once that, though he might have ignored it, this matter was 'news'. And so you went down the drain. And now let us edit my report."

"Of course," said Daphne, "of course it must all go in. It is a true short story. It's very bitter, I know. But it has a terrible punch. If you had written that up, any Editor would have paid you a hundred pounds."

"I don't know about that."

"What were you paid by *The Windsor*, when every month they published a tale by you?"

"I clambered up to more than I think I deserved."

"And America?"

"They didn't take every one. For those they took, they paid a very good price."

"You never employed an agent?"

"I had to in America. In England I never did."

"Copyright?" said Berry.

"I had to be careful about that in the United States.

"The thing was this. By the Berne convention, all countries on earth agreed that if a book was copyrighted in one country, the copyright should be honoured by all others. That meant that, once a book was published in England or France or Germany – where you will, that book could not be published elsewhere without the author's permission for ten years. This virtually secured his right to royalties for as long as he lived – and for fifty years thereafter. I say 'all countries'. Only the United States refused to come in. By such a refusal they stood to gain a great deal. Their output's appeal to Europe was very slight; but Europe's output often appealed to them. And they had a colossal public. So, to save your copyright in America, your book had to be published in the United States within one year. And this wasn't always easy, for publishers wouldn't play. If they waited a year, they knew that they'd get it for nothing. And so they usually did. Only when he feared competition, would a publisher take a book, and thereby stake his claim. The royalties he paid were beggarly. But what could the author do? Jerome K Jerome wrote that classic *Three Men in a Boat*. America waited until one year had elapsed. And then they pirated it. If Jerome had had a royalty on every copy sold, he would have been a dollar millionaire. But he never received one penny, and died a poor man. Things are much better now, but they used to be very bad."

"You wrote nothing during the War."

"Never a line. During the first war, I mean. I had neither inclination nor opportunity. Some people managed to do it – I never knew how. And now, by George, it's your turn."

"Tomorrow," said Daphne, rising. "I can't say I'm tired; but it's nearly one, and I have an engagement to keep at half past nine."

"Not a perm?" said I.

"For my sins."

"How any woman," said Berry, "can – "

"Yes, I know that bit," said his wife. "The blue-based baboons wouldn't do it."

"Of course they wouldn't," said Berry. "When they require de-lousing…"

The hurricane of indignation was, I think, justified.

*

"In remembering Oxford," said Berry, "I find it peculiarly difficult to observe our excellent rules. My own personality becomes immediately obtrusive. I shall, therefore, confine myself to an episode which no one but I can relate, for the other participant is dead. Many would dismiss it as a coincidence. But that, I am unable to do. And I don't think you'll do it, either. God knows, I am no moralist. I'm sure you'll support me there. But I should be, I think, a strange man, if, having subscribed to this business, I thought agnosticism the only creed.

"And now for a brief introduction to this most true report.

"It seemed good to my elders and betters – for I belong to a school that allowed that there might be men who were better than they – that I should take pains to acquire an Honours

Degree. This was, of course, so much tripe, for an Honours Degree is of just about as much use as a – "

"Now do be careful," said Jill.

" – flute in a fanfare. I didn't dare put it like that, for I was afflicted with respect, a vile and malignant malady, now very nearly unknown. I think Lord Dunghill touches for it – I can't be sure. He used to run the dockers' strikes. When he'd lost five million working hours, they shoved him up. Still, I pointed out more than once that academic distinction was not a line of country which I could ride and that it was but the froth upon the tankard of life. But they thought otherwise. In return for a handsome allowance, I had to undertake so to satisfy the examiners that they would award me a class. I made immediate inquiry which was the easiest school. And everybody said 'Law'. And so I turned to Law. But I had many calls upon my time, and I must confess that lectures bored me stiff. The text-books, I couldn't stomach: I don't think they were compiled by understanding men. When I'd still one year to go, I took to a coach. And Cousins was one of the best, as you can testify."

"That's very true," said I. "Learned, efficient, human. And he was very modest. It never occurred to him that he was a brilliant man."

"Well, things got steadily worse. With my last year, my engagements seemed to increase, yet Time maintained his steady, inexorable pace. I wrote down all Cousins said, but I couldn't read what I'd written, and, when I could, it didn't seem to make sense. Now there was a bloke, Roy —, of BNC: and he and I and some others were in the same desperate state. And it came to our knowledge that Cousins had taken an inn in Cornwall for the whole of the Easter recess. And that there he proposed to throw a reading-party... Now we'd read about reading-parties in lady-novelists' works: and I'm sure Dean Farrar must have had one in his 'Tale of College Life'. Till now, we hadn't fallen for the ultra-gorgeous prospect they seemed to present: but 'Schools', as we used to call them, were drawing unpleasantly near, and we felt we must cling to Cousins in whom were all our hopes. So down to Cornwall we went towards the end of March. We didn't do so badly. The weather was set fair and we all got as fit as fleas. Out and about all day. And the village rose to the occasion. I used to strike for the blacksmith – and his wife and his pretty daughters would give us tea."

"A nice reading-party," said Daphne. "I can't believe Dean Farrar's – "

"Not on your life," said Berry. "If they saw a maiden approaching they offered up a short prayer and went and hid in a wood. And the one who didn't was 'sent to Coventry'. Never mind. The blacksmith's wife had a very fat reminiscence."

"Bung it in," said I. "Hadn't the daughters any?"

"Too young," said Berry. "They seemed to live for the present. But there you are, you know – youth must be served. Well, their mother told me this. Her father was a notable smuggler; and a number of kegs of brandy were safely delivered to his house at the moment at which her mother was herself to be delivered of the lady who told me the tale. But on that particular night the excise officers were out. So the kegs were carried upstairs and hidden beneath the great bed. Armed with a warrant, the officers came to the house. They searched the rooms downstairs, but when they came to the bedroom, the midwife barred their path. They were allowed a glimpse. When they saw there was a woman in labour, they searched the rest of the house and went empty away. Very soon after they left, the blacksmith's wife was born. The birth was surprisingly easy. This was because her mother had been anaesthetized. The fumes of the brandy, rising through the mattress, had put her out.

"Well, Time went pleasantly on. March gave way to April, and the weather was that of June. After dinner we always studied, but, after all day in such air, our powers of concentration were not at their best.

"We had three more days to go, and Roy and I were alone, in a ground-floor room. I've called the house an inn, but it was half a hotel. The room was on the small side, but it had a fine French window and this was open wide. And we were sitting at a table, trying to get the hang of a subject called 'Torts'. The time was half-past ten, and the night was windless and dark. We were well up above a cove, and the tide was on the ebb. The regular lap of the waves enchanted the ear. But we were too much depressed to fall under any spells.

"At last I shut my volume and looked at Roy.

" 'We'll never do it,' I said, 'because it can't be done. In eleven weeks from now the slaughter-house doors will open and we shall go in. In gowns and caps and white ties. And after a fortnight of nightmares, we shall emerge. But it won't be worth going in, for the subjects are eight in number and we are familiar with none. I don't know what some of them mean. As for knowing their habits and manners – when Cousins tries to explain them, I cannot construe his words.'

" 'I can't put it better,' said Roy. 'But I can put it more shortly. Dress it up as you please, we both of us know we're sunk.'

" 'But I can't be sunk,' I cried. 'I gave my word I'd get a degree with honours.'

" 'So did I,' said Roy. 'But we've missed the tide. We should have worked for three years. You can't compress three years' study into eleven weeks.'

"This was an obvious truth. And the obvious truth is always the most unpleasant. Like any bull of Basan, it gapes upon you with its mouth.

" 'You've said it,' said I. 'But I'd give six months of my life to get an honours degree.'

"My words seemed to make Roy think.

" 'So would I,' he said quietly. 'And I mean that. Do you?'

" 'I certainly do,' said I. 'What the hell's six months?'

" 'Then let's do a deal,' said Roy. 'A deal with the Prince of Darkness. He gets us through Schools and we give him six months of our lives.'

" 'I'm on,' said I.

"I've no defence to offer for what we did. But we were young and foolish and, I fear, like Gallio, we 'cared for none of those things'. We rose and recited our contract. And then we resumed our seats."

"My darling," said Daphne, "I'm inexpressibly shocked."

"You have every right to be. But let me go on.

"For some moments neither of us spoke. But I think I shall always hear the lap of the waves below. And the darkness seemed thicker than ever.

"I took a sudden resolution.

" 'Roy,' I said, 'we're damned fools. Let's take our words back.'

"He laughed what I said to scorn and accused me of having cold feet. 'You're right,' I said. 'I have. I'm going to revoke what I said and I beg that you'll do the same.' But he only laughed the more.

"I stood up and ate my words. I solemnly revoked my contract, while Roy sat there and laughed. And then I sat down. Soon after, we went to bed.

"The reading-party dispersed. I went back to White Ladies and Roy went up to Scotland to get a week or two's fishing before the term began.

"I went up to Oxford early, and when I was settled in, I had a word with my servant and sported my oak."

"Translation, please," said Jill.

"Every set of rooms in Oxford has a massive outside door, which is called 'the oak'. Except when the owner is 'down', it is never shut. When it is shut or 'sported', it cannot be opened from without, except with a key. The key is in the charge of your servant. If, therefore, you pay a call, to find 'the oak sported', it means that your friend is away or must not be disturbed.

Except in my own case, I've never known an oak sported, unless the fellow was 'down'. But I was determined to work with all my might, and I knew that I could not do this, unless my front door was shut. My acquaintance was too wide.

"For the next eight weeks, I worked ten hours a day. I came out to go to Cousins and dine in Hall. I took no exercise. My servant served my breakfast and luncheon: thereafter he brought me cider every two hours: and a clean towel and fresh water, for I worked with a towel round my head.

"Roy never went to Cousins. One day I asked where he was.

"I was told – in a nursing-home, very seriously ill. Blood-poisoning. Whilst he was fishing in Scotland, he had knelt on a pen-knife's blade. This had entered the knee-cap. He had been within an ace of losing his leg. They might have to take it off yet, unless he improved.

"Time went on, and I worked like any madman, week after week. My system was simple. There were, for instance, two papers on Roman Law. I didn't know what that meant, but I had a first-rate text-book three hundred pages long. One hundred and fifty pages, I learned by heart. I learned half of everything, and prayed for a question or two in the half that I knew. For one subject, I had no time. It was called 'Jurisprudence'. I didn't know what the word meant, but when I looked it up, it said 'The Science of Law'. Well, I didn't know what that meant, either. I had two enormous textbooks on Jurisprudence alone. The sight of them gave me a pain. But their leaves were uncut; so my servant took them back to the shop and they credited my account. But I learned 'Cousins' spots' by heart."

"Translation, please."

"Cousins was a very good coach. And he had been a coach for a number of years. He always kept the papers which had been set, and when he saw that some questions had not been asked for some time he used to select those questions as likely to be asked. This, on every subject. Then to his chosen band he would dictate those questions and follow them up with the answers which they should give. It was the purest gamble. The questions were ten in number. He thought he'd done very well, if he'd spotted three. We called them 'Cousins' spots'.

"I was very scared when I'd only a week to go. I knew half my Roman Law: but if all of the questions came in the other half – well, I was properly sunk. I knew, let us say, a third of everything else. And knew it perfectly. I didn't know what it meant, but I knew the words. But of Jurisprudence, I knew nothing – except 'Cousins' spots'. And the Jurisprudence paper was almost the last.

"At last the day came. We had ten days of it then…morning and afternoon…two papers a day. I had luck all along the line. Two-fifths of the questions asked were in the sections I knew. That meant four out of ten. Not too good, perhaps. But those four answers were perfect, for I knew the stuff by heart. But the Jurisprudence paper had yet to come. You see, the thing was this. I knew Cousins' spots by heart, *but I didn't know what they meant.* Cousins gave question and answer. Very good. But if the question was phrased in a different way, to recognize it would be beyond my power. Do you wonder that I was uneasy?

"When the paper was laid before me on a Friday afternoon, I was afraid to read it, and that is the honest truth. And when, at last, I did, I could hardly believe my eyes. Cousins had spotted eight of the ten questions *in the very same words.*

"I have no hesitation in saying that my papers on Jurisprudence were among the very finest that ever were handed in. I was still writing at the end of the long three hours. Still pouring out Cousins' knowledge. Three hours was not long enough to get it all down.

"So I got my Honours Degree.

"Roy got his, too. He was given an *Aegrotat.*"

"Sorry. Translation, please."

"*Aegrotat* is Latin. It means 'He is sick'. To be awarded an *Aegrotat* Degree, a man must be too ill to enter the Schools. More. He must be in Oxford: the Examiners must see him and must be satisfied that he is too sick to attend: they must also question him, but that is a matter of form.

"Roy was brought down from Scotland by motor-ambulance. He then was carried into The Acland Home. There the Examiners saw him. Then he was driven to London and put back to bed. In time, he recovered completely. But the time from the day on which he knelt on the knife to the day on which he left his nursing-home was almost exactly *six months*.

"I have told you nothing but the truth. And now may I add a postscript to what I've said. The burden of The Bible apart, I've seen so many paintings – all of them works of art – of Heaven and Hell. In all the great galleries of Europe. I've studied their composition and found it beyond belief: I've studied their infinite detail and found it a miracle: but until I returned from Cousins' reading-party, I fear I gave little thought to their *raison d'être*. Thereafter, I did. For I had been taught that the Powers of Good and of Evil do exist. You see, I had brushed against one…one lovely April night…on the Cornish coast."

"Bedford Row," said Berry. "Your office was there, and I find it a comfortable name."

"It was once a most comfortable house. And The Row was a blind alley, so it was very quiet. For all I know, it is now. We had the whole house. Each partner had one floor. There wasn't a typewriter in the building. Every single letter was written by hand. And we had to do many indictments. These had to be written on sheepskin, and the clerk that was writing them out in a copper-plate hand, had to pounce the skin as he went, or the ink would have run."

"The middle ages?" said Daphne.

"Very near. But that was how it was done in 1909. There were any number of clerks and they all worked early and late. But they were always cheerful. And one or two were wits and made me laugh very much. I was very happy there. High and low were terribly good to me."

"You worked damned hard."

"So did everyone else. The work that was done in that office would have made many think. But it was never dull."

"Were you concerned in the Stinie Morrison case?"

"No. But I saw him in court. And I know something about it that didn't appear in the press. And I'm giving nothing away, for it wasn't our case. The Treasury dealt with that from first to last."

"Proceed."

"Well, Stinie Morrison was an unpleasant man. If I told you his main occupation, you'd ask me to leave the house. But he had a side line or two. One was robbery with violence. He'd done seven years for that. And then he added murder. He was a strapping fellow – a great, big Jew. To judge by his demeanour, he rather fancied himself. His features weren't too bad, but they were terribly coarse and more than life-size. His hands were simply enormous – I've never forgotten his hands. He used to strike attitudes – at least, he did in the dock. And his eyes were glittering."

"I gather," said Berry, "that his charm was, shall we say, fleeting?"

"It was not conspicuous. One night he kept an appointment. This was on Clapham Common. The man who also kept it, failed to return. This was because he was dead. Twenty-four hours later, Morrison was under arrest. The evidence against him was clear, but not altogether conclusive. The information against him left no shadow of doubt; but, as I have said before, information is not always evidence.

"At the police-court he pleaded not guilty and reserved his defence. At the Old Bailey he was defended by what is known as 'a thieves' lawyer'."

My sister sat up.

"Whatever's 'a thieves' lawyer', Boy?"

"It was a survival. I don't for a moment suppose that there are any left. I think this particular fellow was one of the last; and he died a long time ago. For convenience, I'll call him Rose. You see, for many years now no man has been called to the Bar, unless a Bencher has vouched for him: but in the old days you didn't have to be vouched for. Hence, 'the thieves' lawyer'. The latter knew no law and never attempted to learn. The etiquette of the Bar meant nothing to him. He touted for work and often enough was never instructed by a solicitor. He was quite unscrupulous; and his name was better known in Seven Dials than it was in his Inn of Court. But – he had the gift of the gab. By God, he could talk. And in his crude way he was able. He knew what prisoners want – and that is their money's worth. And the lower-class prisoner thinks that he has his money's worth, if his counsel browbeats the witnesses for the Crown, harangues the jury, lodges absurd objections and wastes the time of the Court. His conviction, which usually follows, he attributes not to the incompetence of his counsel, but to the malice of the jury or the injustice of the Judge."

Jill laid a hand upon mine.

"Didn't you put 'a thieves' lawyer' into *Anthony Lyveden*?"

"Yes, my darling, I did. I called him Blink, and I must at once confess that I had Rose in mind. I'm afraid I stretched a point, to put him in, for the 'thieves' lawyer' never went Circuit. The Old Bailey and the Sessions were the covers he used to draw.

"The doyen of them in my day was old Daniel —. He provided so much amusement that you couldn't help having a weakness for 'Dannel', as he was called. But he must have been nearly eighty and he was past his prime. He hadn't an 'h' to his name. He knew the practice all right, but he knew no law at all. For him, the rules of evidence didn't exist. He didn't know what they meant. And to hear 'Dannel' arguing in the Court of Criminal Appeal – "

"Oh, go on," said Berry.

"It's true. I've seen him there. The Judges loved him. He was like an old clown. When he made some absurd observation and everyone laughed, he laughed as loudly as any, as if he'd made a good joke. But the Judges were very gentle. Darling would lean forward. 'But, Mr —, if you admit, as you do, that the jury had every reason to bear that fact in mind, there goes your case.' 'That is me point, me lord.' And Darling would sigh and bury his face in his arms, and the Lord Chief would shake like a jelly, and Channell would strive 'n vain to master his voice."

"Who was the Lord Chief Justice – I mean, of your time?"

"Lord Alverstone. He was a splendid chief and a splendid Judge. So far as I ever saw, he had only one fault. And that was that he was impatient. But he couldn't fairly be blamed, for he had a lightning brain. If ever I was before him, I always bore this in mind and cut what I had to say as short as ever I could. With the result that he used to remember my name and was always kindness itself. And now let's get back to Stinie Morrison."

"Who tried him?"

"Darling. And there was a Judge. Taking him all round, Darling was the best Queen's Bench Judge of my day. He was an admirable lawyer. His perception was most acute. He was intensely human. And he had a brilliant wit. The Press very seldom got it – his wit was too fine for them. Real Attic salt. Sometimes he tossed them a trifle which was not worthy of him. The connoisseur sat in his court, when he had time to spare. And savoured his quiet asides. I never once saw him smile. He was always point-device, and his wig was always powdered – the last on the Bench. He was a very fine scholar, as many Judges were. He could jest in Latin and Greek. And French. When his son was at Harrow, Mr Justice Channell used to write to the boy in Greek. I don't commend the practice, but I don't think a High Court Judge could do that today. I may be wrong. And now let's get back to Stinie Morrison.

"Stinie Morrison had a bad record. He had three previous convictions, all for crimes of violence, for one of which, as I've

93

said, he had done seven years. But I don't have to tell you that a previous conviction must never be mentioned in court. The Judge knows all about them – the list's lying on his desk. But, for obvious reasons, the jury must never know. To this rule, there is one exception. If the prisoner (or the prisoner's counsel) should attack the character of a witness for the Crown, then the Crown may give his previous convictions in evidence. If, therefore, you are defending a man who has been convicted before, when you are cross-examining a witness for the Crown, you take particular care to ask no question which might be said to reflect upon his integrity.

"Stinie Morrison's counsel took no such care. He went all out for one of the CID. This was jam for the Crown; and as soon as Rose sat down, Treasury Counsel rose and asked the Judge's permission to prove the prisoner's previous convictions there and then. This, as a matter of form, for he had the clear right. Darling nodded assent, and the three convictions were proved."

"Incredible," said Berry. "I mean, even I knew that."

"So, I confess, I found it, for Rose was an old hand: and, hopeless lawyer as he was, I never could have believed he would make so elementary a mistake. But it was pure ignorance. While he was attacking the policeman, his junior kept pulling his gown. At last Rose turned. 'What the devil d'you want?' he spat. 'Man alive, you've let his convictions in.' 'Good God, have I?' says Rose. 'Well, why on earth didn't you stop me?' A man who was sitting behind him told me that.

"That was virtually the end of the case. I mean, juries aren't fools. So Morrison was found guilty, and Darling sentenced him to death. A week or so later, to everybody's amazement, the Home Secretary commuted the sentence to one of penal servitude for life. No one could understand this, for Morrison was a monster and quite unfit to live.

"I cannot remember who told me what had happened and so I cannot vouch for its truth. But Darling tried the case, and I was so familiar with Darling's outlook that I've never had any doubt that my informant was right.

"When a man is sentenced to death, the Judge who presided at his trial always sends to the Home Secretary his own observations regarding the merits of the case. In this case Darling did so in the usual way. He certainly made it quite clear that there had been no miscarriage of justice and that Stinie Morrison richly deserved to die. But, having a cold contempt for any counsel of experience who could make a mistake which no articled clerk would have made, he added something like this. 'At the same time I venture to doubt whether this man would in fact have been convicted, but for the inexcusable incompetence of the member of the Bar whom the prisoner's friends had instructed – and, probably, handsomely paid – to save his life.'

"The Home Secretary of the day was a very foolish man, and, ignoring the fact that Morrison had been rightly convicted, decided that it was unfair that, because he had been badly defended, the convict should forfeit his life.

"To Darling's horror, therefore, Morrison was reprieved. As a convict, he gave much trouble, but I'm honestly glad to report that he didn't live very long.

"Let me say once again that I cannot declare that that is the true explanation of what occurred. But it is, to me, a very reasonable explanation of the most surprising – not to say, most improper reprieve that was ever granted."

"When you say it's a reasonable explanation, you mean that it is exactly what you would have expected of the personalities concerned?"

"Yes. The only chance which Darling had of chastising the thieves' lawyer was in his report to the Home Secretary. And the man deserved to be chastised. I simply cannot see Darling failing to seize such an opportunity. I mean he was very hot on incompetence in a member of the Bar, when incompetence should not have been displayed. Before Horace Avory was appointed to the Bench, he was appointed Commissioner of

Assize. That is to say, a Judge fell sick or something, and Avory was sent down to take his place. Such an appointment, which is purely temporary, sometimes precedes a Judgeship. When, as Commissioner, he was trying some case, he made an elementary mistake. The man he was trying was convicted – and immediately appealed. When his case came to be heard by the Court of Criminal Appeal, Darling was a member of the Court. He was, I think, presiding, because the Lord Chief was away. Anyway he gave judgment, very properly quashing the conviction, because of Avory's mistake. And in the course of his judgment he said, 'A man might be pardoned for thinking that the learned Commissioner had looked at the wrong page of Archbold' – that is to say, the Bible of the Criminal Bar. That, of course, was scathing. About a month later Avory was made a Judge. The appointment, no doubt, had been made before the mistake.

"Everyone thought the appointment a bad one, partly, no doubt, because Avory was by no means popular. And as Senior Treasury Counsel, he used to press his cases, which nobody liked, which, in fact, he should not have done. He was appointed at the same time as Eldon Bankes, who was very much liked. And everyone considered that his appointment was as good as that of Avory was bad. I saw them walk in procession through the great hall on the first occasion on which they wore the scarlet and ermine. They were side by side. And Bankes was loudly applauded. He never bowed once, but Avory bowed right and left."

"Poor man," said Daphne.

"It didn't matter," said I. "Nobody undeceived him. What is so curious is that Avory made a very much better Judge than Bankes did. That Bankes had a pleasant manner with juries was – unfortunate. I mean, they ate out of his hand. And if juries will eat out of a certain Judge's hand, then, if justice is to be done, that Judge has got to be a most exceptional man; for, though the jury is present, he's really deciding the case. And Bankes was by no means a most exceptional man. (I don't suggest he resembled Weston Gale; but Gale was a fool. In two cases within my own knowledge, entirely thanks to his folly, gross injustice was done.) Avory, on the other hand, went from strength to strength. He wasn't anything to write home about in the Civil Courts, but he became an excellent criminal Judge. And he matured. The older he grew, the better he got. I can't remember who was the Lord Chief Justice, when Avory died in harness: but I remember that he made a public statement which was quite unworthy of any thinking man. 'We shall as soon see another William Shakespeare as another Horace Avory.' That is, of course – and I say it without respect – arrant rubbish. In the first place, I could name off-hand half a dozen Judges of Avory's day, all of whom were unquestionably better Judges than Avory ever was."

"Do it, please," said Berry.

"Alverstone, Darling, Channell, Rowlatt, Scrutton and Warrington. In the second place, the linking of the two names suggests a comparison which is so fantastic as to be indecent. It would be far less preposterous to compare Edgar Wallace with Julius Caesar. But Avory fully justified his appointment to the Bench."

"O-oh," cried Jill. "Do you remember when you were asked to lecture?"

"Yes," said I. "But there's nothing doing."

"This," said Berry, "is a new one on me. What happened?"

"Well they wanted Boy to lecture out here – on English Literature. And Boy said No, he wasn't qualified. So they said, Well So-and-So lectured last week. So Boy thought, Well, if So-and-So can, I can. And he said, What did he say? And they said, Oh, he was most interesting. He completely debunked Shakespeare. He showed what a plagiarist and what a charlatan he was. So Boy said, Well, if you liked him, I'm afraid you wouldn't like me. And no man can debunk Shakespeare. You might as well try and fill in The Caspian Sea."

"What was his name?" said Berry, speaking between his teeth. "I demand his name, that I may load him with everlasting contumely. Debunking the Swan of Avon in a foreign field! Seeking the spittle Notoriety even in the sewer's mouth!"

"That's more than enough," said I. "We'll leave it there. Besides, I want to add something to what I said just now.

"A few moments ago, I said that Weston Gale made a bad Queen's Bench Judge, because he was a fool. That is a strong thing to say, unless I adduce some evidence which, submitted to the average man, will prove my case. This, I propose to do. I referred to two cases 'within my knowledge'. I think I should set one of them out.

"Not long before the first war, the mother of a well-known lady of title determined to give her daughter a run-about car. Neither mother nor daughter had any money to spare. But the mother, who loved her daughter, knew very well that a little run-about car was what she most desired. She could not afford to pay more than a hundred pounds, but she went to a dealer she had heard of and asked him to fix her up. And please remember that before the first great war one hundred pounds was exactly one hundred pounds…one hundred golden sovereigns, if you like to put it that way.

"Well, the dealer fixed her up, as dealers will. He sold her a second-hand car which was worth about fourteen pounds, took her cheque for a hundred and then delivered the car to her daughter's address. The daughter, who knew something of cars, perceived what had happened and told her mother the truth. Her indignant parent demanded her money back. The dealer refused to refund it, and an action was brought.

"The head of my Chambers was briefed, and I went to Court with him, to help and to take the note. The case came before Gale.

"While Harker was opening the case, which he always did very well, Gale looked down from the Bench.

" 'One moment,' he said, smiling. 'Are you going to tell the Court that the plaintiff really believed that she could purchase a car for one hundred pounds?'

"Harker looked up at him – dazedly.

" 'I am, my lord,' he said.

" 'What, a thing that moved?' says Gale.

" 'Certainly, my lord. And I am going to suggest that it was a perfectly reasonable belief. I am going to prove, my lord, that one hundred pounds is a very respectable price for a small, second-hand car.'

"Gale turned and smiled at the jury. Still smiling at them, he replied.

" 'All right,' he said. 'Go on. Of course some people will believe anything.'

"The jury smiled back at him, and Harker and I looked at one another in dismay.

"The thing was incredible – like *Alice in Wonderland.* We had often heard of 'judicial ignorance', but this was beyond a joke. *There were then upon the British market at least half a dozen cars, listed at between one hundred and one hundred and fifteen pounds – NEW. For one hundred and thirty-five pounds, you could buy a BRAND-NEW twenty-horse-power Ford.* (That was the famous 'Tin Lizzie', still to be seen on the roads in twenty years' time.) And this damned fool of a Judge was as good as telling the jury that anyone who was such a fool as to think they could buy a *second-hand car* for a hundred pounds deserved what she got. And the jury was accepting this doctrine. The nice old gentleman knew and was putting them wise. But, you see, the nice old gentleman lived in Belgrave Square and the only cars he knew cost three thousand pounds apiece. That there might be cheaper makes never entered his head.

"We brought our experts, but he laughed the case out of court. And the jury laughed with him. He was the wiseacre. He knew. He really thought he did. His complacency was invulnerable. He was sorry for us, with our hundred-pound second-hand car. But there you were. A fool and his money were soon parted. So long as there really were people who liked to think... He smiled at the jury, and the jury smiled back. He rammed home the truth that a little knowledge is a dangerous thing. He spoke of sadder and wiser women..."

"Oh, I can't bear it," screamed Berry.

"I had to bear it," said I. "And Harker, too. And I tell you, it shortened my life. But hear me out.

"...who would come to realize that cars that could move and have their being were not to be purchased for the sum of one hundred pounds. And while he was talking this slush, brand-new Fords were being driven up Fleet Street, a hundred paces away. And the price which their owners had paid was one hundred and thirty-five pounds.

"The jury didn't even retire. They found for the defendant without leaving the box.

"The plaintiff refused to appeal. For all she knew, there were other Judges like that. In fact, there weren't, but she had had enough of the Royal Courts of Justice. And I'm damned if I blame her.

"Well, there you are. That is exactly what happened, from first to last. And in view of that reminiscence, I think I've the right to say that Gale was a fool."

"One moment," said Berry. "You spoke of another case."

"I know," said I. "But I can't remember the facts. I think it was a running-down case, and a bus was involved. But exactly the same thing happened. I ran into Harry Dickens, the son of the Common Serjeant. I knew him quite well. He'd just lost the case before Gale and tears of impotent rage were running upon his cheeks. He was so mad with the Judge he could hardly talk straight. I remember his catching my arm and crying, 'What about that?' "

"There are men," said Berry, "who can suffer fools gladly. I've always envied them. I knew one once. The bigger the fool, the more he enjoyed his pranks. To watch a fool in his folly was meat and drink to him. But I am not like that. The fool, who has no excuse, I have always found provoking. And when I am at his mercy, it sends the blood to my head. My God, who'd go to law?"

"Except in the last resort – only a fool."

"I'm sure you'll forgive me for saying that I don't remember a Judge called Weston Gale."

"Neither," I said, "do I. Nor does anyone else. In this particular case, I've used a pseudonym."

"Which is considerably more," said Berry, "than his memory deserves."

"There is," said Daphne, "a lot of The Law in your books."

"I'm afraid there is. I'm half a lawyer, you know, and it seems to creep in."

"It may be dull," said Berry: "but at least it's accurate."

"If it wasn't," said I, "I should deserve to be flogged."

"I was always sorry," said Jill, "that you didn't unmask *Rowena* in open Court."

"Let me confess," said I, "that it would have been more dramatic. Unfortunately, it would not have been true to life. Except in plays or novels, no villain is ever unmasked in open Court. It's always behind the scenes that he gets it between the eyes."

"I seem to remember," said Berry, "an occasion in one of your books – a rather famous occasion, if I may go so far."

"You mean *Mr Bladder*? Yes. You have me there. In my defence, let me say that nobody dreamed that the chauffeur would not come up to his proof. Nor did the chauffeur himself, till he saw me in court. So it couldn't have happened 'off'."

"I accept that plea. The case was exceptional. Do witnesses often fail to come up to their proofs?"

"Not very often. In that case the witness went right back on his proof, and that, I must confess, I have never seen, although it has actually happened in many a case. Usually, when they've been got at. A curious thing happened once. When I was a solicitor's pupil, I was sent up to the Old Bailey, to manage an important case. We had instructed Bodkin to appear for the Crown, and, though I didn't do badly, I fear he felt that I was rather too young. (That was the first time I met him. I got to know him much better later on and I have much to thank him for. He was a very good lawyer and he had a delightful wit. He was easily the best Treasury Counsel of my day and I shall always maintain that he should have been made a Judge. He would have adorned the Bench, which is more than some Judges do.) Well, our case had been closed just before luncheon on, I think, the second day. Before the Recorder came back – "

"The Recorder," said Daphne. "That's a new one on me."

"The Recorder of London, my darling. A very coveted post. He has the status of a Queen's Bench Judge, but he sits only at The Old Bailey. Sir Forest Fulton was the Recorder of my day. He was quite good on the Bench, but he liked a long luncheon interval. I always remember that – I may say, with gratitude. I liked a long luncheon interval, too.

"Well, as I was saying, before the Recorder came back, Bodkin sent for me. 'I want to recall one witness, for I have a question to ask.' He told me which witness it was. 'Have him all ready, please.' 'I'll have him all ready,' I said. 'May I know what you want to ask him?' 'No.' Had I been more experienced, Bodkin would not have said that. I was at once uneasy, for I knew the case backwards, though he didn't know that I did: and I couldn't imagine what question he was going to ask."

"Why wouldn't he tell you?" said Daphne.

"I suppose he was afraid that I might put the answer into the witness' mouth. That I would never have done. But to recall a witness for one question only, after your case has been closed, means that you are going to focus a powerful beam of attention upon the question you ask. And I felt that, before he asked it, I ought to know what it was. However, there was nothing to be done.

"The Recorder took his seat. Bodkin applied for permission to call the witness back. The Recorder gave it, and I brought the witness in. He went into the box, and Bodkin rose. Then he asked his question. The answer he expected was, 'Never'. The answer he got was, 'Frequently'."

"Oh, my God," said Berry.

"Yes, it was a fair knock-out. And it couldn't be covered up. Bodkin could only sit down. And the defence were thrilled. It certainly hit us hard, though we just got home. It wasn't Bodkin's fault, for there was a mistake in the brief though not in the witness' proof. But if only he'd told me the question which he was going to put..."

"What would you have done?"

"I should have said, 'But that's wrong. The witness won't say that.' And if Bodkin had insisted, I should have asked the witness before he came into court. Bodkin, of course, was wild: but he was a just man and he didn't take it out upon me."

"Did you get many letters about *This Publican*?"

"He got a lot of rude ones," said Berry.

"Indeed, I didn't," said I. "I never got one. As a matter of hard fact, I've only had about four in forty years. I've had some criticism, of course – nearly always very pleasantly made. Once or twice it's been of very great value."

"Only once or twice?"

"Yes. The other has been – well, curious. One fellow, who said he was a consulting physician, who had read *Perishable Goods*, took the trouble to advise me to consult a doctor before I again described the condition of a dying man. (I need hardly say that I had taken that precaution.) 'You see,' he added, 'a man in *Mansel's* condition could not have a rapid pulse: he would have a very slow one.' In my reply, I pointed out that not only had I not said that *Mansel* had a rapid pulse, but that the word 'pulse' did not appear in the book. Another wrote at some length, about *Lower Than Vermin* – saying that ladies of Scottish descent did not refer to themselves as 'Scotch girls'. He added that he had learned this truth at his mother's knee. In my reply, I pointed out that nowhere in *Lower Than Vermin* had *Ildico* been described as a 'Scotch girl' either by herself or by anyone else. In each case, they had simply got their facts wrong."

"And what," said Berry, "is the matter with people like that?"

"I can beat those two. D'you remember the drive to Bordeaux at the end of *Jonah and Co.?*"

"I do. John Prioleau wrote and asked your permission to include those pages in his *Anthology of Travel*. He said it was the finest – "

"He was very kind," I said. "But I did take a lot of trouble. I covered that ground six times, to get it right. Anyway, Pau to Bordeaux, one hundred and fifty miles – and less than three hours to do it. That meant shifting – in 1922. Well, one fellow wrote me a heavily sarcastic letter, saying that he knew the road from Pau to Bayonne (Bayonne, *not* Bordeaux) and inquiring whether it was really necessary to drive quite so fast, to cover the sixty-seven miles in three hours. He'd mixed up his towns, of course."

"Of course, people like that," said Berry, "should be confined or removed. I mean, they cumber the earth."

"They mean no harm," I said. "But their zeal outruns their discretion. Others correct my grammar. I ought to know, they say, that you don't say 'different *to*'. But these are exceptions. More than once I have had a delightful letter, very gently pointing out a mistake. And I have been immensely obliged."

Jill laid a hand on my arm.

"You've had one more than once that wasn't too good."

"I know what you mean. They're not fan-mail, but blackmail. But they're very rare. I had one once beginning, 'Dear old Pal of long ago, Do you remember how we discussed the shape of *Valerie French*?' Well I didn't discuss the shape of Valerie French with anyone for the very good reason that I had no idea what its shape would be. Added to that, I don't discuss my books. So I wrote back and said that it seemed to me that they had made a mistake. I received a threatening reply, demanding a share of the royalties which had accrued. This, I ignored. Then they began to cable – I was in France. The second cable ran, 'Will not be responsible for tragedy which may occur.' This was inconvenient. The butler took the cables and he was visibly impressed. So I rang up the Postmaster, who was a friend of mine. I explained what had happened and that I was being blackmailed. He quite understood. The French are realists. 'Rest assured, Monsieur. You will receive no more cables from this outrageous source.' Nor did I. I assume that he simply returned them, marked 'Address unknown'.

"Regarding *This Publican*, I had an argument, which I shall always value, with an eminent Chancery Counsel who is now a High Court Judge. It's dry as dust, so I won't say what it was. He pointed out that I'd made a mistake in law. So I had. A judgment of Scrutton's was against me. But I just scraped home, for Scrutton had given judgment in 1937, but my 'mistake' had been made in 1936."

"That was a dirty one," said Berry.

"I know," said I. "But I had my back to the wall. He was the son of a very famous Counsel for whom I had the greatest respect. When he was raised to the Bench, I presumed upon our acquaintance and wrote and rejoiced with him. Nothing could have been kinder than his reply. I well remember his father at the Bar – a most distinguished lawyer, whose very word was law. It was said of him that, when a 'case' was sent to him for his opinion whether or no an appeal should be lodged, he was the only man who would dare to express no lengthy opinion, but simply write at the foot of the document, 'The Court of Appeal (or The Divisional Court) will reverse this decision', and sign his name. When I see my contemporaries, or even men younger than I am, raised to the Bench, it makes me feel very old. I remember the old Judges, and I always regarded them as 'Most potent, grave and reverend signiors', and now men younger than I am are taking their place. I remember Willes J, and that's going back a long way. I remember Grantham's riding down to the Law Courts on his grey: he always did that in the summer, all through the busy traffic right up to the doors. And if it was fine in the evening, he'd ride him back. Morning-dress, of course.

"And now let me finish with my fan-mail. The exceptions which I have mentioned only proved the rule. I have been more gratified and encouraged by the almost invariable kindness and goodwill shewn forth by my fan-mail than by the handsomest reviews which I have ever received. To reply to every letter has meant a lot of work and has taken a lot of time: but I've always been happy to do it – anyone would."

"My gorge is rising," said Berry. "Let's go to bed. And yet – half a minute. Something you said just now flicked a memory into my mind. Bless my soul, what was it? I know it was valuable."

"Boy was speaking of the Judges," said Jill, " and of Grantham riding down – "

"That's right," cried Berry. "God bless your pretty face. But for your wit, a truly glorious episode might have been lost. And this *is* history.

"None of you knew John Dimsdale. I knew him well. In more than one big Trust, he was my co-trustee. He was the best of fellows – a good deal older than me. I should say he was born about 1855. I know he was sent to Eton when he was nine. To the day of his death, he remained an Eton boy. Very merry, a vast appetite, preferred the pantomime to Shaw – and I'm damned if I blame him for that. Years ago I walked out of *Fanny's First Play*. I object to paying to have my intelligence insulted. Of course it's no good talking about the theatre today, because the public's taste has changed. In about 1935 I was taken to a play in the West End which had had a phenomenal run. I had to sit through it, because I was a guest. But I give you my word that, had that play been produced before the first war, it wouldn't have run ten days. It would have been shouted down on the first night. D'you remember when we went to The Gaiety in – oh, it must have been 1936?"

"Shall I ever forget it?" said Daphne. "I thought they'd ask you to leave."

"Do you blame me?" said Berry. "I paid for our seats – eighteen shillings a stall. In the old days you paid half a guinea. The principal comedian, the star, entered – "

"Back to John Dimsdale," said I.

Berry regarded me in silence.

Then –

"Perhaps you're right," he said.

"Well, John Dimsdale was a banker, for he came of banking stock. His bank was one of the best-known private banks, and its office was at 50 Cornhill, in the City of London. It was, of course, taken over years ago. John Dimsdale was born over the Bank, in the house in which his father lived and worked. So he was a true Cockney – a fact of which he was proud. (I do not have to tell you that a Cockney must have been born within sound of Bow Bells.) And it was John Dimsdale who told me the tale which I am now going to tell. And I can vouch for its truth, for John Dimsdale was incapable of telling a lie.

"In the winter, his father and mother always lived over the Bank: in the summer they moved to their country house in Essex, not then very far off. And every morning in the summer his father used to ride to Cornhill. He used to stable his horse at an inn which was close to the Bank, and there was always a stable-boy waiting for him, sitting on a bucket in the yard.

"Well, the years went by and his father began to grow old. He no longer lived over the Bank, and he left the business more and more to his partner and his sons. (The elder brother was Joseph, at one time MP for the City: and the partner was Fowler, also at one time MP for the City of London.) But, though he was growing old, he still used to come to the Bank, to keep an eye on things. He was sitting in his room one morning – and a very nice room it was, with two or three admirable Hogarths – when a Bank servant came in and asked if he would see the Lord Mayor. 'Of course.' So the Lord Mayor came in. 'Well, my Lord Mayor,' says Mr Dimsdale, 'and what can I do for you?' The Lord Mayor sat back and smiled. 'Do you remember,' he said, 'how you used to ride up from Essex and stable your horse at The —?' 'Very well.' 'And how there was always a stable-boy told off to take your horse?' 'I can see him now,' says Mr Dimsdale, 'sitting on a bucket, waiting for me.' 'You were very good to that stable-boy, Mr Dimsdale.' The old man opened his eyes. 'I don't know that I was,' he said. 'But he was a promising lad.' 'Well, I know you were,' said the Lord Mayor. 'You see, I was that stable-boy: and now it will give me great pleasure, Mr Dimsdale, if you will lunch with me at The Mansion House.' "

Jill cried out with delight.

"Berry, darling, it's like a fairy-tale."

"Isn't it? Yet, it's true. A true romance of the City: Dick Whittington over again. No shop-stewards then: but that didn't stop the stable-boy: and it didn't stop Lever, either, from making his famous name: and scores beside."

"Didn't Joseph Dimsdale later become Lord Mayor?"

"That's right. After that, he was City Remembrancer for many years. And now, on that pretty note, let's go to bed."

"I agree," said my sister, rising. "History is seldom sweet: but that's a sweet tale."

*

"The Oxford Group," said I. "I feel you should deal with that."

Grimly, Berry surveyed the end of his cigar.

Then –

"There is," he said, "The Oxford Movement and there is Oxford Clay. There is also The Oxford Manner, which I once asked A E Housman to define. He said, without any hesitation, 'It is an infinite superiority, which we are much too well-bred to show, which is nevertheless apparent.' I thought that was very good. All three belong to Oxford. The Oxford Movement began with a sermon preached at the University Church: Oxford Clay lies under Oxford: the Oxford Manner is attributed to past members of the University. So all three belong to Oxford and have a clear right to bear her famous name.

"But the Oxford Group – which is now, I understand, a Limited Company – was different. It had no more to do with Oxford than had the Balkis Brigade."

"Whatever was the Balkis Brigade?"

"The Queen of Sheba's mounted monkey band. I think there's a bas-relief of the drum-goat in the British Museum."

"I don't remember it," I said.

"Well, they won't let you see it unless you've got your gas-mask on. To return to the Oxford Group."

Berry then spoke for six minutes without repeating himself. When he threw himself back in his chair.

"I hope you feel better," said Daphne.

"He won't in a minute," said I. "That's going to be cut."

"Cut?" screamed Berry. "*Cut*? But you invited me to – "

"Sorry," I said, "but I warned you. For your opinions I have a deep respect; but I have an even deeper respect for the law of the land. I feel very strongly about the Oxford Group; but the very great pleasure which I should derive from your cross-examination would in no way compensate me for the unpleasantness of a writ for libel and its inevitable consequences. Besides, Sir Alan Herbert did what he could; and where he failed, I doubt if we should succeed."

"I entirely agree," said Daphne, " – for what that's worth."

"Oh, all right," said Berry. "Have it your recreant way. Delete a superb appreciation. Deprive the world of a passage worthy of Cicero. And what would Samuel Johnson have said of the Oxford Group? After all, he was at Pembroke... And now, before I forget, Boy made a statement last night which seemed to require a foot-note. 'Not fan-mail, but blackmail.' What did he mean by that?"

"I was speaking loosely," I said.

"A vile and bestial failing, which you have no right to indulge at any time, least of all when – "

"You never do it, do you?" said Daphne.

"Never," said Berry. "The spring of my conversation rises from 'the well of English undefyled'."

"What about your blue-based baboons?"

"Dan Chaucer would have loved them," said Berry. "I'm not sure they don't appear in *The Wife of Bath's Tale*."

"Spare us the quotation," I said. "I don't suggest that Chaucer would not have done them full justice, but his was an outspoken age."

"Perhaps you're right," said Berry. "And now what about the blackmail?"

"The object of the individual who suggested that she had contributed to the writing of *Valerie French* was to obtain money from me. The idea was to bluff me into paying up, to avoid the unpleasantness which would follow a letter to my publishers or even the issuing of a writ. Letter and writ would, as we both knew, be founded on a thumping lie: but to expose this would have been tiresome and not at all to my taste. I've only had two such letters. But authors have to be careful. H G Wells wasn't once, and it cost him three thousand pounds.

"Some woman wrote to him from Canada, alleging that one of his books was really hers. She alleged that she had sent him the typescript of a book which she had written and had asked him for his opinion upon it. That he had never replied or returned her MS; that about a year later, to her immense surprise, she had picked up a book of his, to find that it was *her* book, substantially the same as when it had left her hands. Wells ignored or forgot the letter. The next thing he knew was that heavy damages had been awarded against him in a Canadian court. Horrified, he instructed his solicitors. They wrote at once to their agents in the Dominion, instructing them to lodge an appeal. At very great inconvenience, Wells had to go over himself. He won the appeal hands down, but the plaintiff was a woman of straw and hadn't a penny with which to pay his costs. And that little flurry cost him three thousand pounds.

"What she had done was to buy a copy of his latest book and copy it out on a typewriter, making alterations here and there. Of this, she produced a carbon copy to the Court, alleging that she had sent the original to Wells. As the case was undefended, it went by default. So authors do have to be careful."

"What about people saying they're you?" said Jill.

"Don't be silly," said Berry. "People don't go about defaming themselves."

"Two have – to my knowledge," said I.

"What ever d'you mean?" said Daphne.

"They pretended," said Jill, "that they were 'Dornford Yates'."

"That's insanity," said Berry. "The asylums are full of people who think they're Jack the Ripper or Gandhi's goat."

"I'm inclined to agree," said I. "It must be a form of mania. But these people were at large. And they were believed. Those in whom they confided went about saying they knew me, for what that was worth."

"More mania," said Berry.

"Rubbish," said Daphne. "How would you like it if somebody started using your name and address?"

"Don't be indecent," said Berry.

"There you are. And you've got nothing to lose."

"Or blasphemous. Wasn't it Carson who said, 'Never submit to blackmail'?"

"I believe he did. I imagine a good many counsel have given that sound advice. But you don't have to be a lawyer to issue a precept like that."

"Were you ever concerned in a case?"

"I can't remember that I was. But a few months before I became a solicitor's pupil, the firm I was with defended in one such case, and the clerks were still full of it. It was a famous – infamous victory. *The King against Robert Sievier*."

"By God," said Berry, "that was a hell of a case."

"It was that," said I. "It was a hell of a case.

"Everyone knew Bob Sievier. He was a blackguard: but he had a way with him, and he was a popular man. He ran *The Winning Post*, a most entertaining weekly paper, resembling *The Sporting Times*. *The Sporting Times* was considerably higher class. It was always called '*The Pink 'Un*', for it was printed on rose-coloured sheets. *The Winning Post* was printed on yellow. The main difference between them was, that you didn't mind being seen with '*The Pink 'Un*', but you did with *The Winning Post*.

"Well, every week *The Winning Post* had a column called, I think, 'Potted Personalities'. Anyway, it was something like that. And it featured, as a rule, some well-known racing man. And whoever wrote it didn't mince his words.

"Now in 1908, the famous house of Joel was very well known – not only in the City, but on the Turf. There were two brothers, Solly and Jack; and both were immensely rich. For Solly, I cannot answer, but Jack was said to have a past. Everybody knew that. Including Sievier. One day Sievier went to see Jack at his office in Lombard Street – or wherever it was. He knew him, of course, very well. 'What d'you want with me?' said Jack Joel. 'I'll tell you,' says Sievier. 'Next week I'm going to pot you. I've got the proof here. Would you like to read it, Jack?' Jack Joel read it. Then he looked up. 'Don't be a fool,' he said. 'You can't print this.' 'Can't I?' says Sievier. 'You wait.' 'Well, I'd rather you didn't,' says Joel. 'Yes, I didn't think you'd like it,' says Sievier. 'If you want the type distributed, it'll cost you five hundred pounds.' 'This is blackmail,' says Joel. Sievier shrugged his shoulders. 'Today is Monday,' he said. 'We go to press on Friday. It's up to you.' 'Come back at this time on Wednesday. I'll think it over and give you my answer then.' 'I'll be with you,' says Sievier, and takes his leave.

"Well, Jack Joel thinks things over and rings up Scotland Yard. As a result, on Wednesday his office was enriched by the presence of Chief Inspector Drew and his sergeant, whose name I forget. These men were not to be seen, but they were there. Bob Sievier keeps his appointment. 'Well, Jack,' he says, 'have you thought the matter over?' 'Yes,' says Joel, 'I have.' He pulls out the proof. 'And now let's get this straight. This article goes into your paper as it stands, unless I pay you the sum of five hundred pounds?' 'That's right.' 'But if I pay you the sum of five hundred pounds, the article won't appear and the type will be broken up.' 'I couldn't put it better,' says Sievier. 'Right,' says Joel, and sits back. Then Drew appears with his sergeant, arrests Sievier on the spot and charges him with blackmail.

"Consider for one moment the position. Jack Joel, a Chief Inspector and a Sergeant of the CID were all prepared to swear that in their presence Robert Standish Sievier demanded with menaces from Jack Joel the sum of five hundred pounds, and, by way of confirmation of that statement, they could produce a proof of the very damaging column which Sievier said would go into *The Winning Post*, if the money was not paid. If you can imagine a stronger case than that, I'd love to hear what it is. Talk about *flagrante delicto*... If I had been asked to lay odds, I really think I'd have laid a thousand sovereigns to one. But Sievier knew his onions. He came to my firm and told them to brief Rufus Isaacs for the defence. His choice was good. When Isaacs was very young, he was meant for the Stock Exchange. His uncle was a broker, and he was to learn of him. But before his tuition began, Jack Joel smashed his uncle... The elephant never forgets.

"So Isaacs accepted the brief. Talk about bricks without straw. But Isaacs was out for blood. When he rose to cross-examine, he stretched out his hand, and Joel saw the pointing finger and visibly shrank. His ordeal lasted three hours, and before the end he was weeping, a broken man. Then Isaacs made the speech of his life. And he was terribly clever. He gave the jury their choice – *between two blackguards*...the one a good fellow, the other – not so good. And then he left it to them –

with his charming smile. The Judge tried to straighten things up, but the damage was done. The spell which Isaacs had cast was proof against what he said. And Sievier was found not guilty – and was cheered all down Old Bailey; but Joel was escorted out by another way."

"Terrific," said Berry.

"It was the greatest triumph that Isaacs ever had. He accomplished the impossible thing. He raised that case from the dead. One thousand guineas, his brief was marked. And a hundred a day, refresher. I think it took two days – I may be wrong. But his visits to the Old Bailey were very rare. Once again I remember him there. I'm not going to talk about that, but Muskett gave me leave off, to hear the case. He defended again, in a very difficult case. And simply romped home. Darling was on the Bench and he was extremely cross. He did his utmost to pull the jury round. But Rufus Isaacs' personality was too strong. Darling had the last word, but he couldn't break the spell. I was in court all day. And I saw the spell woven and cast. And I saw Darling try and break it – and saw him fail. Rufus Isaacs was a magician. There was no advocate like him – and that is the solemn truth."

"Wonderful," said Daphne.

"There were giants in those days," said I.

"Back for one moment," said Jill. "Don't people send you things that they have written and ask you to read them and let them know what you think?"

"It has been done," said I. "I always send them straight back by registered post. And if they ask first, I always refuse. I don't like being unkind, but the sheep must suffer for the goats' delinquencies. Then, again, they have no idea – at least, I like to think they have no idea – of the favour they're asking of me. To read a short story and submit a considered estimate of its worth takes a good deal of time. I always tell them that the best of all judges is the Editor of a magazine. If it's worth having, he'll buy it: if it isn't, he'll turn it down."

"You will never criticize?"

"Never, if I can help it. I've had to do it once or twice for people I've known. Of course, there's no danger there: but unless you say it's a winner, you probably lose a friend. And I am not prepared to present an estimate which, to my way of thinking, is false. I suppose one should, really. A fellow I knew quite well once asked me to read a short story which he had turned out. He was very much younger than I and was hoping to make money on the side. So, against my will, I did. To avoid argument, I sent him a criticism in writing. I may say it was very mild: I could have torn him in pieces, but I didn't want to do that. Apart from anything else, it was a piece of bare-faced plagiarism. But I didn't point that out. He never forgave me. I only saw him once more and then he took me to task. I suppose he thought I was jealous and was trying to keep him out. On another occasion, a man I knew – not very well – insisted on submitting his reminiscences. Most of these were unprintable, and, had they all been printed, they would have made a book about sixty pages long. The elementary principles of grammar and punctuation, he had completely ignored. When I pointed this out, he said that all that sort of thing was the publisher's job.

"I said, 'Well, look here. I've pointed out certain shortcomings, because I'm an honest man. The best advice I can give you is to do it up and send it to a publisher and see what he says.'

" 'And have it all pinched?' says he.

"I shook my head.

" 'They won't pinch it,' I said.

" 'Why, they do it all the time,' says he. 'That's why I came to you.'

" 'I can only advise you,' said I, 'to take the risk.'

"He went off, very nettled, and I never saw him again...

"So, you see, it's no good. Be honest with people, and, unless your honesty allows you to say that their stuff is good, they hate your guts. I once had a very pleasant experience. A poor lady wrote to me, in great distress. She said she had no one to talk to, but, as she had read my books, she thought I would understand. And in the course of four sheets she told me the saddest tale. She asked for no assistance – not even for sympathy. She didn't ask for a reply. Well, it was clear to me that her medicine was distraction – something to lift her mind from her piteous plight. And her letter was very well written. (You know that I always maintain that the person who writes a good letter can learn to write a good book.) So I wrote back and said what I could. And then I advised her to write. I told her that she *could* write and that if she began to write, she'd find it a great distraction as well as a valuable resource. A month or two later, I got a most grateful letter, saying that an Editor had accepted her first short tale and had commissioned another five."

" 'Can learn to write a good book.' "

"That's right. *By teaching himself or herself.* No one but you can teach yourself to write well. About that, there is no argument. It is a copper-bottomed fact. If you can write, you can: if you can't write, you can't – and you never will be able to. A lot of people who can't write, do: and a lot of people who can write, don't. But no one can ever teach a person, who can't write, to write: and no one, other than himself, can ever teach a person, who can write, to write well. You can't teach yourself to write: but, if you can write, you can teach yourself to write well."

"I suppose," said Berry, "I suppose you know what you mean."

"I know what he means," said Daphne. "And he ought to know: for he could write and he taught himself to write well."

"Who says he writes well?" said Berry. "Compared with *Essays of Elia*, his books are trash."

"They aren't," shrieked Jill.

I laid a hand on hers.

"They are, indeed, my sweet. Lamb knew how to write. His prose is a perfect thing. But if Lamb were the touchstone, no novel would have been published for years and years. Some of us do our best, but we can't compare with the masters of other days."

"I seem to remember," said Daphne, "that once you had some trouble about the name of the Rolls."

"Years ago," I said, "*Blood Royal* was to be serialized. I saw the editor, to tie up one or two ends. 'By the way,' he said, 'I'm afraid I shall have to ask you to alter the name of the car.' 'Why?' said I. 'We don't give advertisements.' 'I don't want to be obstructive,' I said, 'but the name must stay. I'll tell you why. In the first place, the Rolls-Royce needs no advertisement: in the second place, there are two kinds of automobiles – one is a Rolls and the other a motorcar. In *Blood Royal* I'm referring to a Rolls.' He looked at me, fingering his chin. Then he began to laugh. 'All right,' he said; 'let it stand.' I don't think the point was ever raised again – not even in the USA."

"And they were difficult?" said Berry.

"Very difficult," said I. "*The Saturday Evening Post* would have taken *Blood Royal*, if I had made Chandos an American citizen. I refused, of course."

"Amazing," said Berry.

"The editors love to dictate – I don't know why. And they have queer ideas. America took *Storm Music* and *Safe Custody*. But they wouldn't touch *She Fell Among Thieves*."

"Why on earth?" said Daphne.

"Because the outstanding character was *Vanity Fair*. And they dared not feature a villainess. A villain, yes. But not a villainess. American women wouldn't have stood for that. That's what my agent told me, and I've no doubt he was right. I need hardly say that *This Publican* hadn't a chance."

"God bless my soul," said Berry.

"And now it's your turn. What about the low-down on Napoleon Brandy?"

"Ah," said Berry. "I feel we should have that in."

I began to laugh.

"If you can't deal with that, then nobody can."

"I don't know about that, but I'll try. A little monograph upon that celebrated cognac which used to figure so conspicuously in the more *recherché* wine-lists of England, 'Napoleon Brandy'." He cleared his throat. "It has been offered to me by various *maîtres d'hôtel* again and again: but when I ask, as I do, its age and its origin, the answers which I have received – and they are very few – are at curious variance. The fact is, of course, that there is no such thing. You can bottle a brandy and call it what you please: you can call it Armada Brandy, and no one can say you nay – because you are not saying that your Armada Brandy was distilled in 1588 and lay in the wood unrefreshed for many years. I can hardly believe that if an Armada Brandy was offered, anybody would be quite such a fool as to think that it belonged in any way to the reign of Good Queen Bess. But the Napoleonic era is more recent, and the name 'Napoleon' is French: so a brandy which is labelled 'Napoleon' does suggest to some prospective purchasers that it has to do with the fifty-two years during which that singularly unattractive despot troubled the world.

"Now the *jeunesse dorée*, old as well as young, is particularly sensitive on the subject of brandy: for that a man should be a judge of brandy is an article of its faith. I never quite know why, but there it is. It doesn't feel that, to establish its manhood, it must be an authority on soap or tea or tyres or broad beans. But on brandy, yes. With the unhappy result that again and again it has been fooled to the top of its bent, and has paid an absurd price for a most inferior spirit, which is invariably served to it in a balloon glass – sometimes of grotesque dimensions.

"And now let us have the facts – which not one tenth of them know.

"Distil a good brandy, and let it stay in its cask for fifty or sixty years. Don't refresh the cask – that is to say, add no brandy to it. At the end of that time, have the brandy bottled, and you will have a fine brandy, which you can safely say is fifty or sixty years old. In a hundred years from then, what your great-grand-sons have left will still be exactly fifty or sixty years old – and just as good as it was. But it won't be older and it won't be any better, for brandy does not mature, except in the wood.

"I have possessed a brandy which was ninety years old. It was, in fact, bottled for me, after lying for ninety years in the self-same cask and never having been refreshed. But that was a god-send. I can feel it now just touching the back of my throat – and the wonder is that my throat didn't turn to gold. A good brandy will always just touch the back of your throat: if it doesn't, it's not a good brandy. *La jeunesse dorée* will boast of a brandy which is 'as smooth as silk'. Such brandy is not good brandy: a hundred to one, it has been adulterated. But the *jeunesse dorée* knows – and sets the pace: with the result that, shortly before the last war, all sorts demanded that their brandy should be 'smooth'. And many quite good vineyards were putting gum arabic into their casks – in order to produce a 'smooth' brandy, because, of course, the customer was always right.

"I said of Napoleon Brandy that there is no such thing. Nor there is. But there was once. There was a Napoleon Brandy, and though I never drank it, I believe it was very good. And this was how it happened.

"Somewhere about 1865, the proprietor of a Parisian restaurant was in the Cognac country, probably of design. One day he lunched at an inn, and, after luncheon, he was given a glass of brandy which he found remarkably good. So he asked where it came from... To cut a long story short, he purchased the cask, which was, I think, sixty years old and had never been refreshed. Up to Paris, it went, and there he bottled it. And then he had to think of a name, for he meant it to lead his list. And, very wisely, he chose 'Napoleon'. It was a high-sounding name, and the fact that the brandy was distilled in the year in which Trafalgar was fought probably escaped his notice. But the name was justified. And the brandy became famous, and his custom greatly increased. But that is ancient history. So far as I know, except in his restaurant, that brandy was never sold, so that, after perhaps ten years, there was none of it left.

"Now the name was a selling name, which was, of course, why he chose it. And that, of course, is why it is used today. But his brandy *was* distilled when Napoleon was yet alive. Not that that means very much, for it might have been bottled in the year of Napoleon's death, when it would have been sixteen years old and not worth drinking. But the suggestion conveyed by the name had something behind it. And the brandy was sixty years old, and the soil in which its vines flourished was sympathetic soil. And so it deserved the fame which it certainly won. 'What's in a name?' asks Shakespeare. Of brandy, that's very true. The name means nothing at all. You can call it 'Waterloo' or 'Wapping' or 'Wimbledon'. The only things that matter are whether its soil was good soil and how long it lay in the wood. And the wine-lists don't tell you that. So if you really must know, you must judge for yourself."

"Even I understood that," said Daphne.

"Ah," said her husband, "if every page attained that giddy height of excellence, these idle reflections would be translated – as, I understand, are some lesser known works of fiction – into four hundred thousand different languages, including Swahili and Billingsgate. And now your brother will kindly let the side down."

"Rot," said Jill. "Lots of people will skip that brandy bit."

"Lots of people," said Berry, "don't read *Paradise Lost*. Take us back to the gutter, Boy."

"I was once at Maidstone," I said. "I think it was the Summer Assize. I was in court and was waiting for my case to be reached. They were taking pleas of guilty – they usually do that first. Suddenly a prisoner who was out of the ruck was put up.

He was a gentleman. That he felt his position acutely was very clear, for he looked most deeply ashamed and kept his eyes on the floor. I was terribly sorry for him. He was a nice-looking man: perhaps I should say that he had been, for, though he was young, he looked old. That he drank was obvious. His suit was shabby and stained, but once on a time it had come out of Savile Row. But it was the man's demeanour that got me under the ribs. And then a quiet voice rang out, 'My lord, I appear for the prisoner and I plead guilty. I propose to address your lordship at the proper time.' The prisoner looked something surprised. For a moment he regarded the counsel whose words he had heard. Then his eyes went back to the floor.

"Evidence was shortly given. The man had obtained money by false pretences – not very much, some fifty or sixty pounds. But he asked, as a prisoner may, for certain other cases to be taken into account. There were four or five, I think, all very much the same. What was a good deal worse, he had been convicted before.

"Now I knew the fellow who was appearing for him. I'll call him Slade. I didn't know him well and he was older than I. But he had quite a pretty practice. He didn't belong to the circuit, so he had come down 'special', as it was called. My memory's dim about that, but I think if you went to a circuit to which you did not belong, you had to have fifty guineas marked on your brief and you had to have a junior who was a member of the circuit in question. Anyway, there Slade was. And when the police had finished, he rose to address the Judge.

"I never heard a plea of guilty so beautifully done. It was just right. But the story Slade told was tragic. The man was an old Etonian, and his record was very good. In his way he was brilliant. He had contributed to *Punch*. But he had squandered a fortune before he was thirty years old. So he came to drink and drugs – and so to crime.

"I can't remember the actual speech Slade made, but I know it was very moving, although it was very quiet. But I never shall forget his opening words. 'My lord, I have been instructed to appear for the prisoner by an old friend who desires to remain anonymous.'

"Of course, the Judge sent the man down – he could do no less. But my impression is that he spared him penal servitude. But whatever the sentence was, the Judge made it plain that it would have been a heavier sentence, but for Slade's plea.

"I was dining out a week later, and Slade was among the guests. As soon as I got a chance, I spoke of the case and I told him frankly that to my mind his plea had been a model of excellence. 'You did it perfectly.' He seemed very pleased. Then, 'Listen,' he said, 'let's have a word together, when the women have gone.' When the men were left at table, I took a chair by his side. And then he told me this tale. I'll try to recapture his words.

" 'On the evening before I went to Maidstone, I was working late. I was alone in Chambers; the clerks had gone. I heard a knock at the door, so I went to see what it was. A woman was standing there, an obvious lady. She was young and very well dressed, and she was in great distress. "Are you Mr Slade?" she said. And then, "I've been given your name." "Slade's my name," I said," but what do you want?" "I want your help," she said. "Please let me come in." She looked all in, so I took her into my room and made her sit down.

" 'She had only just learned, by chance, that her former husband, whom she had had to divorce, was to come up at Maidstone for sentence on the following day. And she begged me, with tears, to go down and do what I could. "I can't let him go down," she kept crying. "I must do something to help. He must never know, of course: he must never dream that it's me. But you must go down and do what you can to help him."

" 'Well, I was terribly busy, but she was up against time. If we'd had twenty-four hours, I could have helped her to get hold of somebody else. But it was too late for that. And so I said I'd go down – I hadn't the heart to refuse a woman in such distress.

Apparently, money was no object, so the fact that I'd have to go special presented no difficulty. "But," I said, "you can't instruct me like this. You must go through a solicitor – that's a rule of the Bar." "But there isn't time," she cried. "Besides, I don't know one, except the ones I had: and I'd rather not go to them." So I rang up George — and drove her straight to his house. I explained the matter to him and he said he'd act. There and then he gave me a back-sheet, and another one for young —: I wish I'd thought of you, but I didn't know you'd be there. We got her to tell us something – give me some straw, I mean, with which I could make some bricks. Then I left her with George and his wife and went back to get my robes and leave a note for my clerk. And I left for Maidstone next day, by the early train.'

"That was the end of Slade's tale and this is the end of mine. I've read many better short stories, and so have you: but, for what it is worth, it's true. I've told it out of order, but I saw the second act first."

"It's terribly tragic," said Daphne. "Had the wife married again?"

"I can't remember," I said. "I don't think so. Slade said she was most attractive: and I should say that he'd been an attractive man."

"What's a back-sheet?" said Jill.

"The outside sheet of a brief, with the name of the case and the name of the solicitor. It may contain no matter, but it is counsel's warrant to appear in the case."

"Who," said Berry, "was the Judge?"

"I can't remember. I have an idea it was Scrutton. I may be wrong."

"Scrutton was a good Judge?"

"Very good indeed. And a magnificent lawyer. When he died, it rather upset me to see that *The Times'* obituary notice suggested that his temper was short. I was sometimes before him, and I never found it so. He was always charming to counsel so far as I saw. And on one occasion, I was in a position to judge. The list had fallen in. That is to say that some case had been postponed or had been withdrawn. This case would have taken some time, so the next case wasn't ready, and counsel got in quick and obtained permission for it to stand out of the list. The third case was still more unready, if I may put it that way. As for the fourth case – well, the witnesses were all over the country: they hadn't even been warned. And the fourth case was in my Chambers. I had to go over and make the application. We had been caught right out, but The Law doesn't care about that. Unless you can get round the Judge… It was just after the luncheon adjournment. They'd brought down a silk to try to get the third case postponed. And mine was the fourth. The silk had to fight damned hard, but he had his way. Well, the outlook for me was grim, for Scrutton was getting cross. I mean, his list was melting before his eyes. But I managed to make him laugh… So he did as I asked. Now a Judge whose temper was short would never have laughed."

"Oh, I don't know," said Berry. "Your face under a wig was enough to make anyone laugh. And when you opened it – "

"You filthy liar," shrieked Jill. "Boy looked a love in a wig, and I'm not in the least surprised that the Judges were nice to him."

"There you are," howled Berry. " 'A love.' What did I say about women?" He pointed a shaking finger. "If she'd been on a jury, the 'love' would have had her vote. Merits of the case be damned."

"What about you?" shrieked Daphne. "You said you'd've given yours to the best-looking girl."

"So I would," roared Berry. "No browbeating, blear-eyed hag would have put it over me. But that's my case. Mix the sexes up, and justice goes by the board." He took his handkerchief out, and dabbed at his face. "You must not outrage my emotions. Scratch the divine, and you get the censor of morals."

"A damned nice censor," said Daphne.

"I know my world," said Berry. "And why should I mince my words? Eve got away with the apple, because of sex appeal. And did us all in. 'Looked a love in a wig.' Ugh!"

"So he did," said Jill, stoutly.

"My sweet, you're, what is called, biased. For you, the sun, moon and stars rise and set in the small of Boy's back. And that is as it should be. Any more about Maidstone?"

I shook my head.

"He has," said Daphne. "A winner."

"I know what you mean," said I, "but I'm not telling that."

"Libel?" said Berry.

"No. But one of the principal parties is still alive: and I can't wrap it up."

"You fell for her," said Daphne.

"As better men than I have. But it isn't because of that."

"Let me wrap it up," said Daphne. "Boy had an important dinner in Lowndes Square. And he was kept late at Maidstone, and missed his train. But a chauffeur gave him a lift in an empty car. Boy sat beside the chauffeur, talked to him all the way up and learned quite a lot. The chauffeur's daughter had married a nobleman. He was terribly nice about it and, while he was pardonably proud, he stuck to his job. So he took Boy to Cholmondely Street. Boy had a bath and dressed and went off to Lowndes Square. And he took in the chauffeur's daughter. How about that?"

"Is that really true?" said Berry.

"Yes," said I. "I'd never met her before."

"Was she very lovely?" said Jill.

"She had a lot to her, my sweet: but she couldn't compare with you."

"Well, no one," said Berry, "will ever believe that tale."

"All I can say is," said Daphne, "that, when Boy got home that night, he came and sat on my bed and told me the truth.

125

I've – wrapped it up, of course. But if I told it you naked, you'd get up and walk. I mean, mine is an understatement."

"Oh, well," said Berry, "some people have all the luck."

*

"I suppose," said Berry, "everybody has forgotten the Scots comedy *Bunty Pulls the Strings*. It had a very long run not long before the first war. At The Haymarket.

"Daphne and I went to see it with the Levels. It was a very wet night, and, after the show, the Levels' car was not forthcoming, so young Charles went off to find it, whilst we others waited in the hall.

"People were still coming out, for the house had been full; the Business Manager was standing in front of the Box Office, as they often used to do. I was quite close to him, when a fellow comes up, with his programme still in his hand. He was in evening dress and he looked an educated man. That he hailed from Yorkshire was clear, as soon as I heard his voice.

" 'I say,' he said, 'this isn't *Macbeth*, is it?'

"The Business Manager stared.

" 'No,' he said. 'It's a Scotch comedy. *Macbeth* is running at His Majesty's, over the way.'

" 'Ah,' says the other. 'I thought it wasn't *Macbeth*. I wanted to see *Macbeth*.'

"Now I relate that incident, not so much for its intrinsic value – although, personally, I derive considerable entertainment from its memory – as for its extrinsic worth. I've no idea who the man was or what he was, except that he came from the North: but he was properly dressed and knew how to behave. In his own sphere, as like as not, he was a capable man. But without his own sphere, his intelligence was, let us say, limited. He had sat right through that play for nearly three hours: he had a programme which he had presumably read: yet, though his suspicions were aroused, he felt he must have them confirmed:

he had to be assured that what he had seen and heard was not in fact Shakespeare's *Macbeth*.

"Now when one has witnessed such an incredible display of incapacity by such a man, one is no longer surprised that his numerous inferiors are unable to perceive the respective virtues of 'the blessing and the curse' which are set before them, between which they are invited to choose on the occasion of a general election. And, of course, it follows, as the night the day, that to mislead them by the hundred thousand is the easiest thing in the world.

"To my mind, this is not only the true explanation why so many million Britons consistently choose the curse, but one of the great tragedies of our time. For courage, enterprise, generosity and cheerfulness under misfortune, our race has no equal upon earth. Yet all these invaluable qualities are occasionally rendered useless by a lamentable poverty of mind.

"When Winston Churchill, who admittedly saved the world – and please think what that means – was dismissed from the great office which he had distinguished as it had never been distinguished before, at the very climax of his almost supernatural success, the effect of his dismissal upon the Continent – not to say, the world – was exactly what might have been expected. Myself, I can only vouch for France and Portugal. France, more jealous than ever, greeted the news with the most profound contempt. Portugal, always most friendly, was simply stupefied. But the Continental nations are no fools. And the poorest peasant in France would have shown more common sense than did millions of Englishmen.

"And so I come back to the hall of The Haymarket Theatre, on that wet night. Outside his own sphere, that Yorkshireman was deficient in common sense. If I hadn't heard his words, I never would have believed that a man of that standing could possibly be such a fool. But, bearing that incident in mind, can anyone be surprised that, once they leave their sphere, his inferiors in standing display even less intelligence?"

"I'm not sure you're not right," said I. "By the way, Winston Churchill. He came down to Harrow to lecture after the Boer War. He'd just been elected for Oldham. I can see him now – a slim figure in morning dress, with thick, auburn hair. I don't have to say that his lecture was terribly good, and the school fairly ate it up. We all stood up and clapped as he left the dais. I was then in the Lower Sixth and was sitting behind the Headmaster, Joseph Wood. As Churchill walked off, he turned to us and said, 'There goes another Harrow Prime Minister.' "

"I must have been sick," said Berry. "I don't remember that. Or I may have left – my memory's growing dim. But Joseph Wood was a winner – the last of the great Headmasters of Harrow School."

"So he was," said I. "In every way. Whether he was receiving the King and Queen of England or a new boy, his address was above reproach. I've seen him do both, and I know. He was of the old school. Nobody cares any more, so I won't waste time: but I'd like to relate one little, insignificant matter that meant a great deal to me.

"At the end of every term there was a prize-giving. The school repaired to Speech-room at five o'clock. And such as had won prizes walked up to the dais and received them, while all their fellows clapped. Those who were to go up, took care to be properly dressed: but those who weren't, didn't bother, but came as they were. At the end of my third term, I attended this rout. I had won no prize, so I never changed. Half-way through the worry, to my concern and dismay, Wood called my name. Well, there was nothing for it. I hadn't won a prize, but somebody thought I had, so I had to go up. And so I did. I don't say that I was dirty, but I think I probably was. My boots weren't clean, and I wasn't properly dressed. With twelve hundred eyes upon me, I made my dreadful journey, up to the dais and back. And returned with a prize, to which I had no more right than had one of the servants that swept the Speech-room's floor. A mistake had been made. For the rest of the session, I tried to think what to do. I mean, the book burned my hands. So when it was over, in fear and trembling I made my way back to the dais. All the masters were there, as well as Wood. I went up to my form master, a painfully pompous man. He'd married a lovely wife, who was very rich. And he couldn't get over that. Haltingly, I explained the position. He took the book from me, and turned to Wood. 'Ah, Headmaster,' he said, 'there seems to have been some mistake. This, ah, boy is not entitled to a prize. And so he's brought the book back.' Wood took the book from his hands and looked at me. He was point-device, as ever: but I was probably dirty and certainly under-dressed. I never felt so much ashamed. But Wood looked upon me and smiled. Then he gave me the book again. 'Take it back, my boy,' he said, smiling. 'You'll be worth it one day.' "

"There spoke a great gentleman," said Berry...

And that is no more than the truth.

"A little while back," said my sister, "you mentioned His Majesty's Theatre. That was Beerbohm Tree."

"Let Boy take over," said Berry. "He knew him well."

"I can't say I knew him well, but I met him several times. As President of the OUDS, I saw quite a lot of the Stage. Tree was a *poseur*: but he was most entertaining. And he was a beautiful actor – if he felt so inclined. For some strange reason, he gloried in playing the fool. Arthur Bourchier loathed him, and he loathed Bourchier back. The things they said of each other... Bourchier founded the OUDS and I came to know him well. He was a fine actor, too, though he sometimes played parts which didn't suit him too well. I knew Harry Irving best. He was an awfully nice man. Not the actor his father was, but terribly good. And he always gave all he'd got. After playing *Louis the Eleventh*, he'd hardly the strength to speak. And Henry Ainley, I knew. There was a glorious actor, that went to bits. The son of a miner, he was. And he spoke Shakespeare's lines as they've never been spoken since. I'm glad to say that I saw Forbes-Robertson's *Hamlet* and Waller's *Henry the Fifth*. A fine judge told me they rivalled Salvini's *Othello*. I daresay they did. I can only say that they were the real thing. Of those great rôles, the renderings I have seen since, were just – well, amateur acting: no more than that. But Forbes-Robertson and Waller were trained: and they don't train actors today. Before the first war, an actor learned how to move and to speak his lines. For years he slaved in the provinces, learning to do these things. And then, when he could do them, he came to the West End. But they cut out the learning today. I don't know that I blame them. As like as not, people wouldn't notice the difference. And yet, I don't know. Harry (H B) Irving used to present his father's great melodrama, *The Lyons Mail*. And a damned fine play it was. When I saw it at Oxford in 1906, or thereabouts, he still had in his company some of the old actors whom Sir Henry himself had schooled. The parts which they played were their original parts. Of course they were minor parts, but never before or since have I seen such finished performances. I mean, they stood right out. Each one was a work of art."

"Wasn't Compton Mackenzie up with you?"

"No. I was up with Compton Mackenzie. I had that privilege. We played together in Aristophanes' *Clouds*, and *The Times* said of him that he looked as though he stepped off a Greek vase. So he did. He was the son of a famous actor, Edward Compton, another of the old school, who moved so beautifully that he could play *Charles Surface* when he was over sixty."

"You said you knew no authors, or Berry did."

"Nor I do. I lost touch with Compton Mackenzie before he began to write his famous books. I always find it hard to choose between his first three, for, each in its way, is the most perfect thing. It's strange to remember today that, when *Carnival* was published, an important library banned it from its shelves. I also knew that master, Hector Munro. He's better known as 'Saki'. There was a brilliant man. His early death was a tragedy: but, comparatively little as he wrote, his name will always live. His wit had a polish you never see today. He was over forty when the first war came. He enlisted instantly, consistently refused a Commission, and was killed at Beaumont-Hamel in 1916."

"I remember," said Daphne, "your learning your part in *The Clouds*. How many lines had you?"

"About six hundred. It was damned near the end of me. But, then, I've never had a good memory. They had them in the old days, you know. Wood, of Harrow, told me that, when he was a boy at Manchester Grammar School, every night he was set two hundred lines of either Greek or Latin to learn by heart: this, in addition to his other work: and he used to learn the stuff as he walked four miles to school."

"Incredible," said Berry.

"You met some famous men, when you played in *The Clouds*."

"I did, indeed. Sir Hubert Parry, who wrote the music. He was very kind to me: my voice began to give in, and he put me on oysters and stout. I always thought of him as *Sir Toby Belch*. He was so gay and merry: but he was very handsome in all he did. And Hugh Allen was the conductor. I used to sit in the organ-loft with him, when he played at New College Chapel. He used to shove in the stops with his head. He was afterwards conductor of The Bach Choir. And A D Godley was the Public Orator of Oxford. A wonderful brain, and he looked just like a sheep. Charles Oman, I met later. And Dion Clayton Calthrop, a most attractive man. And Byam Shaw – he looked just like a bookie who's had a good day: and Mrs Byam Shaw might have stepped off a mantelpiece of Dresden China. All these I met at Oxford. And Rudyard Kipling, too. I had to look after him, and I was frightened to death. But he seemed more frightened of me. I couldn't get over that. Then there was Carter of Christchurch: a great connoisseur of old silver, he had the most biting wit. And he didn't care what he said."

"All this," said Jill, "because you played in *The Clouds*?"

"I'm afraid you must put it that way. The fact attracted attention which I in no way deserved. In the first place, *The*

Clouds had not been performed for more than two thousand years – people came from America to see it: in the second place, the part which I played had probably been created by Aristophanes himself. I, therefore, reflected some glory and, as is so often the way, the reflection hung on for a bit, like the grin of the Cheshire Cat."

"I saw it," said Berry, "for I was up at the time; and without desiring to detract in any way from the majesty of your performance, I must most frankly declare that never in all my life have I been so bored. I have a great respect for the Classics, though Aristophanes' particular brand of humour has sometimes seemed to me to be as gratuitously broad as it is unnecessarily long; but three solid hours of nothing but Greek dialogue, of which, I need hardly say, I understood not one solitary word, proved very hard to digest. I was told that the music was superb: possibly it was: I remember a lot of men dressed up as women, yelling their guts out from time to time…"

"That," said I, "was *The Chorus*."

"No doubt. But when you allege that presumably responsible individuals came all the way from America to see that show, all I can say is that if, having sat through one performance, they didn't do themselves violence, their erudition must have been that of the fanatic. I mean, there wasn't one moment's entertainment for the man in the street."

"That was not my fault. If I had had my way, you would have had just ten seconds' entertainment in that dull show. And you ought to have had it, for Aristophanes meant you to."

"What," said my sister, "do you mean?"

"Well, I think this should be on record. You know what I mean by patter?"

"In *Iolanthe*," said Jill. " 'When you're lying awake, with a splitting head-ache.' I love it."

"That's right. Gilbert used it. Properly done, it is truly entertaining. Well, patter's very ancient. Aristophanes used it in *The Clouds*."

"Not the night I was there," said Berry.

"Nor on any other night. Now listen. The patter belonged to the part which I was selected to play. It was some twenty lines long, and all, of course, in Greek. It took me weeks to master: it was a question of the rapid enunciation of unfamiliar words: but at last I could say it, as patter should be said: every word audible, but given at lightning speed. I kept this up my sleeve. There were a lot of important people present at the first word-perfect rehearsal. When I came to my patter, I let go. They were taken completely by surprise: then there was a burst of applause. But the don who was producing *The Clouds* felt otherwise. I was not among his favourites. He insisted that I should say it at the ordinary speed. I begged in vain. 'People won't get the meaning if you say it so fast.' Possibly not. I don't know. True scholars are very quick. But the point is that I had delivered it as Aristophanes meant it to be delivered, and, as likely as not, as he delivered it himself."

"My dear," said Daphne, "it must have broken your heart."

"I confess I was disappointed: but that didn't matter at all. What did matter was that a very great number of people, who were not scholars, would have been most interested to know that patter does not date from Gilbert and Sullivan, but from 423 BC."

"A blasted scandal," said Berry. " 'People won't get the meaning.' What filthy tripe. How many people can follow the *Iolanthe* patter, word for word? But it's the pace they love. Damn it, it's the pace that makes it. The tongue is doing its best to beat the ear."

"That's how I saw it," said I. "But there we are."

"That must go in," said Daphne. "That is a sidelight on history. You must have felt very bitter."

"Oh, I don't know. But I did get back on him later."

"How was that?"

"Well, I wasn't in favour of a Greek Play, for it meant that some of the best amateur actors in the University were washed out, because they couldn't speak Greek. But when the Vice-Chancellor, Jowett of Balliol, gave the OUDS their charter, he stipulated that every four years they should produce a Greek play. And so we had to do it. Well, when I was Secretary, this fellow came to me and said that *The Clouds* had been such a success that the four years must be cut to two. As an Officer of the Club, I told him where he got off. 'You mean you won't do one next year?' 'That,' said I, 'is precisely what I mean.' 'All right,' he said, '*we'll* do one. I'll see to that. And we'll do it at the Town Hall, during the week in which you do your play. And we'll see who makes the most money.' The threat was serious. The Club cost a lot to run, and the state of our finances was not too good. I tried to think what to do. Then I went down to St Aldgates' and saw the Town Clerk. I didn't tell him anything. I simply retained the Town Hall for the week in which we should be doing our play. I paid him a fee of two guineas, which, when they had heard my story, the Committee immediately passed. And now it's Berry's turn."

"Nice work," said Berry. "I suppose it's too much to hope that he remembered you in his prayers. But let that go…

"It is not generally known that Her Most Gracious Majesty, Queen Victoria, once visited a man's Club."

"I don't believe you," said Daphne.

"Yes, she did. And I don't have to tell you that it was all above board. The Queen was driving down St James's Street, when the last of the scaffolding was being taken away from the facade of a fine, new building close to the bottom of the street on the right-hand side. The Queen asked what it was. The equerry told her that it was the new house of the Conservative Club. 'It's very handsome,' said the Queen. Then she added thoughtfully, 'I've always wished I could see the inside of a Club. I'm told they're very comfortable.' A few hours later the equerry informed her that the Chairman and Committee of the Conservative Club would count it a very great honour if Her Majesty would care to visit their new house before the members were admitted. The members were to be admitted at mid-day in a few days' time. One hour before that, Her Majesty arrived. And she went all over the Club from bottom to top. In memory of her visit a very fine bust of the Queen commanded the landing halfway up the magnificent stairs.

"The Conservative was a very old-fashioned Club. When I became a member, with two or three exceptions, I was the youngest member by many years. The spittoon and the goutstool were still in evidence, though I must confess that the former was never used. Old gentlemen used to wear their hats – silk, of course – in the morning-room. Only in three rooms was smoking allowed. The grates were huge, and the blocks of coal were sometimes so large that it required two servants to put one on. Except for the hall-porters and one or two servants in the coffee-room, all servants always wore breeches, black stockings and buckled shoes. And the service they gave was impeccable. Perhaps I should add that they were, one and all, immensely proud of the Club. When they retired, they were always handsomely pensioned, for so long as they lived. The food was cheap and the kitchen extremely good. The cellar was renowned. The peace within those walls, I shall always remember. All was so quiet and dignified. A footfall on a tessellated floor, the gentle closing of a tall mahogany door, the sudden, sprightly tick of the tape-machine – those seem to me, looking back, to have been the only sounds. But then, you know, it was an old-fashioned Club."

Jill was looking at me.

"You put the groom of the chambers in *Period Stuff*."

"That's perfectly true," I said: "and his name and all. The picture I drew was strictly accurate."

"There was someone in *Blood Royal*."

"Something, not someone," I said. "One night I was dining in Curzon Street, at a well-known physician's house. He had attended the old Duke of Cambridge, who had died the day before. When the women had left the table, he called me to sit by his side. 'Would you like to know,' he said, 'what were the last words of the Duke of Cambridge?' I said that I should – very much. 'They were, *Where the hell's the barber?*' So I toned them down and put them into the mouth of the dying Prince in *Blood Royal*."

"And *Duke Paul*?"

"*Duke Paul* was founded on the picture presented by a man I once came across. It was not, of course, a portrait. But, placed as *Duke Paul* was placed, he would, I am sure, have done as *Duke Paul* did."

"In every particular?" said Berry.

"In every particular."

"I gather," said Berry, "that he was unattractive."

"I found him so."

"Rogues," said Daphne. "You haven't met any rogues."

"I'm afraid all my rogues belong to my imagination."

"They work all right," said Berry: "the reason, of course, being that, as nobody else knows what a rogue is like, people have to take your word for it."

"I suppose that's so. At least, I've had no complaints."

"I always love *Punter*," said Jill.

"He's an old friend," said I, "as he once pointed out himself."

"*Brevet*," said Berry, "gave me peculiar pleasure."

"So he did me. I shouldn't say that; but he did."

"Had he run straight, he might have dined out in London almost every night of his life."

"I quite agree."

"His scornful appreciation of Pope when he was virtually standing on the scaffold was a brain-wave."

"The ruling passion," said I, "is strong in death."

"Oh, I know," said Daphne. "Proofs. Don't you hate correcting your proofs?"

"I can't say I enjoy it," I said, "for it's most exacting work. If I can possibly help it, I never do more than, say, two chapters a day. It demands very high concentration, because the author knows his stuff so well that it is extremely easy for him to miss a mistake. Not a big mistake, of course. He'll see that at once – as nobody else will see it. If a sentence is omitted, for instance – he'll never miss that. But 'literals', that is to say, misprints, he may easily miss. 'That' for 'than', for instance, or the omission of inverted commas, or letters misplaced, or 'man' for 'men' – little things that matter.

"I know I'm particular, but I can see no point in doing your best to write the best English you can, if the reproduction of your prose is to be faulty. And so I get down to it.

"There are two sets of proofs which the author should always read. The first are called the 'galley proofs' or 'slip proofs'. These are accursed things to handle. They're about six inches wide by twenty-seven inches long, and the paper is usually vile. But the value of the slip proof is this – that you can alter it as you please. If you want to cut out fifty lines, you can: if you want to add fifty lines, you can. You can do anything you like – to the slip proof. Well, you correct or alter your slip proof and send it back. Then you receive a 'page proof'. Except that the page proof is bound in brown paper, instead of in cloth, it almost exactly resembles the book in its finished form. Title-page, fly-leaves, preface – all are there: and all the pages are numbered. In that page proof should be embodied all the corrections or alterations which you made to the slip proof. Well, you read that: and you are fortunate indeed, if you find no more mistakes. In fact, you find a great many. Some are mistakes which you missed in the slip proof. Others are mistakes, because your instructions upon the slip proof have not been carried out. Others are new mistakes – don't ask me why, but they are. But the main thing is this – that, except in an emergency, no page must be upset: so that any correction or alteration must be very slight."

"Emergency?" said my sister.

"Well, supposing that by the carelessness of a compositor, a whole paragraph has been omitted. Well, it's got to go in. That may upset sixty pages. It may upset the rest of the book. But that can't be helped. *Blind Corner* was a case in point. I was never sent any slip proofs, as, of course, I should have been. When I was reading the page proof, I found that the well-digger's statement, which I had marked to be printed in italic, had been printed in type so small that it could hardly be read. Now, as the whole tale was founded on that statement, it was of great importance that it should be at least as easy to read as the rest of the text. Well, it was up to the printers, for I, of course, declined to pass the proof. It meant rearranging about forty pages. But it had to be done.

"What drives an author quite mad – at least, it drives me quite mad – is to find that some reader or other has amended what I have written, because he prefers his amendment to the original."

Berry was bristling.

"Look here," he said, "if any imitation scholiast presumes to 'improve' any of my monographs – "

"That's all right," I said, laughing. "I'll see they don't. But now you understand how I feel. As I always say, query the stuff by all means. Shove your queries down in the margin, and I'll be grateful to read them: but never alter something, without my consent."

"Are they ever right?"

"In one case in twenty they are. A curious thing happened once. Quite early on, Ward Lock always sent me what is called a 'specimen page', that is to say, two or three pages, for me to approve the lay-out; for these appear as the book itself will appear. They did this, as usual, with – well, one of my books. I thought it looked very nice, and idly enough I began to glance down the first page. After three lines I stopped. A sentence of mine had been altered – that I knew. (You must understand that so far I'd seen no proofs.) I read on rapidly. Sentence after sentence had been altered, entirely destroying the rhythm and generally wrecking my prose. I wrote to Ward Lock there and then, to ask what it meant, for Wilfred Lock knew very well how very particular I was. He was horrified – and went into the matter at once. And this was the explanation. The head of the firm of printers to whom the book had been entrusted had not long succeeded to that position: and he was very anxious to do a first-class job. So he thought he'd begin with the MS and get that right. And so he had been right through it himself, from beginning to end, amending and correcting my English, as best he could."

"God in heaven," said Berry.

"All this, with the utmost goodwill. And then he had given it to the compositors. Of course the whole book had to be scrapped and set again. I had a spare copy, and so they set from that. But one couldn't be angry, for the head of the firm had meant so terribly well. God knows how long it took him to do: but his one idea was to do a first-class job."

"Poor man," said Daphne. "He must have been so mortified. But what an extraordinary outlook."

"It had us all beat. In fact it didn't matter, for they cleared the decks and did a fresh book at once – of course, at their own expense. But it was a queer business. The mercy was, of course, that they'd sent me a specimen page. Otherwise, we should have known nothing until I received the slips."

"One moment. 'Entirely destroying the rhythm.' What does that actually mean?"

"I always think that rhythm is very hard to define. Either you're good at rhythm, or you are not. It's really a matter of ear. When I began to write, I used to read what I'd written over aloud, to see if it was rhythmical. Now I know whether or no it is, without doing that. If, when read aloud, the prose seems to be effortless, then it is rhythmical. If it doesn't, it isn't. That's a very rough definition: Fowler the Great deals with rhythm in his usual, masterly way: but he takes two pages to do it."

"And when you've passed the page proofs, that is that?"

"Yes. Then the corrections are made, and the book goes to press. The next time I see it is when I receive an advance copy. That's properly bound, of course. I always go carefully through that – and if corrections have been missed, I go off the deep end. And I don't think you can blame me. But they very seldom have been. Sometimes there are two or three 'literals' that I have missed myself. These things are put right in the second edition."

"Edition," said Daphne. "That's what I want to know. I've always wanted to know, and I've always forgotten to ask. You often see an advertisement of some book, saying 'Now in its third edition – or fourth or fifth.' How large is 'an edition'?"

"An edition, my sweet, can consist of five hundred copies or of fifty thousand copies or of any number in between. Unless you know the size of the editions printed, the information that a book is in its third or fourth edition means nothing at all. And only the publisher, the printer and, sometimes, the author know the truth. 'Now in its third edition' may mean that over a thousand copies have already been sold, or that over a hundred thousand have already been sold. Without that information, the statement is valueless."

"God bless my soul," said Berry. "And how many poor fools know that?"

*

"The other night," I said, "I mentioned *Valerie French*. I had no idea of writing that book, but my publishers were greatly upset by the end of *Anthony Lyveden* and put great pressure upon me to alter it. This, I refused to do. But they were so insistent that I said, 'Well, I'll tell you what. I'll write a sequel. And at the end of *Anthony Lyveden*, print these words, *To be followed by* Valerie French.' With this, they were quite content, and you can see those words in the first edition today."

"Did you ever alter the end of any book?"

"Once, when the book was appearing in serial form. *This Publican* appeared in serial form in *Woman's Journal*, and the Lady Editor begged me to change the last few words. 'They're absolutely true to life, but they're too savage.' So I laughed and rewrote the last few sentences – only for the serial, of course. The book stayed as it was."

"Very interesting," said Berry. "She knew her public, and she knew it would shrink from the truth."

"Something like that."

" 'True to life'," said Jill. "It was because it wouldn't have been true to life that you wouldn't...you wouldn't..."

I put an arm about her and held her against my heart.

"Yes, my darling. That's why."

"Bung it in," said Berry, fiercely. "Let people know the truth. Hundreds of letters you've had, all begging you to take us back to *Gracedieu*. You always meant to do it. You said as much at the very end of the book. Well, why haven't you? Because we *did* go back...for eight soul-searing months...and had to clear out again. And this time, not because of the Boche, but *because of the French*. And ours was no isolated case. Look at the Duchess of —. Left her lovely villa and fled in front of the Boche. And the Boche never touched a thing. And the moment the Boche was gone, the place was stripped – *by the French*.

"Let *me* tell the sordid story. I don't care. People mayn't fancy the truth, but they ought to know. And, damn it, this *is* history."

"As you please," said I.

"All through the war we were thinking and dreaming of *Gracedieu*. By a round-about route, the servants kept us informed. Our home was inviolate...they had moved the more valuable pictures and hidden them at a farm...they had packed and removed our clothes to a secret place...all was well...the

Gestapo had occupied the villa, but were behaving well...the silver had been buried, the liquor had been concealed...the house was *never* left: food was hard to come by, but one or other of them was always there: they were but waiting for the day when they could once again 'surround us with their devotion'... We continually thanked our God for such fidelity.

"In October 1944, we found ourselves in Lisbon. It was not until February 1945, and then only at the instance of a Minister I happened to know, that visas were issued to us to re-enter France. The war was then drawing to a close, and the South of France was clear. We wired to our faithful servants to expect us in five days' time, and on the following morning we took the familiar roads which would lead us back.

"One incident, I remember. We had been delayed at the Spanish-Portuguese frontier, and night had fallen before we had reached Ciudad Rodrigo, at whose agreeable guest-house we meant to pass the night. The outskirts of the town were not lighted and we lost our way. We encountered a Spanish Officer, whom, having no Spanish, I addressed in French. His manner was rather stiff, but he told me the way. Then he said, 'You're German.' We all yelled 'No', and I pointed to the flag on the car. He peered at this, for the light was none too good. Then he saw it was the Union Jack. Instantly, his manner changed. His face alight with pleasure, he stood to attention and saluted – and stood with his hand to his hat until we had gone.

"Ciudad Rodrigo, Burgos, San Sebastian... And then, at last, the frontier which we knew so well. At eleven o'clock one morning we crossed the bridge into France. Our reception was civil. Boy, who was driving, took out his crowns and put them on to the shoulder-straps of his British Warm. At our request, Cook's representative – a Frenchman – showed us the way to the American Post. Boy spoke to the Officer on duty, who promised to telephone to *Gracedieu* and say that we should arrive in three hours' time.

"Within three hours we sighted the lovely place, and we stopped by the side of the road and looked across the valley, to mark the bulwarks which meant so much to us. Then we drove on through *Lally* and up the familiar road. The faithful servants were there, to wring our hands. I think, to be honest, that tears were in all our eyes. After much tribulation, we had come home again.

"The garden had run to seed...the box had not been trimmed...the lawn didn't look like a lawn...and the fountain was stained... But such things didn't matter. Tea was served in the library, beside a handsome fire: and, later on, a dinner of sorts was produced, with some of our own champagne. But the house was very cold; and two days later I had pneumonia.

"Between you, you pulled me through; and I was myself again, before April was in. But things were difficult. Food was scarce and the beer was not fit to drink. And petrol was hard to come by. But Boy had made friends with the Commandant of the District, an old-type, sad-faced Frenchman, and he had German petrol and gave us what he could spare. We'd just enough to get into Pau once a week. For they said that I must be fed up: and there you could buy butter – under the counter of course, at two pounds ten a pound. But these things didn't matter, for we were at home. And our faithful servants were looking after us. When we went down to Pau, we always took the maid or the butler, to give them a treat. There was one other servant, a little local girl; and, of course, we all pulled our weight.

"And then, almost exactly two months from the day on which we had returned, the storm broke.

"It was after dinner, and we were in the library. The butler came in to take the coffee-cups. Daphne told him she wanted to speak to her maid. Two minutes later, perhaps, the woman came in.

" 'Oh, —, in case I forget, we're not going to Pau tomorrow, but on Monday, instead.'

"The faithful servant stared.

" 'But I have an appointment with my *couturier*. He is to fit the frock which I am to wear at my cousin's wedding next week.'

"We all looked at her.

" 'In that case,' said Daphne, 'you may have leave tomorrow to go to Pau by train.'

" 'And walk to and from the station?'

" 'Yes,' said Daphne. 'We cannot spare the petrol to take you there and back.'

"The woman went off the deep end, shouting abuse in *patois*, like a fish-wife of Dieppe.

"In a flash, Boy had the door open and I ordered her out of the room.

"After a moment or two, the butler appeared.

" '*Madame* will understand that — is greatly upset.'

" 'Have you come to apologize for her?'

"The faithful servant sniggered.

" 'By no means. But as her husband – '

" 'Leave the room,' said I.

"When we were alone, I looked round.

" 'And now,' said I.

" 'Not now,' said Boy. He looked at the door. 'We'll have it out tomorrow on what used to be the lawn.'

"And so we did. I'd been in bed for three weeks, so I hadn't seen or observed what the others had. But they had discovered quite a lot – regarding the faithful servants who had wept for joy to see their patrons again. The reason why I had gone down with pneumonia was that the house had been unoccupied for several weeks. Not a picture had been moved, though we had paid for their transport to and from some farm. The under-clothes which Daphne and Jill had been wearing the day before we left in 1940 were still unwashed in 1945. The shirts which — had been making for me in June 1940 were still unfinished after five years. A pipe had burst in January 1941, and some of the books in the library had been wet. They were still wet on our return, for they had never been taken from their shelves. And that, after four years. Our milk, which had always been delivered, had to be fetched now by the little local maid. The farmer, to whom I had lent money in 1939, asked the maid why I didn't come and get it myself. Boy had come in by the guard-room, wearing his British Warm. Passing through the servants' quarters he had seen the priest of Besse, sitting at the kitchen table, drinking with the butler and the maid. All had risen, so Boy went in to greet the *curé* whom he had known so well. The man had insulted the British uniform. However well we had known them, no peasant uncovered when Daphne or Jill approached. And they never used the third person, as they had always done. In his efforts to obtain petrol, Boy had been grossly insulted by one of the *Prefet*'s staff.

"Well, we were up against it. If we fired 'the faithful servants' we couldn't go on, for the little local maid knew nothing at all, but they obtained the food which we had to have to live. And no hotel would take you for more than two or three nights.

"The nearest British Consul was the man at Bordeaux. He was passing through Pau on Monday. That was why we were going down, for I wanted to visit London for three or four days. And I wanted my passport endorsed, so that I could get back. But now we had to consider whether or no we could stay.

"Finally we decided that we couldn't, and the bitter months that followed proved our decision good.

"And so, on Monday, I had a talk with the man.

"I said we had tried and had failed, and he didn't seem much surprised. Then I asked about visas for Spain and Portugal. 'They're easy,' he said. 'The exit permit's the snag.' 'What, from this country?' He nodded. 'Can't I get that at The Prefecture?' He shook his head. 'Your application must be submitted to the French Foreign Office. You must have a very good reason, which must be supported by documentary evidence. And the application may or may not be granted in two months' time.'

'What, to leave this blasted country?' 'That is so.' 'I'm a British Subject by birth, and you are the British Consul.' 'I know,' he said. 'But I can do nothing at all.'

"No Englishman likes living in a foreign country which he is not permitted to leave. So our applications went in without delay. We made inquiries about accommodation in Pau. This could not be obtained. When we asked about servants, people laughed in our face. 'Do you seek to take a bandit into your house?'

"So there was nothing for it. We had to stay at *Gracedieu* and we had to retain our 'faithful servants', in order to live. As did everyone else, we lived upon the black market – the lawful ration of meat was four ounces a month. And they alone knew the ropes. Why they stayed, I don't know: I suppose it suited their book. But life was more than unpleasant. The hatred, malice and uncharitableness, with which we met, became the order of the day. From high and low. It was intolerable.

"About this time the French Government called in all banknotes. The idea was to reduce the unlawful issue by handing back ten francs for twenty. But the Government lost its nerve. So it handed back twenty for twenty. But at least it knew what money in notes was out. Our parish consisted of just five hundred souls – that was the complement of three villages. If those five hundred souls had handed in six hundred thousand francs in 1939, I should have been surprised. In 1945 they handed in fifty-three million. And I know that that figure is true.

"Nearly three months of hell went by, with things growing worse and worse. We came to hate our condition. Our one idea was to leave for ever the home which we loved so much. The summer was nonpareil. Day after glorious day. But we found no pleasure in it. We stayed on the terrace and on our property: and, when we talked, we talked in the open air. We dreaded being called in the morning. There was no health in us. At last Boy wrote to our Military Attaché in Paris. Five days later we had the visas we sought. We obtained our Spanish visas and those for Portugal. And we wrote to Cook's man at Hendaye, to say that we should be leaving on October the tenth. (I seem to be out in my dates: but I know we were there for eight months and that that was the day we left.) And we asked him to arrange with an agent for the passage through Spain of the car. As is always done. He wrote back and said that he would.

"Boy went to call on the Commandant of the District.

" '*Mon Colonel*, our visas have come, and very soon now we shall go.'

"The Commandant shook his head.

" 'No, my friend,' he said. 'You have your visas, yes. But you will not leave France. You will be stopped at the frontier. I know what I know. Visas or no, they do not mean you to leave.'

" 'Impossible,' cried Boy. 'And what do they want with us?'

" 'I do not know,' said the other. 'I only know that they will not allow you to leave. They will find some fault in your passports or something wrong with the papers concerning your car. They do not mean you to go. Do not think that I blame you at all. I wish I could go myself. And now please listen to me. As the military authority here, I can get you out. But I alone can do it. I have an officer at Hendaye, and, if you will give me the date, I will instruct him myself to do as I say. And you must do as I say in every particular.'

" 'We propose to leave,' said Boy, 'on October the tenth. We have dismissed the servants, and they are to leave on the eighth. On the ninth a responsible caretaker will come in. That day we shall leave for Pau, where we shall pass the night. And on the tenth we shall leave for San Sebastian.'

" 'Today is the twenty-ninth. I shall visit Hendaye in three days' time. Please come to bid me goodbye one week from today.'

"Wide-eyed, Boy thanked him and left. One week later, he took his most careful instructions and bade that good man farewell.

" 'Drive to the Town-hall in Hendaye. The tricolour hangs outside. Be there exactly at two. On no account enter the front: go round to the back. There, in a little office, my officer will be waiting. Do as he says, for he is a faithful man.'

"We did as he said.

"The officer was ready and waiting.

" 'Sirs,' he said, 'the grey car outside is my car. Drive down the Street and turn. As you come back, you will see the grey car moving. Follow me.'

"He led us towards the Bridge. Then he entered the grounds of a handsome private house. He stopped by the door and alighted. 'We must see the Head of the *Sûreté*. The ladies will stay in the car.' One minute later, we were ushered into a salon upon the first floor. A keen-faced, grey-haired man looked up from his desk. 'Sir,' said the other, 'these are the English gentlemen of whom the Commandant spoke.' The other rose and bowed. 'Are your passports in order?' he said. 'Yes,' I said. 'And the ladies?' 'Are still in the car.' 'You will permit me to see them. I will come down.' We left the room and the house. He stepped to the car and bowed to Daphne and Jill, who inclined their heads. Then he turned to me. 'This officer will lead you to the Bridge. As you approach, you will pass him and go on alone. But he will stay behind, until you are gone. I am going now to ring up the Bridge myself.' We thanked him as best we could. Then we re-entered the car, followed the grey car out and drove to the Bridge. As we approached it, the grey car let us go by and pulled in to the side of the way.

"We stopped just short of the pole, and Boy and I got out. Cook's man was there and was grinning all over his face.

" 'Have you got the agent?' says Boy. 'To pass the car through Spain?'

" 'Your passports first,' said the other. 'There is the office there.'

" 'I asked for the agent,' said Boy.

" 'When your passports are stamped,' said the other – and very near laughed in his face.

"Together we turned to the office. A dreadful-looking fellow was standing in the doorway, smiling like hell. As we came up, 'Ah,' says he. 'The Commandants Pleydell, I think. May I see the passports you bear?' And he stretched out his hand.

" 'I think,' I said, 'you have had a telephone message – about our party, I mean.'

"The man shook his head, smiling.

" 'No,' he said. 'And now your passports, please.'

"And, as he spoke, I heard the telephone-bell…

"He turned and entered his office. This was small, and I could see and hear him from where I stood.

" 'But, yes. They have just arrived, sir. I am about to… But, sir… Very good, sir… And the car, also?…Very good, sir… Yes, it is understood… At once, sir… Certainly.'

"When he came back to the doorway, his smile was gone. And his manner was wholly changed. The man was scared.

" 'If Monsieur will give me the passports, I am to stamp them at once.'

"He was as good as his word. As he gave me the passports back, he looked very hard at Cook's man on the opposite side of the way. We walked to where the latter was standing, looking as glum as hell. 'Where's the agent?' said Boy. 'Have – have your passports been stamped?' he faltered. 'Of course,' snaps Boy. 'Where's the agent you said would be here?'

"The man was sunk. He had instructed no agent, because he knew that we should not be allowed to proceed. And now we were being allowed, and our passports were stamped. 'I will find the agent,' he said. 'While I am gone, this officer will clear your car.'

"Looking something dazed, the Customs stamped some papers and handed them back. Then I went off to collect our trunks from the station…

"The agent, who had not been warned, had made no arrangements with Spain and naturally declined to issue a guarantee. But, after what had happened, we wouldn't have slept in France for fifty cars. So our trunks were piled on hand-carts, which porters pushed over the Bridge, and we drove slowly behind them into Spain. The Customs had been so dithered that they'd never inspected the car or opened one trunk.

"The Spaniards were kindness itself. An agent was found, and I explained our case. He'd never seen us before, but he guaranteed the car: by that, I mean that he promised the Customs in writing that he would pay them the duty upon a car which was worth one thousand pounds, if that car was not out of Spain within seven days. He helped us to register our baggage, sealed the trunks himself and gave us the receipts. We had just enough Spanish money to do these things. Then, 'Excuse me,' he said politely, 'but francs are no good in Spain. You will have to stay at hotels and how will you pay your bills?' 'I really don't know,' I said. 'I can give them cheques on Lisbon.' 'You will stay three nights,' he said. 'And Spain is expensive today.' He took his pocket-book out. 'I think you should have fifty pounds.' He gave me the notes there and then. 'But to pay you back?' I said. 'I will send my account to Lisbon. Your bank will arrange.' I suppose that can be beaten. But, after France... I suppose it was strain, but, before I could manage to thank him, I had to master my voice.

"Well, that is the sordid story... And you will bear me out that every word is true. People may refuse to believe it: but I don't care. For all of us know that it's true in every particular. And that is why we shall never go back to *Gracedieu* and why you will never write the book which you meant to write.

"Now it's no good pretending that ours was an isolated case; for it was nothing of the kind. British resident after British resident returned to his home in France, met with the treatment we met with, hoped for a while against hope and finally threw

150

in his hand. I don't say that efforts were made to prevent him from leaving the country: whether they were or no, I have no idea. But, always because of his treatment, he had to go.

"What is the explanation of this astounding *volte-face* on the part of the French? For that is what it was. People who say, 'Oh, the French always hated us', make me tired. The French were never mad about any foreigner, but they certainly liked the English better than anyone else. Up to the outbreak of war, if he behaved himself, the British resident was popular in France. Tradesmen were glad of his custom: servants were eager to enter his service – no servant who had been in an English house would ever again enter a French one. Why? Because in an English house they were properly used. Peasants were always courteous and more than ready to help at any time: officials were, for the most part, extremely civil, and, once they got to know you, would do you proud.

"Let me put on record one single instance of 'service'. On the day on which we entered *Gracedieu*, the bulk of our furniture arrived very late: and when it did arrive, the men to unload it did not – for several hours. With the result that, though we all worked like madmen, the men were not out of the house till nearly eleven that night. We staggered into the library and sank down just as we were. We'd had no tea, we'd not even had a drink, and Daphne was trying to think what would be the easiest food for the chef to prepare and the butler to serve – for the two had worked just as hard as anyone else. Then the door of the library opened and the butler came in, changed and immaculate, with the cocktails, as usual, on a tray. As he brought them round, 'Well done, —,' said Daphne. 'Now about what we're to eat.' The man looked faintly surprised. 'Madame,' he said, 'will be served in a quarter of an hour.' We just had time to wash. Then we sat down to the dinner which Daphne had ordered, perfectly cooked and served. By the time we had finished, it was a quarter to twelve." Berry stopped there and looked round. "Is that reminiscence true?"

"Every word," said everyone.

"Very well. That was the sort of devotion which our servants delighted to render before the war. Why, then, the astounding *volte-face*, which I have described?

"I have spoken with many people who knew the old France: I've spoken with Spaniards: I've spoken with British soldiers, high and low: and I've spoken with diplomats. From what I saw for myself and from what they said, I have formed certain conclusions, and here they are.

"The first is this – that ninety per cent of the French will never, never forgive us for fighting on. When they surrendered, they assumed we should follow suit: it never entered their heads that we should go on. And when we did go on, they were simply wild. Why? Because, by refusing to surrender, we showed them up. For years they had boasted of their honour – a thing which we never did. But, when they were shown the whip, they threw their honour away. And then we were shown the whip – a very much heavier whip, for we were entirely alone. But we hugged our honour more tightly and bade the Germans lay on – so that, while France had no honour left, ours was magnified. Then they comforted themselves by believing, as they had good reason to believe, that we should be broken in pieces – a fate which they had escaped. And then we weren't broken in pieces... And that was gall *and* wormwood, and the very hell of a draught. So they came to hate us like poison.

"The second conclusion is this – that, under the Boche, the French did extremely well. I don't have to tell you that their ruling passion is gain, that it always has been gain. To our way of thinking, that is an unfortunate trait: but they had many qualities. Be that as it may, not only did the Boche pay handsomely, but something which was called 'The Black Market' came swiftly to life. The Black Market meant gain – smart, surreptitious dealing, which not only flouted the law, but always ended in gain...sometimes prodigious gain – two or three months' wages in one afternoon. Now this was right down the Frenchman's street: soon everybody was in it, from bottom to top. The proportions which it assumed were unbelievable. Peasants became franc millionaires: typists smoked cigarettes at ninepence apiece: comparatively poor men's wives dressed at the rate of fifteen hundred a year – pounds, not francs. It was, I think, after V Day, but whilst we were still in France, that a train-load of tyres vanished on the way to Paris from Havre. A whole train, loaded with nothing but tyres – brand-new Dunlop tyres. One of the Dunlop agents told me that. Think of the number of Frenchmen in on that deal: and every one got his rake-off. At that time there were, it was said – with how much truth I don't know – eighty thousand American deserters in France. Many had deserted, bearing their sheaves with them. They would take with them a truck – of American cigarettes. They could live on that for six months. Three pounds fifteen a hundred was what we paid. (They talk about a black market in England. They've never started in England, compared with France.) The French never made so much money in all their lives. And then came the liberation…which dealt a mortal blow to this prosperity. And the nation they hated like poison brought it about. By her cursed interference, doubly *Perfide Albion* deprived the French of their cake. What was so bitter was that they had to pretend they were pleased.

"And here and now let me say this. There were some who did not share this outlook. There were some most honourable exceptions – glorious, gallant men and women, who never threw away their honour, who showed themselves faithful to death. But they were very few… We have heard of '*La Résistance*'. This was negligible. Discussing it with a British General who was in a position to know, I suggested one per cent. He looked at me. 'Point o o one per cent,' was all he said. Had France, as a whole, 'resisted', I doubt if the Boche could have held the country down. He could certainly have done nothing else – look at the troops it took to hold our prisoners-of-war: and they were behind barbed wire. It was fear of such a resistance that kept Hitler out of Spain. Still, as I say, there were some great-hearted exceptions, who loathed the Boche as we do, whose hatred was not for sale.

"Well, there we are. I've told our sordid story: and I've offered an explanation of what occurred. And now let's forget a very bitter experience, which would, I think, have shaken Machiavelli himself."

"One word," said I. "Why did they try to prevent us from leaving France?"

"If you can't answer that question, neither can I. I can only suppose it was malice – they wanted to keep us there and to twist our tails. And, of course, we'd have had to pay through the nose. Nowhere to lay our heads – except at a price. And the one night we spent at Pau cost us over thirty pounds."

"I asked the Commandant, but he never replied. So I didn't ask him again."

"He must have known," said Berry, "God bless his honest soul."

"He was sweet to us," said Jill, "the day you brought him to *Gracedieu*. D'you remember how he kept saying, 'But this is an English house'? And he simply loved the terrace."

"He was honest," said I. "An honest gentleman."

"Give us something to sleep on," said Daphne. "I don't want to dream."

"Once upon a time," said I, "a man and a woman fell out. And the woman went to law. I knew the man slightly. I knew the woman by name. I have always believed that the case was one of blackmail – that is to say that such allegations were made by the plaintiff in the pleadings as she and her advisers hoped would induce the defendant to pay up, rather than let them be repeated, false though they were, in open court.

"Well, it came off.

"The case was never tried. When it was called on, counsel for the plaintiff announced that 'his lordship would not be troubled with the action, as the defendant had agreed to pay the plaintiff substantial damages' – he mentioned a phenomenal sum – 'as well as her costs'.

"I was very sorry for the man, who was one of the best. His father was dead. I was told that his mother had put great pressure upon him to settle the case.

"The solicitors for the plaintiff were Messrs. X and Y, not a very sweet-smelling firm. The solicitors for the defendant were Messrs. A and A, a firm of the best report.

"On the evening of the day upon which counsel made his statement, Mr X wrote a short note to the senior partner of A and A. He did not know him to speak to, but that was beside his point.

Dear Wisdom,
— against —
Our costs in this case amount to five thousand pounds. May we have a cheque at your convenience?
Yours sincerely,
Simeon X

"On his way home that evening, Mr X paid two calls. The first was to a jeweller's, where he chose for Mrs X a very fine string of pearls. The second was to a house-agent's. There he acquired an option to purchase a highly desirable mansion in a highly desirable square.

"When a week had gone by, but Mr X had received no reply to his note, he sat down and wrote again.

Dear Wisdom,
— against —
I think, perhaps, you never received my note, saying that our costs in this case were five thousand pounds. May we have a cheque, please?
Yours sincerely,
Simeon X

"Again he received no reply. But two days later the following letter arrived.

Messrs. X and Y
Dear Sirs,
— against —
  We shall be glad to receive your detailed bill of costs in this case.

Yours faithfully,
A and A

"This was extremely awkward. The making of bricks without straw nearly always is. Mr X was forced to the conclusion that Mr Wisdom was no gentleman.

"After a week's Herculean labour, Messrs. X and Y rendered to Messrs. A and A the detailed bill of costs for which they had asked. This, of course, had been made to amount to five thousand pounds.

"Messrs. A and A acknowledged the bill and notified Messrs. X and Y that they would have it taxed.

"If a solicitor renders a bill of costs which his debtor considers excessive, the latter can require the former to appear before a Taxing Master and justify his charges. The Taxing Master will study the bill and listen to what each side has to say. If he thinks any charge excessive, he will reduce it. If he reduces the whole bill by one third, the solicitor has to pay the costs of the taxation.

"On receiving this notification, Mr X perceived that Mr Wisdom not only was no gentleman, but never had been and never would be a gentleman.

"The two firms appeared before a Taxing Master. The latter studied the bill, listened to all that was said and taxed off – that is to say, reduced it by – very nearly four thousand five hundred pounds.

"Mr X's emotions may be imagined. In any event, the string of pearls went back to the jeweller's shop and the option to purchase the mansion was not taken up.

"And here is a tail-piece, which I doubt if the defendant knew.

"About six months later the plaintiff consulted Mr N, a well-known and popular solicitor, whose office was in The Temple, as some solicitors' are. She looked rather shabby and seemed very much depressed. 'Yes, my girl,' says N, 'and what's the trouble now?' He had her measure all right. 'Well, you know,' says the lady, 'I got — thousand pounds.' 'So I read,' says N, grimly. 'Well, X and Y won't pay me. I've not had a penny yet.' 'D'you mean that?' says N. 'Well, look at me,' says the lady. 'Leave it to me,' says N. 'Your gains may be ill-gotten, but not the Pope himself may confiscate ill-gotten gains.'

"N got the money for her, and that was that.

"Now I knew X and Y: I knew Wisdom: and I knew N. I knew very well a personal friend of X: and a personal friend of Wisdom's was a personal friend of mine. And that is how I was able to piece together this tale. I very much doubt if anyone else in the world knows the whole from beginning to end. But that is exactly what happened some forty odd years ago."

"The iniquity of man," said Berry, "passes belief. Why weren't they struck off the Roll?"

"They should have been," said I. "For that and for other things. But evidence in such cases is very hard to procure. And firms like that are very slippery. And in this case, their course was too easy: they would have got at the woman, and she'd have gone back on her proof. Why did Horatio Bottomley have the run he had?"

"I never could understand that, for he was the Prince of Rogues."

"Let me enlighten you. Twice the Crown went for him. Each time, their case seemed copper-bottomed. Each time they firmly believed they'd got him cold. And if he had gone down, he'd have gone down for fourteen years. And each time, somehow or other, he slithered out of the net. I don't know how he did it – I'd rather not think. The fact remains that he did. And were the Treasury wild? I'll say they were. And, thereafter, they watched him like hell. But Bottomley went straight on and did as he pleased. For years, quite once a year – and I'm putting it low – the information they got was more than enough to convict any ordinary man. So a brief went to Treasury Counsel, asking him to advise whether or no another attempt should be made. And this was the answer which Treasury Counsel gave. 'I will not advise proceedings against this man. Nothing short of the *fiat* of the Attorney-General, will induce me to draw the indictment in such a case.' "

"What's a *fiat*?" said Jill.

"*Fiat* is Latin, my darling, for 'Let it be done'. And Treasury Counsel was right. He knew his man, and he knew very well it would only be riding for a fall. They got him at last, as you know. But I think he was failing then. In his prime, he was marvellous. In court, I mean: for action after action was brought against him, and he always defended himself. And he was a lovely lawyer. I've heard him follow F E Smith on a point of law: and, by God, he was just as good. And always most respectful. If that man had run straight, he could have done anything. I suppose he preferred to be a rogue. They said he was Bradlaugh's son, but whether he was or not, I have no idea. But to hear him cross-examine… Rogue or no, you've got to admire genius. And he was immensely popular."

"Did you come across Arthur Newton?"

"I did indeed. I met him, time and again. He was often against Muskett. And he was charming to me."

"He was a pretty blackguard."

"So he was. But he was a gentleman. He was at one of the very best public-schools. Then he became a solicitor. He had his offices in Marlborough Street. He'd done time before I knew him. He was sent down for getting witnesses out of the way. God knows what he was paid to do it: but he made one stipulation. 'If I do it, they'll prosecute me and I shall be sent to jug. Well, I don't mind going to jug. But a solicitor who goes to jug is struck off the Roll. Well, I must be the exception. *I must not be struck off the Roll.*' Don't ask me how it was managed, but, though he went to prison, he was not struck off. And he came back and carried on. He had a most charming manner, was always well turned out: but I think he lifted his elbow – I can't be sure. I was told – but I can't vouch for this – that, because of Arthur Newton, the staff of Marlborough Street Police Station was always changed every month. Myself, I believe it to be true: but I can't say that it was."

"But why was that?" said Daphne.

"For fear that he'd get at them. You must get to know a man, before you can blackmail him."

"Good God," said Berry. "What company you have kept."

"It takes all sorts," said I, "to make a world. And you couldn't help liking him. He had a most pleasing address. But I always had the impression that most of the work he did never came into court."

"He saw to that?"

"Probably. Anyway, he was very able. And always nice to me."

"The old school tie?"

I shook my head.

"The honour was not Harrow's. He came from another place."

"Any more friends like that?"

"I can't remember one. And that's enough for tonight."

"Would you call that a side-light on history?"

"Frankly, no. But we needn't put it in."

"I don't know," said Berry. "It is not everyone that has a personality so dangerous as to compel the Commissioner of Police for the Metropolis to change the staff of one of his principal stations every month."

"I can't swear to that," said I.

"But you believe it to be true?"

"I do."

"Then bung it in," said Berry. "Damn it, we must consider posterity. What wouldn't we give today for such a reminiscence of the reign of Henry the Eighth?"

"I don't want to damp your hopes: but I can't see this book on sale four hundred years from now."

"Neither can I," said Berry. "But odd copies may survive. The Dark Ages will just be ending. The Barons will be hanging rich merchants up by their thumbs."

"My God," said Daphne, "I thought I told you I didn't want to dream."

*

Berry lighted a cigar and regarded his watch.

Then –

"What about half an hour at the Old Bailey? You know. Something worthy of Hogarth, just to take us to bed."

"You are revolting," said Jill.

"Not at all," said Berry. "Hogarth was a great master. But he never left anything out. And that is what lends to his incomparable pictures a historical value which is beyond all price."

"One day," said I, "whilst I was still a solicitor's pupil, I was at the Old Bailey. Why I was there, I can't remember. But I had been sent up there about some case. I had done what I had to do and was just about to leave, when either some clerk or some policeman touched my arm. 'If you want to see something, sir, which you'll never see again, go into the Judge's court.' I thanked him, and made my way in. The court was pretty full, so I stood in one of the aisles just abreast of the dock. Bench, jury-box and dock were all empty: the jury was out. 'Hullo,' said a man that I knew. 'Come to see some Grand Guignol?' I shrugged my shoulders. 'Somebody gave me a tip, and here I am.' 'Well, don't be sorry for them: they're pure-bred spawn of Satan – and that's the truth.'

"I knew the case. The King against Reubens and Reubens: and the charge was wilful murder. The Judge was Jelf. In fact, I had been in court the day before, for five or ten minutes, perhaps – no more than that. But I was glad that I had, for I happened to see one witness in the box.

"Before I go any further, I'll tell you about the case. I shall have to be very outspoken, but you must forgive me for that.

"Maurice and Mark Reubens lived in a house which they rented in a street in Whitechapel. They were Jews, as their name suggests, and they were brothers. They didn't look like brothers, although they were. Maurice was slim, fair, pasty-faced, with, I think, a small moustache. He might have been a draper's assistant at some rather low-class shop. Mark was animal: he was short, thick-set and dark, with one of the lowest foreheads I ever saw: he looked a hooligan. They did no work. Their income was derived partly from the immoral earnings of the women who lived with them – and others, and partly from the proceeds of the robberies which they committed upon the persons of those unfortunate seamen whom their particular women brought back to their house. Such robberies were lucrative, for the women had orders to concentrate upon sailors who had just been paid off."

"In fact," said Berry, "they were two of the idle rich."

"Precisely."

"Yet, with it all, a thoroughly nice-feeling pair."

"Be quiet," said Daphne. "Go on, Boy. I feel rather sick already, but I've simply got to know that justice was done."

"So much for the men. Now for the two women, who at this particular time were living with them. One was an East-End drab: young, vulgarly attractive, coarse. The other was young, too: she was fair and her face was pretty: her voice was gentle: and, for all her tawdry finery she looked what she was – and that was a lady born."

"Oh, my God," cried my sister.

"A lady born. She was the witness I saw the day before. In the box. I was able to observe her manner and hear her voice. Jelf was pretty tough; but as she turned to leave the witness-box, I heard him say to the jury, 'Gentlemen, this is a sight to make the angels weep.' I cannot better that saying. What tragedy lay behind it, I never knew.

"And now for the case. One evening the women picked up two sailors. I think I'm right in saying that they had just been paid off. As usual, all four went to some public-house, for the sailors had to be sozzled before they brought them home. Now one of the sailors could carry a great deal of liquor: so more than usual was drunk, before he had reached the condition which Maurice and Mark desired. Please bear that in mind. Then the four repaired to the house in the Whitechapel street. Maurice and Mark were there, but were not to be seen. The usual routine was observed. After what the brothers had found was a sufficient interval, the two of them entered the room in which the four were. Mark was carrying a sjambok, just in case. A sjambok's an ugly weapon, as you probably know: you can't kill a man with a sjambok, but you can lay his face open, because it will cut like a knife. Now one of the seamen was out, according to plan: but the hard-headed one was not, and when he saw what was coming, he put up his fists and dared the two swine to come on. Mark did his best with the sjambok, but his best only made that gallant sailor see red. And things began to look ugly – for Maurice and Mark, I mean. Nobody knows what happened – exactly what happened, I mean. But Maurice Reubens had cause to fear for his life – or thought he had. Be that as it may, he whipped out an ordinary pen-knife and opened its blade. And then he thrust this into the sailor's heart. Upon that, the great-hearted man burst out of the room. I imagine that he knew he had had it and hoped to publish the fact. Out of the house he staggered, and into the street, and he ran down the street for a little, with the knife still fast in his heart. And then he fell dead.

"His body was found very soon by a constable walking his beat. The constable knew his job – I'll tell you later why. He didn't blow his whistle: instead, he trailed the blood which led to the Reubens' house. Then he ran like a hare to the station...

"Very soon the house was surrounded, and as soon as he knew that it was, Detective-Inspector Wensley made his way in."

"Wensley?" cried Berry.

"Yes. It was Wensley's show. And, by God, he was a policeman. Rough, as you make 'em, but brilliant. He knew his job."

"You're telling me," said Berry. "Sorry. Just go straight on."

"The five were still there. Now only one would have been there; that is to say, only the drunken sailor, but for the fact which I asked you to bear in mind. And that fact was that more liquor than usual was drunk. As a result of that fact, one of the girls had passed out, and they could not bring her round. The Reubens dared not leave her, in case she had seen what occurred; and in any event, she might have talked to the police. Wensley found them working, drenching the girl with water, fighting like a couple of madmen to get her on to her feet. They'd heard no police-whistle, of course: that may have made them think that they still had time. But they hadn't reckoned with Wensley...

"Well, that is what happened, so far as anyone knows. The two Reubens were charged with murder, and the two girls turned King's Evidence. And that was that. It was a dead case. They duly appeared in the police-court, and they were committed for trial. And now the trial was over, and the jury was out.

"There was a sudden movement in court. I didn't see what had caused it, but I knew what it meant. The jury were agreed upon their verdict. The Judge was sent for, and the jury began to file in. The prisoners were sent for, too. When the jury was back in its box, the Judge took his seat on the Bench. But the prisoners were not in the dock. The whole court waited in silence. And then, from the cells below came roars and yells of protest: these rose into the court, by the stair that led into the dock. The Reubens were showing reluctance to learn what the verdict might be. And the Judge and jury sat, waiting… The roars and yells grew louder: this meant that the brothers were being persuaded to approach the foot of the stair. Phrases could now be distinguished – 'I won't' and 'Let me alone', howled, rather than spoken: but the bellowing was mostly incoherent, and you could hear its echoes beating against the walls of the corridors down below. And the Judge and jury sat, waiting… So they came to the foot of the stair, and the echoes died. But the noise was now much louder. The stair was of polished oak, and it was built to be used by one man at a time. It was, I should say, not more than two feet wide. To bring a man up that staircase, when he did not mean to be brought, presented difficulty. So the warders found. And the stair was slippery. I can't say we heard them coming, for the screams and roars overwhelmed all other sound. But I saw the backs of two warders rising into the dock. I should say that five minutes went by, before they were up that stair. And then at last they were being held up to the bar. A giant warder was between them, with an arm about each of their necks. Four other warders supported him, two upon either side: these had hold of their arms. And four warders stood behind – nine warders in all. And, behind them, the prison doctor, wearing plain clothes. Happily the dock was capacious.

"The uproar suddenly ceased – for no reason that I could see. It was just as though a switch had been turned.

"The Clerk of Arraigns broke the silence, by calling the jurors' names. When they had all answered, he asked the familiar questions. 'Are you agreed upon your verdict?' The foreman replied, 'We are.' 'Do you find the prisoners Guilty or Not guilty?' The foreman replied 'Guilty'. There was a third question, 'And that is the verdict of you all?'; but nobody heard it asked and nobody heard the reply, for the howls and yells of the Reubens filled the court. They roared and bellowed like beasts. The Clerk of Arraigns was shouting. I knew what he was saying: he was calling formally upon them, as is always done. But no one could hear a word. Suddenly, Mark went for Maurice. He never got him, of course: the warders saw to that. But both of them stopped howling, and Maurice drew himself up. He lifted two fingers at Mark, just as does a prelate of the Roman Catholic Church, when he is bestowing a blessing upon some reverent child. In dead silence, 'Marky, Marky,' he said, in a quiet, disapproving tone. 'Please, please.' His brother wilted. Then they looked at the Bench, and saw the black cap. And then they fairly let go. Beside the new explosion, its predecessors seemed pale. Had I not heard it, I never would have believed that only two pairs of lungs could have made so much noise. And it is the only occasion when I have seen the death sentence passed, but have never heard a word. I could see Jelf's lips moving, but that was all. And then it was over, and they had to leave the dock. This they declined to do. They clung to the bar like madmen, they fought and struggled like beasts, and the warders – nine though there were – had all their work cut out to get them to the head of the stair. Not counting the prison doctor, eleven men in that dock, and all of them locked together into a press: and the press was swaying and staggering to and fro: for fear must have lent the Reubens a frantic strength. They hadn't the breath now to roar and yell as before, but they were by no means silent, shouting incoherent refusals and sometimes desires. And, as before, the Judge and the jury sat, waiting... So they came to the head of the stair. There they found fresh hand-hold, and I was beginning to think that they'd have to send for stretchers, to get them down, for the cluster of men was jammed at the head of the narrow stair; when, all of a sudden, I think their strength gave in, for the whole lot fell down together and out of sight. It was just like pouring thick porridge out of a jug: it hangs for a moment at the lip, and then it goes with a rush.

"And now I can give you a tail-piece to this something grim account, and, unless Wensley related it in his reminiscences, I rather doubt if it's ever been told before. It was told me by Wensley himself, and I'll try to recapture his words.

" 'As I expect you know, after an execution, an inquest is always held. So someone must identify the body. Old Mrs Reubens, their mother, was still going strong, but we never ask a relative to do the unpleasant job. We get one of the neighbours to come along. But the name these two brothers had was so unsavoury that not a man or woman in Whitechapel would do the job. So the Coroner's Officer comes to me and asks what to do. "Well, there's nothing for it," I said: "you'll have to ask old Mrs Reubens." So off he went. When I saw him again, "It's all right," he says; "she'll do it. I don't think she minds at all." "What did she say?" I asked. And this was what she said: "I'll come and identify them. And fancy that – my two sons to be hung. Well, it's their own fault. Dreadful, awful, wicked lives they've led. And now it's come to this. All I can say is, I do hope it'll be a lesson to them." '

"My God," said Daphne.

"No doubt it was," said Berry. "A shade late in the day, of course. But what an astounding show! In court, I mean."

"It was remarkable, for violence in the dock is extremely rare. Except in this case, I never saw it once."

"You were very wise," said Daphne, "to tell us their record first. I mean, that hardened our hearts. All the same, it is a most terrible tale."

"I beg you to believe," said I, "that I have exaggerated nothing."

"I'm quite sure you haven't," said Daphne. "All the same, to see Fear rampant like that is a dreadful thing."

"You said you'd tell us," said Jill, "why the constable who found the body knew his job."

"Because Wensley was then at Whitechapel. He knew what he had to deal with, and every man was told to do as he said. Wensley was a great officer. Had that constable blown his whistle, the Reubens would have heard it and would have left the house. And they would have gone to ground. I don't say they wouldn't have been taken – eventually. But the woman they left might not have given them away. She turned King's Evidence, to save her life. But, had the birds flown, that inducement might very well not have been there. So you've got to hand it to Wensley – a splendid man."

"How did the man who told you to go into the Judge's court know that, if you did, you would see a scene?"

"I've no idea, my darling. I'd seen them the day before, but nothing then suggested that they would put up such a show. But they may have given trouble of which I never knew. The man in the aisle beside me clearly knew what to expect."

Berry put in his oar.

"D'you remember Gilbert's *The Hooligan*? He was an East-End Jew. And that master, Jimmy Welch, in the title role?"

"Shall I ever forget it? Women screaming and fainting all over the place. Scene – *The Condemned Cell*. A cut about twelve by eight in a great black cloth. At The Coliseum, not long before the first war. Which goes to show that Gilbert knew his world."

"I'll say he did," said Berry. "And pray allow me to thank you. I did enjoy the vexation of Maurice and Mark. It is so seldom that evil comes by its own."

"By God, that's true," said I.

"I see that I've rung some bell."

"You've rung more than one. But one occurs to me. But I'd rather leave it over."

"As you please," said Berry. "Oh, I know. McCarthy. That won't take long. Why did Mr Justice McCarthy take his life?"

"The answer to that is simple, but very sad. Because his brain was affected. His brain had been impaired by overwork. I remember McCarthy well, when he was at the Bar. He had far the biggest practice of any junior of my time. And he always looked worn. This was not surprising, for night after night, you could see his light in his Chambers till ten or eleven o'clock. And that went on for years. He never took silk, though that would have helped him no end. But, of course, taking silk is a gamble. Had he applied for silk, he could have had it at any time. But he may have been afraid – of crossing the Rubicon. For that is what it is. People who wanted McCarthy as a junior, might not have wanted McCarthy as a silk. For his fees would have had to go up. Of course, he should have done it, to spare his health. And, even if it hadn't come off, he must have made a fortune as a junior, and he wasn't a married man. And then he was made a Judge – taken straight from the outer Bar, a rather rare thing. But the appointment came too late, for he had impaired his brain. He was the nicest of men. Most charming in every way. And he had a very fine brain. But he had worked it too hard: and not for six months or so, but for year after year. And in the end, it gave way. It's a very tragic story. The life and death of McCarthy, a dutiful, kindly man."

"And now, before I forget, I must add a rider to something I said last night. It was said that, because of Arthur Newton, the staff of Marlborough Street Police Station was changed every month. I believe that to be true. But one man was never changed. That was Sub-Divisional Inspector Francis McKay. No finer uniformed officer ever walked his beat. I came to know him quite well, and I would sooner have dealt with Francis McKay than with almost any official I ever met. You knew where you were with him. He personified law and order: his reports were always first-class: and, by God, he knew his world. He was a fine, big fellow, with the heart of a lion: and the malefactor feared him. McKay would walk down courts, which none of his men would have dared to enter alone. But he always stuck to the middle of the court, for he didn't want a flower-pot to fall on his head. And it was for much the same reason that the stage-manager of a theatre in the old days always wore a top-hat. If he was worth his salt, the stage-hands hated him. And it was just too easy to drop a brick from the flies."

*

Berry emptied his glass and crossed his legs.

" 'Let's talk of' ramps, of dupes and sophistry, 'And tell sad stories of the' state of things."

"Now we're off," said Daphne. "What are you going to expose?"

"No vulgarity, please," said her husband. "I am about to contribute to this heterogeneous volume a little dissertation of indisputable value. I don't suppose that, as a result, my remains will be buried in Westminster Abbey: but, though I know my world well enough to realize that it will do no good, I shall at least have set out the honest and considered opinion of many God-fearing men and women, all of whom are impatient of chicanery.

"In my lifetime, I have witnessed two ramps or swindles, neither of which has been confined to the few, neither of which has suffered from exposure, both of which have proved remarkably lucrative to their promoters, both of which are today – such is the credulity of man – firmly established. In each case, with many others, I supposed the ramp or swindle to have attained the ephemeral dignity of the vogue and that, after an indecent interval, those duped would kick themselves – and, possibly also, the promoters – while the ramp or swindle sank into the pit of obloquy. But, with many others, I was mistaken: and I have today the melancholy privilege of witnessing the acceptance of both ramps or swindles as contributions of value to our civilization.

"The first ramp or swindle goes by the high-sounding name of psychology – a word which, I am prepared to wager, not one in a thousand of those who visit and pay a psychologist would be able satisfactorily to define. If my memory is not at fault, the

169

promoter or psychologist really got going between the two wars. (Let me make it quite clear that I am not referring to the true 'nerve specialist', for whom I have always had a great respect.) I am sure that it was about 1932 that, as an ordinary, decent British Subject, I became offended by the hold which this ramp or swindle was obtaining upon my more credulous fellows. I was in France at the time and I mentioned the matter to a distinguished French physician, whom I happened to know. He emitted a sound of contempt which no letters can reproduce. Then he added, 'They tried to start it here: but they didn't last long.' The French are realists.

"But now, in England, psychology and its promoters have come to stay. Men make large incomes by receiving patients, listening to their woes, employing terms and phrases which they can neither construe nor understand, issuing precepts, to obey which is entirely beyond their power, prescribing relaxation, and assuring them that, after a course of 'treatments' at two or three guineas a time, they will discover that they have been born again. They talk about inhibitions and repression: but never of discipline. That ancient and honourable word does not belong to the psychologist's vocabulary. And naughty children are brought to them…and the psychologist says, 'Another problem child.'

"There were no 'problem children', when I was young. But there was discipline. The young were disciplined: their elders disciplined themselves. Relations, friends, doctors, clergymen and lawyers gave us advice. This, they were qualified to give, because they had known us from childhood, often enough. And we never offered them money. Their counsel was not for sale. But all that is out of date: and the bare-faced ramp is in.

"It has actually made its way into the British Army… I don't think 'The Old Contemptibles' had known psychology. Something other than that had taught them to fight. The greatest general of his day, Smith-Dorrien – and when I say 'the greatest', I mean it: neither French nor Haig was in the same street with him – spoke to his 'superior' upon the telephone. 'My men are too tired to march: but they are not too tired to fight.' And he fought and won *Le Cateau* upon the following day. *That* was psychology. His 'superior', French, was proposing to withdraw all troops from the battle zone: he had actually wired to Kitchener, 'I think that immediate attention should be directed to the defence of Havre.' *Havre!* The Channel Ports could go. *Havre!* Two hundred miles from *Le Cateau*, where his 'subordinate' stood and broke the German rush. *That* was not psychology. He didn't know his men.

"That's all psychology means – knowing your man: knowing what you can ask of him, and what you can't: knowing his virtues and failings, sizing him up: and, if he comes to you, helping him when he's troubled, and, if he's playing the fool, making him beat down Satan under his feet. But you can't buy that sort of service. The psychologist can't sell it – he hasn't got it to sell. His wares are pinchbeck wares. And they don't belong to England, although they're there.

"The second ramp or swindle is modernist art. From the point of view of a student of human nature, this ramp or swindle is more interesting than the first; and its triumph, which is unhappily undeniable, is very much more important: for no man had heard of psychology, but many had heard of art. In fact, it was a case of a daw among peacocks; and that, we must all admit, is a difficult role to play. After all, art was established. Pheidias flourished five hundred years before Christ – and even more before Epstein: but that is beside the point. And Pheidias is acknowledged to be the greatest sculptor the world has ever seen. And painting goes back a long way – probably, just as far: but the old stuff has gone. Still, Giotto belonged to the thirteenth century. So we can safely say that in the year of our Lord one thousand nine hundred and ten, art was firmly established all over the world. Everyone knew what it meant – the reproduction in marble or on canvas of natural things; of men and women and skies and scenery; of storms and sunsets; of cattle and cities and battles and hunting scenes; as well as the artists' most humble and reverent conceptions of all we hold most holy in every shape and form. That is what art meant.

"As the centuries passed, the genius of sculptor and painter began to grow less marked. Old names began to stand out – Van Eyck, Claude, Rembrandt, Leonardo, Holbein, Velasquez, and dozens more: they stood out, as mountain peaks, and their followers gazed upon their summits and held their breath. But, though their followers could not attain such magical perfection, they stuck to the great tradition of holding the mirror up to nature, if I may make bold to borrow Shakespeare's deathless words. And Rodin, Winslow Homer and Sargent rose to tremendous heights. So did Munnings and others: but everyone did his best.

"And then the ramp or swindle lifted its shameless head…

"No one knows how it began, for promoters of ramps or swindles don't give their secrets away. But it probably began in Montmartre, where some scamp, like François Villon, who hadn't got Villon's brain, who could borrow no more money of women, who couldn't be bothered to do a decent day's work, determined in desperation to put up a bluff. Perhaps he had seen a cheap-jack, selling his coloured water to country clods. Anyway, he had nothing to lose… So he painted upon a canvas the sort of stuff that a little child would paint – a child who had been given a paint-box to keep it quiet. Before he did it, he probably shut his eyes, for he'd been to drawing-schools and he didn't want what he remembered to get in his way. And then he signed his production and sat down and thought of a name. I don't know what he called it: but, so long as it bore no relation to the blotches upon his canvas, any name would do. And then he took it to a dealer and, clapping a finger to his nose, he said, 'Here's something new.' And the dealer laughed like hell. Then he said, 'One's no earthly. Bring me some more.' So the modernist school was started, and pictures, that were not pictures, began to appear.

"Now that is all speculation, although I fancy it's not very far from the truth. But now I'll pass to the facts.

"It was, I think, in 1912 that for the first time I visited an exhibition of Modern Art. Be sure that I was offended: what is much more to the point, I was inexpressibly shocked. To describe the impertinent rubbish which was hanging, framed, upon the walls would be superfluous: everyone knows it by now, for it's always the same – devoid of every element of draughts-manship and style; and either portraying nothing that any responsible person has ever seen – except when some paint's been upset or the dog's been sick – or representing familiar objects as very young children may be expected to do. What shook me was to see educated people of fashion appraising this rubbish with the air of a connoisseur. They put their heads on one side; they stood back, half closing their eyes; they indicated what they called 'effects' to one another and they used the word 'values' over and over again. I could hardly believe the report of my eyes and ears. It was like a bunch of archaeologists commending the proportions of a dunghill and presaging the rich rewards which its patient excavation would bring. And then it dawned upon me that the old fairy-tale, told, I think, by Hans Andersen, had come to life.

"It is the tale of the king who was to walk in majesty through the streets, clad in a robe of unimaginable splendour, to delight his subjects' eyes. The robe had been specially woven, and, when the grooms of the bed-chamber laid it upon his shoulders, the King couldn't see or feel it, so fine was its texture and so rare its style. But his courtiers were overwhelmed by the sheer magnificence of his apparel. So a procession was formed, and the King went forth. And as he strode through the streets, his loving subjects were, one and all, overcome by ecstasy and vied with one another in declaring the splendour of his raiment and the excellent beauty of its style. And then, at last, hoist on his father's shoulder to see his King, a little child cried out, 'But he hasn't got anything on.' And the King looked round and said, 'Damn it, that's what I thought: but I didn't like to say so, because all these —s about me said that it dazzled their eyes. Give me an overall, someone. Oh, and where are the grooms of the bed-chamber? I'll deal with them here and now.'

"If a little child had been taken to that exhibition and had cried out, as children will, 'Oh, Mummy, that's like I do', the educated people of fashion would have at once avoided each other's eyes. And the gallery would soon have been empty, and modernist art would never have been heard of again. But there was no little child, to speak the truth. And because each of the educated people of fashion was terrified of being found guilty of bad taste, they vied with one another in commending stuff which each of them felt in his heart was beneath contempt – to the great and enduring profit of the promoters of the ramp. Of such is moral courage.

"And now let me bear myself out with a report which anyone who has the time to search the files of *The Times* may verify.

"Not very long before the second Great War, an eminent English art critic went to New York. Having an hour or so to spare he visited the Metropolitan Museum. After renewing his acquaintance with some of the Old Masters, he entered a modernist room. He strolled round this. Then he approached an attendant and gave him his card. 'Take this to the Curator,' he said. The Curator arrived hot-foot, for the critic was very well known. After courtesies had been exchanged, the critic led him to a picture. 'This caught my eye,' he said. 'I'm not surprised,' said the Curator, rubbing his hands. 'We were lucky to secure it. It was in the Salon last fall.' 'I know,' said the critic. 'I saw it there. I suppose you know that it is now hung sideways.' The Curator started. 'Impossible,' he cried. 'Clear the room,' said the critic, 'and have the picture down.' The Curator did as he said. The hooks on the picture had been removed for packing: and there, on the back, were their original holes. Either of design or because they were honestly puzzled, the men who had re-hung the picture had ignored these original holes, with the result that this triumph of modernist art had been hanging sideways for months in the Metropolitan Museum. *And no one, not even the Curator, had perceived that it was the wrong way up.*

"That true report can be verified, as I have said, by reference to the files of *The Times*. And if, after that, anyone is going to maintain that Modernist Art is anything but a ramp and a swindle, then, by God, let us pray for his soul.

"I'm afraid I've said nothing of sculpture. So let me say one thing. William Henry Hudson, the famous naturalist, who wrote that masterpiece *Green Mansions*, lived and died in England in 1922. To do him honour, a memorial in marble was erected in Hyde Park. On this appeared in marble an illustration of *Rima*, Hudson's most famous character and one of the most exquisite maidens that any author has ever created. For *Rima* was Amaryllis, the most delicate child of nature that ever was known. The illustration in marble is as revolting as it is indecent, and it was unveiled by a Prime Minister of Great Britain. Surely, on that memorable day, the ramp or swindle of modernist art touched its high-water mark. But one cannot help wondering whether the famous naturalist turned in his grave.

"And now to sum up. It is written, 'Ye cannot serve God and mammon.' You cannot admire Pheidias *and* Epstein: for if Epstein is admirable, then Pheidias is not. You cannot admire modernist painting *and* the Old Masters. For if M— is admirable, then Reynolds is not. It is, therefore, for every man to choose. But I cannot help feeling that those men and women of all nationalities who have esteemed Pheidias and the Van Eycks for hundreds and hundreds of years can't all be wrong."

"Once again," said I, "allow me to congratulate you upon your restraint. I know your detestation of chicanery as well as your contempt for lack of moral courage. I am also aware of your command of the more violent expressions which signify disapproval and rebuke. It is, therefore, a great relief to me to feel that a monograph which commands my great admiration will not have to be expurgated before it appears."

"Allow me," said Berry, rising, "to pour you a glass of p-port. As you know, I am unhappily very seldom able to commend your outlook. It is, therefore, with a pleasure which is unusual and so the more to be esteemed that I accept a tribute which was never more deserved."

"These courtesies," said Daphne, "are devastating. Last night Berry rang some bell. Boy admitted that, but wanted to leave it there. And the subject was that of evil which does not always come by its own."

"That's right," said Berry. "Come on."

"If you'll allow me," said I, "I'd prefer to withdraw."

"No, you don't," said Berry. "I have my public to consider. And I will not permit my partner to let them down."

"We can expunge the reference."

"That would be most improper. Besides, I want to know."

"So do I," said Daphne.

"Well, it needn't go in," said I. "It means some more plain speaking."

"I have always believed," said Berry, "in calling a jade a jade."

"You're nearer the truth than you think. Still, I must dress this up. When I was in Treasury Chambers, we had to prosecute once in a type of case which invariably presents great difficulty. The offence was extremely grave and can be punished by penal servitude for life. The difficulty is presented by the fact that the principal witness for the Crown invariably goes back on her proof. In this case, she ran true to form; but the case was stronger than usual, and I think we might have got home, if Marshall Hall had not been briefed for the defence. He had a way with a jury, and he got the prisoner off. Well, that was that. But Channell was on the Bench. I remember that he looked at the lady, and she looked back. I can see her now, standing between the two wardresses, small, dark, attractive and terribly well turned out. Then Channell spoke very sternly. 'Margery —,' he said, 'you're a very fortunate woman. You are discharged.' You see, Channell knew, and we knew, and she knew, and Marshall Hall knew a very important fact which the jury did *not* know. And that was that, less than twelve months before, she had been indicted and had stood in the very same dock at the Old Bailey on a precisely similar charge: and Marshall Hall had defended her and had got her off. He was her standing counsel. But, as I say, the jury didn't know that: and so they did as their predecessors had done – and as, for all I know, their successors did. And that is one of the cases in which evil did not come by its own."

" 'Her standing counsel,' " said Berry. "God bless my soul. And what was he paid for that?"

"I wouldn't know. I should say, a hundred guineas. But it was worth her while. If she had gone down, she'd have got fifteen years."

"My God," said Daphne.

"He commanded big fees?" said Berry.

"Oh, yes. And he certainly earned them. He was a very fine advocate, Marshall Hall. Towards the end, he suffered a lot from sciatica, and he used to ask the Judge's permission to sit, instead of stand. Not that those benches can have helped him. But I think his clerk had a cushion."

"When it was very hot, could you ask permission to take off your wigs?"

"I never remember that happening. But Fletcher-Moulton usually had his off. It lay on the desk by his side. But he was a Lord Justice of Appeal, and did as he pleased. He was very old, of course. And another Lord Justice, Vaughan Williams, was even older than he. But there was nothing the matter with their brains. Only their bodies were failing. Old Lady Vaughan-Williams used to come down to the Law Courts every day to prepare her husband's luncheon."

"How sweet," said Jill.

"So it was," said I. "She was nearly as old as he: but she would trust no one else to see to his food."

"A very proper spirit," said Berry. "For the welfare of her lord, no sacrifice was too high. I could wish – "

"That's all right," said Daphne. "I'll prepare your food tomorrow."

"My sweet," said Berry, hurriedly, "I never heard of such a thing. To think of your messing up those beautiful hands – "

"How?"

"Well, making pastry, for instance."

"You won't get any pastry," said his wife.

Berry swallowed.

"We – we mustn't upset Bridget," he said.

"Bridget," said Daphne, "will simply shriek with laughter."

Berry stifled a scream.

Then –

"I withdraw," he said. "I hereby submit to blackmail. It wasn't a proper spirit. Lady Vaughan-Williams went far beyond the dictates of duty. She spoiled the old boy. And I daresay he'd much sooner have had a dozen oysters and a couple of glasses of port."

"That's probably why she did it," I said.

"You are brutes," said Jill. "I think it was perfectly sweet. Did you ever put Marshall Hall into one of your books?"

I shook my head.

"But I put in Bodkin. And though I say it, the portrait was very good. *Mr Quaritch* in *And Five Were Foolish*. He had such a pretty wit."

"Ah," said Daphne. "There's something I meant to ask. *Quaritch* was a Treasury Counsel: yet he was defending a case."

"Oh, yes. That was often done. They had to ask permission – that was all."

"I assume they were well worth having. I mean they knew the ropes."

"Some of them were. But Muir, for instance, was no earthly. I've heard him defend, and he was a fish out of water."

"He had a big name," said Berry.

"Among laymen – yes. So did…others, among laymen. Personally, I never had a great opinion of Muir, as Counsel for the Crown. Give him a dead case, and he'd screw the coffin down as could nobody else. But everything had to go according to plan. He couldn't turn quickly, as counsel should be able to do. But, by God, he was a glutton for work. And he was safe as a house. A very admirable man. No sense of humour at all – he didn't know what it meant."

"Didn't he lead for the Crown in the Crippen case?"

"Yes. And he did it well. But that was a dead case."

"Was it, indeed?"

"We had so much evidence against Crippen, we didn't use it all."

" 'Among laymen'," said Berry.

"Damn it," I said. "I thought you'd pick that up."

"Go on," said Berry. "What the hell?"

"I've got to be careful here. I'm not going to mention names, but I could name at least four counsel whose reputation outside The Temple was in no way deserved. One was definitely bad. Another attained a great name in the nineteen twenties. I'd left the Bar by then, but I went to the Courts one day, to hear him cross-examine. I was never so disappointed in all my life."

"How do they get these reputations?"

"I really don't know. Probably through being in cases which are splashed, because they are 'news'. So the public gets to know their names."

"I've just remembered something. The famous Sir Edward Clarke. I rather think that he was before your time."

"Just before. But I can remember him, for Coles Willing took me to hear him in 1903. Some death-bed Will case. He was, of course, the leader of the Bar in his day: and he actually practised for half a century. Think of the changes he saw in fifty years. It was said that he left the Bar a disappointed man. He'd been offered the Mastership of the Rolls: this he refused, for he wanted to be Lord Chief Justice. But they never offered him that. He was, of course, a famous advocate. He grew very autocratic towards the end."

"*And Five Were Foolish*," said Jill. "Wasn't there something that started one of those tales?"

"I know what you mean, my darling. We were driving down through France soon after the first Great War. And we stopped at a garage, for I wanted some cotton waste. They hadn't got such a thing: but they sold me a box of rags, which, they said, were sterilized."

"The French all over," said Berry.

"Exactly. But I had to have something. The first rag which I took out had once been part of the shirt of a wounded man."

"How bestial," said Daphne.

"The French all over," said Berry.

"I didn't take out any more. But that gave me the idea for the short tale *Madeleine*."

"What gave you the idea for *The Stolen March*?"

"My favourite," said Jill. "It always was."

"I don't know at all. I just sat down and began, and the book carried on. I well remember that I couldn't think how to get them out of *The Pail*. But the book did it all right – and, I think, quite naturally."

"If I may say so," said Berry, "that book has some very high spots. Much, of course, was drivel: but – "

"What was drivel?" said Jill.

"I am happily unable," said Berry, "to retain in my mind such written word as does not attain the standard necessary to merit my attention."

"Plagiarist," said Daphne. "That's *Pride* to the life. Only Boy would have put it better." She turned to me. "I always hoped you'd write a sequel to *The Stolen March*."

"I meant to," I said. "But a lot of people didn't like it, you know."

"That," said Berry, "I can well believe."

"Be quiet," said Daphne. "But, Boy, that didn't stop you?"

I laughed.

"No. That's why I'm not a good author. I've always gone as I pleased. As long as I know that my work is up to standard, I don't care what people like. But my publishers got worried. And so I put it off. And then I did other things, and – well, it's too late now. It could be done: but the sequel would not be a patch on its predecessor. And that must never happen. If you are to write a sequel, it's got to be just as good."

"Was *Rupert of Hentzau* as good as *The Prisoner of Zenda*?"

"No. But the last scene lifted it very, very high."

"What was the best novel written between the wars?"

"That's easy. James Hilton's *Lost Horizon*. About that, to my mind, there is no argument."

"What made you change your style?"

"You mean, start writing romances?"

"Yes. *Blind Corner* was the first."

"Well, I read an article – I think it was in *The Spectator* – in which the writer pointed out that an author who wrote stuff that sold, when he could really write better stuff should be ashamed of himself. That got me under the ribs. For I knew that, if I tried, I could write better English than so far I had. But there didn't seem to me to be much scope for good English in the light stuff I had been writing. And so I wrote *Blind Corner*. Of course I got stacks of letters, saying 'Anybody can do stuff like *Blind Corner*, but nobody else can do your light stuff. Please stick to your last.' "

"What damned impertinence," said Berry.

"It was not meant. And I saw their point. But it wasn't mine. So I wrote three more 'Chandos' books, before throwing back. The author who writes what his public wants him to write, because his public wants him to write it, is doomed."

"It has been done," said Daphne.

"I know. It's a great mistake. In a way, it's writing to order. And that is a thing no author should ever do."

"After the first four '*Chandos*' books, you wrote *Adèle and Co.*"

"To my mind," said Berry, "taking it by and large, you've never bettered that book."

"I shall always think it's the best of the '*Berry*' books."

"Better," said Daphne," than *The House that Berry Built*?"

"That's my belief."

"One thing, I'll give you," said Berry. "For some extraordinary reason, your books don't date."

"That's just an accident."

"Some reviewers," said Jill, "keep on referring to your tales as being impossible. They're quite nice, as a rule, but they will keep on saying that the things that happen are impossible. That always makes me cross, for they're *not* impossible."

"I know," said I, laughing. "It used to annoy me once. But I don't care now. You see, you must remember this. We know that they are not impossible. Take *Cost Price*. Everything in that book could easily have happened. A courageous giant, like *Chandos*, who knew no fear, could have done all that he did. And there was no situation which was unreasonable. But, then, we know the Continent of Europe. And we know that all those things could have happened there. But the reviewer doesn't know the Continent... And so he says, 'Impossible. Entertaining no doubt: but impossible.' Of course such things couldn't take place in England. That is why I always make France or Austria the scene. And I refer to Austria before 1938. In *Blind Corner* I took care to say that, if you had cared to fight a duel with a couple of Lewis guns in the Austrian countryside, before the first war, no one would have taken the trouble to come and see what it was."

"I can bear that out," said Berry. "It's perfectly true. And everything that happened in *She Fell Among Thieves* could perfectly well have happened in France up to the second Great War."

"Well, there we are," I said. "The reviewers don't realize that, and I don't blame them. But it happens to be true. After all, what is a romance? As I have said before, it is a 'tale with scene and incidents remote from every-day life'. And there, I think, lies the answer. I once had a terribly nice letter from a bloke, who said 'What I like about your books is that you never write anything which isn't entirely possible. Given initiative, drive, courage, strength and money, any fit man could do what Mansel and Chandos do. And you always give a perfectly satisfactory explanation of everything. That's why your books are convincing.' "

"That was a rare tribute."

"It was, indeed. And I valued it very much. You see, it's so easy, when A and B are in a jam, for C, the hero, to appear in a waiter's dress and lug them out. But how did C get there? How did he get taken on? How was it that he was there at the critical moment? Well, that's left to the imagination – and must be swallowed whole: for the author doesn't know any more than the reader does. And when the police are coming and you've got to dispose of the dope. Well, you open a panel and you press a lever which drops the dope into a furnace. That's fine, of course. But who installed the contrivance – a rather elaborate contrivance – behind the panelling of a London flat?" I shrugged my shoulders. "Convenient waiters and levers are all very well. But my experience is that in life they are not there. Such work is slovenly. I have always maintained that if you publish a book, you've got to play fair. *The Stolen March* was a fantasy: the action of *Blood Royal* and *Fire Below* took place in a principality not to be found on the maps: but, allowing for the custom of the country, *Chandos* did nothing which a fine fellow couldn't have done. Frankly, I should be ashamed to offer my public something which no thinking man could accept. It is, I suppose, a matter of self-respect."

"Why did you write *Lower Than Vermin*? I mean, that was down a street which you'd never taken before."

"I'll tell you. I waited a year or two for somebody else to write it, by which I mean, to write a similar book: somebody whose position was more important than mine. But nobody did. And so I decided to do it; for I felt that, before it was too late, some author of standing ought to place upon record the truth about the old days, which, because they know no better, today the young revile. Indeed, they are so instructed. They are taught, by fellow-travellers – for they can be nothing else – fellow-travellers older than they, that the old days were wicked days, when the rich oppressed the poor, when no one who was not well-born had a chance of making good, when Great Britain did robbery with violence on nations weaker than she. I have heard such a fellow-traveller, whose name is by no means unknown, declare such things on the broadcast – and he was only a year or two younger than I. We know that such things are lies, and the fellow-travellers who tell them, know that they are lies. We know that the England of our youth was a happy, prosperous land, where most men, high and low, were well content with their lot. And so, before it was too late, I determined to set down the truth.

"Whether this did any good, I shall never know. But I had a great many letters, thanking me for the book. I only received one letter which disapproved of the picture which I had drawn. Two letters, from different countries, whose writers were English-bred, said the same thing. They said, '*Lower Than Vermin* should be made compulsory reading in every school'. So, at least, they got my idea. And now I've talked more than enough about my own stuff. I can't think how I've written thirty books to date. It seems such a lot, somehow. But many authors, of course, have written far more than that."

"I am credibly informed," said Berry, "that some authors set themselves an allotted task. This is always to write five thousand words a day – or three or four or six. And this, they faithfully do."

"So I believe," said I. "Trollope, I know, did that: and so did Arnold Bennett. And so has done many another, for all I know. Now Trollope and Arnold Bennett were both great men: and I can only suppose that they could control their gifts. For I could never do that.

"In the first place I never employ the yard-stick. When I get up from my table, I've no idea at all how many words I have written since I sat down. When I've finished a tale, I've no idea of its length. I know that it's not too short; but no more than that. As a matter of fact, my short stories were always rather long. But they just worked out that way. The book or the tale decides – it's nothing to do with me. They are all eventually measured, but that's my publisher's job.

"In the second place, I never could engage to write so much a day. I've always worked pretty hard, but one day the book will go, and another day it won't. And I cannot possibly force it: the stuff wouldn't be worth reading if I did. Setting yourself to write so many pages a day is much like writing to order: such as can do it – and turn out stuff worth reading, as Trollope and Bennett did, command my admiration: I don't know how they do it, and that's the truth."

"Bear with me," said Berry. "What about dictation?"

I laughed.

"The man who can dictate fair prose is a *rara avis* indeed. I think it likely that Winston Churchill can. So, possibly, can Somerset Maugham. But, then, they probably do it, if they do, as Thackeray did. Thackeray had a magnificent memory. He would stroll in Kensington Gardens, composing his work as he went. And, when he came home, he would dictate the passages he had composed. But wash out the superman, and you may safely say that stuff which is dictated is never fair prose."

"One thing more. You always write your stuff in longhand first?"

"Always. After I've done a few pages, I move to the typewriter. On that I knock out what I've written any old way. I don't care what it looks like, so long as it is in type. You see, when I write, I'm always throwing back – reading over what I have written: when this is in type, it's very much easier to read. When I've copied what I have written, I sometimes go on composing and typing as I compose. But never for very long. After a page, perhaps, I come back to the longhand again.

"When I've done about a chapter, I revise it, that is to say, I cut the typescript about – in longhand, of course. Alter and prune and add, till it looks like nothing on earth. But I keep it legible: for, when the book is finished, the fair copy's made from that."

"So the typescript is really your original manuscript?"

"I suppose it is."

"And he tears them up," said Jill.

"He's not going to tear up this one," said Berry. "It'll probably be sold at Sotheby's for an enormous sum." He sighed. "I suppose it'll go to America. It can't be helped. And now let's go on Circuit for quarter of an hour."

"That's right," said my sister. "Brooch and The Assizes. I used to love to see The Red Judge go by."

"So did I. They're a bit of the old world, Her Majesty's Justices in Eyre."

"What does that mean?" said Jill.

"'Eyre' 's the old word for 'Circuit'. There are two Judges, sometimes. But the 'churching' of the Judge, the state coach with its footmen on the tail-board, the escort, the trumpeters, and The Judge's Lodging – these are all old institutions and stand for dignity. They're very picturesque and very valuable. One day, I suppose, they will go the way of the Grand Jury: and that will be that. But I shall regret their passing.

"In my hearing a member of the Bar once scoffed at the state which is kept by Her Majesty's Justices in Eyre. He was – well, senior to me, so I held my tongue. I remember his saying that he was once engaged in a case which lasted three days – I think, at Lewes. So he stayed in the town. One day, when the Court had risen, he went for a walk. And he fell in with the Judge – Mr Justice Day. The Judge confided to him that he had left the court by an unobtrusive door, in order to avoid being driven back in the coach: and declared his relish at the thought of the coach and its attendant 'flunkeys' awaiting his coming in vain. That the narrator relished this distasteful reminiscence was very clear. Later, he was raised to the Bench, and I used to wonder what he made of it all."

"It doesn't sound a very good appointment."

I shrugged my shoulders.

"I think he did all right. And here let me pay a tribute, in case I forget.

"Nobody ever hears of The Clerk of Assize. He is really the Clerk of Arraigns, and each Circuit has its own Clerk. If he discharges his office with ability, he can become a most important man. It was generally recognized in my day that Arthur Denman of the South Eastern Circuit was the finest Clerk of Assize that ever was seen. Dignity personified, he truly distinguished his most ancient office. His wisdom was infinite, and his address superb. He was severe – I never saw him smile – and most punctilious. More than one Judge feared him: the Bar certainly did.

"Almost the first case in which I appeared alone was heard at the Maidstone Assize. I was frightened out of my life, but I managed to struggle through. When the case was over, Denman beckoned to me. He was sitting below the Judge, so I went and sat down by his side.

" 'Please never again let me see you address the Court with a hand in your pocket.'

" 'I'm very sorry,' I said. 'It was unintentional.'

" 'Perhaps. But it was highly disrespectful. All right.'

"I suppose some people would have resented this rebuke. But I did not; for Denman was qualified to administer it. I never got to know him – I don't think any member of the Bar ever did. But we knew one another in Court. And I have much to thank him for. He was, of course, the author of *Denman's Digest*, a most admirable work.

"The other outstanding personality of the South Eastern Circuit was the Circuit Butler, Smither. He was a splendid servant – the servant of the Bar. He had an inherent dignity, which was compelling. He was always on duty, looking after members of the Bar who were staying the night in the town, and attending other members who were returning by train. He'd carry their robes to the station and get them a seat. And things like that. All sorts of little matters were dealt with by Smither. We always got on very well. Once or twice, if a Judge fell sick, and a Commissioner of Assize came down to do his work, Smither would seek me out and ask me to give him lunch. Why he chose me, I don't know: but, of course, I was very much flattered and very pleased. I only hope the Commissioner enjoyed it as much as I did: but I rather doubt that."

"What did the other members of the Bar think about it?"

"I've no idea. They never seemed to mind. Perhaps it was an honour which they were glad to escape."

"Were you 'The Junior'?"

"Oh, no. 'The Junior' was Gerald Dodson, now Recorder of London – and, I believe, a first-rate Recorder, too."

"To bed," said Daphne, rising. "It's terribly late."

"Not my fault," said Berry. "Your fool of a brother will talk."

"Rot," said Jill. "You're always egging him on."

"I must confess," said Berry, "to a certain squalid curiosity of which I am heartily ashamed. And he seems to be able to satisfy it. But I'm going to tread it under. I will encourage no more of these grisly memories. Some may be side-lights on history: but the glare they cast is sordid."

"They're better," said Jill, "than the stuff you want shoved in.

188

" 'Stuff,' " said Berry. " 'Stuff.' God give me strength. You're a very naughty little girl, and tomorrow you shan't sit up. 'Stuff.' Their intrinsic value apart, drawn from the precious cask of wisdom unrefreshed, the memories I have vouchsafed are literature. Walkup's in all their glory were not arrayed like one of these."

"To bed," said I, laughing, "before he says anything worse."

*

"Tell us some more," said Daphne, "of Madame la Comtesse de B—."

"Yes," said Berry. "She's 'Off-the-Record' history, if anyone ever was. I only saw her once, but I've never forgotten her. She was long past her prime, but her mighty personality hit you between the eyes."

"She was a throw-back," said I, "to another age. Her ancestors were English, and sailed for Virginia when Cromwell killed the King. She married young and spent most of her life in Europe. She was immensely rich in her own right: so was the man she married: and when he died, he left her everything. So when I knew her, money had ceased to count. She had an apartment in Paris, a mansion in Dresden, two lovely *châteaux* in France and a castle in Austria. Of the *châteaux* in France, one was modern and one was very old. The latter was sixteenth century, quite unspoiled: there were fireplaces there into which a car could have passed: much of its plenishing was the lovely English furniture which her forefathers had taken to Virginia in the seventeenth century. She seldom used that house, but she moved between her other residences, as she felt inclined. All were luxurious beyond belief. The servants were trained to a hair: and the table she always kept was such as I never sat to anywhere else. Her castle in Austria was more than forty miles from the nearest town, but her meals were the meals you'd hope for in Grosvenor Square: at breakfast four kinds of new bread were always served. Don't ask me how it was done, for I've not the faintest idea. But that was the way she lived."

"That castle," said Jill, "was *Wagensburg* in *Blind Corner*."

"Yes. The description is very close. But there was no great well, nor, so far as I know, an *oubliette*. But it wasn't called *Wagensburg*. That was the name of a castle not very far away.

"Madame de B— loved a house-party – not a large one, you know. Six or eight. And she always desired her guests to do as they pleased. But they had to be present at meals and – "

"I feel," said Berry, "that that order was cheerfully obeyed."

" – on one thing she insisted: that was that every night, before we went to bed, we should come to her private salon, to bid her good night. You see, when she left the table, she took the women with her and went upstairs. And, when the men left the table, they went to the smoking-room. (You could smoke there, or in your bedroom: but nowhere else.) After a while, she sent the women to bed: and when the men came up, she was quite alone."

"An autocrat," said my sister. "I shouldn't think the women enjoyed their stay."

"Not altogether, perhaps. If you remember, I told you she had no use for her sex. However, when we appeared, she was always alone. And then she'd make us sit down and she would begin to talk. Very soon we were conversing, and her contribution was so brilliant that it improved our own. You've seen a great actor or actress lift up a play, so that the rest of the company never acted so well. Well, it was just like that. I've sat there till two in the morning... All she said was so striking and her wit was so quick and so rare, that, however tired you might be, your weariness fell away, and soon you were talking and laughing as if it was eight, instead of eleven o'clock.

"You could hardly name some eminent figure of her day whom she had not met: she could take you behind the scenes of Court after Court: and her personal magnetism held you as, I quite believe, it had held any number of far bigger men.

"She had an astonishing drive: the consummation she desired, she almost always achieved. She was a most curious mixture of good and ill. She could be quite merciless: withstand her, and she would show you no pity. I've mentioned the playboy before. He'd been her familiar friend: but he'd given her great offence, and she meant to send him down. Yet, she could show a kindness, very rarely encountered in this rough world.

"I remember one summer evening in Austria. I was sitting on the terrace with her about seven o'clock. And far away on the opposite side of the Save which ran below, we saw a cottage on fire. We could do nothing about it, for, though it wasn't much more than a mile from where we stood, that was as the crow flies: you had to drive several miles before you came to a bridge. But Madame de B— was very greatly distressed. Then she called a servant and sent for her maid and a car. 'Poor people,' she said, 'poor people. They're so very poor, the peasants: their home is all they've got. I must make them a present at once.' I begged her to let me go, for she hated driving by night, and to get to the scene of the fire would take a long time. 'No,' she said firmly, 'they'll think much more of it, if I take it myself.' 'Tomorrow morning, Madame.' 'Boy,' she said, 'use your brain. I wish to spare those peasants a sleepless night.' And go she did. I don't know what she gave them – probably more than enough to build a new home. Dinner was very late, for it was fully two hours before she got back. But that night her eyes were shining.

"I remember I said to her once, 'Madame, you have a strange heart. One half of it is of butter: the other half is of steel.' She laughed. 'You're perfectly right,' she said. 'Don't come up against the steel.' "

"I trust you didn't," said Daphne.

"I tried my best not to," said I. "But one of her relatives did, whilst I was there. He was about my age – say twenty-eight. He resented something she'd said or something she'd done – and he had a mean mind. He knew that she slept very sound: and he knew that every night sandwiches were set by her side, in case she should wake in the night and wish for some food."

"Splendid," said Berry. "That's the way to live. I wish she'd asked me to stay. And a decanter of port?"

"No. She was most abstemious. The next morning, when her maid called her, remnants of one of the sandwiches lay on the floor. It had been partially eaten. She told me about it, and I suggested a rat. At once she sent for her maid. When the maid came, she told her to take me to her bedroom. When I came back, 'Still think it's a rat?' she said. 'No, Madame, I don't.' Her bedroom lay in the tower. No rat could ever have gained it, except from within. The floors and the ceiling were sound, and the door was of oak. 'Frederick did it,' she said. 'Perhaps he'll do it again. But he won't do it thrice.' I dared say nothing, but there was doom in her voice.

"The following morning, at breakfast, she turned to me. I was on her right and Frederick on her left. 'Boy,' she said, 'a very strange thing happened two nights ago. One of my sandwiches was eaten... A rat, no doubt. But I am a heavy sleeper, and I never heard a thing. But it left an unpleasant impression. I don't like vermin about me, while I'm asleep. I thought he might come last night. But he didn't. If he had, he wouldn't have gone away.'

" 'You were ready for him, Madame?'

" 'No. But the sandwiches were. I put enough strychnine in each to kill a bull.' "

"My God," said Daphne. "And Frederick?"

"I thought he was going to faint. He turned the most dreadful green that I have ever seen. Then he begged to be excused and left the room. Madame de B— looked at me. 'Well, what about it?' she said. 'Madame,' I said, 'words fail me. Supposing...supposing he'd come last night...' The Countess shrugged her shoulders. 'In that case,' she said, 'he would have been buried on Thursday. But the world would have been no poorer. He's got a small mind.' She looked at me very hard with those keen, grey eyes. 'You think I'm bluffing, Boy. Have you finished? Then come with me.' She led the way to her salon. There she unlocked a bureau. There was a small plate of sandwiches. She lifted one and opened it. The crystals were there all right. I swallowed. 'You believe in rough justice, Madame.' She nodded. 'Yes. To do as he did was great presumption. It was also impertinent. Those are failings, Boy, which I have always deplored.' And if Frederick had broken a leg that same afternoon, she'd have summoned a surgeon from Salzburg and nursed him herself.

"Well, there you are. She showed me once again that it takes all sorts to make a world. But she was a notable woman – born out of date. She could discuss any subject with high intelligence. She always spoke much better than I can write; and her sense of humour was outstanding. I've seen her laugh till the tears ran down her cheeks."

"I do hope," said Berry, " that Frederick saw the humour of that episode."

"I'm afraid he didn't," said I. "For two or three days after that, sandwiches were served at half-past eleven o'clock – and handed round. You should have seen Frederick's face. I didn't take any, either: but I wanted to burst with laughter, when they appeared."

"Had she any Borgia blood?"

"Say, rather, Medici. She had an eye to a jewel."

"I can still see her pearls," said Berry. "They were the very biggest I ever saw. They weren't a rope, like Jill's; but every one was the size of Jill's centre pearl."

I nodded.

"They were more astounding than lovely. They were strung twice a month. Two attempts had been made to steal them: after the second, she wore them day and night. And Borgia isn't fair. She never had that outlook. And she was strictly moral – almost strait-laced. She would neither countenance nor relate a tale which was so much as tinged with impropriety. Only once did I ever hear her break that rule, and then she was relating an historical fact."

"Let's have it," said Berry. "Let's have it. 'A great lady's lapse.'"

"She was speaking of a lady who was in the direct succession to one of the greatest thrones. Of that particular Court, the etiquette was almost inconveniently rigid. She certainly found it so. From being frowned upon, her conduct began to give rise to grave anxiety. At last she was summoned before what I will call a Privy Council. She came gaily. The Monarch himself addressed her. 'Madame,' he said, 'I conjure you to tell this Council the truth. Who is the father of your coming child?' The lady smiled. 'Sir,' she said, 'I haven't the faintest idea.'"

"What ever happened?" said Jill.

"If you'll forgive me, my darling, I'll leave it there. Madame de B— was very illuminating on the Kaiser's mentality. 'He has always had the outlook of a vain-glorious and ignorant child. No one can tell him anything, because he always knows. And he must always be right. Let a man prove him wrong, and that man is doomed; for out of his own mouth, he stands convicted of *lèse-majesté*. The Kaiser has come to believe that he is indeed the All-Highest, who can say and do no wrong. His *entourage* regards him with supreme contempt. But no one stands up to him, for no one has any desire to cut his own throat. His everyday behaviour is incredibly puerile. His idea of humour is painful – and very often vulgar – to a degree. Let me give you two trifling examples...

"'Well-born children were sometimes invited to the palace, to play with his sons. They liked the Kaiserin. She has no brain, but she is motherly. Then the Kaiser would appear. He would stride to some hapless boy, take him by the shoulders and shake him. "What do you mean," he would cry, "by having such a big back-side?" Then he would look round for the laughter, which, of course, always came.'"

"If," said Berry, "we had a vomitorium, I should repair there forthwith."

"Be quiet," said Daphne. "It's quite revolting enough."

"Her second example was this. 'It is well-known,' she said, 'that, if he commands a force at the Army Manoeuvres, that force must always win. What is not so well known is that the Kaiser always breakfasts with the enormous Staff. Everyone has to be standing by his place, when the Kaiser comes in. Then he will take his seat, and breakfast is served. His breakfast always consists of two sponge-cakes and a glass of milk. One sponge-cake he will eat – and wash it down with the milk. Whilst he is doing this, he will cut the other sponge-cake into ten or twelve cubes. Then he will rise to his feet, and everyone does the same. Then he will call the name of a general or colonel at random and pitch a cube in his direction. This, the man will endeavour to catch in his helmet. If he succeeds, the Kaiser applauds his skill: if he fails, as, of course, he usually does, the Kaiser loads him with ridicule, calling him "Butterfingers" and the like. And so on, till the cubes are all gone. Then the Kaiser puts on his own helmet: and that, of course, is the signal to leave the Mess. A sponge-cake and a glass of milk do not take long to consume, and nine out of ten of his staff get next to no breakfast at all. But that does not concern him. Consideration is not among his failings. And it probably does them no harm, for most are too fat.' "

"And that imitation mountebank," said Berry, "who would have been rejected by the meanest circus, was the Emperor of Germany. I saw him only three times – always, of course, on parade. He was, first and last, an actor: but the rottenest actor on earth could never have failed in the part he had to play. The last time I saw him, he was driving through Regent's Park. I was in a car, which had stopped, to see him go by. He was in a victoria and pair – a royal carriage, of course – with the Kaiserin by his side, looking exactly like a cheerful, old fashioned cook, and their daughter, with her back to the horses on the occasional seat. He was perfectly dressed – of course, by Savile Row: a grey frock-coat suit, and, I think, a grey top hat. He had an excellent figure and looked very well. That was in 1911, just three years before the war. And now go on, please."

"There isn't much more to tell. She had so many tales which I have forgotten now. I can't say she wasn't wilful, because at times she was. Go her own way, she would: but she'd never force her opinion on any man. And she would always learn. Once I made bold to correct her upon some point of law: she accepted the correction at once and expressed her gratitude. No argument at all. And I was no expert. She knew a lot about horses, but nothing of cars: so she liked to be told. She was very quick in the uptake – could seize a point in an instant. And she was most punctilious: the slightest service must be acknowledged at once. But, as I have shown, she had this merciless streak... A very remarkable woman, and that's a fact. And, if I may add a footnote, Madame de B— was kindness itself to me. The last time I ever saw her, she set her hands on my shoulders and gave me her cheek to kiss. I shall always value that honour, for that is what it was.

"One more reminiscence. I was staying with her in Dresden in 1913, when a very big man came to tea. He was commanding one of the crack regiments – I can't remember which. He came in uniform, for they never wore plain clothes. And his wife, with him. She was 'the Colonel's lady' – no doubt about that. She was wearing a flannel blouse – "

"I don't believe you," said Daphne.

"My sweet, it's God's truth. That's why *The Caravaners* rings – to me, at least – so terribly true. A beige-coloured flannel blouse and a tweed skirt, bagged at the knee. And white, cotton gloves, and boots: I think they were button boots, but I can't be sure. They may have been elastic-sided, with buttons sewn on – or even painted on."

"That's right," said Berry. "I've seen them. *Buttons painted on*. That was the fashion just then. I wish I'd bought a pair.

Banana-coloured boots, with elongated toes; elastic-sided, with buttons painted on. I can see them now."

"Her husband was point-device and perfectly groomed. His dark-blue uniform – frock-coat – was a beautiful fit. He was dark, which was rare, and handsome: tall and broad, but not fat. I think he's the only German I ever liked. But he didn't seem to be German, except for his wife. He spoke most excellent English and had a sense of humour – another rare thing.

"After tea, we strolled in the garden, he and I. 'Are you in the Army?' he said. 'I haven't that honour, sir.' 'But you will be, when the day comes?' 'My yeomanry will be mobilized, sir.' 'Of course. Well now, look here. You may take it from me that war is a very strange thing. And you and I may very easily meet – in some place other than this.' 'I'll take your word for it, sir.' 'Well, we may. And if we do, you and I, we'll remember this afternoon... and I won't kill you, and you won't kill me.' I laughed. 'Yes,' I said, 'that's a bargain.' He smiled and put out his hand. I never saw him again."

"As certain as that?" said Jill.

"As certain as that. He'd been in England, of course, and spoke so nicely of us. He didn't flatter: I think his liking was real. I was, of course, a civilian. If I'd been a German civilian, he would have treated me like dirt. But I was an Englishman. So he treated me as an equal, though I was much younger than he. You couldn't help liking the man – I wish I could remember his name."

"And his wife like that?"

"Exactly. I haven't overdrawn her at all. She was dressed for poor-district shopping before the first war. Not afternoon shopping – morning. Getting the cheese and matches and a pound or two of potatoes and Brussels sprouts. She only wanted a string-bag. And those were the best clothes she had: for tea with Madame de B— was a great occasion. If it hadn't been, her husband wouldn't have come."

"I know," said my sister, "I know that you're telling the truth; but it's terribly hard to picture. I mean, he was quite a big man."

"I think it's fair to rank him with the Officer Commanding one of the Regiments of Foot Guards."

"And that man couldn't see there was anything wrong with his wife?"

I shrugged my shoulders.

"It may have been a blind spot. If it wasn't, he just didn't care. They, all of them, looked like that."

"And this took place in the year before the War?"

"Yes."

"The Boches," said Berry, "were a most astonishing crowd. Conducive, of course, to vomit. But let that pass. Your man was clearly an exception: but, taking them by and large, they could not learn. Of course, they were civilized – so far as utility went. Railways, power-stations, guns… So far as those things went, they very near led the world. But so far as the elementary decencies of civilization were concerned, they'd made no progress at all. They were damned near barbarian. They'd approach their face to within three inches of yours – and burst with laughter, with their mouth full. If you were bespattered – as you were – they laughed the more – and expected you to laugh, too."

Jill was shaking with laughter, but Daphne was stopping her ears.

"Tell me when it's over," she said; "but don't repeat what he said. I'm not like the Colonel's wife, who was, no doubt, accustomed to beastly things."

"All he said," said I, "is perfectly true. And it ought to be put on record. I haven't set foot in Germany for forty years, but I very much doubt if the leopard has changed his spots."

"Marienbad," said Berry.

"Yes," said I. "In 1905 I visited Marienbad. A very agreeable place. People went there, as you know, to lose superfluous weight. And the King of England, among them: His Majesty

King Edward the Seventh – there was a man. I was never presented, of course, but my visit coincided with his. So I had the great privilege of observing him at close quarters day after day. He had a suite at The Weimar, and I was in the appendage to that hotel. That year he was visited by Franz Joseph, then seventy-five years old, the Emperor of Austro-Hungary, in whose empire Marienbad was. And the King entertained him to luncheon. From my window upon the first floor, I saw the two drive up in an open carriage, and I heard an Austrian maid cry out, 'Oh, there are two in the carriage, but only one King.' That was a compliment, indeed. And King Edward wasn't looking his best, for he was wearing the full-dress of an Austrian Field-Marshal – at least, I suppose it was that – which didn't become him at all: but the Emperor was wearing that of a British Field-Marshal, which would, I think, become almost any man. I was taken to see the table, before they sat down: the decorations consisted of nothing but rose-petals – delicate heaps of rose-petals everywhere.

"Of His Majesty, I hardly know what to say. He was worshipped, because he was worshipful: loved, because he was lovable: however well you felt, the sight of him made you feel better than you had felt before. His charm was radiant and irresistible. His dignity was compelling. His manners were above reproach. All Englishmen – and many others – uncovered when he went by, as a matter of course: never once did I see him nod or touch his hat in reply: *he always took his hat off –* right away from his head: he did so to me, a mere stripling, time and again. One afternoon I was driving with Mrs —: in the course of the drive our horses were walking uphill; and there, at the top, was a car, standing still before it came down. So, *force majeure*, we passed it very slowly. Sitting at the back was the King. Mrs — bowed, and I took off my hat. The King was wearing a peaked motoring-cap, and his chin-strap was down: when he made to raise it, of course it wouldn't come off: but he damned well had it off, pulling it over his face and disordering his hair: then he looked at us and, laughing, inclined his reverend head."

Berry nodded.

" 'Manners makyth Man.' "

"One of my pleasantest memories is that of His Majesty, dressed for dinner, bare-headed, standing alone upon the balcony of one of the rooms of his suite, looking down on the scene below, before he went in to dine.

"And now for Marienbad. I can most truthfully say that, until I went to that spa, I never knew what it meant for a man to be fat. I thought I had seen fat people: but I was wrong. Compared with most of the visitors, King Edward the Seventh was well-covered – no more than that. People used to stop and stare after me in the street – because I was spare. And the fattest were always the Germans. Their bulk was unbelievable. Some couldn't get through doorways."

Jill laid a hand on my arm.

"Darling, do be careful."

"*Et tu, Brute?*" said I. "My sweet, as I live, it's the truth. It would be indecent to describe some of the Germans, male and female, that I saw: but I'll tell you of one. He was making his way to the spring, to drink his dose. He had to walk very slowly and rest by the way. When he rested, he used to do so at some café which lay on his route – with chairs and tables outside, in the continental way: but he didn't sit down: instead, he lifted his stomach and laid it upon a table which was about the right height. That took the weight off his legs. And when he'd rested enough, he lifted it carefully down."

"Have you nearly finished?" said Daphne.

"Shame," said Berry. "What would historians give for such a side-light on manners of the fourteenth century?"

"I've only one incident to add. I believe it took place every day, but I never knew about it, until I was going away. Now, the cure at Marienbad was very strict. I can't remember the diet, but it was very thin. Of course, not a smell of beer – and you know what beer meant to a German… Which is, of course, the reason why all these Germans were there. Swilling down Munich beer, day in and day out. I think I'm right in saying that the length of the cure was three weeks.

"The train that most people took from Marienbad was an express which left pretty early – I think, about eight in the morning. Anyway, when I left, I took that train. So did a great many others, who had just finished their cure. When I arrived at the station, there was a row going on – a crowd of Germans, shouting and struggling a little way down the platform. When I'd secured my seat, I walked down to see what it meant. The storm-centre was the station restaurant: this wasn't very large, and it couldn't receive all the Germans who were fighting for beer. Their cure had finished at mid-night, when all the cafés were shut: so this was the first chance they had of making up for lost time. You never saw such a sight. Those who had reached the bar were reluctant to leave, until, of course, the train was about to depart: but their presence obstructed other less fortunate souls: those in the rear were frenzied, for the precious minutes were passing and trains won't wait. The spectacle wasn't human. And all those men had only that moment completed a very expensive cure to reduce the weight which their indulgence in beer had brought about."

"Such animal behaviour," said Berry, "is touched upon not only in The Book of Proverbs, but, if I remember rightly, in one of the Epistles General of St Peter – God bless his soul. On second thoughts, I realize that such an apostrophe is supererogatory: but it was well meant. I always loved St Peter. At least he put up a show – and cut off Malchus' ear. Malchus dodged, of course: otherwise, he'd've had it. To return to the animal behaviour. This is also comparable with the disgusting practices frequently observed by gluttons in the course of a Roman banquet two thousand years ago."

"I agree… And now may I add one memory, in which Germany is mentioned, which truly concerns the French? I confess that it's right out of place; but I'd like to relate it now, for I've no desire to mention the Germans again. I nearly made this statement the other night. And then I thought that it would mean very little to people who didn't know France. So I held my peace. But, on reflection, I find it a side-light on history: as such, it ought to go in.

"I didn't know France very well, before the first war: but, between the two wars, when a Frenchman spoke of the Germans, he never said 'les Allemands', but always 'les Boches' – more often than not, 'les sales (dirty) Boches'. That practice was always observed by high and low. Do you bear me out?"

"Unquestionably. I never heard a Frenchman say 'les Allemands', until —. But go on."

"When we returned to France in 1945, in conversation with Frenchmen I naturally spoke of 'les Boches'. *When I'd been corrected four times, I gave it up.* I would say, '*Enfin, les Boches sont partis*'. And the reply would come pat – '*Oui, Monsieur, les Allemands sont partis.*' I was corrected by a high official, a physician, a servant and a countryman. When I re-entered Portugal, I told this to a distinguished Portuguese. He heard me out. Then he said, 'Major Pleydell, if anybody but you had told me that, I should have refused to believe it. I know the French, and I should have found it incredible.' I didn't see him again for several months. When I did, he told me this tale.

" 'Since I saw you,' he said, 'I have been over seas. I flew back to Lisbon with one of our Ministers. On the way, for something to say, I told him your tale – how in France today the Boche is no longer "*le Boche*". He flatly refused to believe it. "Sir," I said, "Major Pleydell would never tell me a lie." "I'm sorry," he said, "but I know France, and I must decline to believe that there is a Frenchman alive who will speak of the Boches as '*les Allemands*'." Well, I shrugged my shoulders. After all, he did not know you. We ran into contrary winds and we had to come down at Marseilles and wait for an hour or so. Whilst we were there, we were pleasantly entertained in an officers' Mess. The

Minister was talking to, let us say, the Mess President: anyway to an officer of some standing. He casually referred to *"les Boches". The officer immediately corrected him – "Oui, Monsieur, les Allemands."* The Minister turned and looked at me. Then he said, "I apologize to your friend." '

"I value that confirmation of what, to those who knew France, must seem incredible."

Berry glanced at his watch.

Then –

"Here's something to take us to bed – on a less bitter note. I have often seen used in novels the word 'adventurer': and, when I have seen it, I have wondered whether the person who used it had ever met such a man. Frankly, from their descriptions, I very much doubt if they had. The adventurer, *pur et simple*, is a very rare bird. I have met thousands of people – all sorts and kinds: but only once did I meet an adventurer. But he deserved the name.

"I came to know him – not well, but more than casually. He was a Frenchman, well-bred, good-looking, with excellent manners and a distinguished air. His family was old, and his title was genuine. Few French titles are. I once knew a Frenchman, whom I will call *Monsieur Soeur*. He had a private income and dwelled in a country house. After a while, he decided to take the 'de'. From that time on, he was known as *Monsieur de Soeur*. So for some fifteen years. Then he decided that the time for ennoblement had come. So he made himself *Baron de Soeur*. Very soon he was generally known as *Monsieur le Baron de Soeur*. His promotion was tacitly accepted. All accorded him the honour which he had conferred on himself. He was a self-made man. By now, he is probably a *Vicomte*. Of such is France.

"And now to return to my adventurer. His mother and sister lived at their ancient home, somewhere in France. He kept them going somehow, because they hadn't a bean. He visited them sometimes, but they never came to him. He was, of course, a gambler – in every sense of the word. I'm sure he always played straight and he paid his debts: but no stakes were ever too high. He was, of course, very lucky – gambler's luck. And he had nerves of steel. One week he'd be worth fifty thousand – pounds, not francs: the next, he'd have next to nothing, and a discarded mistress would come to his help. I've actually known that happen. He had no scruples at all. When I knew him, he had three cars, two chauffeurs and a valet. One car was the latest Packard, a beautiful job. I'll say he knew how to live. And he went everywhere. To see him at a *baccarat* table was a revelation. His apparent carelessness was most engaging. He would have to be reminded to take up his cards. In reality, he missed nothing. Often enough he'd play, because he desired to study some other player – see if he was worth playing with, or not. He never touched wine or spirits. I said to him one day, 'I see you don't care for champagne.' He smiled. 'I love it,' he said: 'but I can't afford to drink it.' (His English was very nearly as good as mine.) 'Sometimes,' he went on, 'as a treat, I ask for a very little to be put in my glass of water. So I just get the taste. But you know that I live by my wits. And the wits of a man who drinks alcohol are never quite so quick. Their edge is just dulled.' He was, of course, utterly ruthless – hard as nails. I suppose that he had to be. But many an unhappy woman saw that side. From our point of view, he was a man to beware of. But he was a remarkable production. The finished article. The profession which he had chosen has no name: and those who follow it are certainly wicked men. But he did distinguish his calling – I'll give him that."

"What about a spot of crime?" said Berry. "The wicked brought to book. And wondering whether it was worth it – after all. You know, one of the best things you ever said was in *The Stolen March*. Have we got a copy here?" Jill rose and went to a shelf.

Then she returned with the book and put it into his hand. "Thank you, my love. What a perfect hand-maiden you are. Let's see. It was at *The Peck of Pepper*... Here we are.

" 'Tell me,' said Simon to Pride, 'is outlawry a common punishment within The Pail?'

" 'It's practically the only one,' said Pride. 'It saves the expense of a gaol and it's a great deterrent. To offend the community or to undo a neighbour may be amusing or convenient, but if, as a result, the community (including the neighbour and his friends and any enemy you may happen to have) is to have a day, or a week, in which to offend you, the convenience is apt to wither and the amusement to lose its charm.'

"Now that is sheer common sense. So sheer that it's above comment. A is tried and convicted of robbing B. His punishment is to be outlawed for seven days. Which means that for seven days A can be robbed or beaten with impunity. Put such an Act into force, and after six weeks you wouldn't have any crime. And now lead on."

"Something that you have said reminds me of The Great Pearl Case. To our fathers, The Great Pearl Case meant another trial: a much more dramatic matter: but though I know something of that, I don't know enough to relate it and I should get my facts wrong."

"You've done it now," said Daphne. "Just tell what you know."

"I shall have to keep saying 'I think', and I may be wrong."

"Never mind."

"I think it was at a house-party that a precious pearl necklace disappeared. One of the members of the party was a very attractive girl. She was engaged to be married to a most charming man. Both were well-known in London Society. The lady who lost the pearls suspected the girl of the theft. She certainly had no money, although her *fiancé* was rich. Everyone condemned such suspicion: but the loser stuck to her guns.

Presently she began to say so openly. So the girl brought an action for slander…

"This was heard in the High Court. Feeling ran very high. Everyone hoped and believed that the girl would get exemplary damages. It was an ordeal for her, for the case lasted two or three days. Her *fiancé* never left her side. The two won everyone's hearts.

"Though they hadn't found the thief, the police had found the pearls. They had been sold to a pawnbroker, who had paid for them in five-pound notes. A woman had sold them to him, but she had been heavily veiled. He said that it might or might not have been the girl. He had taken the numbers of the notes, but none had come in. Needless to say, the girl swore that she'd never been near his shop.

"At the end of the second day, so far as the plaintiff was concerned, the case was in the bag. I think it was nearly over. Still, one more consultation was thought advisable, and when the Court rose, she and her *fiancé* accompanied her solicitor to the chambers of, I think, Sir Charles Russell, who was leading for her. Charles Matthews, I'm sure, was the junior. The consultation was in progress, when there was a knock on the door, and Russell's clerk entered the room with a letter for the solicitor. He opened and read it at once.

"The letter was from the solicitors for the defence. It enclosed a five-pound note – one of the five-pound notes which the pawnbroker had paid. It had been cashed at Maples – I'm nearly sure it was Maples – the furniture shop. It was then the practice of a shop, if the customer wasn't known, to ask them to sign their name on the back of the note. In this case, that had been done. The signature on the back of this note was that of the girl."

"My God," said Daphne. And then, "It makes me feel weak."

"Go on," said Berry. "What happened? Or can't you speak to that?"

I laughed.

"As a matter of fact, I can. I'm one of the very few people – at least, I believe I am – who know exactly what happened after that. For, as an articled clerk, Muskett had accompanied the solicitor: and it was he that told me what then took place.

"The solicitor rose and laid both letter and note before Russell. Matthews rose and looked over his leader's shoulder. Then Russell addressed the *fiancé*. 'One of the notes has come in. It was cashed at Maples on —. It was signed, before it was cashed. Here it is. Does the plaintiff deny her signature?' But the girl was already in tears. Her *fiancé* looked at Russell. 'What,' he said, 'do I do?' Russell looked at his watch. Then he turned to Matthews, 'How much have you on you?' he said. Between the two of them, they had about forty pounds. Russell gave the *fiancé* the money. 'My clerk will fetch you a hansom. A boat-train leaves Charing Cross in half an hour. Take her to France. That'll give you a breathing-space. If you don't do as I say, she'll be under arrest.'

"The *fiancé* took his advice, which I think was very good. After a little, she came back and stood her trial. I forget what she got, but, when she came out of jail, her *fiancé* married her. There I may be wrong, for he may have married her, while they were still abroad."

"What a hell of a case," said Berry.

"It was," said I. "I'm only sorry I can't remember more. But, of course, it was long before my day. Russell was afterwards Lord Chief Justice, but I can't remember him. I'm almost sure it was Russell – I may be wrong."

"Now for the second one," said Berry.

"That was very different. The Great Pearl Case was 'news' in 1909, before I was called to the Bar. I saw it from first to last, and, in fact, I managed the case when it came to be tried.

"There was a diamond-merchant, who lived in Cologne. He was, I think, a German: but he was a very big man. His name was Goldschmidt – of the spelling, I can't be sure. Once or twice a year he visited Hatton Garden, bringing his wares. He did so in the spring of 1909. When he came to London, he always used to stay at De Keyser's Hotel. That's gone now, and Lever House stands where it did – at the end of The Embankment, just by Blackfriars Bridge. And he always had his own hansom, to take him about. You see, he wished to take no avoidable risks: for his stuff was always with him, and it was valuable stuff. On this occasion, it was pearls. Eighty thousand pounds' worth of pearls – and that was their rock-bottom value – eighty thousand pounds in a small black leather bag about a foot long."

"Chained?"

"No. Why he didn't wear a chain, I never heard. But he was very particular about his appearance, and the absence of a chain may have been due to personal vanity. On the other hand, a chain would have attracted attention – might have attracted unwelcome attention to his bag. Now, though he didn't know it, a gang was after those pearls – a gang of four. They knew what he'd got, and the gang was out to get it. Two of them travelled with him all the way from Cologne. But he was an old hand and he never gave them a chance. Day after day, one or more visited De Keyser's Hotel – and sat about in the lounge, all ready to spring: day after day, he was followed to Hatton Garden: but all in vain. Time was running short, for very soon he was due to return to Cologne. So they brought in two more men. One was an ex-jockey, Grimshaw, a wiry little man. The other's name, I forget. But he was tall. I'd better call him Payne, though that wasn't his name. Both were known to the police, as men to be watched. Grimshaw, I think, had done time. 'I'll have them pearls,' said Grimshaw…

"On Goldschmidt's last day but one, he drove to Hatton Garden at ten o'clock. He was followed there, but not by Grimshaw and Payne. They were to pick him up there, when he came out. He always came out about one, so they arranged to be there about half-past twelve. Grimshaw was there all right, but Payne was late. The reason why he was late is of peculiar interest. He had gone to a tavern in Holborn – we'll call it *The*

Rose. The Rose was well known to the police, as being a house of call for higher-class thieves. As such, it was frequently visited by plain-clothes men. There was one there that very day – a Sergeant West, of Vine Street, a most efficient man. Payne knew him to speak to and had a drink with him.

"Now West was there on duty. It was part of his job to be on terms with thieves. Whether the practice is still followed, I've no idea. But in my time, the CID were on terms with hundreds of thieves. This contributed largely to the prevention of crime: largely, also, to its cure. If Sergeant West had stayed for another quarter of an hour, the robbery I am relating would not have been done that day.

"So Payne had a drink with West about a quarter-past twelve. Well, that was all right. But Payne didn't want to leave before West left. He wanted to be able to say that he'd never left the tavern before, say, a quarter to two. So he had to sit West out. And West never left *The Rose* until a quarter to one. The moment he'd gone, Payne made for Hatton Garden as hard as he could. He whipped into Grimshaw's taxi just in time.

"Goldschmidt appeared, entered his private hansom and drove to *The Monico*, where he proposed to lunch."

"Where's *The Monico*?" said Jill.

"In Piccadilly Circus – at least, it was. It had one entrance in the Circus and one in Shaftesbury Avenue. So the hansom moved off and the taxi fell in behind. Now, compared with the taxi, the hansom, of course, was slow: so the taxi had to crawl, if it was to keep behind. The hansom went by Holborn, and the taxi followed along. Where the hansom was bound for, Grimshaw and Payne didn't know.

"Now a young man was standing in Holborn. He was employed by a firm, whose offices were near by. It was his luncheon-hour: but he had finished early and was smoking a cigarette before he went back. He was standing on the pavement in Holborn, watching the traffic go by. He was an observant young man, and the taxi caught his eye. For the taxi was crawling by the kerb, as though in hope of a fare: but it had a fare already. The young man found this strange. For taxis with fares inside them don't crawl by the kerb. Then the traffic was blocked for a moment, and the taxi came to rest. So the young man looked at the fares. He could only see one well, though he knew there were two. The one he saw was a small man: and he was standing up, crouching and peering through the window at something ahead. The young man was vastly piqued. He would have liked to follow, if only he had had time. This made him glance at his watch. Almost half-past one, and he must be getting back... The young man's name was Sherlock.

"The hansom reached *The Monico* at twenty minutes to two. Goldschmidt entered the restaurant, followed by Grimshaw and Payne. He reserved his table and went off to wash his hands. The lavatory was long-shaped, with a door at either end. Each door gave into a hall. One hall gave to Piccadilly, the other to Shaftesbury Avenue. Goldschmidt had entered from Shaftesbury Avenue. When he made to wash his hands, he laid his bag on the ledge between himself and the basin. When his hands were covered with soap, the hand of a man who was standing directly behind him stole round his ample waist and removed the bag. Goldschmidt turned about and threw his arms round the thief: but Grimshaw wriggled out of his grasp and streaked for the door to the hall on the Circus side. His victim ran after him, shouting 'Stop thief'. So did another man, who had been washing his hands by the merchant's side. The two collided in the doorway, and both fell down. They picked themselves up and rushed out into the hall. This was empty, and Goldschmidt ran to the doors.

" 'What is it, sir?' cried a porter.

" 'I've been robbed,' cried Goldschmidt. 'The fellow ran out this way. This gentleman saw it happen.'

" 'Which gentleman?' cried the porter.

"But Payne had disappeared.

"That was how it was actually done.

"Within two minutes, Goldschmidt was speaking to Vine Street, reporting his loss. The Inspector on duty promised to send a man down right away. And so he did. The man who was sent was Detective-Sergeant West. This was, of course, pure coincidence: but that is the way in which Fate will sometimes work.

"When Sherlock read the case in the paper, he went to the police. He had seen Grimshaw well, but he had not seen Payne. Goldschmidt had never seen Grimshaw, but only his back. But he had seen Payne. The police got to work. They let the thieves go for the moment and went for the pearls. They knew that pearls of such value would only be received by one or two men. The receiver would lead them to the thieves. Cammy Goldschmidt, of whom I have told you, received the pearls. But the police were just too late. Cammy had been ready and waiting: and before the police could find him, the pearls had been valued and sent to Amsterdam. Eighty thousand pounds' worth of pearls. But, working back from Cammy, the police got the thieves. What Grimshaw said, when he was charged, I do not know. But I know what Payne said. 'This is a damned shame.' He pointed to Sergeant West. 'He knows that I couldn't have done it. I was drinking with him at *The Rose* at a quarter to two that day: and the robbery was committed at a quarter to two.'

" 'At a quarter to one,' says West. 'Not a quarter to two.'

" 'At a quarter to two,' says Payne.

" 'One minute,' says the Inspector. 'How did you know that the robbery was committed at a quarter to two?'

" 'Saw it in the papers, of course.'

" 'I don't think you did. We gave the time to the Press as two o'clock.'

"This was a fact. And the papers, of course, were wrong, while Payne was right. His unfortunate statement had a great deal to do with sending him down.

"For some reason, which I have forgotten, the case was not sent to the Old Bailey, but to Newington Sessions, instead. It was a depressing business, because the pearls were gone. I always felt that Wensley would have had them: but it wasn't Wensley's show. The two men went down all right, but, as though something were needed to enhance the depression we felt, the Chairman of the Sessions put on the lid. To Payne, he gave three years and to Grimshaw four. The two guffawed in the dock – the job had been worth their while. From a High Court Judge they'd have had ten years apiece: Grimshaw, probably more.

"That Chairman has long been dead, but his leniency was a scandal, as everyone knew. Mercy – yes. That is as it should be. But Wallace was absurdly lenient. The leniency which he showed did incalculable harm. Over and over again, it made a crime worth while. And it discouraged the police. 'What is the good,' they cried, 'of doing all this work and getting our man, only to see the fellow laugh in our face?' And, by God, you couldn't blame them. I'd worked damned hard on that case, and I'll say I was sore."

"I'll lay you were," said Berry. "Eighty thousand pounds' worth of pearls. Why, I'd do four years myself for a guerdon like that. How much would they get?"

"I can only guess. I'd say fifteen thousand, between them. And that, of course, was paid them when they came out. Cammy, I should think, took twenty. I may be wrong. Still, fifteen or twenty thousand in 1909 was a very handsome sum."

"And the pearls went to Amsterdam?"

"Yes. That was the market then. All the big stuff went there. God knows how it was carried, but carried it was. I never remember jewels being stopped *en route*. And it wasn't for want of trying. But the carriers knew their job."

"You make a point of that in two of your books."

"I know. *Formosa* and *The Bank of England.* Neither stole, but both of them carried the stuff. All imagination, of course. But I sometimes wonder whether I was so very far out."

"*The Wet Flag,*" said Berry. "I have an affection for that sinister restaurant. And *The Red Nose,* of Montmartre. Your scenes in those two cafés are some of the best you've done. And *Fluff* was a cordial. 'Sweaty knows them cuffs.' "

Jill put in her oar.

"You must have known someone like *Fluff* to make him ring so true. And *Punter* and *Bunch* and *Sloper.*"

I shook my head.

"I never had anyone in mind: but all my life, my darling, I've studied my fellow men. Like everyone else, I've rubbed shoulders with all and sundry. I must have travelled thousands of miles by the Underground, and the Tube gives you every chance of observing your company. I have received all sorts and kinds of impressions on which, I suppose, I have drawn. For the student of human nature, the Tube is a wonderful place. All manner of men take the Tube, and you've only to sit and watch them – or stand, if the coach is full."

"Well, I don't know," said Berry. "You must be damned receptive. You must have a brain of wax, if all your rogues have emerged from impressions made by wallahs you've seen in the Tube. Didn't the Old Bailey help?"

"Not very much in that way. The prisoner at the Old Bailey is hardly himself. And rogues don't frequent the Old Bailey, unless they're brought."

"I knew there was something," said Daphne. "The Great Pearl Case – the first one. When Sir Charles Russell received the damning five-pound note. Hadn't you that in mind when you wrote *This Publican*?"

"I can't be sure," said I. "But I don't think so. I don't think it entered my head. My eyes were fast on what would in fact have happened in such a case. And now pray silence for Berry."

213

"I think," said my brother-in-law, "that a few observations, fat, pungent and brief on the subject of fakes and experts will not be out of place in this authoritative work. The average man takes both at their face value: he can hardly do anything else. He may suspect a fake, but he can't be sure: and if he calls in an expert – well, it's no good calling him in, if he's not going to trust what he says. But a few, more fortunate beings – though not less ignorant – of whom I happen to be one, have, by the merest chance, had the startling truth vouchsafed. And this revelation proved to me once for all that the one and only touchstone which will declare, first, whether an article of virtu is genuine and, secondly, what it is worth, is its sale by auction at Sotheby's or at Christie's Great Rooms.

"I do not suggest that there do not exist experts who are qualified to distinguish between the true and the false, and to appraise. But who can tell which they are? But, if a piece goes to Christie's, the opinion the owner gets is that of a number of experts who are backing that opinion with their own money; and, as more than one expert desires to acquire the piece, the highest market value is paid.

"And now for the fakes...

"I believe it to be a recognized fact that, if a list had been kept of all the period furniture which was made in England up to the end of the nineteenth century, and a similar list were made today of all the period pieces which had survived, the second list would be very much longer than the first. Now the explanation of this flouting of the most elementary principles of simple arithmetic is, of course, painfully clear. But I was never able to focus its detail, until a housemaid, called Bowen, entered the married state."

"Bowen," said Daphne, "was such a very nice girl. I was awfully sorry to lose her. I'm afraid I can't remember her married name."

"Neither," said Berry, "can I. But the point is that the man she married was employed by, er – "

"Very careful," said I.

" – by Messrs. Nottarf and Wotsit, of Stop Street, WC. Is that all right?"

"Admirable," said I.

"And Nottarf and Wotsit, of Stop Street, were a very well known firm. They purveyed antique furniture. If you wanted a really fine set of Chippendale chairs, you couldn't do better than go to Nottarf and Wotsit: if you wanted a refectory table, Nottarf and Wotsit were the people to whom to go: if you wanted a Queen Anne tallboy, Nottarf and Wotsit would have or would find you one.

"Well, in due course Bowen had a baby, and the infant was brought to Cholmondeley Street, for Daphne to see and admire. And Bowen's husband came, too. It was while he was talking to me that he told me about his job: and he interested me so much that I asked him to come and see me next Saturday afternoon. And so he did.

"He was in 'the faking department'. And he told me how it was done. Six copies, perhaps, would be made of a genuine, period piece. But each was slightly different. One was a little larger, and one not quite so large: one stood a little higher, and one not quite so high: but all were in perfect proportion. And when they had all been passed, they were broken down. Tables set out in the rain and thrashed with chains...wormholes inserted in chairs by special tools...and other tools reproduced the traces of rowels, belonging to Cavaliers' spurs... You never heard such a report. That morning he had helped to 'make up' a room. A Tudor dining-room. An American millionaire was due at the show-rooms on Monday: he fancied Tudor stuff: and he had been recommended to go to Nottarf and Wotsit... Before he came, the head expert would scrutinize every piece, to be sure that no proof of age had been omitted or slurred.

" 'How long have you been there?' I asked him.

"He told me, seven years.

" 'Well, you must be an expert, yourself.'

"He smiled.

" 'Well, I wouldn't say that. But I know what to look for, sir.'

"I took him into the dining-room. You remember our Hepplewhite chairs?"

Daphne nodded.

"Ten. And we had two made by Morris, to make up the set. They were beautifully done. After a week, you couldn't tell which was which."

"He could," said Berry. "I showed him the set, and I said nothing at all. He went over every one, and set two aside. 'Those, sir,' he said, 'are copies. They're nicely done.' And he showed me how he could tell, but I can't remember that.

"The point is that he was an expert – a very reliable expert, for he'd had the finest training that any expert could have. 'Set a thief to catch a thief.' By that, I mean nothing against him. He was an honest man. But this was his employment. And he wasn't an educated man. In fact, he was very simple. He never even asked me to keep the things he was saying under my hat. I did, naturally…

"Only once did I use him, as an expert. That was when Madge and Crispin set up their London flat. Madge had fallen flat for some fine old Spanish chairs. Real Cordova leather, two hundred and fifty years old. She found them at —'s. Crispin had them round on approval, and asked me to come and see. Well, I couldn't say: but they looked a hell of a set. So I offered to bring an expert, who'd tell them the truth. 'But on these conditions,' I said; 'that you don't ask him his name or what he is, and that you tell no one about him, for this must be kept very quiet.' Crispin passed his word, of course. 'But he must be a big man,' he said. 'How much is his fee?' 'He'll ask you nothing. If you like to give him a sovereign, he'll be as pleased as Punch.'

"Well, I got hold of Collins – there you are."

"Collins," cried Daphne. "Well done."

"It is wonderful, isn't it? That after all these years, I should be able to recapture – "

"Proceed," said everyone.

"That's right," said Berry. "Defile the crystal fount. Spit into the limpid basin."

"You filthy beast," said Jill.

"That takes me back," said Berry. "When I was St Salmon of Gluckstein, I was operating – "

"Will you go on?" said I.

"Oh, very well… I took Collins round to the flat. He went over each chair – there were eight. Then he stood back.

" :The set's a fake, sir,' he said. 'There's not one genuine chair: not even a made-up chair. I'd say they come out of the Midlands. Shipped to Spain, of course. There's a lot of that goes on.'

"Crispin was so thankful that he gave Collins five pounds.

"Collins stared at the gold.

" 'But I 'aven't done nothing, sir.'

" 'Yes, you have,' says Crispin. 'You've saved me three hundred pounds.'

"And now for the expert by profession…

"Let me make it quite clear that I am speaking of those who declare that they are experts, who ask and receive money for the opinions they give. As an executor, on more occasions than one I have sought their advice. Allow me to place upon record one or two opinions which I was able to check.

"When old Mrs — died, I employed a well-known man. She had some very nice stuff. And the Will had the usual provision – that relatives should be allowed to purchase at probate prices. What was left was to be sold by auction. One of the best things was a Louis Quinze bureau, in a lovely state. I've never cared for them: but most people do. The expert examined that table before my eyes. His examination was thorough. At last he looked up. 'It's an excellent copy,' he said. 'It was made in Holland, by a man called Damuryse (or something like that). It was made for the Great Exhibition of 1851. If it was genuine, it would be worth quite a lot. As it is, I shall put it in at twenty-five pounds.' None of the relatives wanted it, so I sent it to Christie's to be sold. I thought it might make forty pounds, for he was valuing low. That table sold for eight hundred and fifty guineas. It was a fine example of period stuff… And a plate, I remember, he valued at four pounds ten. I sent that to Christie's, too, where it made nearly eighty pounds.

"And the table Boy wrote about in *And Berry Came Too*. We all know that's true. Only, it wasn't Geoffrey Majoribanks. It was a well-known peer. He was having his stuff revalued in 1928. For purposes of insurance. At — House, a stately home of England. And —'s of London valued that very table at twelve hundred and fifty pounds. And it had been made for Lord —: made to his order, some twenty-five years before. And it cost him, I think, thirty pounds.

"Well, there you are. Fakes and experts. They're really synonymous terms. The fake is the frying-pan, and the expert is the fire. It's not strange that, between the two, the purchaser falls to the ground. I don't say the expert's dishonest. But he professes a skill which often he hasn't got. To my mind, that is dishonest; for no man should hire himself out as an authority, unless he knows in his heart that that representation is true. As for the faking of stuff it's purely a criminal offence. Well, not the faking – the selling, as genuine stuff, of stuff that is faked. It's obtaining money by false pretences. And that's what the expert does, too. But that would be hard to prove. Both parties are culpable. Of course, you can talk of fools who deserve what they get. But I say this – that no man deserves such treatment. But, unless the world has changed, a great many people receive it year in year out."

My sister glanced at her watch.

"Something short, Boy?"

"Two flashes," said I. "I'm sorry to have to suppress the names of the cases concerned. But at least I can promise you this – that neither of these flashes has ever appeared in print.

"A man was tried for murder at the Central Criminal Court. Although I was not concerned, I remember the case very well. It attracted much attention. The jury acquitted the prisoner, and that was that. But, always afterwards, at every murder trial – at every hearing of every murder charge, that man was in the front row of the public seats. He was pointed out to me in the Crippen case. One might have been forgiven for supposing that, having been through the hoop, he would avoid the precincts of criminal courts. One would have been wrong. Police Court, Coroner's Court, Old Bailey – if the charge was wilful murder, that man was there."

"Theory?" said Berry.

"I have no theory. I simply find his behaviour very strange.

"And the second flash is this. There was another case, in which I was not concerned. That, too, was a case of murder. The accused was defended – not very well, I thought – by, let us say, Weston Gale, while he was still at the Bar. And after a hearing which lasted for three or four days, the jury found him 'Not Guilty' and he was discharged. Now I felt pretty sure, as did other, wiser men, that the jury had made a mistake. I thought that the man was guilty – no matter why. Some months later, I met the Chief Inspector who had had charge of the case. 'The King against —,' I said. 'Was he guilty, or not?' 'Of course he was guilty, sir. But there was one link in the chain which we hadn't got. God knows I tried hard enough to find it… But there you are. If I could have found that link, the case was dead. You remember we had all his movements on that particular night. From pillar to post we proved them – all but one. That was the gap in the chain, which we could not fill – and, of course, Mr Weston Gale fairly rammed it home.

" 'And now just listen to this, sir. Three weeks after the case, two brothers came to the Yard and asked to see me. They were brought up to my room. I asked them what they wanted. "The — case," said one. "We think there's something perhaps you'd like to know." "A bit late, aren't you?" I said. "The man was acquitted nearly three weeks ago. What d'you want to say?" By God, sir, they closed the gap: they gave me the missing link. Both of them could have proved the very movement I'd tried so hard to get. I won't say how I felt, because you can guess. It was hard to keep one's temper. "I see," I said. "And now will you kindly explain why you didn't report this, say, six weeks ago?" "Thanks very much," says one. "And have to go into the box – to be bullied by Weston Gale." ' "

"Well, I'm damned," said Berry. "What policemen have to bear."

"It was rather hard. You might call it 'rubbing it in'."

*

"You're never yourself," said Jill, "just after you've finished a book. For two or three days, I mean. And then you get all right."

"I'm sorry," I said. "The truth is, I feel so lost. You know I'm a very slow writer. That book has probably taken me nearly a year to write. And all that time I've lived and moved with the people that I've been writing about. I've heard everything that they've said, and I've seen everything that they've done. I know all their thoughts and feelings, their hopes and fears. For eight or ten months, I've lived every one of their lives. And when I suddenly leave them, I feel quite lost."

"Poor little waif," said Berry.

"I simply hate you," said Jill. "And he isn't a waif."

"Back in the wide, wide world."

My wife took her cigarette and pitched it into his lap.

With one convulsive movement, Berry, who was comfortably settled, left his chair.

Searching himself all over –

"Where is the blasted thing?"

"There it is," said Daphne. "Pick it up quick. We don't want to burn the rug."

As he tossed it into the grate –

"And what about my trousers?" said Berry. "Three pounds ten, these cost before the war. Their present value's about two hundred pounds."

"They're quite all right," said Daphne.

"And what of my large intestine? A sudden movement like that lays on that lovely organ a stress or strain it was never constructed to bear." He looked at my wife. "You've been reading comic strips. Just because we let you see them, you don't have to do what Porky and Huckaback do. When your husband makes me feel sick, I've a right to denounce the emetic which he administers."

Jill's hand slid into mine.

"I'm inclined to agree," I said. "It probably sounded precious. As a matter of fact, it's true. I think, perhaps, if you wrote, you'd feel the same. Of course, my people are puppets. But I have heard of actors 'living' their parts. I've actually seen them do it – though not for a good many years. I think, perhaps, they felt lost, when at last the curtain came down. Don't you think Kipling felt lost, when he'd finished *Kim*? I'll lay any money he did. That queer, dirt smell of the East. You can smell that, when you read *Kim*. But he was a great master. His contemporaries shrink in stature when he goes by."

"And there you're right," said Berry, now settled again. "There's a drive in Kipling's work that no one has ever approached."

"Or ever will," said I. "He was a very great man."

" 'Sweet'," said Berry, " 'are the uses of *publicity.*' If you had used publicity, you would have sold about three times as many books."

"I don't know."

"Of course you would. Probably five times as many. Hundreds of thousands of people don't even know your name."

"He's had heaps of letters," said Jill, "saying they've just found his books. He had one the other day. And a man wrote not long ago, saying he'd just read one and gone off to his bookseller and ordered all the rest."

"I can't help it," said I. "I think publicity is wrong. More. I know it's wrong. A book should stand by itself. I've seen mediocre books made into best sellers simply by publicity and nothing else. I've seen mediocre writers made famous – by publicity alone: and while their names were being thrust into the public's mouth, far better writers than they – far better writers than I shall ever be – were being ignored. Well, that tends to put you off. Justifiable publicity – yes. A portrait on a dust-cover, and that sort of thing."

"Blurb?"

"Careful," I said. "I have a gorge, too. The notes on the back of my jackets, I always write myself. They say what the book is and why I wrote it and what I hope it will do."

"I greatly enjoyed the Fable you wrote for *Lower Than Vermin*."

I laughed.

"I had rather a triumph there. I showed it to a man of letters, before the book came out. 'Very appropriate,' he said. 'You've verified it, of course?' It seemed best to say yes."

"Lovely," said Berry. "But you did put *'After* Aesop'."

"I know. But he missed that." I fingered my chin. "You know, all this damned stuff is publicity."

"In a way. But it's under a bushel. If people like to lift the bushel, that's their affair. And now take us back to real life."

I glanced at my watch.

"I have a case in mind, but it will take some time."

"Wilful murder?" said Berry.

"No. There are other crimes. And this, in its day, was rather a famous case. I was then a solicitor's pupil. I saw it from beginning to end; and, when it went for trial, I managed it at the Old Bailey – and anxious work it was. I mean, I was in sole charge, and things went wrong. We got home all right, but my path which had looked so smooth, proved to be rough indeed.

But the public didn't know that. The case was known as 'The D S Windell Case' – a highly impudent fraud, brilliantly conceived and very well carried out."

"I remember it well," said Berry. "Everybody was laughing – except the Bank. 'The d— swindle' case. Talk about nerve. Sorry. Go on."

"Great credit is due to Muskett, for he forced his impatient clients to play a waiting game: and, only by playing that game, did we get our men. I think Jonah would have approved.

"Now, before I go any further, let me say this. It's a long time since all this happened, and on one or two details my memory may be at fault. But I'll do the best I can.

"I hadn't been very long in Bedford Row, when I walked in one Tuesday morning at half-past nine, to be stopped by the clerks from entering Muskett's room. I asked what was up. 'Conference,' was the reply. 'Directors and all. Somebody's done it on one of the bigger Banks.' I knew that it must be big trouble, because of the early hour, and very soon after they'd gone, I learned the truth.

"On Monday morning – that is, the day before – the Manager of the Lambeth Branch of one of the biggest Banks received a letter from the Manager of the Harlesden Branch. The letter said that a customer, a Mr D S Windell, wished to transfer his account from Harlesden to Lambeth: that the money now standing to his credit amounted to two thousand odd pounds: that Mr Windell would shortly call at the Lambeth Branch and make the Manager's acquaintance.

"Mr Windell appeared soon after that letter was received, made the acquaintance of his new Manager, signed the signature book, received a chequebook and drew out four hundred pounds.

"What nobody but Mr Windell knew was that eleven other Managers of eleven other Branches of the same Bank had received eleven similar letters from the Manager of the Harlesden Branch.

"He visited nine of these, and then his nerve failed. Still, he got away with ten cheque-books and, what was more to the point, with four thousand pounds. Even in 1908, four thousand pounds was not a great deal of money. But what was so serious was that it was stolen from a Bank. And not by a hold-up, but by a careful manipulation of that Bank's machinery – machinery which had been designed to make any such manipulation impossible.

"Well, of course, the twelve letters were forgeries. The Manager of the Harlesden Branch had never written one of them. Neither had he ever heard of Mr D S Windell. There was, in fact, no such person.

"In those days letters were answered without delay: and the post was wonderful. With the result that on that Monday evening the Manager of the Harlesden Branch received more than one acknowledgment of a letter, the composition of which had never entered his head. He took immediate action. From this, had sprung the conference of the following day.

"Before twenty-four hours had gone by, we knew all there was to be known. This was that Mr D S Windell was a complete stranger to everyone: that he was not known to the police: that he must have had an accomplice within the Bank: that that accomplice had done the forgeries: that he could not have done them – they were superb – unless he had had access to the handwriting of the Manager of the Harlesden Branch: that that reduced the number of suspects to about two thousand. Two thousand.

"But the General Inspector of Branches – his name was Anderson – was worth his salt. He attended the conference. 'It's one of three men,' he said. He laid a sheet of paper on Muskett's desk. 'There are their names.' Three, out of two thousand. The first of the names was King. And King, it proved to be. I've always considered that a remarkable feat.

"Well, there was nothing to be done but to keep an eye on these men and to 'black-list' the stolen notes. Windell, of course, had disappeared into the blue.

"I forget the name of the Branch at which King was employed. But it was not Harlesden, nor was it one of the twelve. In his luncheon hour on that Monday, King had not lunched. He had made his way to the City, and there, in the Mansion House subway, under the street, he had met D S Windell and received two thousand pounds in Bank of England notes. I don't think the two met again, till both were out of jail. And that was years afterwards. If you ask me how we knew this, I cannot say. I simply cannot remember. But know it, we did.

"Naturally enough, the Press made much of the affair. When all is said and done, it was a hell of a show. I suppose that, reading the papers, King got puffed up. Be that as it may, he did an extremely foolish thing. (I have often heard it said that every criminal makes one bad mistake. I have never found this true. Most criminals make two or three. Some don't make any at all.) King wrote a letter to the Head Office of the Bank, thanking them for the four thousand pounds, and he signed it 'D S Windell'. He wrote it all on a typewriter, including the signature. He wrote it at a house at which he was spending the weekend. But he didn't put an address, and the letter was posted in a district with which he had nothing to do. But he did commit a piece of almost unbelievable folly. He had two shots at his letter, and sent the second one: but, though he tore up the first, he never burned the fragments. These were found the next morning by an inquisitive charwoman, who took them to the police. I doubt if I should have believed that, if I hadn't had the fragments in my hand. But I can see them now.

"That told us, of course, that it was King. But you don't get a conviction for forgery on evidence like that. And so we had to sit still and wait for more.

"Suddenly one of the stolen notes came in through a Spanish Bank. And then another and another. D S Windell was touring

Spain, and, to judge from the way in which he was spending money, was having a gorgeous time. We sent out a man, to make sure – and followed him round. It was very galling for the Bank to have to sit still and watch their money being blown, but King was the man they wanted: and, if we had arrested Windell, King would have been put upon his guard. And that would have been fatal, for he was a very shrewd man. Hardly anyone knew he was suspected. The Manager of his Branch had no idea. In the hope of lulling any suspicions which King might entertain, we arranged for him to be promoted. This was done.

"So we sat still, watching and hoping. All the time, Windell's notes kept coming in from Spain. And the Bank writhed: but Muskett refused to move. King never tried to cash one.

"And then at Whitsuntide, nearly six months after the robbery had been done, King took a short holiday. And he decided to spend it at Amsterdam. So the bankers of Amsterdam were warned to stand by. Sure enough, he walked into one office and laid down five five-pound notes.

" 'Will you change these, please? And what is the rate of exchange?'

"An old Dutchman glanced at their numbers and then at his list. Then he picked up the notes.

" 'No, I won't change them,' he said. 'These notes have been stolen, and – '

"But King was gone.

"The old fellow pursued him in vain.

"King returned to duty with his heart in his mouth. But we were not ready yet. A week or two later, on a Saturday afternoon, King was asked to keep an appointment in Leicester Square. This, at three o'clock. Ten minutes before that time, the old Dutch banker sat down on a seat in the square. He was to keep his eyes open and to raise his hat if he saw anyone he knew. Precisely at three King appeared, and at once the old fellow rose and lifted his hat. King did not see him do so, but two plain-clothes men did. King was arrested and taken to Bow

Street forthwith. On the way, he did an incredibly foolish thing. Though he had already been cautioned, he asked the police a question. 'Tell me,' he said. 'Supposing I'm sent down for this, could they stop me using the money when I come out?' Naturally, this statement was given in evidence against him and had a lot to do with sending him down."

"But what a madman," said Berry.

"It was typical of the man. The fraud was impudent. The sending of the typewritten letter was infernal cheek. His behaviour in the dock was impertinent, and his answers in the witness-box were daring. His attitude conveyed the impression that he would have liked to say, 'Yes I did it all right; but you damned well prove I did.'

"Directly after this, Windell was arrested in Spain: but most of his share of the plunder had disappeared. King's was in a safe-deposit – so much we knew.

"I have entirely forgotten the proceedings at the police court. I imagine that he pleaded 'Not guilty' and reserved his defence. That is what I should have done, for such a case was bound to be sent for trial.

"Bodkin, of Treasury counsel, appeared for the Crown. King was defended by Lever – most ably defended, too. The Judge was Forrest Fulton, the Recorder, whom I have mentioned before. Travers Humphreys was Bodkin's junior.

"At the time in question, no typewriters were used by the Bank. At least, the Managers did not dictate their letters, but wrote them themselves in longhand. So all twelve of the forged letters had been written in longhand, too. And in each case, the hand was exactly that of the Manager of the Harlesden Branch. Not only the signature – the whole text. There was only one tiny, tiny difference. I'm afraid it's hard to explain, but I'll do my best.

"Think of copper-plate writing, and think of a capital Y. The first down stroke of the Y is a deep, bold curve. Now think of a capital H, or a capital K. In these letters, the first down stroke is a miniature copy of the first down stroke of the Y. A copy, but very much smaller – a fifth of the size. Now when King wrote copper-plate, as sometimes he had to do – a name in a ledger, or something – he wrote very well. But his copper-plate hand had one peculiarity. This was that the first down stroke of his H or his K was always almost as large as the first down stroke of his Y. And when he copied the Harlesden Manager's hand, he failed to conceal this one peculiarity. As Bodkin put it in his opening speech, 'Out of his imitation of the Harlesden Manager's writing, there emerged a characteristic of his own.'

"We had several extracts from the forgeries photographed, and some of King's own entries in the ledgers photographed, too. These photographs were greatly enlarged. When the two were compared, there was no mistaking the little peculiarity which was apparent in both. In all other respects, the forgeries were superb. And twelve fairly long letters, remember. It was a great achievement – you can't get away from that.

"I'm not sure, but I don't think we used against him the fragments of the letter found by the charwoman. Why, I don't know. There may have been something unsatisfactory about that evidence. Anyway, it had served its turn, for it led us to King. But with the peculiarity of his handwriting, his identification by the Dutchman, his very foolish question to the police and other evidence, I think we should have got home comfortably, if a sheer catastrophe had not befallen us at the trial. Of course it was never reported, for nobody knew.

"The principal and by far the most important witness for the Crown was Anderson, the General Inspector of Branches. His proof was very long, for he represented the Bank. In that capacity, he was to detail much of the working of the Bank: to explain, for instance, how it was that King had access to letters from the Harlesden Branch and could have abstracted and restored them, without anyone's knowing that he had done so: to speak to discipline, supervision, practices, notepaper, postage – all sorts of things to which only a man in his position could speak with authority. I had no fear, for Anderson was a most exceptional man. He had everything at his finger-tips. And I knew he'd make the perfect witness. As for cross-examination, Lever would get not a pennyworth of change out of him.

"If I remember aright, he was due to be called after luncheon on the second day. As I entered the hall of the Old Bailey about a quarter to ten that morning, Chief Inspector Bower, the principal police witness, hurried to my side. 'Bad news, sir,' he said. 'Anderson's here all right, but he's very ill.'

" 'Ill?' I cried. 'Well, sick, sir. He's got some stomach trouble. The man's in agony.' 'Where is he?' said I. 'Over there, on the bench.' I almost ran to his side. Anderson looked at me, but he could hardly speak. As he opened his mouth, another terrible spasm racked his frame. When it had passed, 'I'll do it somehow,' he said. I asked him if such an attack had occurred before. He nodded. 'I'm subject to them,' he said. 'But they last for twenty-four hours.' 'Have you got a doctor?' I said. 'Yes. If he was here...' I turned to Bower. 'Send a man for his doctor,' I said. 'He's to tell him that Mr Anderson's got one of his attacks.'

"Then I entered the court. Bodkin had just come in. I told him what had happened. 'He's not fit to give evidence,' I said. 'He's got to,' said Bodkin. 'The case can't be postponed.' 'He may get better,' I said. 'If he doesn't, I don't know what will happen. He can't stand up.' 'He's got to do it,' said Bodkin. 'If he doesn't do it, then Mr King will walk out.'

"By way of making things worse, before the case had begun, Lever had requested that all witnesses should be out of court. This meant that, if Anderson went to pieces, no other witness would know and so could not try to repair the damage which he had done.

"When the case was again under way, I slipped out to see what Anderson was like. Whilst I was there, his doctor arrived hot-foot, with a plain-clothes man. 'I must give him an injection,' he said. 'It's the only thing.' The doctor stayed with Anderson all that day. And he kept on giving him stuff, to quell the pain. When the Court adjourned for luncheon, I took the doctor aside. 'For God's sake,' I said, 'don't give him any more dope. You're dulling his brain.' So he was; Anderson's eyes were half shut. 'But I must relieve such pain.' 'Not at that cost,' said I. 'If he were himself, I'm sure he wouldn't let you. He knows what there is at stake.' Needless to say, I got no luncheon that day.

"I'll say that man was game. He entered the box somehow, and he wouldn't sit down. I think he feared to sit down. And there he stood for nearly three hours – examined and cross-examined. I never saw him writhe, but his eyes looked glazed. As I had feared he would, he made a lot of mistakes in examination-in-chief. He forgot: he tied himself up: he contradicted himself: he made mis-statements of fact. Bodkin, of course, could do nothing, for he had to take his answers. I could do less. But I remember wiping the sweat from my face and thinking, 'If this is what he does now, what on earth is he going to do under cross-examination?' "

"I can imagine," said Berry, "few more agonizing ordeals."

"I think it shortened my life. I had to be there and listen: but I was powerless to act. I knew his proof as well as he knew it himself, and, over and over again, I wanted to get up and cry, 'Oh, you don't mean that.' A merciful God, however, tempered the wind. For some strange reason, under cross-examination he did very much better – far better than I had dared hope. And then at last it was over, and he came out of the box. Then the Recorder rose, and I made my disconsolate way to Bedford Row. When I rendered my report, Muskett shrugged his shoulders. 'These things happen,' he said. 'I expect it'll be all right. Have you had any tea?' "

"One to Muskett," said Berry.

"You're perfectly right. My report must have shaken him, for he knew far better than I how vital Anderson's evidence was: and he knew that the Bank would be wild if King got off. (Windell had to be extradited from Spain, and two of the Bank

Managers who had interviewed him were sent out to identify him. They were a little uneasy, for they'd only seen him once, say, six months before. Bower was at the station when Anderson saw them off, and he told me that Anderson's parting words to them were, 'If you fail to identify Windell, you needn't come back.') Receiving such bad news, many a man would have taken it out on me – unfairly, of course: but he would. But Muskett – never. He was very reserved, very just, and always most kind to me."

"I saw the letter," said Berry, "he wrote to Coles, when you left. 'I've lost my right hand,' he said."

"I know. That was far too handsome. And now let's get back to King.

"Muskett was right. I think it was two days later that King went down. But the betting was even right up to the very last. Lever made an excellent speech, and the jury was out a long time. I watched them when they came back, but I hadn't a clue. Neither, I think, had Bodkin. And then the foreman said, 'Guilty' – and that was that. King got seven years – I think that's right. It would have been a scandal, if he had got off. And the Bank would have been beside themselves. King took his sentence in silence, waved to some women in court and turned and ran down the stairs.

"Windell, whose real name was (I think) Bernard, was tried separately. I think he pleaded guilty. He was very young and was said to have mastered six languages. The proceedings seemed to amuse him. After all, he had blown his money. I think he was given two years. He was obviously no more than a catspaw.

"King was as good as his word and went to his safe-deposit, as soon as he was let out. But the police went, too. I think there was some fuss about it: but, of course, he was not allowed to use his stolen notes.

"I think you may fairly say that King cut his own throat: it was his insolent assurance that brought him down."

"Forgery has always been regarded as a very serious crime."

"Quite rightly," said I. "For forgery of a Will, you can get penal servitude for life. Have you ever seen a *Bank of Engraving* five-pound note?"

"That's a new one on me."

"Well, it was exactly like a *Bank of England* note, only, instead of the word 'England', it had the word 'Engraving'. So it wasn't forgery. But I'll lay any money that, if you'd been given one, you wouldn't have noticed the difference. I was shown one at Scotland Yard. They were most beautifully done."

"But what a brain," said Berry.

"It was very clever, for it let the printer out. The man who uttered it could be got for false pretences. I think the law's altered now. But a lot of money was made."

"Let us talk for a little," said Berry, "about Trustees."

"That sounds very dry," said Jill.

"It will be my privilege," said Berry, "to clothe the dry bones with flesh. I have been a Trustee in all some thirteen times; sometimes, a most active Trustee; but always against my will. I have done it, because, as a fool, I conceived it to be my duty. If you except the professional man, such as a solicitor or banker, who is allowed to charge for his services, no Trustee may make so much as a penny out of his Trust. So it's not a paying business. But it can be very trying – at least, I've found it so."

"It's very tiring," said Daphne, "for it means a great deal of work. To give you your due, I think you've been awfully good. But why do you say 'trying'?"

"Because, every now and then, you have to put down your foot. I've always tried to put mine down very gently: but the beneficiary or co-trustee who necessitates that gesture invariably resents it, and unpleasantness usually results. But that's by the way.

"Now I only want to make two points, both of which have emerged from what I have found or discovered as a trustee of many years standing. Many people regard, or used to regard, their trustee as a VIP. 'Got to be careful who you ask to meet

232

him.' To them, a trusteeship resembles a decoration. I'm not sure it oughtn't to be – in which case I should have twelve bars. And now let's look at the other side of the coin. *It is my considered opinion that in the last hundred years private trustees have – almost invariably with impunity – got away with more money than have all the convicts of that period put together.* Often enough, the money has gone into the trustee's pocket: in other cases, it has gone into the pocket of somebody else *owing to the criminal negligence of the trustee.* I could tell you of case after case in which, to my knowledge, considerable fortunes have dwindled to pittances. It was always too late to do anything about it, for the money was gone. Where? Only the previous trustees could tell you that: and they were dead. Of course, the thing's too easy. Look at the *cestui que trusts.*"

"Whatever's that?" said Jill.

"You're one, my sweet. The *cestui que trust* is the person who has a trustee. Sometimes – often enough with unconscious humour – he is called 'the beneficiary'. In nine cases out of ten, these are completely ignorant of money matters and are bored stiff by any attempt at explanation: they accept without question anything the trustee says and do without question anything he tells them to do, such as signing documents. Careless young men and maidens, only too thankful to have someone to think for them: old ladies who can't understand, but always find their trustee a most charming man: casual blokes who never answer a letter and don't care a hoot, so long as they're not overdrawn... They are the sort of people who have trustees. And because nearly all are either grossly ignorant or incurably lazy or both, they are fair game. The vast majority can't be bothered. 'Money's such a bore.' 'My trustee does all that.' Which makes things so very easy – for the trustee. I could have got away with thousands, if I'd been so inclined. And it's The Mint to a monkey-nut that I should never have been suspected, much less pinched. I'm not going to go into details, because it would take too long, but – well, Boy will bear me out in all that I've said."

"I will indeed – as regards the private trustee. The Public Trustee and the Banks and many firms of solicitors are, of course, above suspicion. By no means all firms. And the solicitor-trustee has the biggest chance."

"There you're quite right. He has – because of his special knowledge. And, by God, a lot of them take it. Say a rich fellow goes out, and leaves two trustees to his Will. One's his widow, and one's a solicitor. Well, what does the widow know? Nothing at all. And so the solicitor's virtually sole trustee. If he says, 'Sign here', she signs. Then again, she's much to think of, and she forgets. But the solicitor doesn't forget. She mayn't lose twenty thousand, all in one lump: but she loses a thousand a year for twenty years: by the constant changing of investments, of mortgages, and, of course, in costs. I've actually found it happening, when I've come in.

"And my second point is this. When it was first suggested that I should be a trustee, Coles Willing showed me a textbook. It was by Augustine Birrell, a famous QC. And in it Birrell set out, quite shortly, the nine duties of a Trustee. 'I'll have that passage copied,' said Coles. 'It's little more than a page. And I want you to learn it by heart.' I could recite it now. The point is that from that moment I knew what my duties were. And I will lay you five thousand sovereigns to one that not one trustee in five thousand could today recite three of the duties which, by virtue of his appointment, he has undertaken to do.

"Somebody dies, and a couple of relatives find that they have been appointed trustees. They swell with pride. The Will has dressed them in authority. They can put it across their brothers and sisters and cousins and lesser breeds. Their word is law. It never enters their heads that they have nine duties to do. They know that they mustn't steal, but no more than that. But, then, they knew that before. Beyond that they have some power, they know nothing at all. They don't even know how to wield it. So they're forced to depend upon some solicitor: and often enough they're fooled to the top of their bent. Accounts are rendered to them, which they don't understand: but they daren't say they don't understand them, for that would mean loss of face. And so they pass them – sign them with a hell of a flourish; for their signature is the warrant, without which no man can act.

"Such people are dangerous. And there are hundreds of thousands all over the place. Supposing their luckless victims, the *cestui que trusts*, were to ask them to retire. They'd laugh like hell in their faces. 'Yes, you'd like that, wouldn't you? You see, they've not the faintest idea that, if they are asked to retire, *it is their bounden duty to retire*. If anyone told them that, they'd say he was a liar. In fact, it's true. If a trustee is asked to retire and he won't retire, you can go to the Court. I once came across such a case. The trustee was a solicitor – a low-class fellow; but he was on the Roll. I advised that he should be asked to retire. He blandly refused. So then I wrote to him. After that, he retired all right.

"Well, there we are. The trustee who has no idea of his duties – doesn't dream that he's got any duties, is very nearly as bad as the wilfully defaulting trustee. Shakespeare, as always, has him perfectly taped – 'But man, proud man, Drest in a little brief authority; Most ignorant of what he's most assured, Plays such fantastic tricks before high heaven, As make the angels weep.' No one could call me an angel, but the tricks I've seen them playing have damned near made me weep. In more than one case that I've come across, beneficiaries have been refused information. They have been told, 'That is the trustees' affair.' Such a refusal was a breach of trust. But neither the trustees nor the luckless beneficiaries knew that."

"D'you mean to say," said Daphne, "that, if a trustee is asked to retire, he's got to?"

"Of course. And if he won't, you can apply to the High Court of Chancery. And unless the trustee can show that your demand is prompted by some improper motive, the Court will order him to retire, approve someone to take his place and direct him to pay the costs of the application."

"I'm sure," said Daphne, "most people don't know these things."

"Of course they don't," said her husband. "They grunt and sweat under a weary life – and all the time, the remedy's in their hands. But there you are. Ignorance is responsible for half the ills that flesh is heir to."

"What is responsible for the other half?"

"Lack of moral courage. Will anyone say I'm wrong?"

"I won't," said I.

"You find it everywhere. Look at the way in which people go on with a doctor, whose prescriptions do them no good, in whom they have lost faith. 'Oh, it's so awkward.' They can't even nerve themselves to desire a second opinion." Berry shrugged his shoulders. "Well, it's their body. If they like to pay for it to be mucked about by someone in whom they have no confidence, they can." He looked at me. "*Sir Andrew Plague* was my money. He had no lack of moral courage. Allow me to quote an extract from one of his letters, which always appealed to me.

" 'I regret to say that the manners of the first veterinary surgeon who arrived left much to be desired. I therefore ordered his removal and sent for another.'

"That always did my heart good.

"Oh, I knew there was something. I've meant to return to it for ages, but, till now, it has always escaped me. Darling, the Home Secretary, Stinie Morrison and his reprieve. At the end of that gobbet of scandal, I meant to interrogate you. But before I had time, you ran out – a vile and vulgar practice, which I have always deplored."

" 'Ran out'?" said Jill.

"Ran out. A racing metaphor. Before he had consumed one subject, he fell upon another. Like a dog on a garbage heap."

"I suppose you must be bestial."

"My sweet," said Berry. "I am a realist. And now don't make me run out. The point is this. In his report, Darling said, 'This conviction is just. The man deserves to die. But I am by no means sure that, but for the incompetence of his counsel, he would have been found guilty.' "

"Please," said I, "allow me to emphasize this, as I did when I told the tale. I cannot vouch for that. I have no means of knowing what Darling said. I was told that he had said that; but I can't remember by whom. Personally, I believe it to be true. But I can't put it higher than that."

"Good enough," said Berry. "And now allow the mountain to bring forth its mouse. What I wanted to say was this – that if every prisoner, who would have been acquitted but for the incompetence of his counsel, were to be reprieved, half the jails would be empty."

"That is perfectly true. That's what made the Home Secretary's action so childish. You see, you must never forget what I said – oh, ages ago, that it is perfectly fair to say that no innocent man was ever indicted. I remember the laughter in The Temple over one Colchester Assize. There was a local barrister there who collected briefs for the defence. And he was no earthly. When the Assize was finished, somebody added up the years of penal servitude awarded to his clients during that week. They came to sixty-seven. Some men have the knack of defending: other men haven't. Muir, as I've said, was no good. George Elliot was excellent. He was of the Old Bailey. It may truly be said of him, 'And many a burglar he restored to his friends and his relations.' Juries loved George Elliot. But that was natural, because he was lovable. He was the nicest man. Very simple and charming and gentle, and he had a delightful smile. He was by no means brilliant: but he had the pleasantest ways. And then at last he took silk – and faded away. George Elliot wasn't a leader. But I think he'd made his fortune and wished to retire. But he wanted the honour of silk. I may be wrong. He was one of the old school, and I am quite sure that all who remember George Elliot, remember him with affection. I may have spelled his name wrong. I can't remember."

"Another flash," said Jill, "to take us to bed."

"That's right," said Daphne. "What is the most dramatic case that you have ever known?"

"The one in which I was junior to Gill and Wild. Easily. But I can't talk about that."

"The next one, then."

"You must give me a moment to think... Oh, I know. Yes. But it's going to be disappointing. I was not concerned, and I can tell you no more than the papers did. But the silly thing is this – that at the time at which it happened, the Crippen Case was on, and nobody had any eyes for anything else. But, although this came to nothing, it really was life.

"A lady of easy virtue was living south of the river – I think, perhaps, in Clapham: I can't be sure. Like her virtue, her circumstances were easy: hers was a nice little house, which I think was detached. She was not, on the whole, promiscuous, but she was the mistress of three men. Each of the three believed that she was his mistress, and his alone. For some time she played very well this something difficult hand: and then things began to go wrong. Let me call the men, A, B, and C. Of course she took infinite care so to arrange their visits that none of them met: but something occurred to make – not only A, but also B suspect that, when he was not with her, the lady was receiving another man. Both were jealous men. And both determined to lay that other man out. Accordingly, unknown to each other, both proceeded stealthily to the lady's house on an evening when neither was expected. A arrived first and was endeavouring to scale the porch in the hope of entering or looking through a lighted window above, when B arrived. B was a violent and passionate man. To his mind, his worst suspicions were confirmed. And here was his hated rival. He laid hold of A and pulled him down to the ground. A, very naturally, showed fight. After a very short struggle, B drew a revolver and shot A dead. Then B took to his heels. In fact, at that very time C was in the house. When the shot was fired just outside, the lady was frightened to death. She immediately associated the shot with the dangerous game she had been playing. She besought C to go down and see what had occurred. C did so, only to stumble over the body of A. The night was dark, and he could see no more than that the man was dead. When he ran in and told the lady, she fell down in a faint. Whilst he was attending to her, the police arrived. They, too, had heard the shot. At once they took charge. One of the first things they did was to ask C if he knew who the dead man was. He said, no, that he had not seen his face.

" 'Come and see it now,' said the sergeant.

"He followed the sergeant down, and the light of a lantern was thrown upon A's face.

"C started violently. Then –

" 'No,' he said. 'I've never seen him before.'

"In fact, he had. On very many occasions. *It was his own father*.

"That statement might have cost him dear. People who tell lies, when murder has just been done, are regarded with grave suspicion. He withdrew it the same evening.

"Within the hour, two taxi drivers reported that, while they were waiting on a rank some seventy yards from the house, a man had scrambled over a neighbouring garden wall and disappeared. They had not seen his face. Immediate investigation showed traces on walls and flowerbeds, which left no doubt at all that the man was B. He had scaled three garden walls, to make good his escape.

"Only one person knew who B was: and she would not tell. She swore she had had but two lovers, father and son. No arrest was ever made. An inquest, of course, was held, at which the son and the lady gave evidence. And, as I say, the case was duly reported, but hardly read. But I think it may fairly be called a dramatic case.

"On second thoughts, I must take back something I said: for I seem to remember more than was ever reported by the Press. But at the time in question, I was in touch with the Yard: and I was probably told it by one of the police."

*

With infinite care, Berry lighted a cigar.

Then –

"Last night you mentioned a case for which we have all been waiting in some impatience. I think that the time has come when this duty should be discharged."

I groaned.

"I knew that was going to happen."

"Sorry, but you must do it. For this is history. The case was world-famous. And the great probability is that you know more about it than anyone else. You were in it from the word 'Go' – in fact, you beat the pistol. And you never left it, until the man was sent down. You know it inside and out. Such knowledge should be placed on record, once for all."

"It'll take a long time," I said.

"The night," said Berry, "is young. And your very beautiful wife shall keep your glass charged." Jill rose, to set the decanter within my reach. "That precaution was supererogatory. Supposing I want some more."

"You've had enough port," said Daphne. "And you know Boy's throat gets sore, when he talks for long."

"Ugh," said Berry. "President of the OUDS, and he can't produce his voice."

"Well, you can't, either," said Jill.

"I don't have to," said Berry. "My voice is like a spring that rises, clear as crystal, out of the marvelling earth. When I was Ahasuerus, Esther used to call me her ouzel. I always enriched the palace, while she was pressing my beard."

"For heaven's sake, start, Boy," said Daphne.

"By way of introduction," said I, "let me say this. The Crippen Case attracted much attention – I never quite know why: but the fact remains. It was the handbill, I think, that gave it a flying start. *WANTED FOR MURDER AND MUTILATION.* (Who it was that drafted that bill, I never knew: but I need hardly say that the crime of mutilation is quite unknown to the law.) Then, of course, it was 'the silly season', when papers were hard up for news: then, the woman-in-the-case was arrested, disguised as a boy: finally, it was the first case in which wireless was ever used to lay a man by the heels. Anyway, it attracted such attention as had no other case since the famous Tichborne Trial in 1872. The papers went mad. The whole of each day's proceedings were reported, word for word. *The Evening Standard* would give up as much as eight pages, to get it all in. Nobody seemed to talk of anything else.

"On the day on which Crippen and le Neve appeared for the first time at Bow Street, an admirable photograph was taken from the back of the court. The next morning this appeared in the middle of *The Daily Mirror*. It occupied the whole of two pages. It was really of considerable interest, for several of the big shots of the CID had come down from Scotland Yard, to have a look at Crippen: and there they all were in a bunch. Of less interest is the fact that it included an excellent portrait of me: I was sitting in counsel's box on the Magistrate's left and I was at the moment leaning forward to try and see le Neve's face."

"You would be," said Berry.

"So," said I, "would you. (She was wearing a flat hat, at that time sometimes worn by women who were to drive in an open car: and a veil was, as usual, drawn down tight about it, so that her face could only be seen from the front.) As a result, I was recognized right and left: and strangers would accost me in restaurants, to ask for the latest news of the Crippen Case.

"That's forty years ago, but I don't think the interest has really died today, for the name is still remembered as that of a *cause célèbre*. For twenty years afterwards, it was certainly very strong, and it very often figured in books on crime. I don't suppose that I saw all such accounts, but I can honestly say that more rubbish has been written and published about the Crippen Case than ever has been written and published about any case in the world. Attempts have actually been made to palliate the crime. What is the truth? It was the sordid and barbarous murder by her husband of the Honorary Secretary (or Treasurer) of The Ladies' Music Hall Guild, to whom her many women-friends were deeply attached. Crippen had fallen for his typist: but, because a man falls for his typist, he doesn't have to murder his wife. Why, then, did Crippen do it? Partly because he wished to take the typist to live in his own house, but mainly because he wished to acquire the valuable jewellery which his wife possessed. I have read that Mrs Crippen led him a dog's life. Of that, there was not a tittle of evidence. She certainly had her interests, and he had his. On the night on which she died, they had entertained two old friends. And he used to come and fetch her from The Ladies' Music Hall Guild. What was their private relation, nobody ever knew.

"And now let me say two things. As always, I shall tell you nothing but the truth. I am in a position to tell you certain things which have never been told before. And I shall tell you them. But even at this distance of time, I cannot tell you the whole truth about this case, for there are one or two things which I have no right to disclose. Secondly, all this happened some forty years ago, and upon some details my memory may be at fault. I never held a brief in the case, but I was Travers Humphreys' junior from first to last. With him, I worked upon the case in Chambers, day after day and often till late at night: with him, I attended every hearing at the Coroner's Court, Bow Street and the Old Bailey: with him, I visited the house in Hilldrop Crescent, at which the murder was done: and I never left the case, until Crippen had been sentenced to death. So I do know what I'm talking about, when I deal with the Crippen Case.

"One of my duties was to reconstruct the crime, so I may sometimes state as a fact something which is founded on assumption, and not upon proof. But such assumption was well-founded. Let me give you one example of what I mean. Everyone knows that the luckless woman's remains were found in a grave. Although the head was missing, among the remains was a very little of her hair. This had been torn out. Mrs Crippen was a heavy woman, and there is little doubt that her husband had to get her body down stairs. It was, therefore, assumed that he had dragged her down stairs by the hair of her head.

"And now I will tell you what happened – so far as anyone knows.

"Hawley Harvey Crippen was an American citizen. He was known as Dr Crippen. In fact, he held some diploma which was not recognized. I don't think he practised as a doctor, but he had an office where he made up various specifics, for which there was some slight demand. His wife had been a music-hall artiste. I don't think she ever appeared in the West End, but she was popular in the provinces for several years. Then she threw in her hand and retired. She seems to have been what is called 'a very good sort'. Anyway, she had many friends. Her stage-name was Belle Elmore, and, as I have said before, she was the Hon. Secretary (or Treasurer) of The Ladies' Music-Hall Guild. The Crippens lived in a house in Hilldrop Crescent, not far from Holloway Prison, to which women were usually sent. For some years all went well: then Crippen engaged a typist, whose name was Ethel le Neve. With her, he fell in love. And, after a while, he determined to rid himself of his wife. To which, if any, of the decisions which Crippen took, le Neve was admitted, no one will ever know.

"On, I think, the 31st January, 1910, Paul Martinelli and his daughter spent an agreeable evening at the Crippens' house. If I remember, Martinelli had been a juggler; but he was now retired. They rose to leave about eleven o'clock. As it was raining, Crippen left the house in search of a cab. He returned with one, and the Martinellis left. That was the last occasion on which anyone, except Crippen, saw Mrs Crippen alive.

"Now what happened at Hilldrop Crescent, when the Martinellis had gone, must, to a great extent, remain surmise. That certain things happened we know: exactly how they happened, we cannot be sure. Though much of what I tell you must be assumed, every conclusion was most carefully drawn, and myself I have no doubt that the very gruesome picture which I shall present differs hardly at all from the tale which would have been told, had someone been there to see.

"Belle Elmore was partial to stout. Whilst she was in her bedroom, getting undressed, Crippen brought her a glass of stout. But into the stout, he had put some hyoscine. Hyoscine is one of the alkaloids. It is a deadly poison, inducing convulsions and coma, preceding death. It is very slightly bitter, but stout would conceal the taste. Hyoscine was among the drugs which Crippen employed in the preparation of his specifics.

"Belle Elmore drank the stout, and Crippen undressed. By the time that coma had supervened, Crippen was in his pyjamas. He seized his wife's hair and dragged her out of the room and down the stairs. She was still in her underclothes.

"All this was according to plan, for the crime was premeditated. The grave he had dug was waiting, under the coal-cellar's floor. He had also procured some lime – two sacks, I think.

"Well, he dragged the body downstairs and into the kitchen. He got it on to the table, above which was burning a lamp. This must have meant a great effort for the body was a dead weight and Belle Elmore was not a small woman by any means. That done, he stripped the body, in which, as like as not, there was still some life. His knives and scalpels were ready, and so he cut her throat. The blood he caught in a bucket and poured away. When the veins had been drained, he cut off her head.

"How he disposed of her head, no one will ever know. And a human head is a difficult thing to destroy. And nobody had any theories. The head was gone.

"He then dissected his wife from A to Z. Only a man who had had some surgical training could have done this: and only a very strong man could have completed her dissection within a very few hours. But Crippen, though he was small, was immensely strong. Chief Inspector Dew told me that. It was Dew who brought him back from Canada. During the voyage, he was never out of Dew's sight. So upon several occasions Dew saw him stripped. And I remember his saying, 'Well, I'm a much heavier man, but I should have been very sorry to have had to take Crippen on.'

"When the dissection was done, Crippen proceeded to remove the flesh from the bones. This, too, was a formidable task. But he undertook it because he proposed to bury the flesh, but burn the bones. He could not trust his lime to destroy the bones: and he could not trust the fire to destroy the flesh. By now the monster was working stripped to the waist, for the labour was very heavy, and he was up against time.

"As he removed the flesh, he took the pieces and laid them in the grave. They were difficult to handle – they slipped: so he used the top of his pyjamas, to carry them in. But one piece of flesh, he laid aside. For he dared not trust that piece even to lime.

"Years before, Belle Elmore had had an operation which women sometimes have. It was a major operation. And the scar which it left ran right up the middle of the abdomen. When the operation was performed, she may have been slim. But as she grew stout, the scar stretched, until it became a thin, isosceles triangle – I should say, eight inches in length. Such a scar may fairly be termed 'a distinguishing mark'. So Crippen had to make sure that that scar was destroyed. Accordingly, from the abdomen he cut out a slab of flesh some ten inches square. And this, as I have said, he laid to one side.

245

"For hours the work went on. At six o'clock in the morning, he'd very nearly done. And then something – no one will ever know what – something occurred, to make Crippen lose his nerve. I always think it likely that it was some sound – a milkman's cry, perhaps…which showed that the world was stirring…that people were waking up. Be that as it may, panic was Crippen's portion for half an hour. And his one idea was to get what was left away and out of sight. Almost all the flesh was gone, except the slab which was bearing the tell-tale scar. In his frenzy, he snatched this up and thrust it into the grave. It was, in fact, the very last piece of flesh which he put in. In went his pyjama-top, too, and Belle Elmore's underclothes, and tufts of hair, some false as well as real. But never a bone.

"And now let's go back for a moment.

"I told you that he had ready two sacks of lime. One sack was in the cellar, ready and open for use. And each time he laid a portion of flesh in the grave, he sprinkled it lavishly with lime. He had also a bucket of water. And so often as he sprinkled his lime, he soused that lime with water – he slaked his lime. The lime he had bought was quick lime: by sousing it with water, he turned it into slack lime. He did this thoroughly. He knew what lime could do.

"Well, the last slab of flesh went in, with the other bits and pieces as I have said. Then he threw in lime by the handful, covering everything thick and thrusting lime down by the sides of the shocking heap. And then he slaked the lime, drenching it all with water, as fast as he could. He had some earth ready, some earth he had taken out, when he dug the grave. In this went, on the top and down the sides: and when all was tight and level, back went the bricks with which the cellar was floored. He laid these roughly in lime, for the lime was there. Then he smeared the coal-dust over the top of the grave. Where he hid the bones for the moment, I've no idea. But during the days that followed he burned them in the back-garden, bit by bit.

"And that was the end of Belle Elmore – as Crippen thought. In fact, he was wrong; for he'd made one shocking mistake, which, as a medical man, he should never have made. As I have said, he knew what lime could do. He knew that lime consumes – devours human flesh. In the old days, the bodies of men who were hanged were buried in lime. *But not in slack lime: in quick lime.* Quick lime destroys and devours. *But slack lime presèrves...*

"The lime in the sacks was quick lime. Had he put it in, as it was, in a very short space of time the remains would have disappeared. The tell-tale scar, the organs containing poison – all would have gone to dust. But Crippen was very careful to slake his lime... By doing which, *he preserved, in perfect condition, all that he meant to destroy*. When, nearly six months later, the grave was opened up, all that was in the grave was as good as new."

"The finger of God," said Berry.

"I've always thought so, too.

"Well, Crippen resumed his life, and the weeks went by. But he had to account for Belle Elmore's disappearance. After all, as I have said, she had many friends. So he gave out that she had received an urgent summons from her sister, who was in America; and had left precipitately for the United States. Well, that would serve for the moment: but he had to do better than that. So, after a while, Crippen went into mourning. When people asked him why, he was overcome with emotion. Belle was dead... Belle, his beloved wife...he had had a letter from her sister, just stating the fact. He knew no details at all. But Belle was dead. At the end of the painful recital, he sometimes wept."

"The little darling," said Berry. "Why aren't such people struck dead?"

"I'm damned if I know," said I. "But Crippen wasn't human. I once saw him laugh in court – throw back his head and laugh, at something his solicitor said. He opened his mouth wide and

247

bared his teeth. He looked like a cat, or a tiger – you know how a cat, when it cries, will open wide its mouth and bare its teeth. I was quite close to him, and the startling similarity hit me between the eyes. Crippen was animal.

"Well, his story was generally accepted. After another six weeks, le Neve went to Hilldrop Crescent, to live with him. Presently she appeared in bits and pieces of clothing which Mrs Crippen had worn. People shrugged their shoulders and left it there. 'Men will be men.' There was only one lady who did not leave it there. She was a music-hall artiste, considerably younger than Belle, of whom she had been very fond. Her stage-name, I forget, although she was in demand. Her husband appeared with her. Her private name was Nash. I remember her in the box, a very fine figure of a woman, attractive and full of drive. And she was not satisfied. She had never taken to Crippen, as had most of her friends. ('He had such charming manners,' they used to say. Perhaps he had. To my mind, he was repulsive: but most women seemed to like him, and that's the truth.) And she continually insisted that Belle would never have gone without telling her and that she was perfectly sure that some dirty work had been done. These convictions she declared to her husband, until he was sick and tired. And when he implored her to put the business out of her mind, she always replied as follows. 'If you were half a man, you'd go to Scotland Yard.' Well, Nash was very much more than half a man, but he had all the husband's reluctance to make a fool of himself on behalf of his wife. In July, however, the camel's back gave way. Nash could no longer endure the reproaches of Mrs Nash. So he went to Scotland Yard. He asked to see an Inspector of the CID and was taken upstairs to Chief Inspector Dew. Shamefacedly, he told his story. 'I don't suppose,' he concluded, 'that there is anything in it – you know what women are. But now that I can say that I've told you, perhaps I shall have some peace.' Dew quite agreed. There was probably nothing in it. Still, he'd look into the matter, in case there was.

"Dew was as good as his word. A day or two later, he went to Hilldrop Crescent and, finding Crippen there, desired some information about his wife. 'People are talking, Dr Crippen. They find your wife's disappearance rather abrupt.' 'Well,' says Crippen, 'to you, I can tell the truth. So far as I know, Mrs Crippen isn't dead. The plain truth is that she's left me. We had a hell of a row and she left the house. Oh, more than five months ago. She never said where she was going: she just cleared out. I thought, of course, she'd come back. But, when she didn't, I had to explain her absence. But I was ashamed to tell her friends the truth, and so I made up the story that she was dead.'

" 'Well, where's she gone?' said Dew.

" 'I've not the faintest idea. From that day to this, she's never written a word.'

"Well, Dew told him what he was fit for, for telling so foolish a lie. And Crippen admitted his folly and asked what he was to do.

" 'I must think this over,' said Dew. 'It's a curious case. Will you be here tomorrow about eleven o'clock?'

" 'Tomorrow' was Saturday.

" 'I shall,' says Crippen. 'And if you can help me, Chief Inspector, I shall be very grateful.'

" 'I'll tell you tomorrow,' says Dew.

"Now, why did Dew want time? He told me himself. 'Because,' he said, 'the moment I entered that house, I felt there was something there that shouldn't be there. And I was troubled. And I felt that I must have time to think things out.'

"So much for intuition. First, Mrs Nash and then Dew. Each of those people felt there was something wrong.

"Well, Dew went back the next day. And, after a talk with Crippen, he asked to see over the house. He went into every room, and he entered the coal-cellar, beneath which lay the grave. And, while he was talking with Crippen, he tapped the bricks with his heel: but none of them moved. The house

249

disclosed nothing at all that Dew could suspect: but the feeling that 'something' was there was strong upon him. They, then, returned to the parlour, there to sit down.

"After some discussion –

" 'Dr Crippen,' said Dew, 'you must set about finding your wife. Only by finding your wife, can you silence this talk.'

" 'I quite see that,' said Crippen, 'but how shall I go to work?'

" 'You'd better advertise. What papers used she to read?'

" '*The News of the World* and *The Era*.'

" 'Then advertise in those. If it will help you, I'll draft an advertisement.'

" 'If you please,' said Crippen.

"Dew took out of his pocket a foolscap sheet. It was the paper used at Scotland Yard – azure in colour, with the Royal Arms at the head. On that he wrote out an advertisement. And Crippen was much obliged. He read it through and laid it down on the table. 'It's too late now,' he said. 'But the first thing on Monday morning, in it goes.'

" 'Right,' said Dew. He rose. 'I'll look in again towards the end of next week.'

"But Dew didn't wait so long, for he wasn't satisfied. On Tuesday he called again – to find the house deserted. The kitchen-range was cold. Stuff unwashed on Saturday still stood unwashed. The bedrooms betrayed every sign of precipitate flight: doors and drawers were open and clothes were upon the floor. A bag, half-packed, was gaping, and shoes were lying where they had fallen or been dropped. And down stairs, in the parlour, the foolscap sheet was lying upon the table, exactly as Crippen had left it, three days before.

"Be sure Dew wasted no time. Within the hour his men were within the house. It was searched from bottom to top. Any wall that rang hollow was opened. But nothing was found. Then they turned to the garden, while others interviewed neighbours – to learn that, some months before, Crippen tended a fire in the garden which sent forth offensive smoke. But the garden itself gave them nothing: and after three days of hard labour, Dew threw in his hand. That his intuition was good, he still believed. In fact he now was sure that Crippen had murdered his wife. But evidence was denied him. No warrant would ever be granted just because Crippen had fled. And the Assistant Commissioner was getting restive – Dew and his men were needed for other things.

"So, after another fruitless morning, he sent the squad back to the Yard, with orders to send one car back, for his sergeant and him.

"Now what immediately follows, Dew told me himself. So far as I know, he never told anyone else – outside the Yard.

"He and his sergeant were sitting in the kitchen in silence, waiting for the car to return. Both were depressed. They had been so certain that 'something' was there to be found. And neither wanted to leave, for Dew still had the feeling that 'something' was there. And then he noticed a poker, lying on the top of the range – an ordinary kitchen-poker, which, after years of use, had worn very thin. (Later, he showed me the poker and I examined it.) Dew rose and picked it up. Then, 'Light the lantern,' he said. 'We'll test that cellar again, and this is just what we want.' While the sergeant was lighting the lantern, Dew found a broom...

"The coal-cellar was very inconveniently shaped, as many small coal-cellars were. As I remember it, it was some nine feet high and some seven feet long: but it was very narrow, less, I should say than three feet. There was a plate in its ceiling, through which the coal was shot. The door was some five feet high, by two feet wide. Happily, it was not full: it was very nearly empty.

"While his sergeant shed the light, Dew brushed the coal-dust away. Then he sought to thrust the poker between the bricks. After two or three shots, he managed to force it in. Then he tried to prize up a brick: but the brick would not budge.

"Let me use his own words.

251

" 'Then I got it in again, in a different place: and after a lot of prizing, the brick began to come up. I pulled it out. The next wasn't quite so hard, and the third came away in my hand. I just pulled out another six. Then I sent — for a shovel. Before I'd got out two scoops, I knew we were home... And there you are. If Crippen had taken the trouble to order a ton of coal, he'd be a free man today. The police aren't coal-heavers, and to empty that cellar, when full, would have been a fearful job.'

"The handbill went out that night, and the hunt was up. The sensation it caused was immense. Crippen became world-famous within twelve hours.

"On the 25th July the Master of the s.s. *Montrose* was pacing his bridge. The weather was fair and the ship was two days out. She was bound for Canada, and had sailed from Amsterdam. Among the passengers were a father and son. From the bridge, the Captain saw them, leaning over the taffrail, engaged in talk. He gave them a passing glance, and then he resumed his stroll. The next time he looked at them, his brows drew into a frown. For a little he stood, just looking. Then he called the mate. He pointed to the two, whose backs were, of course, towards him. 'Father and son,' he said. 'Have you ever seen a boy with a behind like that?' The mate considered the case. Then, 'You're right, sir,' he said. 'That isn't a boy: it's a girl.' The Captain left the bridge and went down to the deck. When father and son moved, he engaged them in talk. Ten minutes later, he entered the wireless cabin. 'Get London,' he said. 'A message for Scotland Yard. Say that we think that Crippen and le Neve are on board.'

"Now that is the plain truth.

"The signal was received in London. Questions were sent in reply and the answers came back. The answers were good enough for Dew to board a liner bound for Quebec. She was faster than the *Montrose*, and she came to Father Point the day before. There Dew disembarked. When the *Montrose* arrived, Dew put on a pilot's rig and went off in the pilots' boat. As he gained the deck, he saw Crippen, standing alone. He went straight up to him. 'Well, Dr Crippen,' he said, and took off his cap. Crippen stood still as death. Then le Neve appeared, saw Dew and fell down in a faint.

"Until Crippen had landed and had been lodged in some jail, he could hardly be searched. When he was searched, they found Belle Elmore's jewellery stitched to his vest. I saw it in Court, with the pieces of vest still attached. Brooches and rings. And very fine diamonds, too. I can't remember their value, but they were worth quite a lot.

"On August 1st the arrests were announced in the Press.

"At that particular moment I was at Canterbury. I was playing for The Old Stagers, and the Canterbury Week was nearing its handsome end. I had meant to go on to White Ladies. But when I read the news, I altered my plans. I had been in Treasury Chambers for the best part of a year: and in that time I had learned all sorts of things. And so I was ready to swear that the brief in the Crippen Case would be sent to Travers Humphreys. Travers Humphreys, I knew, was away, because the vacation was on. So were all his devils, including myself. Now it was a tradition of the Bar that the devil or pupil that first got his hands on a brief had the right to stick to that brief and to act as his master's junior throughout the case. And so, on Sunday evening, I took the train for London: and on Monday morning I walked into Paper Buildings at ten o'clock. The clerks looked much surprised. 'Good morning, Hollis,' I said. 'Have any papers come in?' 'Only Crippen, sir.' 'Crippen will do,' I said, and walked into Humphreys' room. 'Bring the papers in.'

"Travers Humphreys returned on Friday: but by that time, I had got the case into shape. I had worked all day for four days on the statements which kept coming in. And the Treasury was delighted to find there was someone there. The senior solicitor, Williamson – one of the nicest of men – rang me up time and again. 'We've tied up that end, Pleydell. The statement's coming along. And Wilcox is doing the analysis. That'll take two or three days.' And so on. Then Travers Humphreys came back, thanked me for what I had done, and we took off our coats.

"Day after day, we worked damned hard on that case. Sometimes we dined at *The Cock* and then went back to The Temple, to work till eleven o'clock. One night we got fed up, and went to *The Empire*, instead. I may be wrong, but I think the Inquest was held before Crippen got back. We attended every hearing, and I always took the note. (The 'note' is a longhand report of everything that is said. So you have to write pretty fast. I always say that the Crippen Case ruined my hand. Be that as it may, after every hearing, the reporters crowded about me to check their notes with mine.) We visited Hilldrop Crescent and went all over the house. I always remember one thing. A glass full of water on a washstand, and a tooth-brush lying across it, with the tooth-paste still on the bristles, waiting to be used. By the time that Crippen arrived, the case was nearly ready – very much more than ready for the first hearing of all. In such a case, the first time the prisoner appears, evidence of arrest is given and nothing else. Then a remand is ordered, mostly for seven days.

"The prisoners, with Dew in charge, landed at Liverpool on a Saturday afternoon. Leaving the boat-train at Euston, they entered, I think, a police car. As it left the station, a crowd of several thousand hooted and booed. Before this demonstration Crippen lost his nerve and tried to leave the car. I forget where they were lodged for the next two nights. They were due to be brought up at Bow Street on the following Monday morning, at ten o'clock.

"I had seen crowds outside Bow Street Police Court, when the suffragists were to appear: but never had I seen such a crowd as was assembled in Bow Street and its environs on that day. Travers Humphreys and I, in a taxi, could not approach the Court: so we drove to the mouth of an alley, and, leaving the taxi there, walked up the alley to the Magistrates' private door. Inside the famous Court there were already more people than I would have said it could hold. But the Bench was empty, and so, with one exception, was Counsel's box. (Who the stranger was, I never knew. But he was very reserved. I think he was an old Civil Servant.) To the box, we were escorted, I think, by the Chief Jailer, Sergeant Bush.

"The latter seldom appeared – the more's the pity. He cut a most striking figure, did Sergeant Bush. He was a fine, big man, with a black, close-cut beard. He was always perfectly groomed and his uniform fitted like a glove. From his belt hung his bunch of keys – there must have been ten to twenty – none less than six inches long: and all were shining like silver and chinking whenever he moved. His manner was superb. Brisk, dignified, firm, Bush was a splendid officer and an impressive man.

"Williamson was already in court and, at Humphreys' invitation, he came to sit by our side. Arthur Newton, who had been instructed for the defence, was at the solicitors' table, just below. Dew was there, of course, to give evidence of arrest. Then ten o'clock struck, and the Magistrate took his seat.

"It was the Chief Magistrate, Sir Albert de Rutzen. That the case came before him was just pure accident; Monday was one of the days on which he sat. But we were glad it was he, for he was the best on the Bench. When Spy's cartoon of Sir Albert appeared in *Vanity Fair*, beneath were printed the words, 'A model Magistrate'. This was a true saying. Very quiet, very firm, very kindly, he truly adorned the Bench. His wisdom was infinite: his understanding, rare. And his polished manner was that of another age. He was a great gentleman.

"Crippen and le Neve were brought in, to stand in the dock, side by side. When evidence of arrest had been given, Humphreys requested a remand for seven days. This was a usual request, and was granted at once. As the prisoners left the dock, Arthur Newton rose. 'I ask your permission, sir, for me to receive a copy of the sworn Information upon which the Warrant was issued for the prisoners' arrest.' This request was also quite usual. Before Sir Albert could reply, Travers

Humphreys rose. 'The Crown, sir,' he said, 'opposes this application.' Sir Albert looked at him. 'Not without reason, sir. But I give the Court my word that by your refusal the defence shall be in no way embarrassed. At next Monday's hearing I will open the case in full, and I will consent to any adjournment which you, sir, may see fit to allow.' Arthur Newton protested with all his might. Such opposition, he said, was unheard of. (So it was.) For years such a privilege had always been accorded the defence. (So it had.) And what were the Crown's reasons? 'I am not prepared,' said Humphreys, 'to disclose the reasons which the Crown has for opposing this request. I have said that it has good reason – and I leave it there.' Arthur Newton replied with some heat. Then he sat down. Sir Albert was very wise. He knew that, without good reason, the Crown would never have dreamed of opposing so usual a request. And, of course, he knew Arthur Newton. And, since he had Counsel's word that the defence should in no way suffer if the request was refused, he refused the request. To do so required considerable moral courage, and I can think of no other magistrate who would have done so. So Newton went empty away."

"And the reason?" said Berry.

"I'm sorry," I said. "It was a very good reason, but I have no right to divulge it."

"Not after forty years?"

"No. I should like to – more than I can say. But that information was secret, and I cannot give it away.

"On the following Monday, Humphreys was as good as his word and opened the case in full. Wilcox had found the poison – traces of hyoscine. (The organs were tested, of course: but until the poison was found, we had had no reason to think that Crippen had poisoned his wife.) Humphreys opened this fact. I was watching Crippen then, for I thought it would hit him hard. I was perfectly right.

"Before my eyes, the blood rose into his face, as I had never seen blood rise into a face before. It was like a crimson tide. It rose from his throat to his chin in a dead straight line...from his chin to his cheeks...from his cheeks to his forehead and hair...till his face was all blood-red, a dreadful sight. And then, after two or three moments, I saw the tide recede. Down it fell, as it had risen, always preserving its line, until his face was quite pale. Twice more I saw this happen – once under cross-examination, and once again. It was a tell-tale flush, beyond his power to control.

"That night, in jail, Crippen broke his glasses and sought to use the fragments to cut his throat. But a warder entered his cell and wrested the fragments away.

"Perhaps I had better describe him. He was on the small side, for a man, and was neither slim nor stout. He had a heavy moustache. This was red, like his hair – a sandy red. Being very short-sighted, he wore very powerful glasses – spectacles. The lenses were unusually thick. Since he had protruding eyes, the effect, when he looked at you, was really most repulsive, for the glass being thick and the eyes very close to the glass, some trick of magnification lent them a horrible look. His gaze was most disconcerting – and that is the truth.

"Le Neve was nondescript. She was not good-looking, but you'd hardly have called her plain. She gave no sign of the lively personality which she undoubtedly possessed. At the first hearing at the police-court, she seemed to have no idea of the gravity of her position: she was charged with being an accessory, and was liable, if found guilty, to be imprisoned for life, if not hanged. During the proceedings, she made no effort to control her amusement and laughed outright more than once, while Dew was relating that, when he arrested her, she was dressed as a boy. I imagine that Arthur Newton let her have it afterwards, for never again did she behave with such impropriety.

"Speaking of le Neve, Dew told me a curious thing. There was plenty of room on the ship on which she and Crippen were brought from Canada: the cabins allotted to them were on

257

opposite sides of the ship. Crippen spent most of his time, audibly lamenting the fact that he had involved le Neve – 'That poor girl,' he kept saying. He need have had no concern. 'The poor girl' was enjoying herself. She was a wag, and her flow of quips and back-chat reduced to helpless laughter the crowd of stewards, cooks and others so often as it found time to collect outside her door. The thing became such a scandal that Dew approached the purser and had le Neve moved to a cabin which was less accessible.

"The hearings at Bow Street occupied several full days, and all the time, between them, our work in Chambers went on. To the best of my recollection, we hardly touched anything else. Sir William Wilcox, the eminent physician, then Senior Scientific Analyst to the Home Office, proved that hyoscine had been found in more than one organ which Crippen, of course, had preserved. Professor Pepper gave evidence – it was, I think, his last case. The famous Bernard Spilsbury spoke to the flesh and the scar. Mrs Nash was called, so was her husband. The Martinellis were called. An assistant from a Holloway drapers' identified the pyjama-top as having been sold by his firm the year before: my impression is that he remembered Belle Elmore as a customer, but of that I cannot be sure. Arthur Newton reserved his defence. The two were committed for trial.

"The Treasury chose Muir to lead for the Crown, and Tobin, QC, was briefed for Crippen's defence. Le Neve was to be tried separately: on her behalf F E Smith was retained.

"In a case so heavy, the Treasury usually gave an extra brief: that is to say, a devil in the Chambers of one of the Treasury Counsel engaged received a brief from the Crown. By the etiquette of the Bar, as Travers Humphreys' leader, Muir had the right to say to whom the brief should go. Naturally enough, the name he submitted was that of Ingleby Oddie, who would work on the case with him and had been his faithful devil for many years. (Oddie was also a doctor and later became a famous London Coroner.) Williamson was kind enough to make a great effort to get a second brief for me, for I had done all the work, and Oddie never came in, till the case was sent for trial. But the Treasury was adamant. One extra brief was all that they could afford. Before the first hearing at the Old Bailey, Oddie came up to me with the brief in his hand. 'Everyone knows,' he said, 'that this brief should be yours.' I thought that uncommon handsome. But it was nobody's fault."

"It was a damned shame," said Jill.

"I never resented it, my darling. I should have liked a brief, and I think the Treasury might have stretched a point. But their argument was that they had allowed a brief and that whose name was submitted was nothing to do with them."

"Muir was to blame?"

"Not at all. Oddie was his rod and his staff: and Oddie would have been by his side, whether or no he had a brief in the case. I don't suppose he gave the matter a thought. Besides, it would have been unseemly that I should have held a brief, while Oddie had none; for Oddie was certainly ten years senior to me."

"Why, then, did Oddie say what he did?"

"Because he was a very nice man.

"The case was heard in October – at least, I think it was. At the Old Bailey, of course. It was tried by The Lord Chief Justice, Lord Alverstone, of whom I have spoken before. It was not his turn to take the Calendar, but he washed out the other Judge and came down himself. I was told that he said, 'This man deserves to hang, and I'm not going to see him get off on a point of law.' Be that as it may, I never remember a case more beautifully tried.

"I think it lasted one week. Humphreys brought in a second devil to help me take the note: this we did by turns, so that I had an easier time. Who was Tobin's junior, I quite forget.

"The defence put forward was this: That Crippen had not murdered his wife or anyone else; that, to the best of Crippen's belief, Belle Elmore was still alive; that Crippen was unaware that any remains were under the cellar's floor; that there was

259

nothing to show that those remains were Belle Elmore's; that the so-called scar was nothing but a fold in the flesh – the mark which had been made when the slab had been folded in two.

"For obvious reasons, I won't describe the trial; but I'll give you a few side-lights which I remember well.

"Tobin, who was later made a County Court Judge, put up an excellent show. How he contrived to do it, I have no idea, but he appeared to have convinced himself of Crippen's innocence. He afforded a perfect example of the way in which Counsel for the Defence should identify himself with the instructions which his brief contains. Of his final address to the jury, the last words were, 'And reconcile your verdict with your conscience and with your God.' As he sat down, I saw the tears on his cheeks.

"Muir was at his best, for the case was a dead case. He fairly screwed down the lid. For Crippen to have declined to go into the box, would have been to commit suicide: though counsel may not comment upon such a failure, the Judge may: and the Lord Chief would undoubtedly have done so. So into the box he went. The papers said that Muir's cross-examination was deadly. Possibly it was. But it was the material that Muir had that was deadly. And Crippen made a very poor witness. He put up no fight. With such material and such a witness, almost anyone's cross-examination must have been deadly. Of evidence against Crippen, we had *un embarras de richesse*. We never even called the man who delivered the lime. It was a dead case. Yet I have read accounts, printed and published in volumes, written by men who knew no more of that case than did the butlers of Mayfair, which have suggested that it was touch and go, that up to the last uncertainty prevailed, that the verdict of the jury was breathlessly awaited and that it is to be hoped that justice was done. Which is, of course, utter rubbish. The case was always dead.

"I think I am right in saying that Crippen declined a chair and stood the whole time. I may be wrong. He stood a little back from the bar and held his hands behind him for most of the time. He was carefully dressed and wore a frock coat, as, of course, in those days many men did. Except upon two occasions, he betrayed no emotion at all.

"Sir William Wilcox was always a deadly witness: and this was not because of the evidence he gave. Having a slight impediment in his speech, he spoke with a deliberation which magnified the importance of all he said. From the amount of hyoscine found in the various organs, he was able to calculate the dose administered. This would have been sufficient to kill half a dozen men. Bernard Spilsbury, fresh-faced and charming – it was his first big case – explained the scar. The slab of flesh upon which the scar appeared, was exhibited in court. It was lying in a large meat-dish – the kind of dish in which sirloins used to be served – soused in spirits of wine or some preservative. It was presented to counsel, and I inspected it. Even I could see it was a scar – a scar which had stretched. Pepper, sitting beside me, indicated various points. 'No doubt at all?' I whispered. 'How can there be? As she grew stouter, it stretched. I've seen them again and again.'

"The defence called two qualified surgeons to say that it was not a scar, but the mark of a fold in the flesh. 'When the slab had been laid in the grave, it must have been folded in two.' Such a contention was manifestly absurd, and the Lord Chief showed that it was. He turned to the leading surgeon, then in the box. 'You say that this is a fold, and not a scar?' 'That, my lord, is my belief.' The Lord Chief held up a sheet of note-paper. This he folded in two. Then he opened it out. There was the line of the fold, quite clear to be seen.

" 'That,' he said, 'is the mark of the fold which you have seen me make. It is a sharp, thin line, of the same width all its length. Now look at that mark on the flesh. That is not a thin line. And it gradually grows wider, until at the bottom it measures nearly an inch. D'you still maintain that that mark on that piece of flesh is the mark of a fold?'

"The surgeon looked embarrassed, as well he might.

"Then –

" 'Yes, my lord, I do.'

"With a shrug of his shoulders, the Judge sat back in his chair.

" 'Go on, Mr Muir,' he said.

"I was told that the Lord Chief was responsible for a something grim jest, which was current about that time. 'Oh, the Crippen Case. Tried for the murder of his wife – and she was in court all the time.' 'Nonsense.' 'She was, indeed. But she was too cut up to say anything.'

"The trial had been going for three days, and the time was a quarter to three. All of a sudden loud snores rang out in court. Everyone looked at the dock, only to see that Crippen's eyes were fast on the jury-box. (I must take back something I said, for I can see him now, and he was sitting down.) So everyone looked at the jury. At the end of the panel, in the front row, a juryman was hanging out of the box, snoring like hell. It was, of course, stertorous breathing. I whispered to Pepper, 'Whatever's the matter with the man?' 'Epilepsy.' My heart sank. If Pepper was right, the jury must be discharged, another jury empanelled and the whole case begun again. But, mercifully, Pepper was wrong. The juror was dragged from the box and carried bodily into an empty court. Wilcox and Spilsbury went with him. The Court sat in silence till Wilcox came back. Wilcox entered the box, and the Lord Chief questioned him. 'What is the matter, Sir William?' 'An acute attack of indigestion, my lord. I think the man lunched too well.' 'Will he be fit to resume?' 'Oh, yes, my lord. If your lordship would please to adjourn for half an hour.' So the Court adjourned, and then went on with the case.

"We called one witness who did not appear at Bow Street. This was Belle Elmore's sister. She had been brought by the Crown from the United States. She spoke to the operation, which her sister had had, as a result of which her abdomen bore a scar. I shall never forget the way she looked upon Crippen. And Crippen wilted and cringed, as he met her gaze.

"And then at last it was over, and the jury found Crippen guilty, and that was that.

"Horace Avory, Clerk of Arraigns, called upon him.

" 'Hawley Harvey Crippen, you have been found guilty of murder. Have you anything to say why the Court should not give you judgment of death?'

"In a very thick voice – it really *was* thick – Crippen replied.

" 'I still protest my innocence.'

"Then came the proclamation, and the doors of the court were locked.

"When the Judge assumed the black cap, for the third and last time I saw that strange tide of crimson rise in a dead straight line from Crippen's throat to his brow. For a moment or two the whole of his face was suffused. Then, exactly as it had risen, the tide went down.

"The sentence pronounced, he turned and left the dock.

"He appealed, of course. So far as I remember, the Crown was not called upon. I remember that the defence suggested that the outlook of the juror, who had been taken ill, might have been affected by the distinguished doctors who ministered to him in the privacy of the empty court. You may imagine how this suggestion was received by the Court of Criminal Appeal."

"How very disgraceful," said Daphne.

"It was, indeed. I don't think Tobin made it, but somebody else. I may be wrong.

"The trial of le Neve took place a day or two later. Our case against her was, of course, very thin. We had next to nothing at all. I mean, we could not prove that, either before or after, she was aware of the crime. Naturally enough, we didn't press the case. Crippen was what we wanted, and he was in the bag. F E Smith came down to defend her and made a lovely speech. But it was supererogatory. Any one could have got her off. So she was discharged."

"Well, I'm much obliged," said Berry. "There's only one question which I should like to ask. You said that the murder was done on the night on which the Martinellis were entertained. And you gave the date – the thirty-first of January, 1910. You were quite definite about it. I know that that was the last occasion on which Belle Elmore was *seen* alive, but how can you be sure that that was the very night upon which the murder was done?"

"I'm sorry," I said," but I'd rather not answer that question. I had an idea that you'd ask it – you don't miss much. But I beg that you'll take it from me that we had no doubt."

"That's interesting," said Berry. "I'll never ask you again, but I can't think how you knew."

I shrugged my shoulders.

"We just did," I said.

*

"Last night," said Daphne, "we had drama taken from life. Which was the most dramatic scene you ever wrote?"

"I think the last scene in the life of *Vanity Fair*."

"I'm inclined to agree," said Berry. "And the way in which it was observed was very neat. Isn't there an orchestra's gallery like that, concealed in the wall of a dining-room at Windsor?"

"Yes. That's how I got the idea."

"Like the table that sank through the floor in *Perishable Goods*?"

"Yes. I saw a table like that in the summer palace of Ludwig, the poor, mad King of Bavaria. At one time he took a dislike to having servants in the room. As he could hardly wait upon himself at dinner, he devised a table that sank through the floor at the end of every course."

"Slightly disconcerting," said Berry. "Supposing one of his guests didn't draw back his feet… And supposing you hadn't finished your Tokay…"

"Be quiet," said Daphne. "Which would you say was your most moving scene?"

"I think, perhaps, the end of *Lower Than Vermin*. But I'm no judge."

"I confess," said Berry, "that hit me very hard. The forced conversation, each trying to cover up...and Philip's last words were exactly what he would have said. It wasn't a brilliant saying: but it was the one remark which such a man would have made.

"You're not a great writer by any means. I doubt if your stuff will live. But every one of your people is true to life. Dead true. And those who say that they aren't, declare their ignorance. Take *Ewart* in *Maiden Stakes* – I've met the man. And the young men and maidens in *And Five were Foolish* etc. – I've met the lot."

"I'm half a writer and half a reporter," I said.

"Rogues, too?" said Jill.

"Yes," said I. "They weren't on the job, when I saw them – so far as I know. I took them out of the bus, or the Tube, or the street, or the bar, and put them in Austria. I got to know them quite well – to recognize *Bunch* and *Punter* and *Dewdrop* and *Rush*.

"Lots of reviewers have said that the well-to-do 'Gadarenes' – as I called them in *Aesop's Fable* – that I have so often drawn, are unheard of...imaginary figures, belonging to a 'never-never world'. The plain answer is that they know no better. If they had attended the opening night of the *Palais Royal* night-club outside Biarritz in about 1925, they would have seen dozens."

"By God, what a night!" said Berry. "George —'s party, wasn't it?" I nodded. "Alfresco dancing on glass, which was lighted from underneath...to the very hell of a band...and the thunder of the Atlantic, breaking upon the headland about thirty paces away. I think we sat down to dinner sharp at eleven o'clock. What were the jewels worth – the jewels that we saw that night?"

"More than three million sterling, I should say. But there you are. We were there, so we know. And at that particular time

265

there were more than twenty night-clubs in and around Biarritz, and all of them paying their way. I don't commend these things – I'm merely stating the fact. And a third of the people were English."

"It was outrageous," said Daphne: "but I wouldn't have missed it for worlds."

"I was at *Irikli*," said Jill.

"And much better off," said Berry. "How did you think of the title *And Five Were Foolish*?"

"As a matter of fact, I can tell you. A fellow was lunching with me – a most amusing bloke – and he would talk about my stuff. And he asked me how I came by my titles. And I said, 'Oh, they just occur to me. It's no good sitting down and trying to work one out. They just come into your head. Some ordinary expression, or quotation – "And five were foolish", for instance. There you are. That will do very well for my new book.' And that is how I chose it. The others came to me in much the same way: but that's the only one whose arrival I actually remember."

"You saw the Spanish Grand Prix?"

"Oh, yes. You've got to see it, to do a tale like *Maiden Stakes*. But that account is dead accurate. In fact, I saw the race twice – once before I wrote the tale, and once a few years later: and I remember thinking I wouldn't have changed a word. And I saw it from the point I described, the point at which *Gyneth* was standing, watching the cars go by."

"Each time?"

"Each time. It was a spot in a million from which to watch such a race."

"Talking of San Sebastian, what about the Casino in *Jonah and Co*?"

"I went twice to San Sebastian to get that picture right. It wasn't so easy as it looked. And I did once see Zero turn up seven times in ten spins. At Madeira, I think. I was on it the last four times, and we broke the Bank."

"Your places are real?"

"A great many are. I could show you the site of *Jezreel* in *She Fell Among Thieves*. I tell you, I'm half a reporter. I report what I've seen and heard."

"You 'hold the mirror up to Nature'?"

"That is what I have always tried to do."

"Will you tell me this?" said Daphne. "Why do so many writers report 'the sordid side'?"

"I can't imagine," said I. "Sometimes they do it very well. And reviewers seem to love it. The more sordid the tale, the higher their commendation. I could have done it, of course. I've seen 'the sordid side' again and again. But I can see no object in presenting it in fiction. Life's sad and hard enough, without adding some sordid picture, to wring men's hearts."

"By God, I'm with you," said Berry. "But, as you most justly say, the viler the picture presented, the better are the reviews. Anyone would suppose that reviewers lived in squalor and never saw anything else. Which is, of course, absurd. Look at the sales of —. And that masterpiece opened with one of the most revolting incidents that a man can ever have conceived."

"Don't talk about it," said Daphne. "I wish I could forget it. I never read any further, but the memory makes me feel sick."

Jill put in her oar.

"Could you have written that, darling?"

"Of course I could, my sweet. As could any writer who knows his job. But it wouldn't have amused me to write it. Frankly, I should have been ashamed to set such things down. Much of this book will be sordid; but then it is, none of it, fiction. Every statement is true. If I was to tell the stark truth of the Crippen case, I had to paint a very sordid picture – no doubt about that. But, when you are writing fiction, you don't have to do the same. The 'mirror' reflects fair things, as well as foul."

"I know one thing," said Jill, "that some reviewers say that always annoys you."

I smiled.

267

"I know what you mean, my darling. But not for long. You see, for me to be annoyed is just what they want."

"When they say that *Berry*'s family always scream with laughter at everything he says."

"That's right. But such statements are made of malice. I'm afraid there's no other word."

"They're completely false," said Daphne.

"They're simply lies," said Jill.

"That shows them to be malice," said I. "If the accusation – for that is what it is – were true, I should be guilty of a very offensive fault – a sick-making fault. That is why the accusation is made – in the hope of prejudicing potential purchasers of the book."

"It ought to be actionable. If they told lies about some tooth-paste, to put people off they'd have to pay damages."

"I entirely agree," said Berry. "And, speaking wholly objectively, I don't think you do it enough. If someone makes an unquestionably side-splitting remark, it is natural for those within earshot to laugh: if they don't, it's unnatural."

"I agree. For that reason, I did it occasionally – as unobtrusively as possible – in my earlier books. But a very pleasant review of one of them – I think it appeared in *Punch* – suggested that it was a mistake. That ruling, I at once accepted: and, since then, I don't think I've done it ten times in four hundred thousand words. And when I have done it, I've done it deliberately, for the reason you've just advanced – namely, that it would be manifestly unnatural for those present not to laugh. Laughter at a predicament, as distinct from a saying, is, of course, different. I *have* to mention that; for, if a predicament is entirely ludicrous, not to declare that the witnesses found it so would be to suggest that they were inhuman."

"Allow me to say," said Berry, "that I think you take it very well. I mean, malice enrages me."

I shrugged my shoulders.

"I can't do anything," said I. "And if I allow it to annoy me, I'm simply playing their game."

"It makes me feel sick," said Daphne. "Let's have a fair reminiscence – to wash out the taste."

"When I was at Harrow," said I, "I got to know Herbert Channell, the son of the Judge. As I think I've told you before, Channell used sometimes to write to his son in Greek. Herbert was younger than I. His father, an Old Harrovian, was always cheered on the steps. But Herbert was ashamed of his dress, as children will be. As a matter of fact, he always looked very nice, in grey morning dress and, always, a grey top-hat. Ten years later, when I was in Brick Court, Herbert arrived as a pupil, and he and I became friends. He never had any work, and I don't know how he'd have done it, if he had: for he didn't take to the Law. But he was most entertaining. We used to lunch together and we would walk home together often enough. To his distinguished father, he must, I fear, have proved a disappointment: his friends were more fortunate. Whenever his father went circuit, Herbert would disappear; for he always marshalled his father, wherever he went.

"Now a Judge's Marshal was a very nice thing to be. I don't have to tell you I've been one, but I think my week with Channell might be set down. The Marshal is a kind of equerry: I fancy he is a survival of the days when the King himself used to go on Assize. The Marshal is in constant attendance upon the Judge. At meals, he takes the head of the table – at breakfast, for instance, he pours out the coffee and tea. When the Judge is on the Bench, the Marshal always sits on his left, and he walks behind the Judge in any procession formed. He takes his Judge out for walks, when the work is done; and he travels with the Judge from town to town. He answers official invitations addressed to the Judge. And he used to swear the Grand Jury – no easy task. For doing all this, he got three guineas a day.

"One Sunday afternoon, when Channell was on Assize – he was taking the Western Circuit – Herbert rang me up. It was in

269

the summer, I know, though I can't be sure of the year. 'Listen, Boy,' he said. 'I've had to come back. I've a carbuncle on my neck, and it's giving me hell. My father wants you to go down and take my place. Can you do it?'

" 'Yes,' I said, 'I can. I mean, I've got nothing on.'

" 'I'll be all right in a week, the doctor says. But if you can take my place, my father will be much obliged.'

" 'I will,' I said. 'Where is he?'

" 'At Winchester. With Coleridge, as the second Judge. The Assize there opens tomorrow, and my father's taking the crime. That means you must swear the Grand Jury. I've got the oaths here.'

" 'I'll come round and see you,' I said.

"I'd never been a Marshal before.

"I went round and saw Herbert, who gave me the dope – more or less. He also gave me a card, on which were printed the oaths.

" 'Only three things,' he said. 'The first is this. Never call him 'Sir', for he can't bear that. The second is, never ride in the coach, for he can't bear the Marshal in the coach – I don't know why. And the third is that you must not *read* the oaths. That he will not allow. You must learn them by heart.'

"With my eyes on the card –

" 'Good God,' said I.

"There were two oaths. The first was addressed to the foreman, and it was one hundred and twenty-six words long. One hundred and twenty-six. The second oath was shorter. This was addressed to the other members of the Grand Jury, and had to be repeated twenty-two times. But the foreman's oath was the devil.

" 'It can't be done,' I said. 'I never could learn repetition. It's now nearly half-past four: and I've got to administer it tomorrow at ten o'clock.'

" 'You've *got* to do it,' said Herbert. 'He's counting on you. But he will never forgive you, if you go and read the oath.'

"I won't say what I said that time, but Herbert only laughed.

"Well, I couldn't go down that night, so on Monday morning I caught the early train. That was due at Winchester at five and twenty past nine. The Judges had to be 'churched', so they would reach the Castle just about ten o'clock. And there I must be to receive them. I should have just nice time.

"I knew what to do on arrival – go straight to the Judge's room and write a note. This, to the foreman of the Grand Jury, asking him, as soon as the Judge had taken his seat, to rise and request the Judge that he and his fellows should be sworn in the old-fashioned way. For the new way would take about three times as long. Then I must send the note off and repair to the Castle's doorway, to meet the Judge.

"All was well – except for the foreman's oath. I knew the other all right: but I was afraid of the foreman's. I'd sat up half the night, trying to learn the thing; and sometimes I could say it, and sometimes I broke down. All the way down, I kept on reading it over and saying it to myself. Suddenly I found, with a shock, that the train was behind its time. We were nearing Winchester, but we were ten minutes late. And the train was slowing down. We reached the skirts of the city at twenty to ten. And there the train came to a halt. Before this new *contretemps*, I forgot all about the oath. But I had the sense to do one thing. I found a scrap of paper, and scribbled my note to the foreman. Then I hung out of the window and stared up the line.

"There were two silks in my carriage. One, I think, was Charles – one of the best of fellows, who later became a Judge.

" 'What's your trouble?' he said. 'They can't begin without us.'

" 'Oh, can't they?' I said. 'I'm the Judge's Marshal.'

" 'The devil you are,' says Charles. 'You're going to be late.'

"We pulled up to Winchester's platform at seven minutes to ten.

"I fairly fell out of the train, and there was the Judge's valet, standing upon one leg. I guessed it was he, because of his frantic demeanour.

" 'Are you from the Judge?' I cried.

" 'Yes, sir. Are you the Marshal? I've got a fly.'

"There were no taxis in those days.

"I left my luggage to him, and the fly-man whipped up his horse.

"As we came to the Castle, I saw the coach coming up.

"I fell out of the fly and ran into the echoing hall.

"I tore off my hat and coat – it was raining hard – and thrust them upon a policeman. 'Take those to the Judges' room.' Then I gave my note to another. 'Take that to the Grand Jury bailiff. The foreman's to have it at once.' He only stared. 'I'm the Marshal,' I said. 'Do as I say.'

"He turned and ran off. As he did so, the fanfare rang out.

"I whipped to the open doorway and stood to one side.

"The coach was there. The High Sheriff was getting out. When the Judges had descended, a little procession was formed. The High Sheriff, in blue and silver, bearing his wand, and the Judges, robed and wearing their full-bottomed wigs. I noticed Coleridge's Marshal, standing, facing me, on the other side of the steps. We let the procession pass and fell in behind. So we passed through the hall to the Judges' corridor. There Channell turned to me and put out his hand. 'I think you're Pleydell,' he said. 'Do you know the oath?'

"For half an hour, I had forgotten the oath.

" 'Yes, sir – Judge.'

" 'Come along.'

"The moment his back was turned, I whipped the card from my pocket and glanced at the print. As we passed a door which was open, I saw my coat on a chair. This, then, was the Judges' room. I pitched the card in, as I passed. I *had* to get through it now.

"But before I came up to Becher's, another fence had to be cleared. I had no means of knowing if the foreman had had my note.

"The Judge passed on to the Bench, and I followed behind.

"The Grand Jury was up on its feet. The Judge bowed to the Grand Jury, and the Grand Jurors bowed back. Then we all sat down.

"I got to my feet and chanced it.

"Looking straight at the foreman –

" 'I think, sir,' I said, 'you have a request to make.'

"He rose and looked at me. Then, to my great relief –

" 'If you please,' he said, 'the Grand Jury would like to be sworn in the old-fashioned way.'

"I glanced at Channell, who nodded.

"Then I administered the oath. I think that a merciful Providence guided my tongue, for I never faltered and I never made a mistake. And then I swore his fellows, twenty-two times. And then I sank down in my stall, by the Judge's side.

"Channell leaned over to me.

" 'I'm much obliged, Pleydell,' he said. 'I have never heard the oaths better administered.'

"I don't know what I replied. But I remember thinking, 'If only you knew the truth.'

"Then he charged the Grand Jury. This, with the natural dignity which characterized all he did. That was the first occasion on which I had heard this done, for no one, except the Marshal, was allowed in Court."

"How could you," said Jill, "how could you have thrown away the card?"

"My sweet," said I, "by throwing away the card, I cut off my way of escape. I *had* to do it then."

"I'm damned if I'd have done it," said Berry.

"I think you would. It forced me up to the jump which I had to take. I couldn't run out then."

"It makes me feel weak," said Daphne.

"When you're desperate," said I, "it's wonderful what you can do."

"I am beginning," said Berry, "to understand how *Richard William Chandos* does what he does."

"That's right," said I. "*Chandos* is sometimes desperate. He's *got* to do the thing: and, because he's *got* to, he does it.

"And now let's go back to the Judge.

"Sir Arthur Moseley Channell was a fine lawyer and an ideal Queen's Bench Judge. He was, without exception, the most unassuming man I ever knew. He had no idea at all that Nature had accorded him a dignity such as very few possess and none can acquire. He was kindly, gentle and wise: but he was very firm. He did his distinguished duty as well as it has ever been done. He was tall and handsome, with thick, snow-white hair and a pleasing voice. I never saw him without his eye-glass. When he put on his spectacles, he put them on over the monocle.

"When that day we adjourned for luncheon, I met the second judge. This was Lord Coleridge. (Two Judges always go the Western Circuit. They usually take it in turns to deal with the civil stuff and the jail delivery.) Coleridge was a son of the famous Lord Chief Justice, from whom his title came. He was a very nice man, though not as good a lawyer, or, indeed, as good as Judge as was Channell. He, too, had his Marshal, of whom I took precedence, for mine was the senior Judge.

"I remember that we were late that day, for, after Channell had risen, there was an application in Chambers, that is to say, his decision upon a preliminary point of some civil action was sought by counsel in his private room. Coleridge had gone long ago, and the coach returned for Channell. When at last he was ready to go, I warned the servants and stood by, to walk behind him as far as the coach.

"As we came to the Castle's doorway, Channell turned.

" 'And what about you?' he said.

" 'I'll get back all right, Judge.'

" 'Have you got a cab? It's simply pouring with rain.'

" 'I'll send for one, thank you, Judge.'

" 'You may find no one to send. Nearly everyone's gone. You will come in the coach.'

"Considering his aversion to taking the Marshal in the coach, I found his gesture handsome.

"As I followed him out of the doorway, the fanfare of trumpets was blown. I entered the coach behind him and took my seat by his side. The footmen, gorgeously clad, shut the door behind me and folded the steps: then they swung themselves on to the tail-board, and the coach moved off. The body, of course, was slung, and the movement was not unpleasant. We lurched and swayed through the streets, with the police clearing the way and people stopping and staring and some taking off their hats. At last we swung under an archway and into the Inner Close of Winchester Cathedral.

"The Judges' Lodging was a fine old house, with a forecourt. I have described this house in *And Berry Came Too*. There a late tea was served, and I had to pour out. After that, the Judge withdrew. I was thankful to do the same.

"To my relief, the valet had collected my luggage and unpacked my things. He later returned to the Castle to fetch my coat and hat. He must have been sick of mopping up that day. I was able to bathe and change, to my great relief.

"For that week at Winchester, life was agreeable, indeed. That night the weather cleared up, and for the rest of our stay we had cloudless summer days. The Judges had their own servants, and we were well cared for and fed. After tea, we always went for a walk. At meals, I took the head of the table: except that one morning, at breakfast, I filled up the tea-pot with hot milk, instead of hot water, I think I got through all right. After dinner, Coleridge and I used to stroll out into the old grave-yard, to look for curious epitaphs. Channell never smoked, but bade me smoke when I pleased. Coleridge used to smoke one

275

pipe after breakfast and another after dinner. A clay pipe. I used to wonder why he was never sick.

"Channell was a staunch Conservative, and Coleridge a fierce Liberal. Party feeling was running very high at the time, and their consideration of their respective newspapers always made breakfast rather a strained meal. Channell would grunt and mutter over *The Times*, and Coleridge snort and blow over *The Daily News*. One day, I remember, Coleridge invited a violently Liberal peer to lunch in the Judges' room. Channell was greatly offended and never opened his mouth. Justice compels me to say that the peer in question looked a first-class crook.

"No doubt everyone has read Barrie's *My Lady Nicotine*. In that, the man who was accustomed to smoke 'The Arcadia Mixture' could smoke no other and would go all lengths to beg, borrow or steal it. I was rather the same about Cooper's Oxford Marmalade. On the first morning at breakfast, some ordinary marmalade was served, but Coleridge had a pot of Oxford Marmalade all to himself. After some hesitation, I asked if I might have some of his. He laughed. 'Go on,' he said. 'Help yourself. I know what it means.'

"Here, perhaps, I may interpose a memory told me by a distinguished officer of one of the Highland Regiments. He was a grandson of the famous Liddell, Dean of Christchurch and Vice-Chancellor of Oxford. His grandmother did her own shopping and did it remarkably well. One morning she entered Cooper's shop in 'The High', which I can remember well. It was as fine a grocer's as ever I saw. 'Mr Cooper,' she said, 'I don't like the marmalade you're selling. Here is a receipt of my mother's. Please make some of that.' Cooper did as she said – and made his fortune as well. For that was the receipt of the famous Oxford Marmalade.

"Every morning at a quarter to ten the coach would arrive, with the High Sheriff in his state dress and the Judges' Chaplain, wearing his cassock and hood. The Under-Sheriff followed them down in his car. The Marshals received them in a withdrawing-room. Then the Judges appeared, and a procession was formed. The Judges, High Sheriff and Chaplain entered the coach: the Marshals and the Under-Sheriff entered the latter's car: the car, of course, beat the coach, so that we were ready and waiting before the coach hove in view.

"If the proceedings were dull, Channell would send me off for an hour or so, with instructions to visit some place of note, to make some purchases for him, or do as I pleased. He was very considerate, and I was always sorry that there was so little I could do for him.

"Though he never knew it, he used to cause me considerable anxiety during our walks. He enjoyed strolling in the lanes and byways, and, once we had reached these, he seemed to assume that such thoroughfares were reserved for pedestrians. He would stray all over the road, as though he were rambling in some park, and nothing that I could do would make him keep to the side – to say nothing of the path. Fortunately the traffic was slight, and there were next to no cars; but many a time I had to make surreptitious signals to some approaching driver, and hope for the best. I think it speaks volumes for the Judge's appearance and bearing that the drivers always slowed down and gave him place and were never once rude about it. None of them can ever have known who he was.

"After dinner one evening I was walking with Coleridge in the Close, when he caught me by the arm.

" 'Pleydell,' he said, 'if you were a Judge, would you ever sentence a man to be flogged?'

" 'For some crimes – frequently, Judge.'

" 'Would you?' he said thoughtfully. 'Would you? I never would. I feel pain too much myself.'

"One of the many old customs at Winchester College is that, so often as His Majesty's Judges visit the City, the Head of the school shall write them a letter in Latin, requesting them to ask the Headmaster to give the school a holiday in honour of their visit. It is the Senior Marshal's duty to reply in Latin to the letter, granting this request. Good enough once, my Latin was not up to the mark. Channell, himself a fine scholar, laughed my dilemma to scorn. Coleridge's Marshal knew rather less than I did. Finally, Coleridge came to my help. But he insisted on composing the reply in dog-latin. This shook me rather, and I often wonder what the Head of the school thought of the reply which, of course, I had to sign. I received a letter of thanks in the best 'Tully'. 'Ulpian' had served my need.

"One afternoon the Judge was trying a most flagrant case of larceny. The accused had pleaded not guilty, but they were not represented and made no attempt to defend themselves. Although invited to do so, neither would enter the box. Channell summed up very shortly.

" 'Gentlemen,' he said, 'I don't think you can have much doubt about this case. The case for the Crown seems to be very clear. And it stands quite uncontradicted. If there is a case for the defence, none of us knows what it is. Consider your verdict.'

"The jury consulted. They did not leave the box. Presently the foreman stood up.

" 'Not guilty,' he said.

"The Judge stared at the jury.

"Then he addressed the prisoners.

" 'You are discharged.'

"He returned to the jury.

" 'Upon my word, gentlemen,' he said,' I don't know where your senses have gone. You'll never have before you a clearer case.' He addressed the Clerk of Assize. 'Empanel another jury, and keep these jurymen here until the end of the Assize.'

"This was done, and another prisoner was put up.

"His case was the reverse of the last. Larceny again, but the evidence offered by the Crown was painfully thin. To put it at its highest, it was a matter of slight suspicion. The accused defended himself with vigour and went into the box. It was clear to me that some mistake had been made.

"The Judge told the jury so and indicated that there was, to his mind, only one thing to be done. 'Consider your verdict.'

"The jury consulted. Then the foreman stood up.

" 'Guilty,' he said.

"Channell stared at him, as though unable to believe his ears. The whole Court was staring at him: and the prisoner was red in the face.

"The Judge addressed the prisoner.

" 'I'm afraid it's my fault,' he said, 'for not making it plain enough to these gentlemen that a verdict of 'Not Guilty' was the only one they could return. Never mind. You will appeal against the verdict, and I myself will see that your appeal is properly lodged. The Court of Criminal Appeal will quash your conviction. Meanwhile you will be at liberty, for I shall grant you bail on your own recognizances.'

"The prisoner thanked him and was released.

"The Judge returned to the jury, now looking very uneasy at what they had done.

" 'Really, gentlemen, I don't know what Hampshire juries are coming to. They don't seem to have any sense at all.' He addressed the Clerk of Assize. 'Empanel another jury, and keep these jurymen here until the end of the Assize.'

"This was done.

"I think we were all anxious about the next verdict, but fortunately it was a reasonable one.

"In another case, three men were charged together with an attempt, if I remember, to steal a cutter. Whilst the jury was considering its verdict, the Judge turned to me.

" 'I think they'll find them guilty,' he said. 'If you were me, what would you give these men?'

"I was taken by surprise.

" 'I don't think,' I said, 'I'd give them very much. I mean, after all, they failed. Twelve months, perhaps.'

" 'What I think would be best,' said Channell, 'would be so to sentence them that they all come out at different times. If they come out at the same time, they'll very likely conspire together again to commit another folly. But, if they don't, they may never meet again. It'll mean giving two of them rather less than they deserve, but that can't be helped.'

"The jury finding them guilty, he sentenced them as he had said. I have little doubt that his wisdom was justified.

"One evening Coleridge was troubled about a point of law on which he had to give a ruling the following day. He laid it before Channell, after dinner, and asked his help. The latter listened carefully, and then very quietly unloosed the Gordian knot. Coleridge put his hand on his shoulder and looked at his Marshal and me. 'There's a good, kind brother,' he said. Channell was greatly embarrassed, and didn't know where to look.

"Coleridge finished his list on Thursday and left for his Devonshire home. Channell did not finish till Friday, and on Saturday we left for Bristol, where I was to surrender my post.

"We travelled in a special saloon, which was attached to and detached from various trains in our journey across country. It was a glorious day, and I sighed for the old days when Judges rode on horseback from town to town. Day was the last Judge to do this, some seventy years ago.

"In the course of this journey to Bristol, we alighted at some junction or other, to stretch our legs. We walked up and down the platform, passing a book-stall each time, for about a quarter of an hour. The Judge was very silent and seemed preoccupied. At last, as we were passing, he turned and went up to the bookstall and bought a copy of *John Bull*. He obviously didn't like doing it, for he thrust it into his pocket and out of sight. As we resumed our stroll – 'You should,' I said, 'have told me, Judge. And I would have got it for you.' 'Well, I did think of that,' he said gently. 'And then I thought perhaps you wouldn't like to be seen buying it, either.'

"Herbert, now quite recovered, was at Bristol to meet us, but, though I had meant to return to Town the next day, the Judge was good enough to insist on my staying the week-end, as his guest. I was very sorry to leave him. Though I fear I had many shortcomings, no one could have been kinder than he was to me. He told me to come and see him whenever I liked, and several times I went to his room at the Law Courts, and sat at his feet. I always count it an honour to have been his Marshal. He was a great man."

"A charming job," said Berry. "The fat of the land, and wisdom while you wait."

"That's very true."

"Coleridge wasn't so good?"

"No. He was sound, you know. But he was undistinguished. And he was a delicate man. And highly sensitive – not a good thing in a Judge."

"A Judge should be tough?"

"A Queen's Bench Judge should be tough. When he is passing sentence, a Judge has to choose between considering the convict and considering the community. I've seen a great deal of crime, and I am more than satisfied that, in ninety-nine cases out of a hundred, it is the community that should be considered. Men convicted on indictment seldom, if ever, respond to leniency. But if the Judge weighs it out, they won't do it again. That is the value of a sentence – to convince the convict – and other potential convicts – that crime is not worth while. If you don't convince him, he'll do it again. All this wash about sending a man to the devil is so much trash. At least, it was in my time. Things may, of course, have changed; though I very much doubt if they have. The scandal of my day was shop-lifting at Selfridge's. I think I'm right in saying that shop-lifting cost Selfridge's six or seven thousand a year. And we couldn't stamp it out, because of one man. I've mentioned him before – Wallace, Chairman of Newington Sessions. The Magistrates at Marylebone Police Court nearly went out of their minds. If they gave a shoplifter more than, I think, two months, the shop-lifter could appeal. The appeal was heard by Wallace – who always let them off. And a sentence of only two months made shoplifting well worth while. I've seen a woman in the dock at Marylebone, with three previous convictions for shop-lifting, caught this time with more than forty pounds of stuff on her person – including a bottle of whiskey in her stocking. If that woman had been given two years hard labour, she'd never have shop-lifted again."

"You wrote about it once."

"I brought it into a tale – the first tale in *Period Stuff*. In that case, a mistake was made – a most easy thing to do. But a very serious thing. Selfridge's had more than one action brought against them, as a result of mistakes. You may remember that I emphasized the uneasiness of the manager, the moment he realized that there might have been a mistake.

"Shop-lifting, of course, is mean. It's a very mean crime. Wilful murder is usually brutal – the crime committed by a brute. Forgery is dangerous; but the forger takes such a risk that I wouldn't call it mean. But I once had to do with a case which shook your faith in human nature more rudely than did any other I came across.

"A timber-yard, owned by two brothers, was a steadily paying concern. I can't remember their name, but I'll call them Brown. The brothers were young and efficient and worked very hard: but the big noise was George, the foreman – a splendid man. He had served their father before them, and even their grandfather, and what he didn't know about timber and timber-yards was not worth talking about. Wise in their generation, before they took any action, they always sought his advice. After all, he had been the foreman before they were born. Though he was over seventy, he might very well have passed for fifty-five. He was a deeply religious man and could be seen on Sunday evenings, preaching at street-corners, with the tears running down his cheeks.

"As I have said, the yard was a paying concern. Masters and men worked hard and harmoniously. The place was of good report. There was only one fly in the ointment – a fly of which no one was aware, except the two brothers and George. For years there had been a leakage, and, do what they would, they could not stop the hole. They could not stop it, because they could not find it. By some means or other, timber which had not been paid for, went out of that yard. It was taken away somehow – stolen and never traced. And no mean quantity, either. The loss to Brown and Brown was between two hundred and fifty and three hundred pounds a year.

"Over and over again, unknown to anyone else, the brothers and George had been closeted with an Inspector of Scotland Yard. Trap after trap had been set. But every measure taken was a failure. The leakage went on.

"The brothers lived together in a house of their own. One evening the elder took his stand in front of the fire.

" 'This cursed leakage,' he said. 'Last year it amounted to more than three hundred pounds.'

"His brother shrugged his shoulders.

" 'Looks like we've got to bear it. Don't say you're going to call in the police again.'

" 'Yes,' said his brother, 'I am. But I'll tell you something, Joe. I'm going to have the police here – and say nothing to George.'

"Joe Brown started to his feet.

" 'How can you?' he cried. 'How can you talk like that? George is the most faithful servant two fellows ever had. If he ever found out that we'd been behind his back, I think it'd break his heart.'

" 'He won't find out,' said the other. 'He'll never know. I'll give you this – that I feel damned badly about it. I'm perfectly sure he's honest. But – well, business is business, and we can't go on like this. Damn it, Joe, the leakage is rising.'

"Reluctantly, Joe gave way…

"Unknown to George, the Yard was called in again, and a conference was held at the brothers' house. Certain measures were decided upon.

"One week later, George was caught red-handed.

"He collapsed on arrest and admitted everything. He was wholly responsible for the leakage and had been robbing the brothers ever since their father had died.

"I assisted the case for the Crown.

"The man pleaded guilty, so it did not take very long. While one could have nothing but contempt for and horror of such treachery, I found it in my heart to pity the prisoner at the bar. He never raised his eyes to the bench or the witness box, and for most of the time he held his head turned to one side and his two hands in front of his face, as a man might do, whom someone was seeking to photograph against his will. When evidence of his religious fervour and activities was given, I thought he was going to crouch down out of sight: and when the police revealed that the money had been spent – not upon his wife and large family, but upon women of ill fame, he trembled so violently, that I thought he was going to collapse.

"I forget what his sentence was, but his exposure had hit him far harder than any imprisonment could do.

"But it's no good blinking the fact that George shook my faith in human nature, as he shook that of everyone concerned in the case and of every hand employed in that timber-yard. And shook it right up. And what about his disciples? And all his neighbours and friends? 'The evil that men do lives after them.' You can't get away from that."

"Treachery," said Berry. "To my way of thinking, treachery's worse than murder. I have an idea that Dante agrees with me."

"Tell me, Boy," said Daphne. "Would you advise a young man to go to the Bar?"

"I'm not qualified, my sweet, to answer that question today. Remember – I left the Bar nearly forty years ago. The Bar was then a great profession. The Bar has produced some of our greatest men. To my membership and to all that I learned as a practising barrister, I owe no end. But, as I have said before, the ladder which the Bar was presenting before the first war was a very steep ladder to climb."

"How did the war affect it – the first war, I mean?"

"Well, I had no practice to lose – at least, not one worth talking about – at the time of the outbreak of the first great war. But a great number of barristers, who were doing extremely well, threw everything up and joined His Majesty's forces as soon as they could. Many never came back. Many came back, to find their practices gone. A few were able slowly to recapture the practices they had lost. Others, great-hearted men, had to start once more from scratch. Now it is, of course, a matter of arithmetic that, if you suddenly remove two-thirds of the Junior Bar, the third that is left will find itself confronted with an opportunity of doing not only its own work, but the work which the other two-thirds used to do. The foundations of some fine practices were, accordingly, well and truly laid between the outbreak of war and the weeks immediately preceding the coming into force of the first Military Service Act in 1916."

"God give me strength," said Berry.

"That is a fact. And I am not biased, for I had no practice to lose. I state what I know."

"Though you had no practice," said Berry, "in those five years you had a hell of a show."

"I did. A hell of a show. Six years of the Law, in all, and what wonderful things I saw! I've told you some of them. There are many that I've forgotten and more that I have not told. I've seen Carson cross-examine – and, by sheer personality, force a hostile witness to play his game. I've heard Danckwerts QC correct the Lord Chief Justice in open court. I've seen Marshall Hall reduced by Lord Alfred Douglas, whom he was briefed to smash. I've seen Darling convulse the court with his exquisite wit. And I've heard and seen the 'whips and scorns' of irony, wielded by that great master, F E Smith. As I have said before, there were giants in those days. And I was lucky enough to see them at work."

"A very great privilege," said Daphne.

I raised my eyebrows.

"Looking back, I fear that I have been very outspoken. I've praised and blamed right and left. Who am I to set one man up, and another down?"

"There," said Berry, "I take you up. And that, with vehemence. You have many lamentable faults. But I'll give you this. Mercifully, you had few briefs. So you were a looker-on. Lookers-on, they say, see the best of the game. And you have the keenest sight of any looker-on that I ever met." I rose and bowed, and Berry inclined his head. "That's not saying much, really. If a hanger-on can't be bothered to use his eyes…"

"The occasions were great," said Daphne. "And Boy took care to improve them." She stopped there and looked at me. "You might have gone back to the Bar, but you took to writing, instead. D'you ever regret your decision?"

"No. For an unambitious man, writing is – or was – the pleasantest profession in the world. Mark you, I was terribly lucky. I never had to fight – my stuff was taken right away. I haven't got very far; but I've never had to look back. I've been very lucky in my publishers and very lucky indeed in my public. Of that, I am deeply sensible. People still read my old books, and write and tell me so. To so faithful a public as that, I owe a very definite duty. So long as I live, I must never let them down."

"By which you mean?"

"Let anything go that isn't up to my standard. I confess that's not very high: but fall below that, I must not. That fear has haunted me for the last three years."

"It has been done," said Berry. "But you must never do it."

"And I'm the judge," said I. "I know if my tankard's a good one. And if it isn't, by God, it'll stay in my safe."

Jill slid an arm round my neck.

"Darling," she said, " you must be terribly tired."

"Not tonight," I said. " Crippen always tires me. But I'm not tired tonight."

*

"No more?" said Daphne.

"No more," said I. "We're both agreed upon that. Though each of us has a number of memories which we have not retailed, they are all too personal. Myself, I feel that that criticism can be levelled at much I've already said. But Berry thinks otherwise."

"Yes," said Berry, "I do. Your comic strips – "

"Comic strips?" shrieked Jill.

"Well, unconsciously humorous insights into the mind of a man who has published thirty books. Such insights have a value. They reveal the haphazard way in which books come to be made; they indicate the refuse upon which the writer draws; and they show how the latter views his completed tripe. Of course, Boy's debunked himself – a work, I need hardly say, of almost criminal supererogation: but for such as like a good, hearty laugh – "

"Boy, I can't bear it," said Jill.

"And what about the stuff," said Daphne, "that you've shoved in?"

"My monographs may be relied on to save the book. I'd an outstanding one on *Titles*, but your brother turned it down."

"Titles?"

"Yes. Why, for instance, the General Overseas Manager of the Hot Drop Forgers' Goose and Loincloth Association and Many of Them, on being raised to the peerage, was not allowed to take the title of Lord Order of Merit. And things like that."

"I must allow," said I, "that your example has an allure that none of my confessions can boast. But not all were so innocuous."

"Perhaps," said Berry, "perhaps. Not everyone has the *entrée* to The Diet of Worms – I mean, The College of Arms. But there you are. As I say, my monographs are the high spots. You can't get away from that."

"I can," said Daphne. "Easily."

"That," said her husband, "is because you have an inferiority complex. On the receipt of five guineas, any psychogeneticalist will confirm what I say."

"Rot," said Jill. "Boy's law stuff leaves them standing."

"*The Police Gazette*," said Berry, "has always appealed to those of little taste. To associate myself with such sensational slush has caused me much pain. But through all the ages people have fought to be taken behind the scenes. And who am I to deny to my fellow creatures a chance of indulging an instinct, however base? Because I prefer gin and tonic, shall there be no more Gooseberry Crush?"

"If you ask me," said Daphne, " I think you're terribly lucky to have a master of English to straighten out your burbling."

"And here's blasphemy," said Berry. "Of course, you'll be struck or something for talking like that. I was going to suggest that you brought me that beautiful decanter; but I shouldn't be surprised if you'd lost the use of your legs."

"I'm afraid," said I, "I haven't displayed much mastery of English in this book. But in my experience, unless you're a Winston Churchill or some other superman, your ordinary conversation is not distinguished by a purity of style. And this is a conversation piece."

"As such," said Berry, "it's human. Homer was an epic poet – the greatest of the four. But I'll lay he didn't call for wine in hexameters. 'Go on,' he said. 'Fill it right up, you fool.' "

"I always thought," said Daphne, "that Homer was blind."

"Not all the time," said Berry. "He had to do his job. Oh, I see what you mean. Well, he probably kept his thumb inside the pot. And now we must have an envoy."

"Whatever's that?" said Jill.

"A send-off," said Berry. "The authors' parting words. They do it in pantomimes. 'And now it's time to go. We hope you've liked the show.' "

"Can't you say something," said Jill, "about it all being true? I mean, it *is* true, darlings – every word. Berry's monograms mayn't be, but everything else is. Every fact, I mean. If people don't believe it, it can't be helped. The thing is, we know it's true. People say all sorts of things about the old days, and lots of them are lies. But these aren't. They mayn't be frightfully exciting, like some of your books. But then you make those up. But Fate made up this book."

"I can't beat that," said Berry.

Neither can I.

DORNFORD YATES

BERRY AND CO.

A collection of short stories featuring 'Berry' Pleydell and his chaotic entourage established Dornford Yates' reputation as one of the best comic writers of his generation. The German caricatures in the book carried such a sting that when France was invaded in 1939 Yates, who was living near the Pyrenees, was put on the wanted list and had to flee.

BLIND CORNER

This is Yates' first thriller: a tautly plotted page-turner featuring the tense, crime-busting adventures of suave Richard Chandos. Chandos is thrown out of Oxford for 'beating up some Communists', and on return from vacation in Biarritz he witnesses a murder.

Teaming up at his London club with friend Jonathan Mansel, a stratagem is devised to catch the killer. The novel has equally compelling sequels: *Blood Royal, An Eye For a Tooth, Fire Below* and *Perishable Goods*.

Dornford Yates

Blood Royal

At his chivalrous, rakish best in a story of mistaken identity, kidnapping, and old-world romance, Richard Chandos takes us on a romp through Europe in the company of a host of unforgettable characters. This fine thriller can be read alone or as part of a series with *Blind Corner, An Eye For a Tooth, Fire Below* and *Perishable Goods*.

An Eye For a Tooth

On the way home from Germany after having captured Axel the Red's treasure, dapper Jonathan Mansel happens upon a corpse in the road, that of an Englishman. There ensues a gripping tale of adventure and vengeance of a rather gentlemanly kind. On publication this novel was such a hit that it was reprinted six times in its first year, and assured Yates' huge popularity. A classic Richard Chandos thriller, which can be read alone or as part of a series including *Blind Corner, Blood Royal, Fire Below* and *Perishable Goods*.

Dornford Yates

Fire Below

Richard Chandos makes a welcome return in this classic adventure story. Suave and decadent, he leads his friends into forbidden territory to rescue a kidnapped (and very attractive) young widow. Yates gives us a highly dramatic, almost operatic, plot and unforgettably vivid characters.

A tale in the traditional mould, and a companion novel to *Blind Corner, Blood Royal, Perishable Goods* and *An Eye For a Tooth*.

Perishable Goods

Classic Yates, this novel featuring the suave Richard Chandos was reprinted three times within the first month of publication, was warmly received by the critics and served hugely to expand the author's already large readership. Typically deft, pacey and amusing, it 'contains every crime in the calendar and a heart-rending finale' (A J Smithers).

A companion novel to *Blind Corner, Blood Royal, An Eye For a Tooth* and *Fire Below*.

Gripping stuff.

OTHER TITLES BY DORNFORD YATES AVAILABLE DIRECT FROM HOUSE OF STRATUS

Quantity		£	$(US)	$(CAN)	€
☐	ADÈLE AND CO.	6.99	11.50	15.99	11.50
☐	AND BERRY CAME TOO	6.99	11.50	15.99	11.50
☐	B-BERRY AND I LOOK BACK	6.99	11.50	15.99	11.50
☐	BERRY AND CO.	6.99	11.50	15.99	11.50
☐	THE BERRY SCENE	6.99	11.50	15.99	11.50
☐	BLIND CORNER	6.99	11.50	15.99	11.50
☐	BLOOD ROYAL	6.99	11.50	15.99	11.50
☐	THE BROTHER OF DAPHNE	6.99	11.50	15.99	11.50
☐	COST PRICE	6.99	11.50	15.99	11.50
☐	THE COURTS OF IDLENESS	6.99	11.50	15.99	11.50
☐	AN EYE FOR A TOOTH	6.99	11.50	15.99	11.50
☐	FIRE BELOW	6.99	11.50	15.99	11.50
☐	GALE WARNING	6.99	11.50	15.99	11.50
☐	THE HOUSE THAT BERRY BUILT	6.99	11.50	15.99	11.50
☐	JONAH AND CO.	6.99	11.50	15.99	11.50
☐	NE'ER DO WELL	6.99	11.50	15.99	11.50
☐	PERISHABLE GOODS	6.99	11.50	15.99	11.50
☐	RED IN THE MORNING	6.99	11.50	15.99	11.50
☐	SHE FELL AMONG THIEVES	6.99	11.50	15.99	11.50
☐	SHE PAINTED HER FACE	6.99	11.50	15.99	11.50

ALL HOUSE OF STRATUS BOOKS ARE AVAILABLE FROM GOOD BOOKSHOPS OR DIRECT FROM THE PUBLISHER:

Internet: www.houseofstratus.com including author interviews, reviews, features.

Email: sales@houseofstratus.com please quote author, title and credit card details.

Hotline: UK ONLY: 0800 169 1780, please quote author, title and credit card details.
INTERNATIONAL: +44 (0) 20 7494 6400, please quote author, title and credit card details.

Send to: House of Stratus Sales Department
24c Old Burlington Street
London
W1X 1RL
UK

Please allow for postage costs charged per order plus an amount per book as set out in the tables below:

	£(Sterling)	$(US)	$(CAN)	€(Euros)
Cost per order				
UK	2.00	3.00	4.50	3.30
Europe	3.00	4.50	6.75	5.00
North America	3.00	4.50	6.75	5.00
Rest of World	3.00	4.50	6.75	5.00
Additional cost per book				
UK	0.50	0.75	1.15	0.85
Europe	1.00	1.50	2.30	1.70
North America	2.00	3.00	4.60	3.40
Rest of World	2.50	3.75	5.75	4.25

PLEASE SEND CHEQUE, POSTAL ORDER (STERLING ONLY), EUROCHEQUE, OR INTERNATIONAL MONEY ORDER (PLEASE CIRCLE METHOD OF PAYMENT YOU WISH TO USE)
MAKE PAYABLE TO: STRATUS HOLDINGS plc

Cost of book(s): —————————— Example: 3 x books at £6.99 each: £20.97

Cost of order: —————————— Example: £2.00 (Delivery to UK address)

Additional cost per book: ————— Example: 3 x £0.50: £1.50

Order total including postage: ———— Example: £24.47

Please tick currency you wish to use and add total amount of order:

☐ £ (Sterling)   ☐ $ (US)   ☐ $ (CAN)   ☐ € (EUROS)

VISA, MASTERCARD, SWITCH, AMEX, SOLO, JCB:

☐☐☐☐☐☐☐☐☐☐☐☐☐☐☐☐☐☐☐☐

Issue number (Switch only):

☐☐☐

Start Date: **Expiry Date:**

☐☐/☐☐   ☐☐/☐☐

Signature: ——————————————

NAME: ——————————————————————

ADDRESS: ——————————————————————

——————————————————————

POSTCODE: ——————————

Please allow 28 days for delivery.

Prices subject to change without notice.
Please tick box if you do not wish to receive any additional information. ☐

House of Stratus publishes many other titles in this genre; please check our website (**www.houseofstratus.com**) for more details.